PENGUIN BOOKS

COSMETIC EFFECTS

Clive Sinclair was born in London in 1948 and educated at the universities of East Anglia and California at Santa Cruz. His first novel, *Bibliosexuality*, was published in 1973. In 1980 he was awarded a Bicentennial Arts Fellowship, which allowed him to spend a year writing and teaching in the USA. In 1982 he was one of twenty writers chosen as 'Best of Young British Novelists'. He was literary editor of the *Jewish Chronicle* from 1983 to 1987 and in 1989 was the British Council Writer in Residence at the University of Uppsala, Sweden. His first book of stories, *Hearts of Gold* (Penguin, 1982), won the Somerset Maugham Award. This was followed by a second collection, *Bedbugs* (Penguin, 1983). He is also the author of *The Brothers Singer*, a critical biography; *Blood Libels*, a novel; and *Diaspora Blues*, a personal view of Israel. His work has been translated into eight languages. He lives in St Albans with his wife and son.

Clive Sinclair
COSMETIC EFFECTS

PENGUIN BOOKS

PENGUIN BOOKS

Published by the Penguin Group
Penguin Books Ltd, 27 Wrights Lane, London W8 5TZ, England
Viking Penguin, a division of Penguin Books USA Inc.
375 Hudson Street, New York, New York 10014, USA
Penguin Books Australia Ltd, Ringwood, Victoria, Australia
Penguin Books Canada Ltd, 2801 John Street, Markham, Ontario, Canada L3R 1B4
Penguin Books (NZ) Ltd, 182–190 Wairau Road, Auckland 10, New Zealand

Penguin Books Ltd, Registered Offices: Harmondsworth, Middlesex, England

First published by André Deutsch 1989
Published in Penguin Books 1990
1 3 5 7 9 10 8 6 4 2

Printed in England by Clays Ltd, St Ives plc

For Fran and Seth

A large part of this book was written while the author was the British Council Guest Writer-in-Residence at the University of Uppsala. He wishes to thank both the University and the British Council for the opportunity afforded him.

1

And all the people saw the thunderings, and the lightnings, and the noise of the trumpet, and the mountain smoking: and when the people saw it, they removed, and stood afar off. And they said unto Moses, Speak thou with us, and we will hear: but let not God speak with us, lest we die. And Moses said unto the people, Fear not: for God is come to prove you, and that his fear may be before your faces, that ye sin not. And the people stood afar off, and Moses drew near unto the thick darkness where God was.

'Is he going to come back?' I whispered to my mother. 'Wait and see,' she replied. I was also in thick and smoky darkness at the time, though mine was pricked with a shaft of light, at the end of which danced Charlton Heston and a cast of thousands.

My father always referred to the St Albans Hippodrome as the local fleapit, but to me it was a stately pleasure dome. A lady in some sort of chocolate-coloured uniform sat in a glass booth and dispensed purple tickets at the touch of a button. These were subsequently torn in half under torchlight, whereupon we were permitted to descend a flight of densely carpeted stairs which led to a large, dimly lit hall on whose walls were gold charioteers in bas-relief. Swing doors led from this antechamber to the auditorium proper, each portal being manned by an usher who scrutinized our tickets a second time before admitting us. Within was organ music and a screen so large I felt as insignificant as an extra at the foot of Mount Sinai.

'What did you think of the picture?' asked my father as the credits finished rolling. 'I know it was called *The Ten Commandments*,' I said brushing the choc-ice wrapper off my lap and rising from my springy seat, 'but I liked the plagues better.' Except for the last, I could have added, which scared the living daylights out of me, being a first-born myself.

As a matter of fact it was to celebrate the ninth anniversary of my nativity that we had come to see Cecil B. de Mille's much trumpeted epic. Nor did the outing end when the house-lights came on, for the manager, a personal friend so my father often said, suddenly appeared in his penguin suit and beckoned me to follow him. He led me out of the auditorium, unlocked an unmarked door, ran up a narrow flight of stairs and entered a small room at the heart of which stood a giant machine that looked like one of Buck Rogers's more formidable enemies. It stood upon a central leg, which supported a black body with silver flashes and translucent red knobs. Growing from its side were two round heads, one on top of the other, divided by a single eye out of which poured light as pure as creation. The sweaty projectionist was leaning over the gleaming apparatus, apparently removing the contents of its brain, a spool of crackling film. 'Behold the Ashcraft Suprex,' said my father's friend, 'the machine that burns but does not consume.'

The Ten Commandments, being a film of exceptional duration, had caused the booth to become as stifling as Luxor. The projectionist, now stripped to the waist, glistened like a stevedore. 'Does it always get this warm in here?' I asked, concerned about the fellow's well-being. The manager laughed. 'Tell this innocent what it used to be like, in the old days,' he said, 'before there was electricity.' The projectionist winked, skirted the still hot Ashcraft Suprex, and placed his perspiring arm around my shoulder. Then, leaning forwards, he whispered in my ear: 'My father used to tell me that when he was a little lad he could earn a few extra pennies by sitting, with his mates, on a big bag of gas. Their combined weight forced the gas out in a jet, which was ignited and directed on to a piece of lime.' I must have looked perplexed, because the manager felt the need to add: 'You've heard of limelight, haven't you?' I nodded. 'Very effective, but very dangerous,' he continued. 'Isn't that so Mr Reffold? Tell our young visitor what happened to your father.' 'One day the bag he was sitting on went off like a bomb,' said the projectionist, his face still close to my ear, 'and he lost a leg. But he was the lucky one. The rest of his friends got blown to bits.'

.At bedtime, aware that my mother was not in the habit of smearing our lintels with lamb's blood, I asked her, 'How do we know that the Angel of Death won't come one night and get me by mistake?' 'Because you are Jewish,' she replied. 'But how will the Angel of Death know that?' I persisted. 'God will tell him,' she replied, 'because God knows everything.'

This, if true, was a mixed blessing. I certainly wanted him to have a word with the Angel of Death on my behalf but, equally, I didn't want him to be privy to my Saturday morning secret; or, if He was, I hoped He'd be a good enough sport not to tell my parents, who thought I was saying my prayers in the neighbourhood synagogue alongside old Mr Rosenthal when, in fact, I was in the Hippodrome on the edge of my seat.

I went the first time for a dare and had to go the following week just to find out how the hero avoided the certain death that seemed to be awaiting him. And such was the nature of Saturday morning serials that the same thing happened on the second visit, and the third. How would he escape from the raging torrent, the descending ceiling, the runaway car, the assassin's knife, the ticking bomb, the bullet with his name on it? This was not the stuff of nightmares, you understand, but of diurnal speculation, engaging the rational side of my intelligence. The answer, the way out, could be found by the same process as a mathematical solution, because you knew that there always was a logical outcome. But what if there wasn't? What if the hero couldn't outwit the Angel of Death, as happened in other films I saw in the company of grown-ups? Then the irrational fears began and nightmares stampeded through my sleep.

After one such movie I became convinced that a herd of maddened elephants would trample down our house. The fact that there was no precedent for such an event in the annals of Hertfordshire was no solace, for I had seen it happen with my own eyes, or I would have if I had kept them open long enough; to this day I do not know whether Elizabeth Taylor survived to the end of *Elephant Walk*.

What did get trampled down eventually wasn't our home but

the Hippodrome itself, not by elephants but by bulldozers activated in the name of progress. 'History always repeats itself,' said my father. 'When I was your age I stood on this very spot and watched them demolish old Arthur Melbourne-Cooper's Picture Palace. That was what you call a cinema! At the portico stood a commissionaire in a coat of claret and gold who touched his peaked cap every time a customer went past. Inside all the ladies were given phials of French perfume, in case the film proved too strenuous for their female sensibilities to bear. Those were the days,' he said as the last walls of its successor fell to earth.

Arthur Melbourne-Cooper was one of the pioneers of the British motion picture industry. He was born at 99 London Road, not far from the present ruins. His father, who moved to St Albans in the 1860s, was a professional photographer. I think my father identified with the Melbourne-Coopers. I remember that he took me, when very young, to the old fellow's studios in Alma Road, where I was shown one of his very first features, *Dreams of Toyland*, in which the contents of a nursery came to life. The film gave me a nightmare which made my fear of elephants seem an exercise in realism. Nevertheless, in the morning I declared: 'I want to make pictures like Mr Melbourne-Cooper.' My father looked as pleased as punch, though things haven't turned out exactly as he hoped. Nor are there many elephants left in the world, either. Their tusks, designed to protect them, have led to their near extinction. They also led, by a strange quirk, to the motion picture industry, celluloid being a by-product of the search for an ivory substitute that would allow the mass-production of – among other things – billiard balls. I'd have preferred a cure for mortality, but I'm grateful for science's small mercies, like penicillin, organ transplants, cornea grafts and the aforementioned movies, which provide me with employment if not eternal life.

In the beginning film was made out of a celluloid variant called cellulose nitrate. Although the likes of Charlie Chaplin, Mickey

Mouse, Greta Garbo, Gary Cooper and Jean Gabin are often accorded immortal status they were actually in grave danger of immolation, for nitrate film is chemically related to gun cotton, a volatile substance liable to self-combust or even explode. Their divinity was only assured by the invention, in the 1950s, of the more stable cellulose triacetate. Personally, I'm still at the cellulose nitrate stage, being cursed with labile hypertension, which can burst my heart at any moment (though my doctor, a believer in the efficacy of beta-blockers, is somewhat more sanguine, according what he calls my 'white-coat hypertension' to hypochondria). Combine this with my sympathy for the overwrought alarm that awakens me in the mornings and you have an animated time-bomb.

At the appointed hour I half-expect to hear the tiniest of clicks in the cranium, whereupon the nervous system will deliver the shock, the arteries the shudder, to the little tick-tock in my chest, which will stop mid-beat, and the great Abu Nidal in the sky will chalk up another victim. Here on earth, it must be said, even Abu Nidal's terrorism has some purpose, but what does the celestial scarifier want of me? The sort of exemplary behaviour that would satisfy the Hays office? Or just a bended knee and blind terror? Well, I confess, I'm scared.

I walk to my place of work as gingerly as Yves Montand drove his truckload of nitroglycerine in *The Wages of Fear*, convinced that if I put one foot wrong, do something as trivial as break the second commandment, I'll go up in a cloud of smoke. Just look at how I behave on the busy thoroughfare, where the Hippodrome once stood. When other pedestrians pause to consult their wristwatches, I stop to check my pulse, to ensure that I am not the late Jonah Isaacson, nor likely to be for the duration of my journey. I don't want the embarrassment of detonating on the street — give my imagination a metaphor and it'll have the mise-en-scène worked out in no time — nor do I want to be responsible for the death of the pickpocket who is toying with the idea of fingering my wallet, or the man who is urging me to purchase an umbrella, or the girl who is as prettily made up as Queen Nefertiti. They are all innocent passers-by, but then so am I. I give to charity, I am faithful to my wife. At least once a year I visit God's holy dunams in an El Al jet, longing to give myself up to their security staff. 'Don't let me on the plane,' I want to cry, 'I am too dangerous. A walking bomb!' But I am never given the opportunity, because my wife is a travel agent and knows the right people. In this instance we have *proteksia*. So no one hears my plea: 'Defuse me, please!'

My wife flies out to examine new hotels or discuss novelty packages with her distant colleagues, while I tag along to see for myself how the Zionist dream of building a land where Jews may lead normal lives is progressing. Really, that's all I want for myself; a normal life. For which you need a wife and a job, both of which I have. Just as a state has its constitution or its laws, so a normal person must have a routine, which I also have. Every day starts at precisely seven-thirty when the aforementioned alarm goes off, allowing me exactly forty-five minutes in which to shower, dress and eat my breakfast (always pink grapefruit, toast and muesli), after which I kiss my wife and make my way to the campus where I work. The phrase 'a normal life' has a dark side, of course, which is death, since the average person inevitably dies. To become normal is therefore to eschew the possibility of immortality. But abnormality is unnatural, which is not so great either. The obvious solution is to have a child, thereby at least ensuring genetic continuity, but for every gene there is a germ, and I don't know if I would be able to stand the strain of worrying about an offspring as well as myself. Imagination, like free will, is a hard thing to handle though, given my desire to mate with every attractive woman I see, I'm not sure how free my will actually is.

I envied the animals of the field, who are strangers to such forebodings, until it was pointed out to me by Professor Gutkes, my colleague from the University of Frankfurt, that they too must fear death. Why else would the antelope flee from the cheetah if it didn't already anticipate the jaws on its jugular and the claws slicing into its flesh? 'Surely that's simply instinct,' I said. 'And where did the instinct come from in the first place,' replied the professor, 'if not from some distant but still distinct memory?' 'You mean animals have a collective unconscious?' I asked. 'Why not?' he replied. 'If you observed them a little more carefully you'd appreciate their refinement. For example, just the other day we made a little expedition to Whipsnade Zoo where I saw a wonderful thing: the consummation of a courtship. Six little clouds of dust rose from the ground as the male of the species mounted his mate, and more dust escaped as he made himself comfortable on her back. It wasn't a quick coupling as you see with lions, but a slow pleasurable business, a shiny pinkness showing between his belly and her back at the conclusion of each thrust. And how can I say with such confidence that the business was pleasurable for both parties? Here I must anthropomorphize, but I make no apologies for it. You see, I know what it means for me when my partner sinks to her knees with her eyes closed and her body relaxed and I slump on the length of her back and lay my head on her shoulder. All this before I have withdrawn, just to prolong the moment of intimacy. If anyone were to see us then – other than my wife – they would say, this is a couple in love, as I say of that pair of rhinos who stood thus as the dust settled. If they have learned to fear death why shouldn't they also have learned to savour love? And what enviable love they had! If I were forced to retract from the backside of my mistress in public I would display a very shrivelled thing, certainly nothing like the magnificent instrument that was revealed to us. It was as long and as thick as my arm with a bend in the middle that corresponded to my elbow, something I would gladly have given my companions there and then, for both acted as if they had never seen a penis before. But then Polly or Petra kissed me on the cheek and I thought, poor caged beast, to be stuck with one mate, and I thanked the Lord that I lived in a university and not a zoo, where what we remember isn't a matter of life and death, but a fact that can be checked in the library or the diary. We have the written word, that is the chief difference between us, a blessing and a curse in equal measure.'

He's right. These words, written in a blank notebook purchased by my now obscure grandfather in his native Grodno, will be a blessing unto me when my descendants revive me through their agency (which I cannot do for my unfortunate *zeide* who did no more than write his name on the expensive rag paper) and a curse if my wife should ever happen upon them. For in order to interest you I must do things that will necessarily upset her.

Professor Gutkes is famous, which is why he is at the University of St Albans, being a world authority on the English romantics: Shelley *et alii.* He is with us for a term, though the contract was almost terminated on the first day when he discovered there was no sauna on the premises. He insisted that the Vice-Chancellor inspect his skin-tone and sun-tan and demanded to know how these could be maintained without the assistance of sauna and solarium. In the end the Vice-Chancellor gave the professor his wife's sun-ray lamp and paid a plumber to fix a sink in Gutkes's office. Some students were taken aback, upon entering the professor's room, to see on shelves in place of scholarly tomes, bottles of Johnson & Johnson's baby oil, pots of Vaseline and Nivea, and jars of various corporeal lubricants; others were even more surprised to see the professor, attired in nothing but sunglasses and a pair of briefs, supine upon a rug, basking not in the glow of knowledge but in the light of a megawatt bulb.

Polly and Petra came together for a tutorial and stayed, so the story went, long enough to re-enact the infamous scene in Antonioni's *Blow-Up,* wherein two aspiring models wrestle each other out of their clothes before doing the same to David Hemmings.

I teach Film Studies, as you may have guessed, which is how I met Professor Gutkes in the first instance. He came to my office (at the other end of the corridor, in the Department of English and American Studies), knocked on my door, and said: 'Dr Isaacson, I need your help. Explain to my why I hate Meryl Streep.'

The problem, we soon discovered, was *Sophie's Choice.* You may have forgotten the William Styron novel upon which the film was based; if so let me remind you that Sophie Zawistowska, a Pole defiled by her experiences in Auschwitz, seeks forgetfulness in various ways, one of them being untruthfulness, another being sexual abandon.

'Sex in the cinema is much more significant than most people credit,' I explained to my visitor. 'In the old days, before topless bathing, when a woman showed you her tits, it was a signal that she was prepared to go all the way. That's why the coming of bare bosoms to the screen was such an important victory for verisimilitude. I mean, what real woman would hold a sheet to her breasts after a night of abandon? She obviously wasn't trying to stop her lover seeing 'em, therefore she must suspect that someone else is out there watching — us — and bang goes the illusion. Goodness knows why the breasts are so important since the nipple, the defining characteristic of the mammal, is one of the commonest things on God's earth. But I, for one, worship them to the point of contravening the second commandment. It is not, I could almost swear, nostalgia for lactating ducts, but something much more pagan. Love is an abstract best represented — from a masculine point of view — by the female form. This is generally hidden from our eyes, like the face of God. We may deduce the lineaments of the body from its apparent shape, but unless we see the unencumbered flesh with our own eyes we cannot be sure that we are not being deceived. And such is the nature of mankind that even then we are not satisfied with the numinous, but also demand the embrace; we lose patience with the invisible promises of Moses, and require a Golden Calf of Aaron, and an ankle and a thigh and a hip and a vagina and breasts. Above all it is the breasts that put flesh on the abstract concept of sexual desire, they are love's epitome. Consider how many movies have been compromised by the director's need to conceal his star's chest, either for reasons of censorship or because of the lady's amour-propre. Only Hitchcock got away with it in *Psycho* (when you don't think that the whole point of the murder-in-the-shower scene is *not* to show Janet Leigh's tits, though he has subsequently revealed that it was). Or compare Vanessa Redgrave's performance with that of Jane Birkin in *Blow-Up*; the former spends ten minutes without her shirt dodging the camera, making a monkey out of Antonioni, whereas the latter doesn't give a damn who sees what. I'm not saying that Birkin is a better actress than Redgrave, of course, simply that in her scenes there is a greater sense of

9

danger, because we know from what we have seen that the girl is prepared to go all the way — where we do not know — and it's that titillation, that spice of danger, which keeps us in our seats.

'Now, in some films this peek-a-boo type of performance doesn't make much difference, but in *Sophie's Choice*, when Streep is being paid and subsequently praised for pretending to be a concentration camp survivor, it matters a lot. Her performance, as far as it goes, is flawless, a perfect piece of mimicry; her Polish accent is wonderful, her gestures are a carbon copy of the original, when she is called upon to look sick you believe she is going to die, but I wasn't convinced for a minute, and I'll tell you for why: because she didn't show her tits in the sex scenes. Okay, maybe she's shy, maybe she has a right to protect her privacy; but that's just my point, she's playing a woman who had no rights. She is pretending to give her all and yet, when it comes down to it, she is prepared to give nothing of herself. And when you think what she's doing, this is downright obscene; her biggest danger is not the gas chamber but not getting an Oscar. Streep looks like victim Sophie, but you know that she's the one who's really in control. It's all manipulation, at no personal risk. And that's why you hate her. She is the prostitute who fakes her orgasm so well you believe you are a superstud until you go home to your wife. You hate her because she has made a fool of you, has taken you in without giving you a thing of herself.'

'Dr Isaacson,' said Professor Gutkes, 'I think we are going to be good friends.'

I was flattered. After he'd gone I wondered if what I'd said could form the basis of a future course. Would I then be accused of sexism? Surely not if I added an attack on Marlon Brando for keeping his private parts well off-screen in *Last Tango*. Only when I got to thinking about concentration camps did I recollect that Professor Gutkes was German, and that maybe his hatred of *Sophie's Choice* was not one hundred per cent artistic. And I remembered also what Nestor Almendros, the great cinematographer, wrote about the making of that film, in particular his description of how Meryl Streep's memories of Auschwitz were manufactured. These flashbacks were shot on regular Kodak stock which was then desaturated, which means that the lab technicians toned down the original colours, thereby producing more subtle shades, literally faded images. Before the final take Almendros and his director — Alan Pakula — ordered some laboratory tests, as a result of which they decided to dress Sophie and her fellow prisoners in loud colours, as these survived the desaturation process best. Red, blue, but not yellow (Sophie, being gentile, wouldn't require a yellow star anyway). And that is why in the film the garden of Rudolf Hoss, the commandant of Auschwitz, is planted with red and blue blooms. The finished product, Almendros observed, resembled that obtained by Nazi film-makers with their Agfacolor, a fact that he thought would create the 'appropriate conditioned reflexes' in the memories of older viewers. As it happens, I do not approve of conditioned reflexes, though sometimes these cannot be helped. For example, I find it difficult to warm to Germans, my feelings not having been sufficiently desaturated. How much more so for those who were actually there; among whom may be numbered the late Primo Levi. Not for him the pastels of Agfacolor; for him Auschwitz was 'an out-of-focus and frenzied film, filled with dreadful sound and fury devoid of meaning: a hubbub of persons without names or faces drowned in a continuous, deafening background noise ... A black and white film, with sound, but not a talkie.'

Nonetheless, the professor was right; we have become great friends, so much so that he keeps urging me to join him in his triplicity. 'My good doctor,' he trills, 'I invite you to enter Tripoli, my pretty Polly; or, if you prefer, take Petra and her rose-red titties.' But fear of destabilizing the trinitrotoluene that throbs in my chest always prompts the same response, *'Nein, mein professor.'* Nor will I even accept the offer of a wardrobe from where I might spy upon the tritagonist and his two leading ladies. 'At least', says Professor Gutkes, 'admit you are tempted.' Not a difficult confession. 'Then why not give in?' He pauses. 'You don't believe in God, do you?' 'Not in a beneficent deity,' I reply. 'What then,' he asks, 'a sort of Otto Preminger?' 'No,' I say, 'my model is not the movies but international terrorism. And Abu the Ubermensch has given me an unacceptable set of demands, without the option of free will. A sort of ten commandments with knobs on, to which I must surrender of course. Otherwise — boom!' 'My dear doctor,' says the professor, 'we Germans once suffered under such a regime, which we also called upon ourselves. Now those who did not rebel are called cowards and worse. Your name is Isaacson, not Prometheus, so live and show your bare arse to the bastard.'

Instead I show my class *Deep Throat,* as well as the ins and outs of Linda Lovelace, a great performer according to my theory, about to be put to the test. Professor Gutkes turns up, as do Polly and Petra. They make a handsome trio: the professor, sun-tanned, sandy-haired, in good shape for his fifty years; Polly and Petra, each in their early twenties, well-made, as both their outfits reveal in different ways. Petra is curly, from the top of her head, through the curvatures of her masculine shirt, right down to the curvilinear jeans. Polly is straighter. Her brown hair hangs loosely, as does her extremely low-cut dress, which criss-crosses her otherwise bare breasts, a state which I can confirm every time she inhales.

I am therefore rather surprised when she approaches me after the screening with the following complaint: 'There is a question I must ask you, Dr Isaacson. In the films you have already screened there was much sexuality and some near pornography. Mostly you were able to explain why this should be so, but tonight I can see no justification for the obscenity you inflicted upon us. It made me wonder if the other movies you praised so lavishly were as empty of content. In short, Dr Isaacson, it made me seriously question your judgement. Why did you do it?'

When Polly was much younger she had an accident which

resulted in the loss of an eye. The replacement is a perfect match, at least as far as pigment is concerned, but of course the pupil does not dilate. In daylight this is hardly apparent, but in the dark of a movie theatre the disparity is very noticeable, so much so that I do not know whether it is ruder to stare into her eyes or down the front of her dress. As I dither between those upper and lower orbs it occurs to me how similar they are in design if not function, and I begin to wonder if the female torso might not be a replica of the face, wherein the organs of sight, smell, taste and hearing have fleshy equivalents. A naked woman promises so many secrets, but long before she can even be approached you have been turned into a piston, a mechanistic slave of the old double helix, life's mainspring, trading messages with your lover's genes and not her soul as previously intended. 'Sometimes I think that fucking is all there is,' I reply, 'that everything else is a bloody pantomime. Can you think of a better medium than the movies to test the truth of this? The general reaction to *Deep Throat* — and I do not doubt that your response is typical — seems to suggest that I may be wrong.' 'You are wrong in at least one respect,' says Professor Gutkes, putting his arm around Polly's shoulders, 'there is certainly fucking, but there is also eating.'

So we go to Alberto's in St Peter's Place, which happens to be next door to my wife's travel agency in the new precinct, a coincidence that is anything but accidental. Alberto and my wife are cousins and the parvenu parade was constructed by their paterfamilias, notwithstanding the protests of local residents, who preferred their Victorian garrets to the characterless units that have replaced them.

My wife's parents both died from unpleasant ailments when their only daughter was just in the teens and her bereaved uncle assumed responsibility for her, treating her with no less consideration than his own son Alberto, a concern that continues, despite her marriage. Thus when Alberto was offered one of the shops for his restaurant at a peppercorn rent my wife was given the same opportunity.

I do not wish to question this generosity by ascribing

motivation, but it is a fact that my wife's uncle was, in his turn, raised by his Aunt Bella, who now, in her turn, lives under his protection. She is in her late eighties, but acts as though she were twenty years younger.

Born in Milan in 1899 she was, by dint of her precocious beauty, posing nude for various artists by the age of fourteen, a small piece of art history she lets no one forget. Her most notable appearance, however, is in Giacomo Balla's *Dog on Leash;* an attempt, heroically executed, to compress an entire motion picture into a single frame. The impression conveyed, though, is of a woman with twenty legs rather than a graceful walker. This was called Futurism. Its chief propagandist was Filippo Marinetti. At the age of sixteen my wife's great-aunt became his mistress. Hitherto she had been known as Balla's Bella. Now the wags called her Marinetti's marionette. The liaison ended abruptly and Bella migrated to Paris where she dallied with Dali, was more earnest with Hemingway and Ernst, posed for Picasso, and wore greasepaint for Luis Buñuel. All the racy anecdotes in my famous essay 'Surrealists in the Cinema' come from her.

Bella's good times lasted till the Second World War when, with her orphaned nephew in tow, she fled to Britain, where her niece (the boy's sister) already lived with her English husband.

At school the immigrant boy was called Ice-Cream Man or Organ Grinder. He vowed revenge and today heads the richest Italian family after the Fortes. His one remaining ambition is a peerage, to which end he agreed, when asked, to spend millions on the University of St Albans which is, I blush to inform you, a private institution. Others, less charitable, maintain that this was the price he had to pay for the planning permission required to build St Peter's Place.

The lights are still on in my wife's shop and, through the moonshine that turns her windows into umpteen affordable variations of Eden, my wife can be seen conversing silently with her computer, drawing invisible lines between happy families or illicit lovers and their tropical dreams. I tap on the palms of Tahiti and she looks up, as does a lonely man lost in a reverie about distant climes. I point to my mouth and rub my belly and she nods, acknowledging that my mime has been understood.

She joins us as we drill into the *antipasti* with our forks. I observe at once that Professor Gutkes, who has not met my wife before, is keen to make a good impression upon her. Perhaps he is anxious to discover what a woman who wears a baggy double-breasted pinstripe suit (albeit with a silk blouse underneath) would be like in the sack. Motivation in the human male, I continue to believe, is based primarily upon genetic principles, though we disguise it in various pretty garments, just as the true purpose of my wife's agency (which is to make her money) is concealed by picturesque promises of paradise.

Consequently, it does not surprise me to hear the professor say, as he slices into his veal, 'Mrs Isaacson, you clearly have two levels of sexuality; the first seems a forbidding place, but the other is altogether more alluring. One day I shall talk to you about it.' My wife, though no semiotician, comprehends his unspoken message as clearly as she did mine about dinner; she knows that what he is really saying is, 'I bet you're wearing black lace briefs beneath those trousers. One day I'd like to get in them.' Perhaps I am being a little over-sensitive but I think I recognize in the subtext a suggestion that only he can play Prince Charming to her long-dormant sexuality. 'Professor Gutkes,' she replies, bless her, 'I'm sorry to disappoint you, but I'm no Marlene Dietrich.'

More like Joan Crawford, if you ask me, being far too ambitious these days ever to make love without a contraceptive. My wife shields herself from birth with a rubber sheath, and from death with material possessions, in the belief that the grim reaper, like a tradesman, would be too intimidated to rap upon the front door of our residence.

Protected by my reluctant good behaviour and my wife's ability to accrue wealth we have achieved a harmonious *modus vivendi*, though we are no longer so close as Polly and Petra who are eating off the same plate. I regard this as a domestic tragedy. When we began married life copulation was the norm, a nocturnal metaphor for our diurnal intercourse. We lived in a state of perpetual nudity, nothing was hidden between us, nothing closed. We each haunted the other's body. I entered her through the vagina, anus and mouth, she penetrated my mind, heart and soul. Then came leaves such as those that once coddled the figs on the sweet trolley, now being wheeled toward our table by Rudolf Valentino's double. And after them rules as censorious as those that nipped Hollywood's second efflorescence in the bud. Life became a routine, which gradually eroded the spontaneous correspondence between us. My wife had entered the safety-conscious age of cellulose triacetate, and what had once been vivacious became vicarious. Thus our anarchistic realm was turned into a condominium, and poor King Priap crowned with a condom. But how could it have been otherwise? I might envy the peach being flayed by the Italian heart-throb at Polly's behest, but I'm realistic enough to know that the skinless fuck I crave, as intimate as open heart surgery, will be an apotheosis rather than a precedent. And so as Polly sinks her gleaming teeth into the exposed flesh of the golden fruit I brush my wife's cheek with a fingertip and receive a dusty reminder of mortality: the rouge that now reinforces her healthy complexion.

Petra, meanwhile, pulls a pipe and a silver tobacco pouch from the pocket of her jacket and fills the bowl with St Bruno, not for Professor Gutkes but for herself. 'Christ,' she says suddenly, between puffs, 'I hate this country.' Words spoken with such vehemence that all other conversation stops. 'Anything in particular?' asks my wife, as if she were taking down holiday requirements.

'The people,' begins Petra, 'their conventionality, the culture, or lack of it, the conservatism, the smugness, the dullness, the blindness, the lousy food, the absence of excitement, the climate.' Here she looks accusingly at the windows, which drip anaemic blood from invisible wounds. 'I'll tell you all a secret,' she says. 'If Adolf Hitler were standing at the next election I'd vote for him, just to shake things up.' Professor Gutkes shifts uncomfortably in his wicker chair. 'Mrs Isaacson,' he says, 'you know the world's most exotic nooks and crannies. Where shall we send this jaded girl to brighten her life?' My wife reels off a list of places from Alaska to Żanzibar. Then Polly says, 'Wouldn't it be great if we could travel in time as well as space?' 'Where would you go, Professor Gutkes?' asks my wife. He is a man of letters, not a historian, English letters to boot. I should have guessed the answer, but I didn't, I thought he'd say 'Auschwitz'.

'Easy,' he says, 'I'd go to the Villa Diodati beside Lake Leman in the month of June 1816. Not for the weather, it was a wet month, nor even for the scenery, but for the company. Lord Byron was in residence with poor Polidori, his physician and his poodle, doomed to kill himself with prussic acid at the age of twenty-six. The night of the 15th was especially stormy, providing a perfect background to the story Byron read to entertain his guests — Percy Bysshe Shelley, Mary Godwin (not yet Mrs Shelley) and Claire Clairmont (her half-sister, pregnant with Byron's child) — the sort of Gothic fantasy in which my fellow countrymen once excelled. The combination of atmosphere and highly-strung company prompted Byron to suggest they all try their hand at such a tale. Claire dropped out, intimidated by the literati, but Mary persevered, though for days she was devoid of inspiration.

'The weather did not improve, the tension in the villa increased, until one evening Shelley had a fit, occasioned by listening to Coleridge's *Christabel* under the influence of laudanum. Byron had just got to the bit where Geraldine unties the cincture from beneath her breast,

> Her silken robe, and inner vest,
> Dropt to her feet, and full in view,
> Behold! her bosom and half her side —
> A sight to dream of, not to tell!

when Shelley sat up as if he'd seen a ghost. In fact what he'd seen, or thought he'd seen, were Mary's naked breasts, but with eyes where the nipples should be. Later, retiring to bed past the witching hour, Mary herself had a nightmare, not about the withered dugs Christabel had seen, but about a pale student of unhallowed arts kneeling beside the thing he had put together. "I saw the hideous phantasm of a man stretched out," she later reported, "and then, on the working of some powerful engine, show signs of life and stir with an uneasy half vital motion." Surely this is an excellent boost for your argument, Dr Isaacson. If Geraldine hadn't bared her boobies to Christabel, Shelley wouldn't have had his fancy, nor Mary her nightmare, and there would have been no *Frankenstein.*'

At which point the clock in St Peter's church, just up the road, begins to strike midnight. 'I'd give my soul for a night at Diodati,' concludes the professor, 'but just now the only thing I've got on offer is my body.' Polly giggles, though Petra continues her sulk. My wife's body is also on offer, as it turns out. Afterwards she flushes my posterity down the lavatory, sets the alarm, and goes to sleep. Cursed with insomnia I look at the clock's face and see my own distorted in the convex glass. We are indeed brothers; I send her to sleep, he wakes her up.

Inspired by Byron, Professor Gutkes proposes we swap stories of our sexual conquests. But as Polidori was to his lordship, so am I to the professor. His adventures make me feel like a eunuch (which is the reverse of their intention, of course). So much so that I begin to regret our weekly exchange.

But here he is again outside my door, for it is six o'clock on a Friday and he is as regular as clockwork. And so we sit in the easy chairs before my office windows, warmed by the spring light and the Jack Daniels, discussing in the pedantic detail usually reserved for Wordsworth the proclivities of Petra and Polly. What is the purpose of such candid detail? What good does it do me to hear that while Petra's anus is hairy, Polly's is as clean as a babe's? Do I really need to know that in the occasional lacunae between intercourse and orgasm Petra is able to fart with her vagina? Does it increase my appreciation of Dvořák's cello concerto to learn that, arriving late, Polly and the prof performed mutual masturbation in an otherwise deserted vestibule of the Albert Hall?

My attention wanders out of the window over brilliantly bilious fields of new wheat, and even brighter meadows of oil seed rape that look as though the sun has melted upon them, towards Gorhambury and the ruined house of the university's patron saint, Sir Francis Bacon. A particularly appropriate avatar for, like him, our avuncular benefactor, having been ennobled by the Prime Minister, was accused of financial irregularities — leavened, in his case, with antisemitic insinuations.

'The place was full of Jews,' continues the professor, meaning the Albert Hall. 'It seems that the soloist was a refusnik recently released by the Soviet Union. How do I know they are Jews? Not by their big noses, don't worry, but by the labels on their heads. Why do they wear those knitted skullcaps that wouldn't cover a shrunken head? Because they are designer Jews, that's why, just as the women of the Corniche are designer women. My friend, I would no more want to discuss religion with one of those Jews than I would want to fuck a woman who parades around in a G-string. Both lots probably think that Meryl Streep is a great actress. But I don't want signs, I want the substance.' The professor sips his bourbon. 'You don't think I'm a racist?' he asks suddenly. 'A German should be careful what he says.' 'Of course not,' I reply. 'Good,' he says. 'Now it's your turn.'

'Summer was in the air,' I begin, having well-rehearsed my pathetic contribution, 'the wind was coming from the west and was warm and the girls were in their cotton frocks. I was driving across the campus when I noticed one such in hot pursuit of some wind-blown letters. They flew into the road and I stopped to allow her to pick them up. Immediately I saw that she had a problem; if she bent to pick up the letters her dress would choose gravity over modesty and depart from her chest. Nor could she use her left hand to cover herself, as this was already full of papers. Actually she had a go, but only succeeded in dropping more. Already the drivers behind me were becoming impatient. So she looked at me, shrugged as if to say "You win," and knelt down. Her dress descended in accordance with Newton's prediction and her breasts suddenly appeared like the headlamps on a Lotus. It was a beautiful moment.'

'But is that all?' asks Professor Gutkes. 'What more do you want?' I ask. 'Here was a girl prepared to show her all for the sake of letters, which is more than you can say of a certain actress.' 'But what of you?' replies the professor. 'What have you given? The narrator is supposed to participate in these stories, not merely observe. This is life, not the movies. The simple function of our erotic tales is to produce an erection. If they don't, they fail.' 'I got a hard-on,' I protest. 'Maybe you did,' he replies, 'but some of us require more than seeing. We want to do. To be. To be in the story, in the woman. We admire the word made flesh — or whatever — a vital transformation. But you — you are like that man who stood outside your wife's shop, tempted by the posters but too scared to go in and make a reservation.'

Unlike Mrs Richmond, who stumbles into my arms one afternoon while I am minding my wife's business. Although she is old enough to be the first Mrs Gutkes her hair is still blonde, unnaturally so, and her face artfully made-up to conceal the passage of time. If a single brush-stroke had been out of place I'd have put her down as an alcoholic, but nothing is smudged, nor does her breath smell.

'Whatever must you think of me,' she says, regaining her composure, 'I'm always falling over. I've fallen over in the street and broken my wrist. I've even taken a tumble and cracked a femur in my own kitchen. All because I was rushing about for Stella. Just like today. That time I was helping her pack. She was due to go to Babylon, seeing she was Queen Nadia's beautician. What a bitch that woman was. But she wasn't proper royalty, she was just a German the king married. She treated my daughter really badly, kept her waiting for hours. And not only her. Even Charlie Kedourie, the photographer. She kept him hanging around too, her ladyship. Anyway, they put two steel rods in my leg and packed the top with concrete. I was in bed about a fortnight. Stella postponed her trip, of course. She went the following week, when I was no longer in pain. She must have done well, because they've invited her back, though God knows why she wants to go. I'm not so keen, there's always some sort of trouble in that part of the world, but she's set her heart on it. So tell me, sir, has AlBa got a good reputation? Is it safe?' 'AlBa?' I say. 'The Royal Babylonian Airline,' she replies, taken aback by my ignorance. 'Safe?' I say. 'Of course it is. King Melchior flies it every time.' 'Now *there's* a gentleman,' she says, relieved.

Thanks to his testimonial Mrs Richmond makes the following reservation for her daughter: London–Babylon–London.

If only my wife hadn't behaved like Queen Nadia I wouldn't still have been in Dream Time when Nefertiti came in with the deposit. St Albans is not a big place and I have seen Stella in the city centre on several previous instances, but never before in close-up. Her face is a living advertisement for her art. It is as perfect as flesh can be. In her mother's case her task had been to outwit time, in hers she has merely to enhance its handiwork; the enemy has become an ally. Each decorated feature seems to have a life of its own. Her large brown eyes look positively radioactive, as though they had been coated with luminous paint. And then she smiles and I can think of nothing but a sentimental song which goes, 'And that laugh which wrinkles your nose touches my foolish heart,' which, even now, is sending out warning signals.

'What should I do?' I ask Professor Gutkes the following Friday at six-fifteen. 'What do you want to do?' he asks. 'Date Stella, dine her, maybe even fuck her,' I answer. 'Despite the consequences?' he asks. 'I can't help myself,' I reply. 'Dr Isaacson,' says Professor Gutkes, 'I believe that you are under the influence of the progenitive impulse which, I warn you, can be suicidal. At Whipsnade Zoo I heard tell of certain frogs whose mating call not only attracts the female of the species but also bats which specialize in eating them. So at least put an eye in your backside when you are courting, to ensure that you do not fall into the clutches of some predator. This shouldn't be too difficult as your brains are already in your bollocks.'

'You don't seem to have come to any harm,' I reply. 'Ah,' says the professor, 'but I am a member of a cursed tribe. Since I am foredoomed I try, in the meantime, to enjoy myself. I have nothing to lose.'

'Listen,' I say, 'for weeks you've been urging me to take the plunge. Now that I'm finally ready, what happens? Do you welcome me with open arms? No, you try to persuade me to remain faithful to my wife. Why?'

'Because, my dear Dr Isaacson,' says the professor, 'I have become convinced that you are not cut out for adultery. You like to look at other women, that's undeniable, but I'm pretty sure by now that you'd flee from any tactile engagement.'

'You may be right,' I say, 'so let's assume you're in my position. You've seen Stella, you want her. How are you going to get her?'

'The first step is easy,' he replies. 'She has booked a flight to Babylon. The ticket will arrive in a few days. You have her address. Deliver it by hand. The rest is up to you.'

The Richmonds live in a red-brick Victorian terrace near the station, though their particular house is disguised by stone cladding to look like a Gloucestershire cottage. The front door is made of opaque glass, which obscures as much as it reveals, likewise Stella's Japanese wrap-around. 'What must you think of me,' she says, 'not dressed at this hour? But we've had high drama here this morning. Mummy was bringing me breakfast in bed when she missed a step or something and fell down the stairs. You should have heard the clatter.'

'Good lord,' I say, 'is she all right?' 'Near enough,' replies Stella. 'Daddy just telephoned from the hospital. The doctors think it's a dislocated shoulder. It will take more than that to stop me going this time.'

I give her the ticket. Our fingers touch. Stella does not withdraw her hand. Is it a hint? What would my mentor do? 'Will you have dinner with me?' I ask. 'Come in,' she says, 'and tell me what I owe you.' 'You haven't answered my question,' I say. 'I know,' she says. I follow her through the hall toward the inner sanctum.

If the outside is meant to resemble an English aristocrat's country retreat, the interior is someone's idea of Madame de

Pompadour's boudoir. As we enter the ornate living-room an ormolu clock on the marble mantelpiece chimes the quarter hour, causing the miniature nymphs and shepherds on its flanks to quiver with delight. I know exactly how they feel when Stella suddenly says, in the sweetest of voices, 'Yes, I'd like to.'

My heart, now thumping, gasps, 'Look at this place. Look at the trollop. She probably thinks Truffaut is a kind of chocolate.' My mind, always less emotional, advises, 'At least ask her what movies she likes.' 'Anything with Richard Gere,' she replies. Then asks me to name my favourite movie. She hasn't heard of it, but is not uninterested. She enquires about its plot, stars, director. Finally she makes a guess, 'Are you a film buff or something?' 'Something,' I reply, before elucidating. 'I don't usually mix with brainy men,' she says, 'but don't go thinking I'm stupid, because I'm not.' I can see that she is beginning to adjust her personality to suit my requirements. Christ, I think, she's as good as Meryl Streep. 'Don't be taken in,' pleads my heart. 'Sorry fellas,' I inform my organs, 'but I'd swap the lot of you for a glimpse of her in the noddy. Not to mention my immortal soul.'

'To whom should I make it payable?' asks Stella, opening her cheque book. 'My wife,' I say. 'You're married?' she says. 'Yes,' I say. 'Does it make any difference?' 'Not to me,' she says. And what about to me? My wife would be hurt of course, were she to find out about a night both candle-lit and clandestine, not because my two-timing would break her heart, though that cannot be ruled out, but because I would be bringing disorder into the house, thereby granting death its entry. There is a syllogism that has me half-convinced, as you know. Everyone commits adultery. Everyone dies. Therefore don't commit adultery and you won't die. On the other hand, who wants the kind of life that doesn't include knowing the likes of Stella? I mean that in the biblical sense. I am ripe and ready to fall. Like Eve I'm prepared to spit in the face of Abu Nidal or whatever he called himself in those days. When I depart I kiss Stella on the cheek and feel, in return, a slight pressure where our bodies are accidentally touching.

*

23

Founder's Day is a moveable feast at the University of St Albans. It falls on the first Monday in June and, by tradition (to use the language of our prospectus), it marks the end of the academic year. All members of the faculty and their spouses are invited to take sherry with the Vice-Chancellor in his walled garden, if the weather permits, or otherwise in the great hall of New Gorhambury, the regency mansion wrested from the hands of Nell Gwyn's descendants by 'the parvenu Jewboy' we honour today (my wife's black-sheep uncle, of course). This year it is raining, so we are all in the great hall, famed for its gilded mouldings, huge murals depicting martial achievements, and a ceiling decorated with angels, cherubim and other winged hominids.

Tradition also demands a speech. In the enforced absence of our benefactor this is made by the Vice-Chancellor. He walks, a tall man with close-cropped grey hair quite at home in his business suit, to a podium carved, absurdly, in the likeness of an ostrich. The Vice-Chancellor flattens a piece of paper upon the giant bird's unruffled feathers and begins to read from it. As soon as he opens his mouth it becomes obvious that while the voice may be his the words are those of my wife's uncle.

'My dear friends,' the Vice-Chancellor says, 'it gives me great pleasure to see you here today at the end of another year of high academic achievement. Far be it from me to recommend summer reading to such an awesome collection of intellects, but allow me to urge those of you who are not already familiar with it to take a look at a book penned in 1624 by Gorhambury's most illustrious tenant, our great predecessor here, Sir Francis Bacon. *New Atlantis,* written in the last years of his life, contains, as its name suggests, a vision of Utopia — the one, I may add, which inspired me to create a university in this place. Bacon believed that the universe was a great machine governed by eternal laws, and therefore susceptible to a mechanical explanation. If humanity as a whole wishes to establish and extend power and domination over this universe, to recover that right over nature which belongs to it by divine behest, it must, with our benign assistance, dismiss superstition and abstraction in favour of rational thought and empirical experimentation. Thus wrote Sir

Francis Bacon, not a stone's throw from this very spot. He proposed that scientists and thinkers should labour together in an institution which he called Salomon's House. Therein our ancestors wore robes not unlike those we ourselves have donned today. We have a great inheritance, my friends, but do not let us be shy about adding to it.' The Vice-Chancellor pauses and taps the ostrich-like podium. 'My thought for the summer is this . . .' he smiles at his audience, '. . . keep your eyes upon the heavens and your head out of the sand.'

Afterwards the first question in every conversation is entirely predictable, even Professor Gutkes (accompanied by his two unofficial wives) asks it. 'And where, Mrs Isaacson, are you going this summer?' 'As a matter of fact,' replies my wife, 'we're off to Israel on the 19th. Jonah's giving a talk at the Jerusalem Film Festival and I've got a few deals to settle.' 'Excellent,' he says, 'and before you go you must prepare your tender skin for the desert sun in my little solarium.'

The news is clearly not so excellent for Polly and Petra, however. 'Israel,' cries the former, as if my wife had said Uganda or Cambodia. 'You mean occupied Palestine, don't you?' says the latter.

'Dr Isaacson,' says Polly, brushing her long hair with her hand, 'don't you feel guilty about going there?' 'Guilty?' yells my wife, taking a canape from the shining tray of a passing waitress. 'Why should we feel guilty? If you want to know about real guilt ask your boyfriend.' She waves her hand and launches a prawn in the professor's direction. It somersaults across the space between them like a pink crescent moon and, lubricated by mayonnaise, slips slowly down his lapel, leaving behind a permanent slick of grease.

'The Second World War was a long time ago,' says Petra, raising her voice, 'we're talking about now. About Israel's involvement in Iran, in South Africa, in Nicaragua, in Washington. Let me tell you something, Mrs Isaacson, when American jets took off from our country to bomb Libya I felt defiled. Not by the Yanks, but by their paymasters, the Zionists. I don't want to become a part of Greater Israel, thank you very much.'

'Don't thank me,' says my wife, trying to clean the professor's jacket with a tissue moistened by her tongue. 'Why not?' demands Petra. 'Doesn't your uncle own all this? And isn't he also responsible for the phagedaena called St Peter's Place? Why are so many of you into demolition? Is it because you Jews, having no terrestrial memories of your own, save those that were celestially inspired, are jealous of those of us that do? So much so that you want to destroy everything we hold dear — our heritage, if you like. St Peter's Place wasn't much, but it was ours. Now it's your brave new world in microcosm; rootless, characterless, temporary and, above all, profitable. It is your revenge upon the world for the holocaust — cultural genocide. We are in the same boat as the Palestinians, following our memories down the drain. For Jaffa read Tel Aviv, for St Albans read Brent Cross.'

My defence is to wonder if it would be possible to fuck someone with such views, which are a bit much even for a girl with a hairy anus. My wife is more aggressive. 'Can you be the same young lady who said, not four weeks ago, "I hate this country"? Why the sudden change of heart?' she demands. 'It's not me who's changed,' says Petra, 'it's England.' 'Petra thinks we're giving up without a fight,' explains Polly. 'Talking of which,' says the professor, 'aren't you worried about hijackers?' 'No,' says my wife, 'El Al's security is the best there is.' 'Pity,' says Petra, permitting a somnambulistic wine-waiter to refill her crystal glass with chilled Chablis. 'So you and Polly support the PLO,' says my wife. 'You like the idea of innocent citizens being blown out of the sky?' Polly shakes her head, but not Petra. 'There are no innocent Israelis,' she says. 'All are eligible for call-up, so all are legitimate targets.' 'Professor Gutkes,' says my wife, 'you have lovely friends.'

'Oh, don't let them upset you,' he replies, 'you know how radical the young can be. To them Israel is just another expression of western imperialism and racism. They feel sorry for the Palestinians. And they don't remember the holocaust.' 'Perhaps you should remind them,' says my wife.

'There are plenty of others, more than ready. Too many, if you want my opinion, Mrs Isaacson,' replies the professor. 'Perhaps you are unaware that we had a similar controversy in Frankfurt; old residences demolished and replaced by inhuman office blocks. Our city, once the pride of Germany, was ravished and prostituted. All for the sake of a few shekels. You may not like this, Mrs Isaacson, but many of the profiteers were Jewish, though no one mentioned this at first. In those days children were told, "Look at that man over there; he is a Jew. We must be polite to him." One such, Rainer Werner Fassbinder, grew up to break every rule in the book, including the only-say-good-things-about-the-Jew taboo. He dared to write a play on the subject of the destruction of Frankfurt, and my late friend was brave enough to put these words into the mouth of a Jew: "I buy up old houses in this city, pull them down, build new ones and sell them for a good price ... I couldn't care less if children cry, if the old and infirm suffer." Of course the play was never performed. Mrs Isaacson, isn't it time the Jews grew thicker hides? The truth is like the sun, it only burns those whose skins are too thin.'

'I've never even read *The Garbage, the City and Death*,' I answer, 'but I did see the movie they made from it. So I know that Fassbinder's Jew was not only a speculator, as you have described, but also a sex-obsessed murderer. Moreover, with his shaven head, his thyroid eyes, his greedy tongue and his long fingers, he looked like Nosferatu's brother. Indeed, as I recall, a burgomaster complains that the Jew drinks his blood, sucks him dry, then puts him in the wrong because he is a German. "I rub my hands," he concludes, "when I think how he would have choked in the gas chamber." '

'Dr Isaacson, I'm surprised at you,' replies the professor. 'You know those words were said by a Nazi, and in no way represent Fassbinder's own opinions.' 'Do I?' 'It's like accusing Walt Disney of being in favour of wicked step-mothers because he includes them in his cartoons,' continues the professor.

'Are you saying that an artist has no historic responsibilities,' I ask, 'that you'd be perfectly happy to accept Leni Riefenstahl's *Triumph of the Will* as a brilliant documentary and nothing more? 'My dear doctor,' replies the professor, 'life is short, but art is long. Posterity will be the judge of such things, not us.' 'Then artists are no better than Nazis,' says my wife.

Polly, long silent, gives me a strange look. 'Dr Isaacson,' she says, 'I was under the impression that you were against all forms of censorship, especially self-restraint. Or does that only apply to Linda Lovelace?' 'Why must everything be reduced to the absurd?' cries my wife, her own self-restraint vanishing in advance of her person. Never one to forget his manners the professor, though now addressing her rear, says, 'Enjoy your holiday.' Then, with the pale skin of her exposed back in mind, he adds, 'My offer is still good. It'll save you getting sun-burned.' But she doesn't turn round. I start to follow. 'Not so fast,' says Professor Gutkes, taking my arm. 'Before we go our separate ways tell me one last thing: when are you taking her out?' 'Tomorrow night,' I reply.

Stella is one of those women who manage, within minutes, to create the illusion that you are the most important man in their lives, or so it seems to me as we waltz into the dining room of St Michael's Manor. Summer sunshine pours across the lake and the lawns and floods through the french windows of the restaurant, galvanizing everything it touches: the silver cutlery, the sparkling glasses, my emotions, Stella's hair. Thanks to this copper and gold fireball I now understand why bulls run at matadors. The maître d'hôtel positively skips as he shows us to our table.

Stella has obviously spent hours preparing for this date, but then so have I; starting with a haircut this morning and finishing with a shower just an hour ago, after which I dusted vulnerable areas with my wife's favourite talc. A fact which does not escape Stella's attention. 'You smell nice,' she says, 'a bit feminine, but never mind.' She notices my haircut and that my blue shirt matches my eyes. Listen, I deal with insubstantial shadows born of transparent celluloid every day, and in the night I might just as well be one myself for all the notice my wife takes of my bodily presence. I know that marriage has made recognition of my mating potential unnecessary, but it doesn't do to forget entirely the games our genes have programmed into us. In ten minutes Stella has spoken more about my masculine attributes, my attractions, than has my wife in the last ten years. I am not especially vain, but I am flattered, and want more. As do the waiters, who show an embarrassing preference for our table.

'What will you have?' I ask, glancing at the menu. 'You order for me,' she says. Christ, I feel masterful! I am drunk even before the wine reaches my head. I see that a waiter, dazzled by Stella's décolletage, sneaks a glance down her dress as he refills her glass. Envious of this freebee I do likewise when I help her out of the chair after the meal. She is, I observe, wearing a black brassiere. I am glad to inform you, however, that the satisfaction denied my sense of sight is subsequently granted to my sense of touch.

Grass grows grey in moonlight, water stands like mercury. We stroll over the former and around the latter in the grounds of the hotel-cum-restaurant. Coots rustle in the weeds, ducks glide over the meniscus, silently breaking its surface. 'Stop,' I say, 'just for a minute.' In the adjacent park an owl hoots. 'I wish I were Richard Gere,' I say. 'No you don't,' she says. 'At least I would have kissed you by now if I were,' I say. 'So what's stopping you?' she says. I take the hint again. Her tongue comes out of its lair. It is then that I place my hand upon her left breast. 'I wish I'd booked a room as well as a table,' I say. 'So do I,' says Stella. 'You return from Babylon on the 18th,' I say. 'You remember,' she says. 'Of course,' I say. 'You get back on the 18th, and I go to Israel on the 19th. It doesn't give us much time.' 'God will provide,' she says, as a peckish pipistrelle flitters above the waters. I make my third wish which, if repeated, won't come true.

Red brick turns phosphorescent under firelight, glass opalescent. My wife's travel agency is burning down. I had dropped Stella and was returning home when I saw a devilish glow over St Peter's Place and heard the banshee cry of fire-engines on heat.

The temperature is tremendous. It is as though the thousand suns contained in brochures and posters had simultaneously gone supernova. The windows can withstand it no longer, they burst, showering the fire-fighters with bloodthirsty rain, and releasing a stream of charred paper which mutates into flocks of deformed bats. Everyone's eyes are full of tears, but only my wife's are genuine. 'This is my Kristallnacht,' she says.

I recognize in this eloquent description two subsidiary meanings: that this is the beginning of the end, and that Professor Gutkes of Frankfurt or his acolytes are somehow responsible. Surely not! Role models were plentiful for Baader and Meinhof in Germany, but there has been no terrorist in St Albans since Boudicca burnt the place down. It could be argued, I suppose, that Gutkes had infected Polly and Petra with alien ideologies, and financed my philandering with his golden example but, in truth, none of us were innocents. Though less guilty, I suspect, than the man now conversing with the police, who seems to be balancing the Leaning Tower of Pisa on his head. This is Antonio's chef who, we soon learn, left a pan of olive oil above a flame while he took time off to telephone his fiancée in Roma. The unattended oil combusted and quickly consumed the cheapskate partition that separated Antonio's kitchen from my wife's office.

God spoke to Moses out of a burning bush. Well, he doesn't have to say a thing to me, his actions have sufficient grandiloquence. I've been to enough movies to recognize a mafioso-style warning when I see one. On the other hand, I know the difference between life and art, and recognize that tonight's misfortunes are real enough and that they all belong to my wife.

She is inconsolable, beyond the reach of everyone, including me, though I try. And my efforts are genuine, for I am suddenly reminded how much I love her. She is wearing an old blue jumper she must have pulled on hurriedly after the police telephoned with the bad news, and faded jeans, and her hair is uncombed. It's the first time she's been out sans make-up in years, and she looks just like she used to, in the days when we were both idealists. It's a pity I can't introduce her to Stella, who could teach her how to enhance her natural good looks without resorting to the cosmetic mask that is distancing me, but I cannot because I've also got too much to hide.

At last we are alone. The firemen have gone, the police have gone, the insurance man has gone, even Antonio has stopped wondering how he can run a restaurant without a kitchen. Only Mrs Isaacson, kicking about in the soaking, smoking ashes and her husband trailing behind, trying to find something hopeful to say.

And then it dawns upon my wife that all is not lost; the safe, of course, has survived the fire, but so has the computer, with its elephantine memory. We lug it back to the house, along with the contents of the safe, where it puts an immediate damper on the new affection that rose phoenix-like from the ashes of Dream Time.

'Let's go to bed,' I say, meaning, Let's make love. 'Sorry,' she replies, plugging in the computer, 'I'm too busy.' By morning she has become so addicted to its small screen that she seems part computer herself, a calculating woman.

Not that I am much better being, in effect, an animated calendar, whose only function is to register the passing days. My wife, zealously remaking her life in advance of our forthcoming vacation, barely notices me, let alone my obsession with time. And if she thinks about my new interest in men's fashion at all, she probably assumes I am frequenting the boutiques in St Peter's Place to find clothes for Israel.

My chief worry is that Stella won't phone on the 18th, or that if she does it will be merely to report insurmountable obstacles to our coupling, which I will interpret as excuses. That's if I live to the 18th, of course. Maybe God is so malignant he'll push the button before I've done anything to deserve it. But I survive, and at two-thirty precisely on the appointed afternoon the telephone comes to life and my vigil is over.

'Good news,' says Stella, 'my mother had a fall and broke her arm. And for once it wasn't her fault. Someone spilled a packet of frozen peas in the supermarket, and over she went. Daddy made a big fuss, of course. As a result of which they're both at a posh hotel in Bournemouth, all expenses paid. So I'll be alone in

31

the house tonight.' 'No you won't,' I say. Now you know the gist of my third wish.

I inform my wife that I am going to the Film Museum at Bradford to attend a lecture by Elem Klimov on the new Soviet cinema and a reception thereafter. 'The chance of a lifetime.' I give my word that I'll be back in good time for our flight. She is not pleased, but provides a lift to the station.

I catch the inter-city to Sheffield, alight at Luton, and get the next train back to St Albans. Then I walk to Stella's. 'Come upstairs,' she says.

Her bedroom looks like it belongs to a teenager rather than a woman of twenty-five. Posters and photographs of movie stars are pinned to the walls, many of the latter signed to Stella. There is a framed portrait of King Melchior and his Queen, also signed. On a table beside the bed is an alarm clock with the figures of Noddy and Big Ears on the dial. Noddy's head moves to and fro, registering the passing seconds, a fair representation of my former self. The alarm, I notice, is set for eight. I feel as if I am at five-to, with one hand on her neck and the other on her buttock. Then it's midnight as she starts to unbutton my shirt from the top. 'Why should women always get undressed first?' she asks.

I keep telling myself, don't let her take control, keep to your own pace, don't rush. But already I have failed to take the advice proffered by Bernard Malamud in *Dubin's Lives*: always urinate before an orgasm.

'My turn,' I say as I begin to undo her blouse, revealing the black bra underneath. I don't know if Tonto ever saw the Lone Ranger without his mask, but he couldn't have been more jubilant than me when the veil drops and I see the real Stella for the first time. Where Shelley saw eyes I find nipples so engorged that the areolas have disappeared. Just above the right one is a crescent-shaped scar, like a surgical love-bite.

Stella is no less observant. When my dick, disconcertingly detumescent, makes its debut she asks, 'Are all circumcised penises the same? Yours looks just like King Melchior's.' I do not

32

enquire how she knows. Her pubic hair is trimmed to accord with the latest line in bikini pants. This should add to the eroticism, as the hinterland stubble emphasizes the secret nature of the hair itself, but the ragged rectangle is actually less aesthetically pleasing than nature's triangle. Perhaps because it diminishes the importance of the naked fundament, which has been despoiled to satisfy the vulgar desire for a tan. It is a sacrifice made on behalf of appearance, giving the poolside gigolo — played by Richard Gere, inevitably — priority over the lover. This is a disappointment, but not as big as the one I must be giving her.

'Let's go to bed,' she whispers. She is supine, I am superior, but in position only. I kiss her perfumed throat which smells sweet, but leaves a bitter taste. If my impotence is simply the result of first night nerves, a psychological defect that is curable, it is something I can live with; but if it is the by-product of cardio-vascular irregularity, if my overworked heart cannot pump enough blood down to the pertinent extremity, then I might as well be dead, and probably will be soon. Either way, it doesn't look as if I'll be fucking Stella tonight. Instead my fingers penetrate between her thighs, causing her to groan softly. The sounds gradually become rhythmic until it's like she's playing modern jazz on an invisible saxophone. But it's a duet she's after, not a solo. 'Please, Jonah,' she gasps, 'I want you to fuck me.' But all she gets is the consolation prize as I sullenly rub her clitoris. She sits up suddenly, grabbing my arm for support, so that her long nails dig into my flesh. Even though I can feel the skin peeling I make no sound. What right have I to complain? It is Stella who screams, a long throaty cry.

'Move over,' she says, having recovered her breath. 'Now I'll fuck you.' Kneeling down she sucks my balls and would surely swallow my penis if it weren't attached. God's cruelty is exquisite, this is worse than being blown up, this defeat snatched from the jaws of victory.

'I'm sorry,' I say, though whether to Stella, my wife or God I'm not sure. Perhaps the last named assumes it's for Him, because a miracle occurs. How else to explain my new-found potency? Quickly I roll on to and into Stella, whose unblinking eyes open wide as if in shock. 'Slowly,' she hisses, trying to control my thrusts with her hips, 'slowly.' But I am beyond advice. Within seconds I am an adulterer. Stella, however, is not impressed. 'Why are you doing this?' she asks. 'Because of Franz Kafka,' I reply. 'How so?' she asks. 'He had this woman called Milena,' I say, 'and he took her to a hotel where — so far as we can tell from the letters — he backed out. Now his biographers speculate upon his sexuality and wonder if he ever really had a woman. Well, I want my descendants to know that I did — and more than one. I want them to know for sure that — despite being scared — I became an adulterer.' 'So this is your first time with another woman?' she asks. I nod. 'I should have guessed,' she says, 'but never mind, the second time will be much better.' 'How do you know?' I ask. 'Because you'll have taken this,' she replies, holding up a finger-sized phial filled with brown powder. 'What is it?' I ask. 'A little something for the amateur philanderer,' she replies, 'all the way from Babylon.' The label, I note, is printed in Arabic. 'You really want me to take it?' I ask. 'Jonah,' she says, 'I want you to fuck me till I come. If you think taking that will help, then I really want you to take it.' 'What's in it?' I ask. 'Rhinoceros horn,' she replies. 'You're joking,' I say. 'Jonah,' she says, 'do it for me.' 'I'll need a glass of water,' I say. Still naked she brings wine for us both. I tip the contents of the phial into my hand. It's like swallowing sand. 'Thank you, darling,' says Stella, getting into bed. 'I'm going to take a nap. Wake me when you're horny.'

Unwilling to stay, but unable to leave, tired but too depressed to sleep I turn on the television and flick through the channels until I find a late night movie. It takes only a few seconds to recognize James Whale's *Frankenstein*. I watch with growing desperation as Colin Clive, the modern Prometheus, flees from the monster he has created. And what a monster Boris Karloff turned out to be! Misshapen, malevolent, but also the acme of inarticulate despair.

Unfortunately it is an old print and the picture keeps wavering, which makes me feel dizzy as well as miserable. I shake my head to clear it and see out of the corner of my eye that the quilt has slipped off Stella's slumberous body, leaving her breasts and more completely unprotected. And so, as the monster forces his way into the bedroom of Frankenstein's fiancée, I lurch towards my mistress's open sex like a beast overcome with passion. I have become a monster dreamed up by my own desires; I am the id personified, King Priap unfettered. I don't ask Stella, I take her. She wakes, feeling me stiff within, and stares at me in amazement, until her eyes begin to roll and nothing is showing but the milky whites. Who's in control now, my friend? Taken to the brink Stella raises her head and cries, 'That's it! That's it!' At which point I erupt.

The next thing I know I am alone in the bed. Stella is across the room, on the telephone, saying something that sounds like, 'Is that the Syrian embassy?' There is a pause. 'I need to speak to Said,' she says. Another pause, then, 'Tell him it's the girl from Babylon. He'll know who I am.' Finally, after a long delay, she says, 'Everything's ready.'

I try to get up, but cannot move a muscle. 'What's happened to me?' I ask, but Stella doesn't answer. I'm not even sure that I'm properly awake. This is what Mary Shelley (née Godwin) must have experienced that night at the Villa Diodati, trapped in the desert between sleep and thought. But there the resemblance ends; what she saw 'with shut eyes, but acute mental vision', was but a sweet dream compared to what I am about to experience.

Said is a handsome man, brown-haired, doe-eyed; kitted out like an American academic in button-down shirt, red tie and charcoal grey pin-stripe, though I cannot explain the incongruous duffel bag. Stella, beautiful but dishevelled, remains stark naked, a comment upon the nature of their relationship, confirmed by Said's next gesture. He dips a finger in Stella's belly and sniffs it. 'I see that your sacrifice was very great,' he says. 'We shall undoubtedly name a square for you in Jerusalem — after the victory.'

Oh God, I've heard that Syrians, before killing a prisoner, like to turn his testicles into gob-stoppers. The only question in my mind — or what remains of it — is whether Said's revenge is political or personal. He opens the mysterious bag and I wait to see the murderous glint of a carving knife; instead he withdraws a lump of plasticine the size of a bag of sugar. Then he puts on a white coat which I don't like at all.

'Are you sure he's relaxed?' he asks. 'See for yourself,' replies Stella. He leans over me. 'Dr Isaacson, I presume,' he says. 'My name is Dr Habash, Dr Said Habash, doctor of medicine. I regret to inform you that I must inflict a little pain upon your person, but I'm sure you'll agree that a broken arm is a small price to pay for the pleasure Stella provided. Moreover, I can assure you that the break will be clean and that it will be expertly reset.'

Turning away from me he whispers, 'Let's get it over with,' and Stella reappears, ball hammer in hand, looking like the Soviet goddess of labour, which is a relief. I must be hallucinating, otherwise I'd surely feel more than a tingle when the hammer snaps my radius. 'Cyclonite,' says Said. And Stella, bless her, returns with the sugar to sweeten my wound. This is rolled into strips and wrapped around my arm between layers of plaster. 'Best let him sleep it off,' the doctor advises.

When you go to the movies you're actually participating in a complicated perceptual exercise, not fully understood even now. What the eye sees through its lens is a series of individual pictures, all upsidedown, which is hardly the continuous movement our sense of vision seems to be showing us. Between the 'seeing' and the 'showing' there is, deep in the brain, a time lag in psychological perception, while the images are decoded. I spend the night stuck in that interstice.

'Oh my God,' I say next morning, upon seeing my arm, 'it really happened.' 'It's all my fault,' says Stella. 'I shouldn't have made you take that aphrodisiac, though I cannot put my hand on my heart and swear that I'm one hundred per cent sorry.' Here she smiles, letting me know that I came good in the end. 'The second time was sensational, so wild that we both fell out of bed. And that's when you broke your arm.' 'Then what?' I ask. 'I phoned for a taxi,' she replies. 'The driver was a young

Moroccan — you seemed to think he'd come to harm you — but he was wonderful. Together we got you to the City Hospital. Luckily it was a quiet night in casualty. We were back within the hour.'

Having had my memory restored it is time to think of a lie to take home. I look at Noddy, who shakes his head affirmatively, but also as if to hurry me. No wonder, it is already nine-thirty. 'What am I going to tell my wife?' Stella comes to the rescue, as she does in the shower, when I try to wash off the evidence of my mortal sin with only one available hand. 'Tell her the truth,' she says, 'that you fell out of bed. Look on the bright side, at least you won't have to explain away the scratches.'

After breakfast I walk to the station and wait for the first train from Sheffield to arrive. Then I go to telephone my wife. Fishing for the necessary coins in my pocket my fingers find a cool tube. I smile, expecting to pull out the magic phial, a strange but sentimental memento. But no, it's something better; one of those flashy ball-points with a digital clock incorporated in the top and my name engraved on the barrel. Attached is a note which reads, 'Now you'll have no excuse not to write.' My wife, much to my relief, accepts mine, and not without sympathy. She even asks if I am in pain.

The El Al flight to Israel is fully booked, and the departure lounge is already crowded with school parties from north-west London, Christian pilgrims from Bath, curious Japanese, Hasidic Jews from Stamford Hill, and sacrilegious semites from all over, including my wife's Great-aunt Bella, a woman with a past who retains at least the skeleton of her notorious loveliness. The security officers recognize my wife and wave our party through. True, they ask questions about my arm, but these are more concerned than suspicious. Because of it I no longer feel the need to denounce myself to them as dangerous. It was crime and punishment all in one night, and surely even God does not practise double jeopardy.

The take-off is perfect and some of the passengers clap the

pilot. There are a lot of us sitting anonymously in the jumbo's whale-like belly. Jumbo. None of our names are likely to last as long as that poor elephant's, to become synonymous with a whole species or type, like Hoover and Xerox and, maybe, Technicolor. The original Jumbo, if I remember aright (my dictionary is on my desk at home), served out a life sentence at the London Zoo. How I empathize! And I don't think I am alone in this. Women in their face-paint, men in their strait-jackets and ties, we all prepare for our diurnal parts in the circus called civilization, pretending that we are sentient beings with all our senses tamed. But in our hearts we yearn for the jungle or savannah, where death is not invisible, but a palpable thing you are taught to outwit or outrun.

The jet begins to climb to its cruising height. *Per ardua ad astra.* Why was I prepared to risk everything, just to fuck Stella, to put my life on the line for someone as hollow as Meryl Streep? I'm not daft enough to expect spontaneous intercourse in this day and age — no Jane will swing my way — but I am vulnerable to the command performance meant for an audience of one, in which Stella has a talent acknowledged by royal appointment. But even she cannot outface death, though she has discovered how to smooth away its fingerprints, those marks time leaves upon our physiognomies. Perhaps that is enough, the illusion of immortality.

After the in-flight movie, after the plane has crossed the last coastline of Europe and is casting its shadow on the purple sea that gave birth to Aphrodite, when my blasé wife is drugged with the tedium of her umpteenth flight and her Great-aunt Bella out cold, I'll take the brand new biro from my breast pocket, check how much longer there is to go, click the button at its top, and begin my first letter to Stella, informing her at last — coward that I am — of the little lump I felt in her left breast.

2

Zap! Pow! On the screen people are dropping like flies! It's difficult to decide who's the more bloodthirsty, the director or the great dictator whose bio-pic this is. Either way some of their power has devolved upon me; I, too, can bump off a character with a stroke of the pen. Shall I pretend that I never felt that extraneous lump in Stella's bosom, and thereby withhold vital information from her? My mistress's consequent removal would certainly spare me a lot of potential distress. What was her last message? 'Now you'll have no excuse not to write.' Correct me if I'm wrong, but doesn't that suggest a wish for our affair to continue? A desire I'm not sure I share. Certainly I lusted after Stella, but I only wanted to fuck her once, to prove that I could make out with other women, not become the sort of man who does, though I'm well aware that the memory of the first copulation will ensure subsequent capitulation. Is this a new definition of love? My wife is a moral woman but, even so, I think it would be difficult to convince her of the necessity of renewing contact with a trollop on the grounds that it is better to be her lover than her murderer.

'The people who made this film must themselves be Nazis,' says Great-aunt Bella, echoing the complaint her great-niece made to Professor Gutkes. 'Most artists are, in my experience.' Extensive, as you know, Great-aunt Bella's life having been as scandalous as that of the nephew she is on her way to see. 'Take Marinetti,' continues Great-aunt Bella. 'Ask me now and I'll tell you he was crazy, but then everyone called him a genius and I believed them. To me he was a god. We went everywhere in his racing car, which he drove at top speed. Heads turned as we flew past, to see the flashing meteor, the dashing officer and the beautiful girl. "Bella," he would say to me, "I am a mystic of action. I worship four things: speed, danger, war and you." '

He would have screwed Stella, that's for sure, but not written to her; memory meant nothing to him, the eye everything, as he believed in sensation rather than contemplation, consciousness rather than conscience. To be fair, the instinct for self-preservation was another casualty of this *Weltanschauung*, though I can hardly criticize him for that these days.

'By some miracle he survived the First World War,' continues Great-aunt Bella. 'The Great Iconoclasm, he called it. He came home claiming that he felt reborn, though it would have been better if he'd never returned. He was right to have called himself a Futurist, he should have been young now, not then. These flights were made for him; to be travelling at 600 miles per hour, while some movie stutters to a morbid conclusion. Instead he went to Rome, fell in love with Mussolini, wrote *Futurismo e fascismo*, and broke my heart.'

Great-aunt Bella is right, we are inhabitants of a futuristic Utopia, we four hundred quiescent citizens of a subsonic city state, whose charter is a timetable, whose *raison d'être* is movement, whose aim is to shrink the world. Within the cabin the pilot's rule is absolute, while our role as the *hoi polloi* is to offer unquestioning obedience to the handmaidens and stewards who secretly police our behaviour. Not that we mind! We don't want to scare ourselves with the problems of aerodynamics. Give us an inkling of the potential flaws that could turn our triumph over the atmosphere into a catastrophe and there would be anarchy on board. No, it's better we don't know how fragile are the walls that separate us from infinity's blue beyond.

Like the Futurists, who chose cinematographic effects to convey the illusion of motion, airline companies also demonstrate movement in a way you've often seen on the screen. In the same package that contains the emergency drill and the disposable bag (unpleasant reminders of the frailty of machine and man) you'll find maps, upon which our routes are represented as thin red lines, as though the motion of jets through air was exclusively laminar, and their invisible trails were really the province of cartographers, in the manner of geographical phenomena, rather than insurance salesmen.

My wife, being a travel agent, is an essential part of the cartel, which is why she is able to sleep so soundly, an example her great-aunt copies, leaving me awake with my subversive doubts. I have watched too many movies and read too many newspapers not to fear the hidden bomb and the zealous hijacker, as well as other natural and unnatural occurrences such as human error, metal fatigue, food poisoning in the cockpit and clear air turbulence without; the latter being especially reserved for high fliers like us.

At 35,000 feet, our present height, we are well above the small-scale turbulence which characterizes the lower atmosphere, but right in line, if unlucky, for its big brother, the terror of the upper atmosphere. Clear air turbulence, with its 100-mile per hour verticals and helter-skelter troughs, may well be of sufficient intensity to strain our aircraft's very structure. In the quotidian there are certain things you avoid because you know they are trouble, just as an alert pilot will skirt thunderously high cumulus clouds; but every so often you get lured off the straight and narrow, as I was by Stella, and thereafter, as a resident in life's fast lane, you'd better be on the lookout for turbulence though you'll be lucky to see it coming, laminar motion being a thing of the past.

All things considered, I ought to forget Stella, if only for the sake of my wife, but I cannot because — beat this for perversity — I have the aforementioned moral obligation to contact her, for the sake of her life.

Let's get it over with, while my wife is still snoozing. I give her a sideways glance, just to make sure, and am unexpectedly moved by her vulnerability and beauty, so much so that I want to preserve the moment forever, forgetting that the only immortal instrument I have to hand is the biro, presented to me by Stella, which I must soon use to inform my benefactor that she probably has breast cancer. I roll the pen between my fingers, ever surprised that such a nondescript little item (even this one, which is personalized and ticking) can be the repository of so much power.

41

When I was a boy I loved coloured pencils for the magic they contained and, inspired by romantic reveries of the artistic life, I drew in the evening after school until one of our German au pairs, delivering my supper of milk and a biscuit, warned me grimly that pencils were as deadly as adders. 'Impossible!' I cried. 'They contain lead,' she said, 'and lead is poisonous.' Here she picked up one of the crayons and pressed its point into her breast, as if she were Cleopatra with an asp. 'Prick your finger with one of these,' she said, 'and you'll see a red line start to move towards your heart. It is death that is creeping up your arm. And nothing can stop it.' 'Nothing?' I ask, horrified. 'Nothing,' she replies calmly, as I place my thumb on the biro's propellor in readiness for the words that Stella least expects.

The plane, however, has other ideas. It suddenly ascends like a pole-vaulter, pausing shudderingly at the perihelion, so much so that my wrist shakes like a seismograph over the San Andreas faultline, before dropping as if pole-axed, with such abruptness that the pen slips from my grasp and rolls down the aisle, coming to rest at the feet of a frail woman with thin red hair atop a ravaged face still showing signs of remarkable beauty. She bends with difficulty and, wrapping her long fingers around my biro, examines with weak eyes the name incised upon its side, then taps the shoulder of the man in front of her, a white haired old devil sporting a seadog's patch, who looks famously familiar. His name may be on the tip of my tongue, but it certainly isn't on my pen; nevertheless, he nods his gentlemanly thanks to the lady and pockets it.

Alas I am in no position to retrieve the thing, being pre-occupied with remaining in my seat, which I'm hanging on to like the greenhorn traveller in Lewis Falcon's great Western, *Deadwood Stage*. Actually, I'd be less concerned if the crew were mocking my efforts, calmly chewing tobacco like Andy Devine and, between gobs of brown juice, saying to John Wayne in that sing-song way of his, 'That dude don't know he's bin born,' but they are equal victims of gravity's uncertain embrace, and most are slithering on the floor or falling in the laps of fearful pilgrims.

My wife, now wide awake of course, straps up her dozy old relative and hugs my plaster cast, as if comforted by its properties as a healer of fractures. But it's a bigger hand than mine that has the plane in its grip, maybe even the invisible fist of God, intent upon shaking the last secrets out of us.

One by one the luggage compartments burst open, spilling their contents upon the unprotected heads of the passengers beneath. We are fortunate in that only overcoats and soft bags fall upon us, but others have pates bruised and foreheads split open by duty free whisky and ghetto blasters. The sight of blood dribbling through hair and staining the antimacassars on the seat-backs is a touch too much verisimilitude for many of the passengers, especially the elderly party from Bath, whose screams of panic overwhelm the genuine sobs of pain. Between their banshee yells and the rhythmic throb of the engines the insistent buzz of prayers can be heard, though even this becomes somewhat more demanding when the oxygen masks drop unannounced from the ceiling, and sway upon their umbilical cords.

'We're going to crash!' cries a woman, old enough to have survived worse dangers. 'Are we?' asks my wife. 'I doubt it,' I reply. 'Well, if we do,' she says, 'I want you to know that I love you. Always have done, always will.' 'If we get out of this,' I say, 'let's make a baby.' 'It's a deal,' says my wife. 'I want that in writing,' I say. 'Then give me a ballpoint,' she says, 'You had one in your hand a few moments ago, a rather swish one if my eyes didn't deceive me.' Shaken by this observation, not to mention our predicament, and shamed by the use proposed for my undeclared souvenir, I am tempted to confess its provenance, but all I reveal is its terminus. 'Pity,' says my wife.

I notice that several other people, notably the Israelis and the Japanese, are attempting to write last testaments in notepads, passports or on the back of landing cards. The latter, having inscribed their ultimate word (or so they think), sign off with an inkan, their personal seal made of ivory, for which no substitute has yet been sought, though four thousand elephants are still being slaughtered every year to satisfy this vanity. Perhaps I am to be the unwitting victim of their revenge, my juvenile nightmare realized at last. I look along the aisle and remark that the pirate who pilfered my pen does not share this need for a final message. Who is he? Perhaps some old Futurist, enthralled by the practical demonstration of relativity now being offered by El Al.

One minute, as we encounter heavenly resistance, it seems that we have stopped, the next (which feels more like an hour than a minute) we are catapulting through space at brain-teasing speeds. Nor is it only the cerebellum that is bewildered: some of the passengers are having out-of-body experiences, evidence of which is piling up in the puce bags that accompany the route maps. Thus we hurry toward our destination or our destiny while below, on the laminated waters, the Cyclades and the Sporades bask like turtles.

'Ladies and gentlemen,' says a voice over the intercom, 'you have just survived an act of God. Clear air turbulence, like the Almighty, moves in mysterious ways, being invisible, unpredictable and undetectable. Hence the unscheduled aerobatics, for which I apologize. If anyone received a knock please contact a member of the cabin crew for immediate assistance. The rest of you may relax and enjoy the remainder of your flight with my assurance that it will be as smooth as Jacob's backside.'

We all applaud, moulded into one people by the supernatural trial and the hard-won knowledge of external danger. This has made us sceptical of predetermined routes, but even more dependent upon the skills of our captain, now transformed from Mussolini into Moses. We have crossed an invisible boundary up here and become Israel in miniature, just as the stagecoach may be said to represent America in Lewis Falcon's film.

Therein, you'll recall, the Deadwood Stage (meaning also a time to cut down and build anew) survives nature's hostilities – the desert – and Apaches – denizens thereof – on its way to Lordsburg – the heavenly city – wherein all the human problems that motivate the journey and the movie are resolved. The hero and the heroine ride off into the sunset to build their log cabin and raise a family, the last words of the film being: 'We'll plant trees. We'll make the land green.'

As it happens, that's what they said about Israel when I was a kid, and it is a comparison I intend to make in my introduction to the movie, when it is shown as part of the Jerusalem Film

Festival's homage to Falcon. I still have, in an old chest, a document, decorated with idealized kibbutzniks, certifying that a tree has been planted for me in an Israeli forest. It could even be that some of my leafy alter ego's exhalations were among those that buffeted our plane and prevented me from writing to Stella. For what reason? Self-preservation? Paper, after all, comes from wood pulp. Less writing, more trees. Or was there some other arcane intention in that arboreal mind? Oh foolish tree, to think that blowing in the wind could change the course of an aeroplane, let alone history. Oh naive boy, to imagine that one tree would make a bosky paradise.

No, Israel is more like a jungle, to judge by the behaviour of some of its citizens. One such — an obese man in a bespoke jacket spoilt by a spilt drink — breaks up the harmony on board with his vociferous, multilingual complaints. 'Thanks to your pilot's clumsiness,' he screams at the stewardess, 'I shall have to cancel a meeting and jeopardize a deal worth millions of dollars. I'm going to sue you for billions!' Good luck to him! Truculence may be unpleasant, as turbulence is scary, but both are symptoms of autonomy, and therefore to be valued. They are blows against obedience and the preordained route, they are the contra-indications of individuality and free-will.

Taking their cue from the fat man other voices begin to grumble, or to tell the tale of our breezy escapade umpteen various ways, though surely only Great-aunt Bella slept through the whole ordeal to awaken with the words, 'I dreamt I was young again,' all of which is also to be welcomed; so long as there is pluralism, a proliferation of stories and interpretations, then the future won't be fascistic. Though, according to Petra and Polly, our destination already is.

The same couple, incidentally, picketed the showing of *Deadwood Stage* during my Western season the term before Professor Gutkes's arrival. They branded Lewis Falcon a racist and called the film an unacceptable tribute to social darwinism which, in the name of progress, sanctioned the genocide of the native American people. 'Viva Geronimo!' they cried, just as more recently they chanted, 'Arafat, Arafat!'

And why don't I join in? Why do I salute the turbulent, but

damn the terrorist? Because a terrorist is not some wind-blown privateer freebooting his way to a fortune, but a person who wants to rework the map according to a different — but no less determined — world view. Nor do I like the idea that these new red lines won't be drawn with ink.

Just consider an electro-cardiogram, that visual representation of our bloody impulses; up and down signifies alive and kicking, straight means dead, which may be why the imagination is stirred by mountain chains rather than the plains, always excepting the coastal one we are now descending upon with our undercarriage lowered.

The Futurists were right, it is a small planet. Standing in the baggage hall, just beyond passport control, where only arriving passengers should be, is my wife's uncle, sleek, muscular, and obviously at home in his land of exile. We wave from our place in the queue and he responds, though he seems equally surprised to see us. 'Did you tell him we were coming?' I ask my wife. 'No,' she replies. 'So why is he at the airport?' I ask. 'I can't tell you,' she replies, though I can tell you the reason he is in Israel, why he couldn't make Founder's Day at the University of St Albans.

Because he's on the run, wanted by the fraud squad in connection with a financial scandal in the City. It seems that one of his cronies, chairman of an even larger company than his own (itself the biggest property developers in private hands), had given him the wherewithal (written off as a payment for 'professional advice') to invest millions in his firm, in order to create an artificial demand for their shares. And this, it turned out, was in breach of company law. Unfortunately the high flier's profession of ignorance didn't cut much ice with the salt of the earth types who knew things in their bones and joined the fraud squad to put the likes of my wife's uncle where they belonged: behind bars in Richbell Place, their Holborn headquarters. Looking at him as suspiciously as the immigration official is now eyeing me, the boys in blue said, 'You're going to have to do better than that, sir.' My wife's uncle knew he couldn't and so, rather than face a second interrogation and almost certain incarceration, he approached his niece and begged her to get him to Israel as soon as possible, which she did, via Belfast, Dublin and Rome.

At Tel Aviv he invoked the Law of Return, whereby all Jews are potential citizens of Israel, and within days persuaded his new government's Ministry of Industry and Trade to back *Cisco*, his acronym for the Cinematographers of Israel Corporation, which he ran from a small office on King Solomon Street. The Minister thereof took to my wife's uncle immediately, so obviously that the press soon dubbed them the Cisco Kid and Pancho, not inappropriately, as my unlawful uncle's aim was to construct a frontier town in the Negev desert, wherein he would produce a series of Westerns, each based upon biblical originals, and the paunchy Minister had the morals of a Mexican bandit.

In order to attract capital for this proposal my wife's uncle suggested that the Minister should offer the locals a tax shelter if they put their shekels in Israeli-made movies. 'It's a great idea,' said the Minister, 'but how am I going to sell it to a Cabinet made up of humourless bastards with high moral principles?' 'Easy,' said my wife's uncle, 'remind them of *Three Coins in a Fountain*. Who wanted to go to Rome before that movie? It put Italy on the tourism map. My films will do the same for Israel. Everyone will want to come here. Tell your colleagues how much foreign currency that will earn.'

Cabinet meetings are held on Sundays in Israel. The following Monday (about the time we were toasting him in the Vice-Chancellor's sherry) my wife's uncle invited his fellow citizens to participate in the razzamatazz of movie-making by investing in *The Six Pointed Star*, as King David's story was to be called. 'It will be an Israeli film, shot here with local actors,' he promised, 'but it will also have a director of international stature.' Most Israelis thought he was lying, but they have a soft spot for such barefaced cheek, and they gave him their money.

Our own passports duly stamped, we approach the sun-tanned scoundrel, who, having given his aunt a dutiful peck on the cheek, cries: 'So where is he?' 'Where is who?' I ask. 'Who?' he cries. 'Lewis Falcon, that's who! Here to be an ornament of our Film Festival and, though he does not know it yet, to do a little work. Wasn't he on your flight?' The man with the eye-patch! No wonder I suddenly recalled *Deadwood Stage*. But why hadn't I recognized its creator? The fact is that though I've read the descriptions in all the unauthorized biographies, and seen a few photographs, none of them contemporary, I don't really know what he looks like now, except that he wears an eye-patch, but then so did Moshe Dayan, and who's more likely to be on the flight to Tel Aviv?

Nevertheless, when he shows up at last on our side of the barrier he is unmistakably Lewis Falcon, and I wonder at my failure. There is a dangerous look to his septuagenarian features, as though he could do or say anything. My wife's uncle, who clearly wants him to say 'Yes' to something, fusses around him like an ox-pecker on the back of a rhino. 'My God,' I whisper, 'you don't expect him to direct *The Six Pointed Star*?' 'Mr Falcon,' he says, gesturing towards his aunt and my wife, 'meet my family.' While the ancient son of capricorn examines the women with his one good eye my wife's uncle looks at me as though he's forgotten who I am, so I make the introduction myself. 'My name may be already familiar to you, Mr Falcon,' I say, 'I'm Jonah Isaacson.' 'Never heard of you,' he replies.

When Marcellus, in dusty battle fatigues, cocks his machine gun and says, 'Something is rotten in the state of Denmark,' many in the audience cheer, whoop or applaud, to inform the cast that they know this *Hamlet* is about warmer places than Scandinavia, and that they are with them.

Some years ago my scholarly interest in the Old West took me to the National Cowboy Hall of Fame in Oklahoma City. Nearby was Tsa-La-Gi, location of the Cherokee Cultural Center, where I saw performed, in the only artificially cooled al fresco amphitheatre on the continent, a production entitled *The Trail of Tears*. Although the lachrymose appellation suggested an evening of lamentation, the play was actually an upbeat celebration of statehood, enacted in the dramatic equivalent of capital letters. But even here, a few miles from Muskogee, the red-neck capital of America, the audience clapped when a Cherokee, ill-used by illegal settlers, said: 'The United States, as usual, is backing the wrong side.' They'd had enough of the South Vietnamese, and they didn't care who knew it.

I turn to Lewis Falcon in order to explain that the Israelis feel the same way about the Lebanese, but his ears are blocked by the headphones that are providing him with a simultaneous translation of Shakespeare's famous soliloquies etcetera.

We are at the National Theatre to watch the intemperate young actor playing Hamlet, earmarked by my wife's uncle for the lead in *The Six Pointed Star*; though the yellow one, pinned to the cloak of the ghost, now yelling blue murder at his frantic son, signifies the late king's martyrdom rather than his status as marshal of hellfire. His last words – 'Adieu, adieu! Hamlet, remember me' – are somewhat redundant in this context. As if anyone in the theatre could forget – in Israel of all places – the fate of those the star denotes. And so Hamlet, palpably burdened by the terrible disclosure, staggers off to regain his kingdom from his uncle.

My wife's uncle, I observe, is somewhat discomforted by Claudius, who has been padded out to resemble his friend the Minister. Worse than that, he is wearing jackboots. Gertrude, 'the imperial jointress of this warlike state', is decked out seraglio-style like a voluptuous daughter of Jerusalem, in so loose-fitting a blouse that she is effectively bare-breasted. A pearl, milky-white, adds an opaque glow to her navel. As to her private parts, even these are on public view, through her transparent pantaloons. She is the state, and the state, as all can see, belongs to the strongest. No wonder her only son eats his heart out.

Dudu Wolf's performance as Hamlet has caused a sensation in Israel. He has managed to capture, in lines left over from the English renaissance, all the agony of his generation; a haunted generation, haunted by an unquiet past, a betrayed generation, betrayed by its parents, a lost generation, with no direction known. The cheer that arises from his contemporaries when the prince stabs Polonius, a self-righteous rabbi from Mea Sherim rather than a Lord Chamberlain, is frightening. It is frightening because they are endorsing the very act that leads, eventually, to

Hamlet's destruction. In their confusion and their rage they want, like Hamlet, to strike blindly at their enemies who are, of course, rejected parts of themselves. The deed has become more important than its consequences.

By the final act Dudu Wolf looks like Wittgenstein on speed, his world delineated not by language but by action. It is action not words that has won him the pearl, that obscure object of his desire, the treasure of the state deposited in the treasury of its queen, which does for them all — king, queen and prince — with its poison.

Now there's no pretence that the action is taking place in distant Denmark. The queen dies first, killed by the bitter fruit of her navel. As she writhes upon the ground crying, 'I am poison'd,' Dudu Wolf rises to his feet and rises further than that for he has become the avenging angel, death personified. The audience shivers involuntarily, half convinced that divine retribution is being enacted before their eyes, a punishment so severe that it will be visited upon the people as well as their ruler. Dudu, possessed, stabs the king, calling him 'damned Jew' instead of Dane, then forces the venomous juice between his lips, draining the dregs himself. There is stillness on the stage, and a chill in the auditorium, as though a new ice age for the Jews had just commenced. And then the spell breaks, proving Hamlet wrong; the rest is not silence, but glorious summer for another nation. The sound of grenades and kalashnikovs precedes the entrance of Fortinbras. Stepping over the illustrious corpses he unwraps his Palestinian keffiyeh and pronounces the words, 'I have some rights of memory in this kingdom.' Then there is real silence, but only until the resurrected cast takes its bow. Yassir Arafat at the United Nations didn't get a bigger ovation.

'What the hell was that all about?' asks Lewis Falcon. He must be the only person in the Habima who doesn't know. The director's warning is clear to the rest of us; victory will go to those who, in the name of some remembered wrong, do not commit suicidal folly. We understand also, for the first time, the significance of the opening scene. The sentries posted to watch for Fortinbras see instead the ghost, thereby bringing about the very event they were stationed to prevent.

This production, unsurprisingly, has not been a palpable hit with those who wish to retain the West Bank for reasons of security, especially those settlers who claim — when forced by politics to put aside their messianic motivations — to be the eyes of Israel. Indeed, their patron saint, the Minister of Industry and Trade, asked the Knesset to ban it. I open my mouth to explain all this to Lewis Falcon, but no more comes out than came out of Cordelia's at the end of *King Lear*.

'Forget about the play,' says my wife's uncle, 'what did you think of the boy's performance?' 'I'll tell you this,' says Lewis Falcon, leading us to the bar, 'that kid has more emotion in his foreshortened pecker than Gary Cooper had in his entire body.' 'Then you think he's right for *The Six Pointed Star*?' asks the would-be mogul. 'I didn't say that, Mr Jacobi,' replies the great director, downing his whisky in a single gulp. 'I meant he'd be a hit with the faggots and such like who dress up as cowboys. They'd lap up his histrionics. Not my audience. They know their heroes suffer, but they don't expect them to show it. They don't give a shit about acting, they want reality. And that's what we gave 'em. And that's why — since the Gary Coopers, Jimmy Stewarts, Henry Fondas and John Waynes retired or died — I don't make movies any more.' There's a tear in his eye. 'That's bullshit,' whispers my wife's uncle. 'The reason he hasn't made a film in seven years is that no one will back him. Westerns are old-fashioned, Falcon's a has-been, and both are box-office poison — that's the conventional wisdom, and he knows it. So you'd think he'd show a bit of gratitude to someone who's saying — "Mr Falcon, I think you're a genius. Here's five million dollars. Go make a movie."'

By the time we get back to the Hotel Splendide on Tel Aviv's new esplanade Lewis Falcon is drunk. Although it is nearly midnight Great-aunt Bella, equally spirited, is slouched in a flapper's outfit on a sofa in the bar. 'Enjoy the play?' she yells upon seeing us, causing the other lounge lizards to turn their heads sleepily in our direction. At the airport Lewis Falcon had hardly given the old lady a second glance, but now he is transfixed by the octogenarian siren, and gladly joins her on what her jealous nephew quickly calls the geriatric casting couch.

'Do you think there's a chance he'll say Yes?' he asks. 'Do you?' I reply. His face does not register hope. 'I'm taking him to meet the Minister tomorrow,' continues my wife's uncle, 'whose expectations are somewhat in advance of the actual proceedings.' The Minister is famous for many things, but patience is not one of them. The Cisco Kid looks like he's heading for the last round-up. 'Good night, auntie,' he says.

'What's your hurry?' cries Lewis Falcon. 'I want to know why you didn't introduce me to this lady earlier, instead of dragging us all off to see that pansy wet his pants. It turns out that this woman, your aunt, actually appeared in *L'Age d'Or*, one of my all-time favourite movies. Listen, I met Buñuel once, at George Cukor's house. We were all there: Billy Wilder, William Wyler, Alfred Hitchcock, John Ford — who was carried in and out by his muscular black manservant — and yours truly. Buñuel was a charming man who had compliments for all our films, including *Deadwood Stage*, but when I asked him about *L'Age d'Or* all he could say was, "I haven't seen it since it was made, so I can't really tell you anything about it." Now, Mr Jacobi, I have a second chance and I don't intend to let it pass.'

'I'm sure my aunt will be happy to oblige,' says her nephew in a way that could hardly be described as respectful. Bella ignores the remark and gives her full attention to her new admirer.

'*L'Age d'Or* is, as you know, a hymn to *l'amour fou*,' she says, flirting with her new conquest, 'Buñuel being a surrealist and all that. But there was method in that man's madness, believe me. His script left very little to chance. So, providing the actors were sympathetic, he didn't have to do much directing. Max Ernst got me a part — only a small one. My real moment of glory came when the Italian Embassy — misconstruing the performance of Picasso's friend Artigas, whose moustaches were almost as big as his body, as a slight upon our equally diminutive king, Victor Emmanuel — filed a complaint. Being Italian myself I was sent to mollify the ambassador, a most ungracious gentleman who called me Buñuel's *buñuelo* — Buñuel's doughnut. I don't have to tell you what he meant by that.'

'I'd have shot the bastard,' growls Lewis Falcon, convincingly. 'Exactly what Buñuel proposed,' continues Bella. ' "A duel to the

52

death," he cried, "what could be more surrealistic?" It took a lot of persuasion to make him see sense. In the end he changed the location of the film from Paris to Rome, just to spite the Italians. Buñuel was an extraordinary man; capable of the most outrageous acts, yet always a gentleman, especially with the ladies. If you want to know the truth, Mr Falcon, I think he was a little scared of us.'

'Lewis, not Mr Falcon,' says the director. 'Well, Lewis, as you know, there was a scandal when the film was eventually shown at Studio 28. For six nights all was peaceful, but on the seventh the cinema was attacked by the Camelots du Roi who threw purple ink at the screen and screamed, "Down with the Jews!" '

'But Buñuel was a Catholic,' protests Lewis Falcon. 'My dear friend,' replies Bella, 'you are an American, you do not understand such things. To the European a Jew is anyone who threatens the established order.' 'Then I am a Jew too,' says Lewis Falcon. My wife's uncle looks at me, seeing in this conversion a glimmer of hope.

'Tell me,' says Lewis Falcon, 'the famous scene when the woman, out of her mind with desire, sucks the toe of a statue, whose idea was that?' 'Mine,' replies Bella. Lewis Falcon claps with delight. 'Mr Jacobi,' he says, 'your aunt is a great woman.' 'And a tired one,' she replies, accepting the compliment graciously. 'Of course,' says Lewis Falcon, 'it's been a long day.' He summons the waiter, who brings the bill for signature. 'I'll get it,' says Lewis Falcon, removing a pen — my pen — from his jacket. 'Nonsense,' says my wife's uncle, 'you're my guest.' Out comes his wallet, back goes my pen, at which I breathe a sigh of relief. I do not relish explaining to my wife why my name has been engraved thereon — an uncharacteristically vain gesture — and therefore resolve to let Lewis Falcon enjoy the benefit of his crime indefinitely.

'I'll pick you up in the morning,' says my wife's uncle to the aforenamed, 'we've got an appointment with the Minister of Industry and Trade at ten-thirty.' 'Exactly when I'm due at the beauty salon,' exclaims my wife.

*

While she is being pampered by the Hotel Splendide's version of Stella, I remember my obligation to the original and telephone St Albans, though I probably get Beer Sheva as it's an Arab voice that says hello. I reach her on the second attempt. She sounds upset, rather than pleased. 'Why didn't you write?' she says. 'How do you know I haven't?' I say. 'I've only been gone a day.' 'Have you?' she says. 'No,' I say. 'I knew it,' she says. 'Listen, Stella, I've got something to tell you,' I say. 'What?' she says, as though she dreads the answer. 'I felt a lump,' I say, 'in your left breast.' At which she laughs, with something like relief. 'Oh,' she says, 'is that all? I've had one before, as you probably noticed. It wasn't malignant, and I don't suppose this one will be either. Still, it was sweet of you to worry.' Silence. 'I miss you,' I say, surprised by the fact that the sentiment is suddenly true. 'And I was really looking forward to your letter,' she says. 'Most of my men friends don't bother with such niceties.' 'To tell you the truth,' I say, 'I almost started one on the plane.' 'What changed your mind?' she asks. 'I dropped the pen,' I say. 'Which pen?' she asks. 'The one you gave me,' I reply. 'Why didn't you pick it up?' she asks. 'Because someone beat me to it,' I reply. 'Who?' she asks. 'You'll never guess,' I reply. There is a pause, as though Stella suspects that I am leading her into a trap. 'Who?' she asks. 'Lewis Falcon,' I say. 'Who is he?' she asks in a lighter voice. 'A famous movie director,' I reply. 'So the pen is lost?' she asks. 'Not irretrievably,' I reply. 'It turns out that my wife's uncle — the one who built the University of St Albans — is ready to finance his next movie, providing he makes it in Israel.' 'Will he?'

That's the question! My wife's uncle is obviously beginning to think he will, because he invites both of us out to a celebratory lunch in Jaffa, Tel Aviv's ancient port, founded (some believe) by Jopa, daughter of Aeolus, the ruler of the winds, who seems to have been taking an uncanny interest in my affairs of late.

The interior of the Dolphin is cool and smells of charcoal and seafood, the cause being a barbecue which smoulders eternally on a patio overlooking the small harbour.

'Follow me,' says my wife's uncle, as he leads us through the kitchen, beneath a grand stone arch (left open to admit the offshore breezes) and on to the terrace where a fashionably dressed young Palestinian paints sardines and mullet with olive oil before laying them upon the griddle.

'Sami,' says my wife's uncle, 'I'd like you to meet my niece and her husband.' He nods in our direction, hardly taking his eyes away from the fish. A few hours ago they were in their watery element, now they are sizzling above the flames. We smile back.

'You know him?' asks my wife. 'I ought to,' replies her uncle, 'I own this restaurant. Or rather Alberto does. In case he should ever find it expedient to return to Zion.'

When the fish are ready Sami flips them on to a long blue dish which he offers to my wife's uncle who says, gratefully, 'Here's a boy who enjoys his job.'

'Do not patronize me please, Mr Jacobi,' replies Sami, holding another pair of sardines by their tails. 'I am your employee, not your servant. And if I look happy it is because my work puts me in mind of the parable which Rabbi Akiba told to Pappus, concerning a fox who, seeing some fish swimming for their lives from men with nets, says, "Why not join me on terra firma where you will be safe?" The wise fishes decline, preferring to remain with the devil they know, and most survive. Today, I fear, the fish are not so sensible, and many have risen to Zionism's foxy propaganda, with predictable consequences. That is why I smile as another tail curls over the heat.' Sami looks at us with something like pity. 'Mr Jacobi,' he says, 'I know that you and your people have had very bad experiences over there' – he points toward the western skyline, shimmering in the afternoon heat – 'but it is truly where you belong. Not here.'

'You are wrong, Sami,' says my wife's uncle, 'we have not jumped out of the European frying pan to end up in some Levantine fire. No, we are here to stay. And you can stay too, Sami, providing you remember who's boss. God gave us dominion over this land, over all its animals, over all the birds that fly through its air space, and over all the fishes that swim in its territorial waters.'

He makes an expansive gesture with his free arm that takes in the stone buildings of Jaffa, the wooden boats in its harbour and all the Mediterranean as far as the eye can see. 'Do you recognize that rock down there, Sami?' he asks, pointing to a jagged protuberance at the mouth of the harbour. 'That is where Andromeda was left in chains, just as was Palestine when we found her. Thank us, Sami, do not hate us.' 'It is not thanks you want,' replies Sami, 'but our love. And that you will never get.'

'Why don't you sack him?' asks my wife, when we have found an al fresco table on the curve of the world's oldest port. Just below us, at the foot of the sea wall, water laps at the ragged rocks, while above our heads dry palm leaves provide shelter from the midday sun. 'What for?' replies her uncle. 'For telling the truth?' He dips his flat bread into the spiced aubergine. 'On the subject of gratitude,' he continues, 'I do not think I have thanked you sufficiently for your help in saving me from an unmentionable fate. It is an omission I wish to rectify immediately.'

So saying he hands her an ebony box containing a white sphere the size of a billiard ball which, on closer inspection, proves to be a globe of the world. 'Solid ivory,' he says. 'Take it home through the green channel. It's not the sort of thing you can declare.' 'Thank you, uncle,' says my wife, kissing him indelicately on the mouth, 'you seem in a generous mood today.'

'With good reason,' he says. 'The fact of the matter is that the Minister and Lewis Falcon got on like a house on fire. Falcon is mad on guns, so what does the Minister do? Only presents him with a pair of Colt .45s. Not replicas but genuine antiques. I should know, they cost me a small fortune. Plus two hundred and fifty dollars for the holster. Falcon looks as pleased as punch. "May I?" he asks. "Be my guest," says the Minister. So Falcon buckles on the gun-belt and makes to go out of the office. But at the door he swivels on his heels, like he's the hero of one of his own pictures, whips out the pistols and fires. Bang! Bang! The bullets thud into the maps pinned to the Minister's wall. "Excuse me," says Falcon, "I got carried away." "I understand completely," says the Minister, examining (with some envy, I believe) the crater that used to be Lebanon. "Tell me," he says, "are they good guns?" "Excellent," replies Falcon, "except for their handles. Tortoiseshell looks good, but it's too slippery if your palms happen to sweat. I prefer wood." Then the Minister invites Falcon down to his ranch near the Red Sea for some real shooting and Falcon accepts. If you want my opinion, we're half way there! *We*? It seems as though he is talking about us, his relatives, rather than Cisco, his company, a suspicion confirmed when we learn that we are included in the invitation. 'Great-aunt Bella too?' asks my wife. 'At Lewis Falcon's insistence,' replies her uncle. 'Why not?' she says. 'Sounds like it might be fun.' 'What's eating Jonah?' asks her uncle. 'He looks like he doesn't agree.'

He's right. I ought to be delighted at the opportunity afforded to study Lewis Falcon at work, but I'm actually depressed at the thought of the great American auteur succumbing to Anthony Jacobi's blandishments. A falcon tethered to a gloved hand is not the same as a falcon on the wing.

'Another Jonah sat in this same spot a few thousand years ago looking just as glum, but for a much better reason,' says my wife's uncle. 'Why doesn't he cheer up? He's not going to Nineveh.'

If it weren't for the wadi that drains it, Makhtesh Ramon would be another Dead Sea and Mitzpeh Ramon a port like Jaffa. But Makhtesh Ramon is a barren crater, as efflorescent as the Painted Desert, and Mitzpeh Ramon merely the settlement that overlooks it. Perched on the edge of steep inland cliffs more than 500 metres high it had tentative beginnings.

In 1948 there was nothing here. Then the site was selected as the summit to which the Ascent of Independence aspired, and tents were put up to accommodate the men who would have to build that vertiginous highway.

If you've seen Lewis Falcon's *Iron Road* you'll know what happened next. Others moved in to satisfy the needs of the workers and pretty soon the tents had become prefabs which were themselves abandoned in favour of more permanent accommodation.

Nowadays the inhabitants work in the nearby gypsum quarries, which supply the busy cement factories of Israel, or serve mitz to parched tourists. Not surprisingly, Mitzpeh Ramon's most notable feature is a water tower.

We have paused in its shadow en route to the Minister's ranch at the request of my wife's uncle who has, it seems, a business associate in the vicinity. 'Here we are,' says the Minister's khaki-clad driver, pointing to a café-cum-souvenir shop. 'Mifgash Nevatim.'

The few stragglers still on the street stare at the gangsterishly proportioned American limousine as we emerge from its air-cooled interior into the sweltering day.

The restaurant, sparsely stocked with anorexic furniture, is without customers save for a ghostly man smothered in white powder, who stands involuntarily when he sees my wife's uncle, causing dust to rise around him in little clouds. 'Order drinks for yourselves,' says my wife's uncle, 'I'll join you in a minute.'

He sits opposite the spectre at his formica table where, judging by his reaction, he hears something not to his liking. 'What the fuck is a placodent?' he yells. The shade speaks quietly and we do not hear his answer. Subsequent enquiries reveal that a placodent is an extinct reptile with a flattened body and toughened shell something like a turtle, the discovery of whose fossilized remains has stopped work in the pale man's quarry, though why this should bother my wife's uncle remains a mystery.

Such is the perversity of history that the revolutionaries who made the Ma'ale Ha'atsmaut — the Ascent of Independence — possible, provide an inspiration to the Palestinians who want to replace them. Their successes prove that terrorism can have constructive ends; that road to the bottom of Makhtesh Ramon, the largest of the Negev's three craters, being one of them. These spectacular depressions were formed when the upper crust, weakened by the action of underground watercourses on its subsoil, caved in, thereby setting a precedent for anarchists in other lands who see terrorism as a metaphor, a puny substitute for an impossible dream: to take the ground from beneath our feet.

As we spiral down through the various strata like microbes on a corkscrew it soon becomes clear that our journey also has a didactic purpose. 'Does this remind you of anywhere?' my wife's uncle asks Lewis Falcon. The answer is obvious to any movie-goer; we could be in Arizona, Utah or New Mexico, travelling not in an Oldsmobile but in the Deadwood Stage itself. There's the same expanse of sand, rock and scrub surrounded, an unquantifiable distance away, by similar canyon walls, ochre, pink or even red, according to the light and the minerals deposited therein; in brief, the same beautiful hostility.

'I wanted you to get a feel of the place,' continues my wife's uncle, 'that's why we're driving down instead of flying. Maybe you'll even find a location or two.' 'It's like enough,' says Lewis Falcon, 'but it's not my America.' 'Does it really matter?' asks my wife's uncle. 'No one will know the difference.' 'I will, Mr Jacobi,' replies Lewis Falcon, as the road takes another twist and enters the triassic period.

'It's not just a question of resemblance, it's something else. You must understand that I do not pick a landscape just because it's picturesque. I audition the land, exactly as I would an actor. And I okay it for the same reason. It has to feel right to me. This doesn't, and I'll try to tell you why. It's like your Dudu Wolf, it's too showy. It looks like it's wearing make-up.'

'Is that such a bad thing?' enquires Great-aunt Bella, as we reach the bottom of the canyon which, in this upsidedown world, is of the same geological epoch as the top. 'It is if you're making a Western,' replies Lewis Falcon, turning towards my wife's uncle. 'Integrity is what they're all about, Mr Jacobi,' he says, 'and I don't intend to sell you mine.'

There is a long silence while we all look out of the windows as if weighing up the resemblance between this canyon and those of the American West. It is broken by my wife who suddenly cries, 'Stop!' The driver, sensitive to such imperatives, obeys and my wife, looking like she has caught something from the man in the café, runs to the side of the road where she adds the contents of her stomach to the desert's eco-system.

For a few moments it looks as though she might even faint, but instead the colour returns to her cheeks, and her concerned relatives breathe sighs of relief. As we stand around, waiting for her to feel sufficiently recovered to resume the journey, it occurs to me that we are unconsciously replaying the scene in *Deadwood Stage*, when those travellers pause in Monument Valley to give some comfort to the pregnant passenger and the driver, taking a gulp from his canteen, looks up toward the inscrutable sky and sees vultures circling there, a sign that carrion lies nearby. It is, in fact, the fulcrum of the film, the moment when life and death are in perfect balance — thereafter the scales will tip one way or the other.

I wonder if the coincidence has occurred to Lewis Falcon, who is kneeling beside Great-aunt Bella, his white hair blowing to and fro in the hot wind like the pages of a book.

Closer examination reveals that he is not proposing but observing a large beetle as it stumbles over the broken snail shells that have accumulated in the gap between two rocks. Progressing past these into the shadow it steps upon a glistening thread.

'Watch,' says Lewis Falcon, as the trap springs and the unfortunate beetle finds itself dangling from a webby platform, in the centre of which sits the black spider that will devour it.

'Could be the opening scene of a Buñuel movie,' says Lewis Falcon. 'Or one by Sam Peckinpah,' I add, thinking of *The Wild Bunch*. 'Enough,' says Great-aunt Bella, 'you're making me feel as sick as Sophie. How is the poor girl?' 'Better,' I say, 'but I'm getting itchy. Sweat evaporates in the desert, except under a plaster cast.'

Lewis Falcon, still on his knees, prods the doomed insect with a pen — my pen — prompting an unavailing impersonation of Harry Houdini. The spider, alerted by the vibrations, darts toward its prey. Is Lewis Falcon playing a similar game with me? For what reason?

'Correct me if I am wrong, Dr Isaacson,' he says, as he rises to his feet, 'but I assume you see, in this little confrontation, the Middle East in microcosm. Perhaps the spider is the Arab, waiting to ensnare the innocent Israeli, or maybe the spider is the industrious Israeli, prepared to defend its territory by all means possible. Either way, the interpretation remains indigenous. Your Israel, like my America, is a state of mind.' He touches his head, as if to suggest its real location.

'Some scholar — perhaps you know his name — once claimed that the true Western landscape requires five significant components. I'll list them for you: astonishment, plenitude, vastness, incongruity and melancholy.' He takes in the whole panorama, from the mountains of Edom in the east, across countless miles of inhospitable rock, to Har Ramon, the Head of Ramon, in the west.

'They are all here, to be sure, but I need something else. I tried to explain what to your wife's uncle, and now I shall make the endeavour again for your benefit. An archeologist can, by dint of spadework, recreate the past of any given area. Agreed? Well, I try to do the same. My methods, however, are impressionistic. In this I am like Remington, and those other heroic painters, who somehow managed to extract moments of dramatic action from terrain that was already highly charged. I just add the causes and the consequences, which are present anyway. All I need is my imagination, to pick up on them. And pretty soon the land is populated by ghosts who, believe it or not, all resemble my favourite actors. Finally there is the film which, if it is successful (and I don't mean financially), will convince the viewer that I have made the very stones speak, and told a tale that could not have happened elsewhere. Christ, I surely don't have to lecture you people on the uniqueness of certain locations! Here, try as I might, I see caravans not wagon trains. Dr Isaacson, your wife's uncle needs Cecil B. de Mille, not Lewis Falcon.'

So saying he links arms with Aunt Bella and leads her back to the Oldsmobile.

My wife's uncle, though advised of this opinion, remains of a different persuasion. 'The fact is,' he says as we approach the car, 'that even if he had the backing for a film in America — unlikely in itself — he still wouldn't be able to make it, because he's been banned from his beloved valleys by the Navajo and their neighbours, who take a dim view of the way he portrays Indians in his movies. It seems to me that if Mr Falcon wants to make another movie he's going to have to make a compromise first.'

Having traversed the high plateau of the Negev we descend upon the desolate plain of Arava, which translates as prairie, though no cattle cool off in its salt marshes or shelter under its umbrella-shaped acacias.

Only at Yotvata, a kibbutz in the middle of nowhere, are there cows, and these all congregate, like the atoms of a giant breast, in an open-sided shed — hardly the masculine imagery required by Lewis Falcon. Here also are the wells that provide sweet water for Eilat, still some twenty-five miles distant.

Thirsty ourselves we stop at the roadside milkbar. 'Whose car is that?' asks the healthy-looking girl behind the dusty counter. The Minister's driver tells her.

The Minister divides the country. Half the nation idolizes him, the other half wishes he would drop dead. The girl, we discover, is in the latter category.

'It's a pity he's not with you,' she says, wiping her hands on her apron, 'because there's a big question I would like to ask him. I want to know why he gives so much money to the settlements in the occupied territories when we have to beg for every shekel. We are the people who are building the country, not them. The West Bank isn't Israel, Yotvata is. Though everyone seems to have forgotten that fact. Once we were the miracle workers who made the desert bloom. The green-fingered stars of a thousand propaganda movies. Now we are crazy idealists. The sort your Minister doesn't give a fig for. And why? Because there are no quick bucks to be made from cultivating the wilderness — which gives us the answer to my big question. Your boss doesn't give us any support because he is a corrupt bastard!'

'Be warned, young lady,' says my wife's uncle, 'that is a slander. Uttered before witnesses. The Minister may sue.' 'Not such a pretty girl,' says his driver. 'Finish your drinks,' she replies, 'I want to close.'

I do not wait to be told a second time. Dissociating myself from my travelling companions I wander across the sand in the direction of something that may yet be a mirage: an isolated square of brilliant green. Arriving I discover that it is what it seems: a meadow, so vibrant that it appears to be growing as I watch.

Beyond the field, stretching to the foot of the mountains, are groves of date palms, their braids of red fruit glowing beneath feathery headdresses that flap in the desert wind. Otherwise nothing but sand and stone, and a sun smouldering in an empty firmament.

A naked land, as dangerous as a virgin goddess, unlike old England, so carefully clad in its pelt of green.

This is the land my ancestors are supposed to have hiked across for forty years, but I have no memories of the place, my recollections all concern St Albans; my school, the *shul*, the cinema, my father's photographic studio.

I have stumbled upon the third day of creation and, despite my promethean ambitions (I should like to present the milkmaid with a brave new world), I feel as dumbfounded as Frankenstein's monster. I pick up a handful of dust from the desert floor, as God did on the sixth day.

The Hebrew alphabet has twenty-two characters. Find the correct permutation and you too can vitalize that red detritus, create another golem of your own. Some claim that God made a golem before He made Adam, a dissatisfied brute blessed with every human attribute save one: a soul. More philosophic sages say a golem is nearer Caliban, being one whose potential has not been properly fulfilled — which makes me the golem of Jacobi the Magician and his beautiful niece.

In Anthony's institution I step up to the lectern at the appointed hour, prop my wristwatch on its sloping surface, and talk about film, itself but a shadow of reality; while in Sophie's bed I am just as distant from the truly creative act, being forced to smother my own progeny. No wonder I grabbed the opportunity provided by Stella's promiscuity.

She should have had a biopsy by the time we get back to Tel Aviv. I'll telephone her then and, if all is well, maybe make another date.

The horn summons me to the car. Returning I pass the girl, walking in the opposite direction, away from the kiosk. The horn sounds again.

'Go,' she says, 'they are waiting.' Her cheeks are so red they look as though they have been slapped. 'Are you all right?' I ask.

She stops. 'No,' she says, 'your friends have nearly killed me. I am sick. That's why I am here. To lead a peaceful life.' 'Then why did you pick an argument with them?' I ask. 'Because certain things are so important that even a person with familial hypercholesterolaemia must sometimes raise her voice,' she replies.

Familial hypercholesterolaemia? It makes labile hypertension sound rather benign. 'Familial means it's hereditary, an inheritance from my European ancestors, with their sachertorte and strudel,' she explains. 'Thanks to them I manufacture too much cholesterol. It sits inside me like a bomb, awaiting its detonator.' 'Yotvata is worth that risk?' I ask.

'You have read the Torah?' she asks. 'No,' I reply, 'but I've seen *The Ten Commandments*.' She smiles. 'So you remember when Charlton Heston smote the rock and water poured forth?' she asks. I nod. 'Well, that's what we do here,' she says. 'We tap the sandstone that's beneath our feet. True, the water that rises is brackish, but it suffices. For ourselves we have the wells. But Yotvata possesses more than mayim, water, it has hayim, life. Just look around you.'

She points to a thorny branch still quivering from the arrival of a masked bird in an emerald cape on the lookout for lunch. 'When the little green bee-eater decided to make aliya it chose Yotvata for its first home,' she continues. 'Why Yotvata? We're nothing special, not even mentioned in the Bible. So why? Because here we believe in live and let live. Noah sent out the dove and it brought back an olive branch. To me an even greater symbol of hope is the sight of that bird with a bee in its beak. In fact I'm prepared to die for it.' 'May you live till 120,' I say, a greater possibility, now her cheeks are no longer bright enough to illuminate a brothel.

Having abandoned any notion of settling down with her, on account of the unlikelihood of either of us surviving prolonged love-making, I sink into the seat beside my unfructified wife.

Heads turn admiringly as we enter the steamy port of Eilat

where the streets are flanked by wooden crates instead of houses, each stencilled with its exotic place of origin; here Somalia, there Uganda or Burundi. Dockers, stripped to the waist, pause from their unloading to show proper respect as we cruise past in our ostentatious limo. All I know about ports I learned from *On the Waterfront.* Indeed, at the moment, I feel rather like Rod Steiger surveying his crooked domain. As in the aforementioned movie there is a feeling that here, in this no man's land between the sea and the state, the normal rules of society do not apply.

We glide through the boulevards of Eilat proper heading south, so that the brilliant shore of the Red Sea is always on our left. Once we have quit the city there is nothing on our right save the granite rocks they call Hametsuda, the Stronghold. Nothing, that is, until we reach Nahal Shelomo, a sluggish brook that runs down from the mountains into the Gulf of Eilat. At its outlet, overshadowed on either side by massive boulders, stands a solitary house, shockingly white in the late afternoon sunshine. We have arrived.

'If this is a ranch,' says Lewis Falcon, quoting the advertising slogan that scuppered Gary Hart's chances of winning his party's nomination for the 1984 presidential elections, 'where's the beef?'

No beef but plenty of ham. The Minister, having flown down, is there to greet us. He is wearing a stetson. Beyond him, in the cool interior of the thick-walled house (built originally by an English mineralogist), loiter half a dozen men (minor actors, promised roles in *The Six Pointed Star*) dressed in cowboy outfits, complete with holsters and tooled leather boots. 'Welcome,' he says. 'Make yourself at home.'

Here is at least one of the properties Lewis Falcon demands of the land: incongruity. Behind our backs in Saudi Arabia the Midian mountains, as if demonstrating the effects of the desert sun, begin to blush, a colour that is reflected in the quiet sea which separates that kingdom from Israel, whose own citizens do not seem entirely at ease in their foreign attire. If anything they resemble Eli Wallach's desperadoes in *The Magnificent Seven*, itself a transplant from Japan.

'You probably want to freshen up after your long drive,' says the Minister, 'so retire for as long as you require, then, when you are ready, join us in the back-yard.'

The driver unloads our luggage and we are shown to the guest rooms, situated on the south side of the house, so that each looks out upon the Red Sea. 'What do you think?' asks my wife, seating herself on the edge of the bed, which has a spectacular purple and gold cover. 'It's a nice room,' I say.

This is not what my wife wants to talk about. 'I mean, will Lewis Falcon do it?' she says. 'Not in a million years,' I reply. 'What makes you so sure?' she asks. 'He's got integrity,' I reply. 'Oh,' she says, 'is that all?'

Silence ensues as she concentrates now upon the removal of her shirt, shorts and underwear. 'Jonah,' she says as she falls backwards upon the bed, 'be a darling and fan me, my body needs air.' So I stand above my spread-eagled wife, a pocket Aeolus, single-handedly waving my own shirt to create a breeze, watching her pubic hair and wondering why, in the space beneath it, my clones are not doing their much greater work. 'That's good,' she says, closing her eyes, though her breasts look at me accusingly, as if to say, 'We're very happy as sex objects, thank you, why do you want to turn us into little Yotvatas?'

But I have my own question. 'Why is it such a big deal?' I ask. 'What?' she says. 'The movie,' I say. 'My uncle told you,' she says. 'Tourism.' 'Is that all?' I ask. 'All?' she cries. 'Jonah, my dear, tourism is a multi-million dollar industry. One that is going to make us rich, if this project comes off. So show a little enthusiasm for it. Please.' I smile.

'Does the name Sede Boqer mean anything to you?' she asks. 'Sure,' I reply, 'it's the kibbutz in the Negev where Ben Gurion's buried.' 'True enough,' she says. 'But I meant what do the words actually mean.' I shrug. 'They mean Rancher's Field,' she says, sitting up, 'and the place is literally crawling with cattle and horses. All we need do is open a luxury hotel there — call it a Dude Ranch — import a few covered wagons, and charge a fortune for the experience. When that's established we'll open a theme park in Eilat, like Knott's Berry Farm in California, and have daily shoot-outs.'

'If people wanted that,' I say, 'they'd be flocking to Gaza, where they can have it for real.' 'Jonah, you spend all your life looking at movies,' she replies. 'You, more than anyone, should know that reality is exactly what people don't want.'

There is a barbecue in the Minister's back-yard and, some distance from the heat, blocks of ice, upon which stand cans of Budweiser beer. A confederate flag on a white pole, which is planted at the end of a well-kept lawn, as in many a good American home, makes token efforts to fly. Hamburgers and hot dogs sweat over the coals and remember, for the last time, the bodies whence they came, beasts that roamed ranges far from the Minister's spread.

One of the pseudo cowboys serves the meat, which we eat seated upon the spiky grass. Bella, on more comfortable rugs, is doubtless telling Lewis Falcon about her bohemian years in Paris, while away in the shadows, where the lawn ends and the bushes begin, my wife's uncle and the Minister conduct a whispered dialogue which leaves neither looking happy.

The bushes at their feet bear no berries, instead their branches are covered with thousands of tiny snails whose shells are as white as skulls. Stretching my legs I observe that larger snails have colonized the ground near Solomon's Brook, which itself teems with slow-moving molluscs. The Minister, seeing my curiosity, dips a hairy arm into the water and plucks an amphibian from its shallows.

'This clever fellow', he says, severing the unfortunate creature's columella muscle, thereby separating it from its shell, 'is blessed with a gland in its rectum which secretes a single drop of yellow liquid thus,' he points to a duct on the outer arch of the snail's glistening back where a droplet is indeed forming, 'which turns as purple as permanganate on exposure to light. You are looking at the legendary murex dye, discovered by the Phoenicians of Tyre. The robes of Roman emperors were dipped in it, as was the bedspread in your room. Sixty thousand of these sacrificed their lives to produce enough for that. Sixty thousand.'

Laughing, the Minister tosses the homeless gastropod on to the grass where it is subsequently squashed by an unknowing cowboy boot.

'End of lecture,' he says. 'It is time to give centre stage to our guest of honour.'

What a pity that Lewis Falcon hadn't been more attentive when we took him to the Habima, or he would have known not to accept the Minister's wager.

'My boys have heard how you removed Lebanon from the map,' says the latter to the former, 'and, sick of my retelling, would like to see you perform the trick for themselves. Have you, by any chance, brought your guns?' 'Yes,' replies Lewis Falcon, 'but the light is no good.'

Not good, maybe, but beautiful. The sky looks as if some divine barman had poured lemon, green and blue liqueurs over crushed ice, some bits of which glitter like stars.

Floodlights, the sort that petrify terrorists, bring about the required improvement. A map is pinned to a board at the far end of the garden and Lewis Falcon, having buckled on his gun-belt, repeats his party piece and then, to much applause, spins the smoking gun around his trigger finger.

'My boys are very impressed,' says the Minister, 'but – forgive their arrogance – think they are faster. Since I am, in a sense, their leader, I must show them loyalty and – please do not take offence at this – I am ready to gamble several thousand shekels on the best of them beating you to the draw.'

'Against what stake?' asks Lewis Falcon. 'Well,' says the Minister, 'these gentlemen are all aspiring actors who want nothing more than to be in a Lewis Falcon movie. Does this sound fair? Ten thousand shekels against your signature on a contract.' 'Fair enough,' says Lewis Falcon. Then, turning towards the extras, he adds, 'Who fancies his luck?'

The rules of engagement are quickly established. The two men will face each other and, on the count of three, will draw and fire, at which time the gun must be clear of the holster, or the shot will not register.

Bella, carried away by the memory of the duel that Buñuel nearly fought on her account, gives Lewis Falcon a favour to wear, though all he has asked for is a little powder to dust over his palms in order to improve his grip on the tortoiseshell handles.

It is obvious that he is taking the contest seriously, judging by the way he lifts the shining guns from their holsters, peers down their barrels to check for obstacles, spins their cylinders and, finally, plugs their chambers with brass and copper bullets. Blanks, we are assured.

'God speed, my champion,' says Bella, kissing him on the lips, as though death were nevertheless a distinct possibility.

His opponent, presumably no stranger to battle, balances himself, his hand hovering like a kestrel over the pistol butt. Lewis Falcon, moving from foot to foot, looks like he's receiving serve at Wimbledon.

Selected as being the nearest thing to a neutral I am instructed to begin the count.

'One.' My voice is surprisingly unsteady. It's silly but I'm beginning to act as if this is for real.

'Two.' There's no denying the tension now. All movement has ceased, as everyone waits for me to utter the magic word that will bring this tableau to life.

'Three!'

Like fugitives from a futurist painting, their arms in twenty places at once, the contestants snatch their weapons. But only Falcon fires.

We clap and cheer, making no connection between that phenomenon and the red stain on the loser's chest, an object of infinite interest to the man who is growing it. He turns towards us, as if to show it off, stretches out his hands, and drops to his knees. Great-aunt Bella screams, a silvery sound, that awakens the moon.

'Oh God,' says my wife's uncle, 'the man's been shot.' The fellow in question, as if to confirm the accuracy of this observation, keels over and comes to rest in a prone position. The Minister kneels over him, trying to find a pulse in his neck. 'Is he ... ?' asks my wife, leaving the sentence uncompleted, in the time-honoured way.

At which point Lewis Falcon, to our astonishment, starts to laugh.

'Cut,' he says.

'What are you implying?' asks the Minister.

'My dear sir,' replies Lewis Falcon, 'I've been making movies too long not to know a special effect when I see one. I have no doubt that, were I to open that carcass's shirt, I would find, not a bullet hole, but a little sack of pig's blood, if such a thing can be obtained in this country. I am equally sure that one of his amigos has a small detonator in a pocket which burst the bag at the appropriate moment. I will admit, however, that it was professionally done.'

'Please accept my apologies for this little charade,' says the Minister, reviving the corpse with a pat on the shoulder, at the same time as trying to strike my wife's uncle dead with a look of frightening hostility, 'and I promise that I shall make up for it tomorrow by taking you out for some real shooting.'

Lewis Falcon, ten thousand shekels the richer, still wants to know what would have happened if he had not seen through the scheme. 'Nothing,' my wife's uncle assures him, though even in the darkness it is clear that he is uncomfortable. The night has not yet ended, and we are on the Minister's private beach. Watching the black waters wobble under the lunatic sway of the moon I wonder what this pocket Neptune has in store for us next. Standing red-hued on the perimeter of a driftwood fire, harpoon in hand, he will only say, 'All will be revealed.'

The sea is an inkwell into which God, the great plotter, dips his quill. Many a page is discarded before he presses the final draft against the celestial blotter; these we experience as dreams or, more likely, nightmares.

Once, travelling in the footsteps of Lewis Falcon, I spent the night in a motel at Mexican Hat, a few miles from Monument Valley. Sophie was with me. In the morning I reported a strange vision to her; I had dreamed I was hitting her on the head with what looked like green onions of gigantic proportions.

Later that day, in the Hopi village of Shongopovi, we witnessed a rain dance, at the completion of which the masked celebrants slapped one another with the stuff of my dreams, now identified as saplings.

At another time I dreamed so vividly that my teeth were broken, the relief was enormous when I discovered, on waking, that they were whole — until lunch when one really cracked.

I have come to fear my dreams and so told no one that last night, in Tel Aviv, I saw myself burning to death in a smashed car. It did not seem tactful to describe — just before setting off on a long drive — how it felt to be trapped within an upturned wreck, experiencing the panic and the heat, or how it felt to be standing outside at the same time watching the paint peel. I only mention it now because of what is about to happen.

Suddenly the cowboys whoop and the Minister, beckoning us, strolls toward the animated circle. We follow. 'Now you know my secret,' he says, pointing to the slow-moving animal his minions have surrounded. 'I run the only turtle ranch in Israel.' He pats the beast, still dragging itself along like a wounded soldier, on its shell. 'This particular species — prized for its tortoiseshell — is not indigenous. So I imported some fertile eggs from the Celebes and planted them here, where we are standing. They hatched and, unlike the Jews, quickly made themselves at home in the waters of exile.'

'Perhaps they are like the Jews in that they carry their homeland on their backs,' I say, quoting Heine for the defence. 'In which case we are in for a hot time,' replies the Minister.

Sluggish at best, this turtle is exhausted by its prodigious nocturnal achievement — somewhere beneath the beach are the two hundred eggs it has just laid. The Minister carefully hooks his foot beneath the turtle's underside and then, unmercifully, hoofs it into the night. It lands on its back and though its fins still function they find no purchase in the air.

Just as the soldiers depositioned to guard Elsinore brought about its fall, just as the elephant's fearsome tusks have led to its near extinction, just as the settlements designated to make Israel invulnerable may put an end to it altogether, so the hawksbill's armour has been its downfall. Called a hawksbill because of its beak-like upper jaw, presently opening and closing to no effect, it has no real defence except a horny shell of thirteen plates assembled like the leaves of an artichoke, which serves against most enemies, except its worst.

To prove this point the Minister, eyes as red as rubies, holds the terrified creature upsidedown over the fire until the heat makes the semi-precious shields spring away from the bony base of the carapace; simultaneously the masks of concern drop from the faces of my wife and her great-aunt to reveal acquisitive smiles.

'Was that really necessary?' I ask. The Minister, putting down the turtle, looks at me with the sort of contempt Josef von Sternberg is said to have reserved for the ingenuous Marlene Dietrich.

'Do you know what differentiates us from the animals?' he asks. It is a rhetorical question, for he also supplies the answer. 'Amnesia, the ability to forget. The woman who wears a diamond forgets the sweat of the men who mined it, just as easily as the Jews who boast about Israel's morality forget the sins that were committed in its name by the likes of me. I am not proud of the bad blood I spilled, but I am not ashamed of it either. Because it was necessary. And if your wife likes tortoiseshell and you want to make her happy and buy some for her it is necessary for someone, somewhere, to do what I have just done, or worse. And don't you forget it.'

Meanwhile the half-cooked turtle has dragged itself across the beach and into the cooling sea. Noticing the attempted escape the Minister summons the gun-fighter who played possum and, pointing to where two nostrils break surface, passes him the harpoon. The marksman, surprisingly, aims the shot skywards whence if falls vertically straight into the back of the unfortunate turtle and lodges like death's periscope.

'That also was not very nice,' says the Minister, 'but I guarantee that tomorrow, as soon as you smell the soup we make from the fins — which we boil up with a few vegetables, a little mace, some sherry and some lime juice — you will forget what you have just seen.' From which I deduce that the Minister only wishes nightmares upon the ungrateful.

*

The following day, like the turtle, we cook on the beach and cool off in the sea. Since our stretch of sand is more or less secluded my wife decides she only requires the bottom half of her bikini. Her breasts, under continuous assessment by the beach bums who were yesterday's cowboys, look up at me in triumph.

Dinner is a more formal affair. The Minister, at the head of a great wooden table set upon a flagstone floor, looks every inch the Western patriarch. His wife, newly arrived from Tel Aviv, wears a tight black dress and a pearl choker. She does not say much, unlike Great-aunt Bella who, surprised by the splendour, will not stop apologizing for the poverty of her attire.

A great chandelier, purloined from an Ottoman palace, is suspended above us, making it seem that our crystal glasses are filled with distilled light, rather than a prize-winning white from the Golan Heights, a perfect complement to the turtle soup now being poured from a silver replica of the late animal's shell. The Minister is right, the butchery we witnessed does not detract from its bouquet.

It is followed by a bowl of white leathery eggs, the dead turtle's deposit in the genetic bank, some of whose yolks have been scrambled. The taste is oily and very savoury, not unlike anchovy.

The main dish arrives upon a silver platter, a large beef-like joint roasted in its own skin.

The Minister, poised over it like a matador about to deliver the coup de grâce, slices away with absurd generosity. 'What is it?' asks my wife impressed, like me, by its meaty juices and distinct flavour. 'God knows,' I reply, as she cuts it into smaller pieces for my benefit.

Half-way through the course the Minister rises and raises a glass filled with a velvety Burgundy. 'Ladies and gentlemen,' he says, 'I have an important announcement, to the effect that Lewis Falcon has, after all, agreed to make a film in Israel. Let us drink to its success.'

My wife looks at me. 'Never in a million years,' she says. 'My husband's some prophet!'

No wonder her uncle has been looking so pleased with himself since the hunting party returned. How did they do it?

Lewis Falcon's face remains as expressionless as Buster Keaton's as we all respond to the toast.

'The press have been informed,' continues the Minister, 'and the contract will be signed tomorrow at Sheba's Palace.'

'Okay,' I say to my wife's uncle between the coffee and the brandy, 'what happened?' 'Let's just say that Mr Falcon succumbed to the creative urge,' he replies. 'I don't believe you,' I say. 'I didn't think you would,' he says. 'In fact it was the opposite impulse — the desire to destroy — that trapped him.' He takes a sip of coffee.

'We set off in the jeep before dawn and got to Hai Bar just as the sun was rising over Edom.'

'Wait a minute,' says my wife, 'Hai Bar's a wildlife reservation.'

'True,' says her uncle, 'but Lewis Falcon didn't know that. All he cared about was shooting something. Preferably the rhino that the Minister had promised him. To which end he is carrying a state of the art sporting gun. We quickly pick up the rhino's spoor and spot it, chewing on some bush, long before it sees us. Rhinos being stupid, as well as half-blind, it lets us get very close before acknowledging the squawks of the birds that breakfast upon its parasites and taking off at a swift trot. Then, I must admit, it got exciting.'

He has another gulp of coffee and wipes his lips. 'As soon as it realizes that we mean business it breaks into a gallop but, fast as it is, it is no match for a jeep and in a few moments we have over-taken it. Being stupid, as I said, the brute holds its course and, as we slow down to let it thunder past, Lewis Falcon stands up and, given its whole length to aim at, shoots at its face, opening up a third eye, through which the rhino sees its approaching death. But it does not falter. Instead it bravely turns to attack what has hurt it. Falcon makes out that the first shot was too easy and that this is what he was hoping for. He orders the driver to stop broadside to the charging rhino. Then, when we can actually hear the rumbles in the beast's belly the driver accelerates, spins the wheel, and offers Falcon the shot he desires. This time the bullet passes straight through the eye and into the animal's tiny brain, stopping it in its tracks. Involuntary shudders demonstrate that the great body is receiving the brain's last message: you're on your own. Not knowing what else to do the rhino drops upon its front knees, as if seeking guidance from above. But God is either silent or He imparts the terrible truth, for the rhino begins to tremble without remission. Its mouth is open and its tongue reaches the dust, which is stained by blood and saliva. The stench of its noisome breath is almost unbearable. Finally, like a man undergoing electro-convulsive therapy, its muscles go into spasm and, with a last great and stinking exhaltation, it rolls over and dies. Falcon happily poses, foot upon its head, for a victorious snap. "Hemingway once told me," he says, "that a great killer needs honour, courage, a good physique, a good style, a great left hand and much luck. I don't want to boast, but I don't think you'll see better." "Correct me if I'm wrong," says the Minister, "but didn't Hemingway include a good press in that list?" "He may have," says Falcon, getting wary. "Tell me," says the Minister, "what kind of press do you think you'll get if they find out you've slaughtered the only rhinoceros in Israel?" You should have seen his face when he realized how we'd tricked him. He called us every name under the sun, including "dirty Jews", but he soon saw that h: had no choice. We had him, good and proper.'

My wife's uncle finishes off his coffee. 'How the hell are you going to get rid of a dead rhino?' I demand. 'No problem,' he replies, 'we butchered it on the spot. You've already eaten its hump.'

Having digested the information I approach my fallen idol and say, 'Thanks for dinner.'

The Minister, pleased as punch, walks round the table, anxious to be loved in his moment of triumph. He has gifts for us all; tortoiseshell polished for the ladies into a warm translucent yellow, mottled and spotted with rich brown tints; and, for the gentlemen, a disturbingly familiar phial of prepared rhinoceros horn.

My wife is anxious to test its efficacy and so I, unable to pass on what I already know, am forced once again to swallow a handful of agglutinated hair. While waiting for it to take effect I remind my wife of the pact we made on the tumbling jet. 'How could I forget?' she asks, kissing my neck. 'In principle I'd love a baby tomorrow, but I don't think I want to start one tonight.' 'But I do,' I say. 'Not with me you won't,' she says, rubbing baby lotion into her blushing breasts.

Let me refresh your memory concerning Buñuel's *L'Age d'Or*, that story of unrequited love, a love so mad that it justifies everything, including murder. According to Buñuel's friends its philosophy catered for the 'masochism of the oppressor'. The crime I have in mind is no less passionate, though not as bloody as a rule. I intend to rape my wife. Having only one good arm would normally make this a near impossibility, but tonight as predicted the proposed victim is colluding by being naked, on her back, and certainly in the mood for love's benediction.

'It seems to be working,' she says encouragingly as I pull the genetic garbage bag over my cornucopia. There is no question of forcible entry, you see. On the contrary, my wife manually buttock-shoves me deeper into her belly, until her hips take over the job, and her arms involuntarily rise above her head so that I can smell the scent of her exertions.

She endeavours to keep her eyes open, seeing that I am propped up and watching her face, but after a few more pushes from me their lids also fall from her control and shut out the light. It is the moment I have been waiting for. I withdraw.

'What's the matter?' she asks, taken aback. 'Turn over,' I say. Obediently she kneels on the bed, facing the blank wall. After the Founder's Day fracas my wife made up with Professor Gutkes and availed herself of his amateur solarium, so that the back that presents itself to me is already as sunburned as the desert.

Looking between her thighs and her pendulous breasts I satisfy myself that her eyes, like her nipples, are covered by cupolas of skin.

Then, under the equally sightless stare of her posterior, I remove posterity's glistening blindfold.

Separating her buttocks (as well as I can with one hand) to improve access to the womb's rear end, I release the pheromones that arouse me to my very chromosomes. 'Okay, boys,' I say to my genes, 'she's all yours.' And grabbing the flesh that pads her hips as if it were a handle I enter her as God intended.

Purple fruits decorate the coverlet upon which this exercise in immortality proceeds; pomegranates, figs, dark cherries and grapes wobble as if loose on the branch or vine. I am the zephyr that shakes them thus, I am the khamsin that brings forth sweat. I am Ramon, the God of the Negev, after whom the fertile pomegranate is named. I rage over the desert and wells overflow, filling the wadi that runs from the nape to the coccyx.

It was a wild wind that extracted the fruitful promise from my wife, and it is a sirocco that will blow the seeds into their proper furrow. My wife's head rocks from side to side then suddenly stops. 'Oh God,' she says, 'I'm coming!'

Now nothing can stop my sperm which races up the vas deferens like mercury in a heatwave. Breathless, I collapse over my wife's dewy back, and rest my chin upon her shoulder, so that each of our exhalations enters the other's mouth. 'I feel wetter tonight,' she whispers, too dozy to work out why.

During the night, as we sleep our dreamless sleep, death, floating on the warm thermals used by raptors, crosses the five-mile security zone and the border fence that separates Israel from Lebanon. Spotting a rocky field of dry thorns, otherwise empty except for a few olive trees, the unwelcome stranger glides to terra firma and, unharnessing himself, is guided by the glitter of God's discarded fingernail toward the nearest habitation, a living nightmare about to invade sleep.

In the subsequent exchange of fire seven are killed: six Israelis and the Palestinian, who is left in the dirt, where he falls, so that flies can breakfast on his blood.

What isn't done in the name of love? The soul of the dead Arab has no regrets. He compares himself to a husband who, returning home, finds not one man but a whole nation in bed with his wife. 'Your wife divorced you,' chant the murdered Israelis, 'on the grounds of neglect. Look at the difference.' They point to the orange groves that surround their kibbutz. 'She is blooming again,' they say, 'it is the dawn of a new golden age.' 'This is not the result of husbandry,' snaps the Arab, 'but of rape.'

It's a bit much, don't you think, for a killer to harangue his victims for a lesser crime? I know I did wrong to impregnate my wife against her will, but at least my aim was to create life rather than end it. Okay, I confess that my motives were selfish. But doesn't everyone look twice before crossing the road? We all want to survive. And if my own body is too unstable to sustain me for long, who can blame me for taking root in someone else's? Maybe that's why I have become indifferent to Stella, because she is carrying death's button over her heart.

Different badges are pinned to our chests by the security officers of Sheba's Palace, a necessary precaution as we have to pass through several more checks before reaching the inner sanctum chosen by the Minister for his press conference.

Sheba's Palace, standing at the very edge of the strand, looks down the gorgeous sea in the direction of distant Ethiopia. The Romans, adept at utilizing such watery proximities, constructed palatial piscinas at places like Caesarea, and the proprietors of Sheba's Palace wanted no less for their property. So they sank a spiral staircase like a stack of dollar signs, laid out a perspex tunnel and, one hundred yards from the shore, built a large aquarium-in-reverse, a room with walls of glass behind which schools of pilot fish are suspended like silver drapes.

There is a strong sense of being watched, such as Polonius induced in Hamlet, explained when undersea currents part the curtains to reveal the trans-sexual antheus, the nudibranch in its red and yellow pyjamas, the chevron barracuda, the pregnant male seahorse, the coral crunching humphead rasp, the moray eel, the lion fish, scorpion fish and angel fish, the hermit crab and the lobster, the terrapin and the turtle — all spying upon their terrestrial counterparts with fishy eyes.

We enter this undersea world to find the Minister strutting around like Captain Nemo, while nervous staff in yellow blazers uncork bottles of wine and make pyramids out of triangular sandwiches.

Attracted by this activity twelve-foot sharks, tipped with white, begin to patrol our liquid hinterland, like carnivorous eggs hungrily eyeing the amorous sperm trapped inside a durex.

The expression upon Lewis Falcon's weathered face makes it apparent that he considers the Minister and my wife's uncle close relatives of those cold-blooded omnivores. He takes his appointed seat and stares glumly at the contract, which is weighed down by a greenish stone as if it would otherwise float away. Alongside it are several plastic biros bearing the hotel's logo.

'Do cheer up,' says Great-aunt Bella, squeezing his shoulder, 'it isn't the end of the world.'

When all immediate appetites are gratified the Minister rises to the microphone and proceeds to list the manifold benefits Cisco and its works will bring Israel, not least of them tourism. My wife nods approvingly. Then the Minister, getting down to specifics, explains the Western project and describes how the great Lewis Falcon, overwhelmed with enthusiasm, volunteered to help get the first production — *The Six Pointed Star* — off the ground.

'And now, ladies and gentlemen,' he concludes, 'the moment you have been waiting for.'

With what looks like a last gesture of defiance Lewis Falcon rudely brushes aside the proffered plastic pen and, instead, removes Stella's stylo from his pocket. Having engaged the point he signs his name on the dotted line at the end of the contract as if it were an innocent man's death warrant.

Small flashes punctuate the air, startling man and fish alike, none more so than an Arab journalist as he flees along the tunnel that leads back to Sheba's Palace. What's his hurry? A deadline to meet? No one seems interested, least of all the Minister, who crows so much you'd think Lewis Falcon was an opposing general who'd just signed the instruments of surrender. He prances around the tables holding the contract aloft; he dances the hora to an invisible sailor's hornpipe while the reporters clap and the photographers snap tomorrow's front page. The three Jacobis jig up and down.

'Come on, Jonah,' calls my wife, 'join in.'

But I prefer to stand quietly beside my crestfallen hero. By now the Minister seems to have lost all sense of proportion, has probably even forgotten what the fuss is about; anyway, he wants to hug everyone. He hugs my wife, a bit too tightly for my liking; her uncle, his partner; Great-aunt Bella, who doesn't want to let him go; and then me, who does.

'Ouch!' I cry. 'What's the matter?' he asks. 'It's my bad arm,' I say, 'you're squashing it.' 'Sorry,' he says, withdrawing his sweaty face from my cheek. And then, with such surprising gentleness that I begin to feel guilty for not liking him, he lifts my sinister limb so that when he delivers his second bear-hug it rests on his back, out of harm's way.

3

In the beginning God created the heaven and the earth. And the earth was without form, and void; and darkness was upon the face of the deep. And the Spirit of God moved upon the face of the waters ... And God said, Let the waters bring forth abundantly the moving creature that hath life ...

My doctor, having assured me that my sperm count was normal, added that, being average, I could expect to produce 400,000,000,000 of the little devils in my reproductive lifetime. Of which maybe two will come to fruition. This means, according to my calculations, that in the wake of every fuck a potential world is wiped out. Even with this information I never gave a thought to the sufferings of the multitude that were called into existence by me merely to perish in the maws of man-made predators. Until now, that is, now that I am fighting for my life in the full knowledge of what I really am; an insignificant by-product of God's spectacular potency.

Oh you may mock, you salt of the earth types, secure in your little house, with your little family, in your little country, on your little planet, but one day – like me – you are certain to be shaken out of your illusory paradise, to confront the awful realization that you are no more to God than our sperm is to us. Something like shazam. That's all it takes.

God is not an average man, notwithstanding those sentimentalists who, unable to accept their ephemerality, have dressed up the truth with a sweet metaphor wherein God, instead of destroying us with his procreative powers, fathers a child upon a virgin, whose son subsequently goes one better and gives birth to himself, having died meantime. They would have us believe that self plus destruction equals self, which is like saying that five minus six equals five; it is the illogical dialectic of a frightened intellect.

I'm terrified too, but I refuse to find comfort in an equation that insults my intelligence. God is not manageable, does not want to settle down with an immaculate girl, needs more than an individual womb to receive his ejaculate; in fact he requires a sea, which is where we find ourselves after the crash we could not listen to and the flash we dared not look upon, after the discharge that blew us off our feet and into the womb of eternity.

It is chaos, without beginning and without end. An ultramarine infinity, filled with golden specks, transparent-bodied glass fish, silver shards sharp enough to sever limbs, colourless moon jellyfish and naked men and women begging, at the dawn of creation, for the breath of life.

Those that can swim toward the light, others struggle in the depths with expressions as eloquent as screams, but most float motionlessly awaiting the sea-change or worse. A woman waves before being swept away. Who was she? Drifting past, like a multi-finned fish, goes a notebook from which my life streams in tendrils of blue.

Already I can barely recollect my former existence. I think I had a wife, who had an uncle, who had an aunt. But I can no longer picture their features or even remember their names. If I concentrate I can just visualize a celebration full of forgotten faces, one of which was pressed against my cheek as the crescendo commenced. The owner does not seem to have survived the impact intact; though, it must be said, the division is not entirely inappropriate. For all of us, not just him.

Crustaceous creatures tug at the bloody tentacles that spill from the top of his trousers, while his upper half bobs around like a demi-god in a constellation of pink bubbles he has created himself. To what purpose? To what purpose are any of our endeavours, be they mock animal or mock divine, if our final destination is on the snout of a blood-crazed shark, such as the one now feeding freely upon the innards of my erstwhile companion? Is he the victim of an omnivore, or is this what always happens when the sperm meets the egg? How did my doctor put it? The successful sperm penetrates the egg. He got the wrong verb. The penis penetrates. The seed is devoured. That's what it looks like down here, awaiting the half-man half-fish synthesis. Amphibiousness has its advantages, to be sure, but I'm not convinced they outweigh the trauma of the merman metamorphosis, which exceeds even my own worst fears.

Therefore when another shark, attracted by my own far from negligible wounds, begins his approach, I do an unnatural thing; I swim for my life knowing quite well that I have no function other than to embrace change or die. But it's not so easy outdistancing a ravenous leviathan with only one fully articulated arm, and I would surely have undergone an equally excruciating evolution if I hadn't been snatched away by strange ichthyophagi with shiny skins, webbed feet and external lungs. They drag my body from the volatile brine and deposit it in the soft belly of an albino automaton whose bloodshot eyes rotate upon stalks.

Concealed beneath its steely skin is the source of the great motive power which suddenly propels us in an unknown direction, reminding me also that my head is as painful as my arm. The sound of blood-chilling screams fills my ears, though whether they come from the creature or from me I cannot say; either way they portend no good. 'Hang on,' I tell myself, 'concentrate upon the pain. Do anything. But keep a hold on yourself.' It is at that instant, on the verge of unconsciousness, that he realizes he no longer knows who he is.

It is days before he shows signs of life again, before he stirs with an uneasy, half-vital motion. His ears open, as it were, before his eyes. He hears two people speaking: a man and a woman. 'Aḥot, ma matsavo?' says the male voice. 'A'bayin meḥoosar hakarah,' replies the female. 'Im yesh lo sechel hoo yisha'er kach,' concludes the man. The words fill him with panic, precisely because he cannot understand them. Think, think, think, he repeats to himself until the word itself becomes sound without meaning, and is replaced by a pictogram of a hand and a fish. The hand is his mind, the fish is reality. It is, of course, impossible to grasp. Nor are his feet upon terra firma. He has dropped into the hollow centre of a whirlpool which possesses sides but, as yet, no bottom. He reaches in vain for a handhold, but the sides are not solid. His brain sends out a desperate command: Swim! But his limbs do not respond. You know how to swim, dammit, screams his brain, do the crawl or, if you prefer, the breast ... Suddenly a terrible word invades his consciousness: Stroke! He has had a stroke; his disorientation is explained, as is his lost comprehension.

When he is sure that the visitors — his parents, his makers, his keepers? — have departed he opens his eyes. At least he is not blind, though he does not seem to be fully sighted either for, according to his eyes, the room does not appear to have a left side. Nor, now he comes to consider it, does he. He can feel his right arm and right leg, can see their shapes beneath the sheet, but there are sinister blanks where their opposite numbers should be. By way of experiment he moves his right leg until it comes up against an obstacle which observation (achieved by a slight turning of the head) reveals as the missing limb. He can see it, but still cannot feel it, which seems to suggest that his earlier diagnosis was substantially correct. As for his left arm, that he can neither see nor feel. But there must be something on that side (his heart?) to account for the wires than run out of his nightshirt, through the bars of his cot, to a pale cabinet that houses a phosphorescent screen. Across the glowing surface a green dot nonchalantly glides until inspiration seems to strike and it reaches for the *mot juste*, only to subside again, like a word processor without a vocabulary. Listening to the machine's regular bleep he realizes how quiet the room has become since the departure of his unknown guests, a silence that finds a correspondence within, the terrible silence of a self that is so lost it sees no point in crying out. All he knows is that he is in bed in a darkened room. He could not feel more isolated if the world were flat and he had dropped off the end of it.

Then, to his astonishment, he sees that he is not alone. There, in the obscurity of the room's farthest corner, an unusually attractive woman dozes in an armchair. Her face shines out like a half moon, one side silver-bright, the other lost in the shade. Like him she appears to have been bisected, though in her case it is certainly just a trick of the light. She is simply dressed in a white blouse and short denim skirt, which could almost be a uniform. He cannot see her feet. A single curl of black hair has fallen out of place and hangs across her forehead like a comma on white paper, separating clauses which have yet to be written. He wants to say something to her, some recognition of their shared humanity, but utters 'water' instead, thereby discovering that his overriding physical discomfort is thirst.

Despite appearances her slumber is not profound and is easily penetrated by the insistent whistle and click of his whisper. She rises and then advances upon his bed. It is a most peculiar progress, a series of discontinuous poses, spliced together to produce the semblance of motion, like a movie projected at the wrong speed. His eyes are faithfully recording all her actions, but his brain seems incapable of translating them into coherent movement, just as he was earlier unable to find any meaning in what must have been an exchange of everyday words.

She has moved to the bedside table. She has picked up a plastic pitcher and is pouring him a glass of water. But he has ceased to believe in the reality of the images; they are an optical illusion, a mirage. An arm proffers the glass. It is as though it has passed through an invisible portal into the third dimension, for it is indisputably made of flesh. The remainder of her body follows.

'Welcome back, Jonah,' she says, and he could kiss her, because he can make sense of the words again, though where he has been and why she is calling him Jonah is as much a mystery as her identity.

Gently she raises his head with her hand and slowly introduces the water into his mouth watching, with some satisfaction, the rise and fall of his unshaven Adam's apple. 'Who are you?' he asks. 'My nurse?' 'Jonah,' she says, 'are you teasing me?' 'Is Jonah my name?' he asks. She is still leaning over into the cot so that he is overwhelmed by the sweetness and variety of her perfumes and by the proximity of her breasts, which have become visible thanks to the open buttons of her blouse. He is surprised by this intimacy, but also gratified. His instincts, it seems, have not been erased. Unable to stop his arm, which seems to be moving under its own volition, he tentatively touches the newly-exposed plump flesh, only to withdraw his hand as if sensing that he has done something wrong.

'It's all right, Jonah,' says the woman, 'I'm your wife.' 'Wife?' he says. He is not seeking a definition of the word – which he actually understands – but confirmation of the fact that he has one. 'Listen, Jonah,' she whispers, 'if this is some kind of act because you're in serious trouble I'm prepared to go along with it, but I must know.' He stares back at her with such incomprehension in his eyes that she feels like a widow. Clearly upset she steps back into the penumbra and suffers a partial eclipse, as though her left side were soluble in darkness.

The screen beside his bed remains blank, except for the green dot, whose light now illuminates her visible surfaces, transmuting them from living flesh into the chilly glitter of emeralds. Her motions have also broken down into their constituent parts; instead of two arms she appears to have at least twenty.

Once again he feels like a man who has fallen out of the known world into a *pays inconnu*; without recognizable landmarks he has no means of deciding what is real: the warm palpable breast or the cold stony heart. 'Please,' he says, 'tell me where I am.' 'You're in hospital,' she replies, in a voice that gives him no help. 'How long have I been here?' he asks. 'Nearly a week,' she replies. 'What happened to me?' he asks. 'You were in an explosion,' she replies.

An explosion! The word, though unexpected, comes as something of a relief; at least the injury to his system, great though it seems to be, isn't self-inflicted.

'How badly am I damaged?' he asks. Now she seems to be hovering between states, between the cold beauty of her crystalline form and the living symmetry of her human shape. 'The blast tore away the bottom half of your left arm just below the elbow and dislocated the rest at the shoulder,' she says in a voice that has lost all its hardness. 'It also did some damage to your head which, they assure me, is not permanent.' She is so near he can feel her breath on his cheek.

'Oh Jonah,' she cries, 'I'm so glad you're alive. Nothing else matters.'

'How do you know?' he asks, not meaning to question the prognosis of the doctors or the veracity of her outburst but, rather, her version of his history. 'Because I was there,' she replies.

'Tell me what happened,' he demands. 'A bomb went off,' she replies.

A bomb! Is it credible, he reasons, that I should have no recollection of such a cataclysmic event?

'Then what?' he says. 'I don't know,' she replies, in some distress. 'I can only describe what happened to me.' 'Go ahead,' he says, 'I'm listening.'

'Well,' she says, shifting uneasily from foot to foot, 'a waitress was refilling my glass with orange juice. She was smiling. I was smiling. Even the sharks were smiling. We were, you may need reminding, in the Queen of Sheba's Grotto. At the bottom of the sea. To tell you the truth, I was smiling at your discomfiture. You obviously weren't enjoying the Minister's embrace. It turned out to be his last. That's why the sharks were smiling.'

She pauses briefly, so as to let her feelings run on ahead, thereby ensuring that they cannot be ambushed by the words already gathered on the tip of her tongue.

'Always,' she continues, 'without fail, just before the plane takes off, an air hostess stands at the bulkhead and performs, in dumb show, the art of survival. Well, in the split second between the blast and the breaking of the glass, I realized that the waitress was doing the same. She kicked off her shoes, took down her pants, and corked her vagina with the latter. So did I. Then, as the waters hit us she reached behind and slid a finger up her anus. So did I. Many that didn't were sodomized by sea water. Menstrual cycles were accelerated. One poor woman — formerly pregnant — was induced to miscarry. I shan't ever forget the sight of that foetus rolling slowly in the blue sea like a naked cosmonaut. Aunt Bella, believe it or not, was spared such a humiliation by her incontinence pads.'

There is a trick here, but the man does not fall for it, because he genuinely does not know who Aunt Bella is. Nor does the news that Uncle Anthony and Lewis Falcon are also both alive and, though suffering from various internal ruptures, likely to stay that way provoke any response from him. Instead he is assailed by a new thought. 'Who planted the bomb?' he asks. 'And why?'

'Good questions,' says a deeper voice emerging from the shadows that have hitherto concealed its owner. A man, wearing a shiny mask of simulated skin, steps out of the darkness and into the greenish spotlight. Where his nose should be there is just a bump and two holes. His lidless eyes seem to be fixed in a permanent stare. Nor does his lipless mouth close over his teeth. Two ragged ears complete this parody of the senses. He glances at the woman, who registers no particular surprise at his sudden appearance, and then gives his full attention to his new acquaintance. He is dressed in a sleeveless sweat shirt and tight denim jeans like the archetypal movie tough guy. The man with one arm stares admiringly at the biceps on display and considers, perhaps for the first time, the implications of his injury.

'The answer to the first question, my friend, is you,' says the faceless one, with the trace of an accent, 'the answer to the second remains unknown, at least until you are prepared to enlighten us.'

The erstwhile sleeper can hardly believe his ears. Why, if he thinks of me as a murderer, does he use the words 'my friend'? How can he be? And if he isn't, does that mean that the woman who calls herself 'my wife' isn't either? Are both simply figures of speech? The man's other words certainly don't contain any hint of concern or affection, nor does his bedside manner, perfectly exemplified by his aggressive grip on the side of my cot. It seems that those bars were deployed not to restrain me, as I had assumed, but to protect me from the likes of him, in which case I am almost certainly in a lunatic asylum and must humour my fellow inmates. They, poor things, must have been moved by my unconscious presence to create fantasies that could incorporate me into their own sad stories; to one, left at the altar by a fleet-footed lover, I am the ideal husband; to the other, disfigured in some meaningless fire, I am a black-hearted anarchist. It only remains for me to convince the authorities hereabouts that I am sane, concludes the man in the bed, and await a transfer to a more appropriate institution. To which end the word 'doctor' forms in his mouth.

It never emerges, for the tough guy, a reader of lips if not of minds, gags the would-be speaker with his horny hand. 'Not just yet, my friend,' he whispers, 'not before we've had a little chat.' 'Don't hurt him,' says the woman. 'Please.' The tough guy relaxes his grip. 'Are you willing to talk?' he asks. The man in the bed nods. 'What do you want to know?' he asks. 'Why you did it' says the faceless one. The man in the bed looks up at the head of his interrogator but can discern no recognizable expression in the shiny skin that is stretched across its features. He is a robot with the rudiments of a human face, thinks the man in the bed, who has been programmed to believe in my guilt. 'Give me one good reason why I should blow myself up,' he says.

'Because you are a self-hating Jew,' comes the mechanical reply. 'Impossible,' says the man in the bed; 'how can I hate what I do not know?' 'Because you are prejudiced, my friend,' comes the reply, 'like all our enemies.' The fellow's paranoid as well, thinks the sane one; still, I suppose it's a way of making sense of his fate. 'But I'm not your enemy,' he says, soothingly. 'Then why did you assassinate our Minister of Industry and Trade?' snaps the faceless one. This is too much! 'Go away,' says the man in the bed, 'you're crazy.' The faceless one says nothing. Instead he turns the handle that turns the screw that raises the mattress, he turns the handle until its unresisting occupant rests at the ten to three position. Then he walks robot-like toward the dark side of the room whence he returns, moments later, with a black case from which he removes some full-plate photographs.

'My friend, we have heard your wife's version of the assassination,' he says as he sorts out the black and white images, 'and what has it taught us? Only that you were not cuckolded by Neptune. This, pleasing as it must be for you, does not help us to resolve the outrage.' He looks at the woman who seems to be blushing (the green light makes it impossible to be sure), causing him to go as far as a tough guy can go toward an apology. 'I did not intend to be personal, Mrs Isaacson,' he says, 'it is the same with all the survivors; they remember only their own salvation.

They all say the same; first there was a bang, then this or that happened to *me* — it's not an accident that *me,* in your language, is also the first syllable of memory. My friends, the only eye-witness worth anything is the camera, of which there was no shortage. But do you think the editors of our esteemed free press would let us examine the film from those that we salvaged? Not likely, as you would say. Hold on, they howled, we are birds of prey not stool pigeons. My friends, we said, you are either for terrorism or against it. But if we give in to you this once, they squealed, the next time there's trouble our cameramen will be looked upon as spies and treated accordingly. We had no sympathy and took them to court where, only yesterday, we won our case. It is true that the judge ordered us to return the films, but he set no date, and ruled that we could develop them in the meantime. You never know,' he says to the man in the bed, holding the incendiary images in front of his face, as if he were offering pornography to a potentate on his divan, 'perhaps one of these may jog your memory.'

The sequence begins innocently enough. Two men are hugging in a crowded room: a thin man and a fat man. Laurel and Hardy, thinks the man in the bed, without knowing why; then, from a deeper place, he brings up the names of Owen Wister, the beanpole scribe, and Frederic Remington, his beefy illustrator. The thin man's left arm is in a plaster cast. In the penultimate picture, surprisingly, his arm is replaced by a brilliant white flash. The last photograph is less well defined, has begun to break up into its constituent grains, which is appropriate as it displays, shockingly, the disintegration of human flesh.

'What have these got to do with me?' asks the viewer, his memory untouched.

By way of an answer the faceless one selects a small mirror from the bedside table and, raising it aloft, allows the witness to incriminate himself at the one-man identity parade. I am the thin man, he thinks, but says nothing. 'What makes you so sure', says the woman, who has also been scrutinizing the photographs, 'that my husband was responsible for the bomb? Hasn't it occurred to you that he might have been trying to protect the Minister? How do you know my husband isn't a hero?'

'You are a lucky man, my friend,' says the faceless one, 'to have such a loyal wife. She is, of course, quite right to draw my attention to the ambiguity in the evidence. Indeed, we would probably have given you the benefit of the doubt, if it hadn't been for one thing.'

'Which is?' asks the woman, impatiently pushing the hair from her eyes. The tough guy waves his hands in the manner of a conjuror and plucks a new object from the open case. 'Do you know what this is?' he asks the man in the bed, pointing a silver pen at him as if it were an accusatory finger.

An image comes unbidden into the mind of the man in the bed. A memory? He sees an elderly gent wearing a black skullcap and a zebra-skin shawl picking out, with a similar silver pointer, strange letters drawn upon a yellowish scroll. Beside the man is a boy who is trying without success – this is what his expression indicates – to make sense of that indecipherable alphabet. Both faces, though suggestive, are anonymous, bearing more resemblance to those de-individualized visages favoured by many modern artists. A third person enters the scene: the boy's mother, perhaps? She is clearly known to the pedagogue, because he raises his head from the parchment and winks at her. This is no memory, concludes the man in the bed, but an intuitive warning; the faceless one is in cahoots with the woman, who is not *my* wife but *his* stooge!

'Read the name on the pen,' demands the faceless one, 'if you still remember how.' The man in the bed screws up his eyes and peers at the gold letters inscribed on its side, at the curious curlicues and loops, and a single word enters his mind: *italics*!

He sees a boy in a blue blazer stooped over an ink-stained desk laboriously copying out disjointed phrases in the same ornate script. Was he that ill-used youth? Or was he the teacher in whose privileged shoes he seems to be standing? Either way there is a name on the tip of his tongue.

'Jonah Isaacson,' he reads. 'Do you know who that is?' asks the faceless one. 'Me?' enquires the man in the bed, knowing what is expected of him. 'Congratulations,' says the faceless one. 'Now we're getting somewhere. Here's the next problem. Whose pen is it?' Logic dictates the answer. 'Mine?' says the man in the bed.

'A brilliant deduction, my friend,' replies the faceless one.

'What does that prove?' asks the woman. 'It proves that your husband is a murderer,' replies the faceless one. 'For God's sake,' says the female half of the double-act, studying the gilt barrel with its golden trim, 'it's just an ordinary pen.' 'Except for one thing, Mrs Isaacson,' replies the faceless one. 'It contains the timing device that detonated the bomb.'

He looks at the man in the bed with eyes made luminous by victory. 'What we want from you, my friend,' he says, 'is the name of the man − or woman − who gave you this. Who knows, you may even be able to persuade us that you were a dupe, a victim − like Austria! I concede that a man experienced enough to construct such a sophisticated device is unlikely to sign his handiwork.'

The man in the bed turns from the robot to the ice queen in the hope of seeing some sign of a conspiracy, but only finds an inscrutable man and a woman whose tears look hot and real.

His right hand twitches, the memory of her bosom still fresh upon it, and he, in consequence, sees for an instant a female breast with a crescent-shaped scar incised above the areola − sees not in front of him, but flashed upon that interior screen where memories once were seen. The nipple is very dark, almost brown, with five pimples circulating around it like little moons. He experiences an overwhelming desire to take it between his lips and suck, though he is in some doubt as to whether this would be to give pleasure to its owner or to find comfort for himself.

It is certainly true that he needs the latter, for he has also been convinced by the circumstantial evidence and has accepted, in lieu of any other explanation, that in some earlier life he was more than capable of murder. If he were the judge his verdict would assuredly be guilty. This conviction enables him to comprehend more fully the loss of his arm, which he regards as a form of poetic justice, his body's atonement for its master's crime.

His right arm, the survivor, rests uneasily upon his chest, not entirely devoid of jealousy for its disembodied twin; since perpetual banishment, when observed from another point of view, looks like eternal freedom. It considers all the wonders it could finger if it weren't for the constraints placed upon it by the metaphysical considerations of its keeper. Why, for example, did he terminate the voluptuous pleasure afforded in such abundance by the intimate contents of that woman's blouse? No such scruples will restrain its sinister sibling; neither memory nor conscience will proscribe its search for new experiences; veritably it is the sense of touch made flesh.

The spoilsport in question also contemplates his amputated appendage, imagines that St Elmo's fire crackles upon the surface of the water, quickening the scapegoat limb that lies five fathoms deep. See how it makes its crab-like way, unencumbered by its former integuments, out of the wreckage of the Queen of Sheba's Grotto and along the sandy bottom of the Red Sea, relentlessly following the evolutionary path toward the promiscuous sensations of dry land. Its motivation is simple: to feel but not to interpret. Such a journey, as must be expected, is not without pain. What is surprising is the fact that the incidental agonies which accompany a traverse across broken glass and jagged coral should transmit themselves to the bedridden brain of the libertine's erstwhile travelling companion, for it is beyond question (the assertions of his self-appointed instructors notwithstanding) that feeling is returning to the very tips of the abandoned area.

The importance of this revivalist phenomenon is apparent to him at once; if his left arm is not missing after all he is in mendacious company, be it malicious or merely mad. Either way, he is innocent of the abominable crime he had half-believed himself capable of.

The sensations continue: pricks and stabs but mainly small charges that leap across nerve ends, seeming to reconnect the sinews and muscles of the injured limb.

At the same time, deep in his mind's dark screening room, he reviews a sequence of strange images, obviously inspired by his present predicament.

A misshapen half-human creature is strapped to a mortuary slab by a hyperactive alchemist, whose mental condition is echoed by the raging storm without. Kite-like conductors are released through open casements to attract the heavenly fire which, when concentrated by glowing coils and condensers, has divine power enough to reanimate the moribund body – which, for a moment, the dreamer believes is his. Surely the shocks now ripping into his left side have the same high-voltage source controlled, in this instance, by that box of tricks beside his bed to which he is wired. Voltages of astronomical magnitude must be coursing through its cables even now, for the pain has become more than he can bear. 'Doctor,' he screams, 'come, come and switch off the resurrection machine!'

Actually a nurse appears who, without showing the least surprise at the patient's awakening, efficiently injects a syringeful of morphine into his left shoulder. She then disappears as quickly as she came, but only for as long as it takes to find the doctor. The man in the bed, pacified by the painkiller, is now more confused than ever, numbness having once again gobbled up his left side.

A different figure flickers into focus – a doctor to judge from his white coat and in-pocket stethoscope – who promptly shoos away the discomforting duo. This new arrival, clearly a man of some authority, appears to be his best hope for clarification; so he forces his befuddled brain to find some questions that may elucidate answers to the matter of his identity, his injuries and his guilt. But upon closer inspection the doctor, despite his confident gestures, baggy eyes and hang-dog expression, turns out to lack the gravitas that will distinguish the genius capable of restoring life to him; he looks far too immature to be the required father figure. Moreover, he seems exclusively interested in the semiotics of the body, with no time for the ambiguities of the mind. Having allowed but one exchange – 'Good morning, and how are we today?' 'Confused.' 'I'm not surprised. For a while we thought we had another Rip Van Winkle on our hands' – he cuts off verbal communication by the simple expedient of blocking his ears with the horns of his stethoscope which, in the manner of his profession, he uses to record the health of his patient's lungs and bronchial tubes, not to mention the state of his cardio-vascular system.

While the man in the bed breathes in and out, as requested,

he is remembering the doctor's words which have, quite unintentionally, given him much to think about. 'Good morning.' His room apparently has no windows, so is not subject to the approximate temporality of daylight. Indeed, until a few moments ago he had forgotten that days were divided into various sections. Now it frightens him not to know whether it is morning, afternoon, or the middle of the night. 'Today.' He hasn't a clue what day it is, or what month, or even the year. The fish returns to torment his hand. 'Rip Van Winkle.' Why should he be another one? Who was the first?

The doctor is noting down, upon charts taken from the foot of the cot, the indicators that will help him to foretell the immediate future of a stranger who, it is quickly established, doesn't know the first thing about his own past, despite the provocative promptings from state security's muscle man. Good God, the poor sod even requires to be told that he is missing an arm! Did he lose it in an explosion? Of course. Could he have been carrying the bomb? Certainly not! Otherwise he would be in the same state as the late Minister.

'You are wrong,' interjects the faceless one. 'It so happens that the Minister was wearing a new flak jacket, filled with steel wool and ribbed with a flexible alloy. It didn't save the Minister but that, plus his fat, sufficed to shield our friend from the worst of the blast.'

At which the parvenu medic turns upon the resident tough guy and a dispute ensues which, though conducted in an obscure tongue, clearly concerns the condition and ownership of the bed's occupant.

'What language are they speaking?' he asks, remembering the conversation that awakened him from his coma. 'Hebrew,' replies his wife. 'Hebrew?' he repeats. 'The language of Israel,' she explains. 'Oh,' he says, 'can you understand it?' 'A bit,' she says. 'Enough to understand their discussion?' he asks.

'The doctor is furious,' she says. 'He wants to know what else he hasn't been told. Nothing, the other assures him. The doctor reminds him that while you are here you are the responsibility of the hospital. The other disagrees. He argues that you belong to the police – not exactly, the security services. He thinks you are faking your memory loss. The doctor is not so sure. He suspects retrograde amnesia.'

'He's right,' says the man in the bed, 'I don't even remember why my arm, my ex-arm, was in a cast to start with!' 'You told me that you fell out of bed and broke it after painting the town red with Elem Klimov and a few of his embassy minders,' replies his wife, 'and I believed you.' Why the past tense, wonders her forgetful husband?

Behind them the guttural cross-talk suddenly ceases, to be replaced by silence; for two words have attracted the attention of the faceless one — 'embassy minders'.

'Mrs Isaacson,' he cries, 'you didn't tell me your husband's drinking companions were Soviets on official business.' 'Does it make a difference?' she asks. 'Don't you see, Mrs Isaacson?' laughs the faceless one, 'it could explain why no hospital in Bradford had a record of Dr Jonah Isaacson, on that night or any other. His accident was no accident. The Soviets almost certainly broke and reset the bone themselves.'

'Are you expecting me to accept that my husband voluntarily stuck out his arm and let someone snap it?' she asks. 'Something like that,' he replies. 'You're crazy,' she says, 'it's completely out of character.'

'He may have been anaesthetized,' concedes the faceless one, 'there were traces of tubocurarine in his blood and urine, which certainly suggests an involuntary sacrifice.'

'I don't believe what I'm hearing,' she says.

'Didn't it strike you as odd that he suddenly had to go to Bradford,' he demands, 'on the very eve of your holiday?' 'He said it was a chance of a lifetime,' she says. 'Did you believe him?' he asks. 'Half,' she says, 'Half?' he asks. 'I half believed he was going to spend the night with another woman,' she replies. 'It seems to have been worse than that,' he says.

'But why?' she cries. 'Why what?' he asks. 'Why would the Soviets do it to him?' she asks. 'In order to blow up flight LY 316,' he replies.

Sophie suddenly stands very still, as though trying to cope with a severe internal pain. 'Do you realize what you are saying?' she asks quietly. The faceless one nods. 'And you expect me to believe that the Minister was assassinated by accident and that the real purpose of the plot was to blow up a plane in which I happened to be travelling?' The faceless one nods a second time. 'Why,' she cries, 'tell me why?'

'There is a multitude of possibilities,' he says, 'maybe the Russians wanted to destabilize the Middle East, maybe they wanted a war which would enable their surrogates to test some new weaponry in battlefield conditions, maybe the KGB wanted to embarrass the reformers in the Kremlin, maybe they just like killing Jews.'

'I know my husband,' says Sophie Isaacson, 'he is Jewish, he loves me, he isn't suicidal and he is no communist, so what was his motive?' 'That's what I'm here to find out,' the faceless one replies. 'We know why the bomb didn't explode in the plane. Because Mr Falcon stole the detonator. What we don't know is why it went off when it did. Was it a plan or was it plain lucky?'

'Lucky?' she asks. 'Lucky,' repeats the faceless one, relaxed, even cheerful, now that he has the beginnings of a useful scenario, 'lucky for them and, in my opinion, lucky for us.' 'I don't understand,' she says, 'I always thought it was unlucky to lose a Minister in such circumstances.' 'In the short term, perhaps,' he says, 'but in the long run we may be able to use this undeniably tragic misfortune to unlock the doors and release a million of our co-religionists from their Soviet prison. Failing that we'll at least get an exchange of ambassadors out of it.'

Lucky, unlucky; both words seem equally inappropriate to the man in the bed. They conjure up a pagan world prey to the disinterested vagaries of chance. No, the words he would choose must evoke good and evil. Wicked! That's it! That's what he is! Wicked to have joined the bolshevik conspiracy to sabotage an aircraft; wicked to have become a living bomb. 'Doctor,' he cries in his despair, 'do you possess such a thing as morphine for the conscience?' He wants something, anything, to induce anterograde amnesia, so that he can forget that he is — or was — a ruthless mass murderer prepared to exterminate hundreds of people — including his wife — for what? For what?

*

The faceless one, the dweller in shadows, has a name. It is Gideon, diminutive Gidi, by which he is known to his colleagues in Shin Bet, the state's internal security service.

His present commission is to recover from Jonah Isaacson's lost recall the eventful eve of his flight to Israel. It is confidently anticipated that this version will coincide with the politically convenient mise-en-scene already established in the mind of his boss who has, in fact, drafted a confession implicating the Soviets in a terrorist outrage; something that will convince their beleaguered leader that someone, somewhere in the Kremlin, planned this clandestine operation for the purpose of domestic and foreign destabilization.

In exchange for his verification Jonah Isaacson will be made an honorary Austrian; which is to say that he will be counted as the plot's first victim. Sceptical at first, in accordance with the rules of his profession, Gidi has begun to believe that the man in the bed really does have amnesia. He has even forgotten his religion, and therefore knows nothing about the country in which he has reawakened, ignorance exceptional even in an Anglo-Jew.

'Let me get this straight,' he says, 'the Jews left Europe after the defeat of the man whose political platform was their destruction, to live among another people dedicated to their expulsion. Why?' 'Because Israel is our homeland,' replies Gidi. 'Didn't you tell me that your parents were born in Poland?' asks Jonah. 'But they were not Poles,' replies Gidi, 'they were Jews a long way from home.' 'How long?' asks Jonah. 'Two thousand miles,' replies Gidi, 'and two thousand years.' 'Two thousand years!' exclaims Jonah. 'The Jews have a long memory,' explains Gidi. 'Except me,' says Jonah. 'Except you,' agrees Gidi. 'And what do they remember?' asks Jonah. 'God's promise,' replies Gidi. 'What of those who are atheists?' asks Jonah. 'They remember our history,' replies Gidi. 'Then I am doubly excluded from Zion,' laments Jonah. 'I do not believe in God and I have no sense of history.' How can he be expected to list all the ancient pogroms, massacres and catastrophes when he cannot even recollect the colourful incidents of 18 June?

And it is not for lack of effort. More than anything Jonah wants to please Gidi, whom he has come to admire to the point of hero-worship, but try as he might he cannot remember the train ride to Bradford, Klimov's lecture, too much vodka, the broken arm, Soviet aid, the loaded keepsake and the fond farewell. He knows that all these things must have happened but, despite Gidi's vivid descriptions, he cannot place himself in the picture. A comparison comes to mind, from where he does not know; he is like a cinematographer, that invisible presence whose only trace is the film itself. He knows that he must have participated in the drama outlined by Gidi, because otherwise Gidi would have nothing to relate. It is just a matter of location. Where was I?

But he finds it far more pleasant — and much easier — to imagine Gidi's heroic exploits. Twenty years ago or more little Israel prepared to defend its existence against mighty enemies. Fearful battles were fought in the desert. See those tanks racing across the sands of Sinai. In one of them, behind brave Colonel Iska, is Gidi, hell-bent for the Mitla Pass and the road to Suez beyond. Great the victory, great the rejoicing. But it doesn't last. Israel's foes do not sleep. In 1973 Gidi goes to war again, and fights at the ghastly battle of Hushniye where, under the ghostly light of a full moon, the last Syrians are driven off the Golan Heights.

Gidi, veteran of three wars and numerous campaigns, squeezes his shoulder. 'I know what you're going through, my friend,' he says, 'I've been there myself. Relax. Take your time. Assuming that it is lost, your memory will almost certainly return. Which is more than can be said for my face.'

And so it happens that Jonah asks Gidi about his third war. 'Israelis are veterans,' replies Gidi, 'Europeans are survivors. That's what I believed, until 1982, when I also became a survivor.' 'I don't know what you're talking about,' says Jonah. 'My friend,' replies Gidi, 'in 1982 the man you blew up was our Minister of Defence. He had a big plan. He wanted to invade the Lebanon. And I was one of the faceless Israelis he sent to do the job. We hit that accursed land like a storm. And people in countries I have never heard of took one look at me and my buddies and began to hate us because, in their eyes, we were nothing but cogs in the world's most efficient fighting machine. What really hurt was the realization that this was a view shared by our superiors, especially the fat mother-fucker who pulled the strings. What were we to him? Human beings? Don't make me laugh. You know what a golem is, don't you, my friend? A circumcized zombie, whose role model was vitalized by the Maharal of Prague in the year dot. Its orders were to protect the local Jews. Four times the army, our latter-day golem, saved Israel – in '48, '56, '67 and '73 – but in '82 it was on the rampage, answerable to no one but its master in the Cabinet. Some of us began to fear his next command. We could see the day when we would be turned, despite our better judgement, upon the body politic we had been trained to protect. I shouldn't be telling you this, but when the RPG hit our tank I cursed the man, and when my face began to melt I wished him dead. I didn't want him weeping crocodile tears over my coffin, lamenting the loss of another of "his boys".

'After the war there was a big debate; some, like Dudu Wolf the actor, were prepared to go to jail rather than serve in Lebanon or the occupied territories; others believed that without their restraining hand the army would become a blood-crazed juggernaut. I took the latter view, which is why I am here now.'

Jonah Isaacson is confused. What could have happened between '73 and '82 to turn a nation of heroes into a brute bent upon self-destruction? Does it mean that he must now side with their enemies? He looks down at his armless sleeve. Perhaps he already has. Then he recollects Gidi's unusual choice of word to describe the Minister's disappearance from the scene. Lucky. Even his wife had commented upon it. Was Gidi secretly pleased that the Minister had been done away with?

'Gidi,' he asks, 'why did you use the word lucky?' 'I explained to your wife,' he replies; 'it gave us something to use against the Soviets. If Syria had bumped off one of our top men we could hardly have gone to them and said, "Look, chaps, we know what you've done and, if you don't do so and so, the world will know too," because they'd be only too pleased to accept the responsibility. But the Soviet Union sees itself – and wants others to see it – as a civilized nation, not a nest of terrorists like Syria or Libya. And they'll pay us in kind – maybe let out a few more Sharanskys, or even exchange ambassadors – to forget the evidence to the contrary. Because they know no one will believe them if they rubbish our charges. They won't believe it themselves, because in their byzantine power structure – forgive the expression, my friend – the right arm never knows what the left is doing.' Jonah Isaacson, looking like a choirboy in his white hospital gown, and conscious that all these redeeming consequences depend upon his reminiscences, wishes that he could sing for Gidi. He glances up at his damaged hero and witnesses a strange phenomenon: the present overlaid by the past. Instead of gaping holes there are handsome features, as if the ravaged face still contained the memory of its former glory. As of course it must, for between the bone and the charred flesh the blueprint remains, sending forth its insubstantial images. What if my memory is in a similar fix, thinks Jonah Isaacson, beaming out its messages as hopelessly as a movie projector without a screen? Or maybe there is a screen. How else can Gidi have obtained such a detailed picture of my movements on that fateful night? Why not? I see his face as it was, he experiences my past life as it happened. Are we in telepathic communication?

Jonah Isaacson is beginning to feel better about himself. If Gidi can read his mind and not be appalled by what he finds there, then perhaps his former deeds are not so terrible after all. Even the murder, which he is prepared to believe that he committed by accident, does not seem to have caused Gidi much anguish. On the contrary, there are grounds for assuming that he regards it as a *mitzvah*. Where did that word come from?

'Correct me if I'm wrong,' says Jonah, 'but I think *lucky* was a little Freudian slip. You're glad the Minister got blown away, aren't you?' Gidi looks down at the prisoner on the bed, who has assumed a more confident pose, his head resting upon his right hand, and fears that his authority has been transferred to him. He feels so uncomfortable that he cannot keep still, and wanders over to the window with its view across ochre hills and olive groves that eventually merge into the wild and wooded valley of Rephaim. Behind him is the whole of Jerusalem. The time has come to decide whether meaning should be added to his characteristic form of address.

'My friend,' he says, turning around, 'the Jews were a dead

people. That we are alive again is a miracle. But it is not natural. We are like the monster brought to life by Baron Frankenstein. Here, in Israel, the remnants of the world's Jewish communities have been stitched together and reanimated by the force of a single idea – that we have returned to the place of our birth. Abortive attempts were made to destroy us, but we survived. We were like you, we had to learn everything anew – including a language. As we grew, our founding father taught us all he knew, until he wearied of the task and retired to the desert. And other guiding lights appeared. But, oh my friend, they were not the same. They flattered us, because they were not sure of our love. And their words acted like wine upon the cerebellum. One, in particular, took advantage of our intoxication. "You are strong," he cried, "you are strong enough to take whatever you want. You have a *casus belli*. So take." And we succumbed to his forked tongue and we shamed ourselves. My punishment is written upon my face. I have become the embodiment of my nation's history – my nation's, your nation's, any nation's – always available to the most able decorator, never fixed, always liable to reinterpretation. You are right, my friend, I do think it was a good thing that the man who misled us was blown to bits. He would have been a father to us like Abraham was a father to Isaac.'

Two days later – it is 4 July – Jonah renascent is to be found strolling, arm in arm with his wife, through the hanging gardens of the Hadassah Hospital. This signifies two things: that his physical recovery is almost complete, give or take an arm, and that he is no longer regarded as a danger to the state. What it does not signify, unfortunately, is that he recognizes his wife; though, increasingly, he wishes he did.

Early evening and the perfumed air is cooling around the hills of Jerusalem, a premonition of the coming ice-age that makes the diurnal effusions of the luxuriant flowers all the more poignant. Jonah stares at their variegated blooms in wonderment. Such a variety of species! 'What is that?' he asks, pointing to the red trumpets that blare out upon a climbing plant. 'Hibiscus,' she replies. 'And that?' he asks, referring to its neighbour upon the yellow wall, which is adorned with white stars. 'Jasmine,' she replies. A tiny bird, a whirring blur of metallic green, alights upon a stem of the hibiscus and, bowing, dips a curved bill into the sweet engine of its fertility. 'A sunbird,' says Sophie, in anticipation of her husband's question.

They wander on, disturbing all manner of lizards, some seemingly dipped in chlorophyll, others camouflaged as dead leaves, which seek refuge in the wall's hot crevices.

The earth, of course, is very dry. It is red, like clay, and cracked. Scattered upon its surface are pink or honey-coloured stones, some of which display rings, as if they were once growing things.

At the end of the path is a tree with herring-bone leaves, and flowers like yellow pom-poms. Upon one of its thin thorny branches sits a plump bird crowned with roseate feathers, too regal to be disturbed by the newcomers. Taking its time it spreads its black and white wings and, in a series of graceful undulations, glides down to the spiky lawns where, beneath the sparkling spray of a dozen sprinklers, its fellows are digging for worms. Mimosa. Hoopoe. The naming of names continues.

Jonah's accident, as it is now termed, did not greatly diminish his vocabulary; it merely separated a considerable number of nouns from the objects whose representatives they are. Thus he remembers generic words such as flora and fauna but, until he steps out of the hospital and enters its fragrant back-yard, he has no idea what they entail.

If he had been asked to describe a bird he would have listed the following: beak, head, breast, wings, tail, legs. And that would have been it; no colours, no heterogeneity, just the ur-bird. It was the same with *wife*. He knew what one was in theory — she on whose account shall a man leave his father and his mother — but he didn't know that he was married until Sophie introduced herself. Likewise with *pain*, which had no meaning for him until the morphine wore off. Now he half suspects that there are, lurking somewhere in his body, somnolent predators called *pains*.

103

He is even more confused about the word *love*, which is what his wife says she feels for him. Apparently he once loved her and, she hopes, will do so again. He is equally optimistic, having been convinced by empirical evidence that nouns are indeed born of objects, cannot in fact exist without them. His problem, at the moment, is to be at home only in the shadowland of words. Well, with the help of his wife, he has taken his first steps back into the real world.

'It's like the Garden of Eden,' she says. Jonah, looking around at his brave new world of brilliant colours and inebriating smells, sees, crouched on parched earth between clumps of prickly cacti, an elderly gentleman hiding behind a camera.

'Look,' he whispers to his wife, but she is slow to respond and reluctant to confront the ancient voyeur. 'He's an old man,' she says, 'what harm can he possibly do?' 'I want to ask him why he's taking pictures of me,' says her obstinate husband, pulling her down the uneven steps and along the uncultivated border between the ornamental beds and the diamantiferous grass upon which the hoopoes still dine like clockwork toys.

But their route around the perimeter is longer than his diagonal exit line, which cancels the handicap of advanced years and enables him to make his escape. His flight is further facilitated by Sophie's fall, occasioned by the coincidental encounter of her foot with a green snake-like hose. She tumbles over it into a thick shrub whose leaves look like the hands of alien supplicants, until they receive her body, whereupon appetite becomes the dominant feature. They finger her breasts and thighs, caress them when she tries to rise. Not even a plant can take such liberties with a wife, especially in front of her husband. In one bound Jonah is at her side and, single-handed, pulls her from their clutches.

She is wearing white shorts and a powder-blue blouse, so fine that he can see the naked contours of her chest beneath. His hand, at the end of its tether, all but screams out, 'Touch!' His other senses take up the cry, especially the olfactory receptors, which have been seduced by the lemon-laced aphrodisiac hanging heavy on the air. He looks at his wife, as if seeking acquiescence, for he feels that his better judgement is now at the mercy of a biological imperative, something that not even amnesia can erase. And gets the nod. For Sophie is also under the influence of the geranium's narcotic perfume. She reaches out and, taking her husband's itchy palm, places it upon her left breast. Then, open-mouthed as if expecting to bite into an invisible apple, they kiss. And Jonah's hand begins to move. To explore. And Sophie can tell, by its tentative manoeuvres, that it is exploration.

Though, once or twice, she has the strangest feeling that another more knowledgeable hand is also negotiating her intimacies. An impossibility, she knows, and can only suppose that her whole body remembers what her mind is at present reliving: their last fuck upon Caesar's cloth, only a fortnight before, when he took her from behind and made her so wet inside. Jonah, on the contrary, cannot recall any such precedents, and can only anticipate the pleasure in store. Whence comes this prophetic vision? Surely from some collective memory, an understanding that pre-dates the fall. There are certain things the body knows better than the mind. This, obviously, being one of them.

But, wonders Jonah, is there a difference between desire and *love*? Is one the metaphysical justification for the colonial activity being undertaken, in my name, by this greedy hand; which, it must be said, is meeting no resistance from the occupied? Am I, then, in love? No, says a mocking voice, you are in Sophie's pants. The implication being that the two states are synonymous. Sure enough he feels the pressure of elastic on his wrist and soft flesh, in two parts, at his fingertips. The fingertips of his left hand!

He opens his eyes just in time to receive a conspiratorial wave from his cursed arm before it turns and slithers away to its lair in the undergrowth. 'I'm sorry,' he says, not entirely certain that he need be. 'Don't be silly,' says Sophie, 'it's not every day that a woman is courted so passionately by her husband.'

Upon that thought they return to the hospital, a married couple reliving their relationship in reverse.

The septuagenarian is in situ the following afternoon and this time Jonah, a quick learner, ignores the objections of Sophie and the decorum of the garden. He jumps down the steps and sprints across the lawn, thereby cutting off the observer's line of retreat. The old man, no fool, tries to dodge past on his pursuer's left flank, but Jonah is too quick and, side-stepping, grabs the old boy's safari jacket as he passes, putting an end to his flight.

'Now,' says Jonah, 'you'll tell me who you are.' The blanched photographer, white of hair and face, looks at his captor and says, in a voice that is far from steady, 'Don't you recognize me?' Jonah, beginning to worry, shakes his head. 'I'm your father,' comes the reply.

Jonah examines the lined face with its fleshy nose, searching brown eyes and colourless moustache, but not one of the features is familiar, neither on its own nor in combination with another.

'Hello, Toby,' says Sophie, catching up with father and son, 'I warned you this would happen.' Jonah drops his hand. 'Adieu, my boy,' says Toby. 'Try, try and remember me.'

These are the things that Jonah remembers. He remembers that he was in an explosion; that he, in fact, caused it. He remembers the Russians who planned it. He remembers that he is in Israel. He remembers that state's turbulent history. All these things he remembers to please Gidi. To please Sophie he remembers that he is her husband. But he does not remember his parents, though he wants to please them too.

They visit him in his hospital room, his father and his mother. It is a difficult meeting for them all; for the parents who are denied by their son, and for the son who sees only strangers. So hard that both mother — Queenie — and son are struck dumb. It is left to Toby to do the talking.

He tells of his little studio on Holywell Hill, which he ran for nearly half a century, from the age of the Thornton Pickard to that of the Nikon and the Hasselblad. His forte was the Jewish wedding. Like Boris, his great rival, he was something of a missionary; what he wanted was to bring Hollywood to the East End (which was forever moving west — by the end of his career he had to travel no further than the marquees of Radlett, Elstree and Bushey). But in the beginning he would pack his precious equipment into the back of his old banger and rattle down Watling Street towards the glittering ballrooms of London.

How did he get those first commissions? By reading the personal columns of the *Jewish Chronicle*, noting whose engagements had been announced, and contacting the happy couples. He could charm the birds out of the trees in those days. He also had the good sense to ingratiate himself with caterers, wine merchants and florists who, when asked, would recommend Tobias the photographer — if Boris hadn't got to them beforehand.

Unlike his rivals Toby — or Tobias — chose to work on location rather than in the studio; he preferred the vulgar but vivacious bustle of the Imperial Ballrooms or Stern's Hotel to the waxwork atmosphere of an unnaturally lit cubby-hole. If Boris Bennett was Ernst Lubitsch he was John Ford; a man attuned to the small pleasures of ordinary life.

Not that he couldn't say to the besotted groom, if the occasion demanded (as it usually did), 'Imagine you are William Powell,' carefully naming a star who was famously dapper, but not impossibly handsome, 'Imagine you are William Powell arriving at the premiere of your new movie.' What screen goddess he selected depended upon the appearance of the bride. This was the *shmoos*, the gilding of life with macassar oil, and it came to interest Toby less and less.

These were, in truth, terrible years for the Jews and Tobias the photographer set himself a mighty task: to capture the spontaneity of the moment, the gaiety of the night, to illustrate the *joie de vivre* that gave the nod to the next generation. But, alas, in the cold light of their cramped apartment the couple who had been king and queen for an evening felt embarrassed by the images of their unbuttoned jollity and chose, instead, the conventional portrait with the slicked down hair, the razor sharp crease and the pool of Brussels lace.

Sometimes the crease was not straight enough or, worse, the bride had one chin too many or the groom's gut was too pronounced and his customers would sheepishly ask the photographer to varnish the truth. Which Toby could do, no problem, much to the delight of his young son, who became so fascinated by his father's ability to retouch reality that he ended up teaching Film Studies at the University of St Albans.

'You don't remember a thing, do you?' says Toby. 'Not a thing,' agrees Jonah. 'I thought you'd never forget those Mondays — our Mondays — when I was the sorcerer and you became his apprentice. I won't,' says Toby. 'I can still hear your feet on the stairs. God knows why you never fell. And then my door would burst open and there you'd be, fresh from school, with a glass of milk in one hand and some of Queenie's famous cookies in the other.' There is a beat, a moment's silence, in recognition of the thing that is irrevocably lost. ' "You haven't started, have you?" you would say, and I would always reply, "No, I've been waiting for you".'

Toby cannot go on, once again he is waiting for his son. 'I'm here,' says Jonah, wanting to be of help, 'but I wish I was there. Please continue.'

Toby, restored, speaks with renewed enthusiasm. It is catching. As he describes the shared thrill of watching a photograph gradually emerge in the developer, so a picture slowly demists in his son's mind. Of a boy who watches open-mouthed as his father, illuminated by a red bulb that glowers in its wall-socket like a one-eyed devil, removes the camera back and extracts the film, film whose memory he will now reactivate with various chemical processes. If only he could drink something, some panacea for amnesiacs, and thereby regain his past. Instead he gobbles up Toby's words. But it is his imagination that responds, not his memory. He has never seen the boy in the darkroom before.

Tobias didn't become a household name like Boris, but he always had plenty of work and would probably still be in business if it hadn't been for the minor tragedy that put a stop to his optimism. His negatives, especially the early ones, had been deteriorating for years, but it never occurred to him that they might vanish overnight, taking his entire collection with them.

On an otherwise insignificant day last March Queenie woke him up in the small hours and said, 'I can smell something burning.' Toby descended. (They continued to live in the flat above the studio, which was small, but had a spectacular view of the cathedral.)

Entering the darkroom he found his negatives in a state of self-induced combustion. He subdued it quickly, but not quickly enough. 'To me this was the end,' says Toby, 'the end of my dream. It wasn't just celluloid that had gone up in smoke. It was the collective memory of Anglo-Jewry. Not that anyone noticed.'

The only survivor of the catastrophe was Toby's family archive, which was stored elsewhere.

He has brought a selection of prints from it in the hope that Jonah will, through their agency, rediscover himself. Jonah looks and despairs; the boy shown on his first day at school, on holiday, with family and friends, bears no resemblance to the lad he has just seen in the darkroom. He remains, perhaps forever, a stranger to himself.

In a way this is a bigger blow to Toby than the loss of his life's work, for this archive was to have been his legacy, his contribution to generations of Isaacsons as yet unborn, and likely to remain so. Sophie is a modern girl, not given to parturition.

It has become, in all senses, a negative legacy, destined to end up in an indifferent dustbin, because it is meaningless to his son, for whom it was intended. It is a lesson from which he is too old to benefit: do not base your immortal hopes upon flimsy substances such as a son's memory and shadowy film. Queenie was right when she begged him, all those years ago, to follow the example of Boris and go into property development.

The perfect opportunity arose when Jonah married Sophie and Anthony Jacobi became his *machuten*. At that time Anthony was planning St Peter's Place. He invited Toby to join him. 'It's a great opportunity,' he said. Toby hesitated. 'Please,' said Queenie, 'the man is a wizard with money.' A wizard indeed! He waves his wand and buildings grow, everywhere from St Albans to Judea and Samaria. When he dies he'll be able to say, like Christopher Wren, 'If you seek a monument, look about you.'

*

And what of Toby Isaacson? What will be his memorial? At the moment it stands, one metre high, upon the linoleum-covered floor of his son's hospital room. Built, not with bricks, but with the *cartes de visite* left behind by the heart-broken photographer. It is a slow business, balancing the load-bearing trestles with only one arm, but after many involuntary demolitions the edifice is finally complete.

Surveying his triumph the architect wonders, why did I do it? To please my father, whom I do not recognize as such? A somewhat disingenuous disclaimer!

Jonah Isaacson knows he was formed when the said father lay atop his mother and planted his seed in her belly. He knows this in the sense that he knows the sun will rise tomorrow. It is the way of things. He knows this even though he feels more like Adam newly made in Eden, a man who entered the world unencumbered with ancestry. But Jonah Isaacson is no creationist, he knows about evolution and how he is descended from apes and, somewhat more evidently, from those gentlefolk whose ghostly faces stare out at him from the House of Isaacson.

The structure has been artfully designed so that the sturdier portraits with the more glamorous studio marks — Cracow, Lvov, Kiev — form the foundations, while photographs from Whitechapel and Limehouse comprise the middle stories, holding aloft the flimsier postcards from St Albans.

Staring at this ascendancy of triangles Jonah, still groggy at times, has the illusion that he is looking at the world through the eye of a fly. He sees a kaleidoscope of faces whose features are extraordinarily animated; for example, the nose that once belonged to his grandfather, the one who sailed from Odessa to Tilbury, has jumped on to the chops of his father's brother, from where it leaps at Jonah, landing right between his eyes. Likewise ears fly from behind the coiffure of a Cracowian dandy in order to alight, like a bisected butterfly, on either side of the head of his English descendant. As for eyes! They roll from socket to socket as if in perpetual motion.

There is some comfort to be drawn from this display of familial continuity, but it is as nothing when compared with the disquiet now lodged in Jonah's breast; for he has recognized in these unknown people the proscription of his own potential. What is amnesia to the genes? Merely a sideshow. The real business was done in the womb. From birth his body has been on automatic pilot! Receiving its orders not from his mind, but from that control tower, that house of cards! Just at that moment of depressing revelation the door of Jonah's room bursts open, letting in the tail end of a khamsin, and the whole construction, inherently unstable, folds in upon itself.

Enter Anthony Jacobi, no idle man. As soon as he is able to walk without risk of further ruptures poisoning his innards he decides to visit his stricken nephew-in-law. Not for him the agonized silences and intermittent lamentations that characterized the unavailing encounters between Mr and Mrs Isaacson and their only boy. On the contrary he is cheerfully loquacious, for he sees in the untidy fellow looking at his scattered family not some pathetic reliquary devoid of contents but *homo novellus*, the man of the future.

'Hello,' he says, leaning heavily on his ebonite cane, 'I'm your wife's uncle. You knew me once.' No apology for the havoc wrought.

Jonah turns away from the monochromes to confront a glossy gent in a purple gown, grey pyjamas and red slippers, who looks as though he has just stepped out of a manicurist rather than a hospital bed. 'I've heard of you,' says Jonah, in no mood to be accommodating.

'Leave those where they are,' says Anthony, pointing imperiously to the photographs, 'they belong to the past, not you.' He strides forward, intending to release Jonah from his familial responsibilities, but his stick misses the floor and accidentally prods the stern visage of a black-bonneted village crone from the backwoods of Poland, who responds by scooting across the room, causing Anthony to fall flat on his face. Whereupon Jonah laughs for the first time since the explosion that changed his life, laughs till his eyes fill with tears and his sides ache.

'Don't mind me,' says the source of his amusement from a prone position, 'I approve of laughter. Gravity is my enemy, by which I refer both to Newton's universal magnet and the sobriety that smothers life's little joys. That is why I put up buildings and produce movies, despite the objections of folklorists and puritans.'

He rises to his knees. 'It is also, incidentally, why I have chosen to live in Israel. So that I can throw my weight behind those who plan to build a new society, as against those who only want to dwell in the past. My dear Jonah, if you want my opinion, you are better off without a memory. It means that you are your own man, beholden to no one. Now, if you have finished wetting yourself, perhaps you could assist me to my feet.'

Made light-headed by excessive laughter Jonah unsteadily guides his wife's uncle to the safety of a chair, the one Sophie occupies every afternoon. Nor are his senses assisted by the seductive aromas of after-shave and talc that emanate from the body he is leading.

'Right,' says Anthony, as though he had just alighted upon a throne, 'let's get down to business. Time is money, even in this place. So. Have you ever heard a word against the Italian Renaissance? I doubt it. Michelangelo, Leonardo, Raphael, Machiavelli. Everyone loves 'em. Well, we've got one here. A Jewish renaissance. Thanks to Mother Eve's indiscretion no birth is without pain. Okay. I can live with that. It's a small price to pay for progress. And progress is what it's all about. It is the opposite of gravity. It is the life force itself. To oppose progress is as futile as to deny evolution. You wouldn't do that, would you, Jonah? Silly question! You may have lost your memory, but I have it on good authority that your marbles are all there. That's why I want to enlist you as an ally. After all you are, literally, a renaissance man; having had the good fortune to be reborn with all your faculties. You are consequently in the happy position of being able to pick your past as well as your future.'

He leans forward in the chair and lowers his voice. 'I wouldn't dream of trying to replace Toby in your affections, but I would like to offer myself as — shall we say? — a paternal-style adviser. In which capacity I commend the following position: Executive Producer on *The Six Pointed Star*. You know what I'm talking about?'

Jonah nods; thanks to Gidi he remembers nothing but knows everything.

'I have great faith in you, despite your recent problems and, what is more important, Lewis Falcon seems to have taken a shine to you. He's even prepared to let you work over the script with him. Most lecturers in Film Studies would give their right arm for such an opportunity.' Anthony pauses but does not consider it worth apologizing for his little *faux pas*.

'By the way, your new appointment won't prejudice your position at the U of SA. In case it's slipped your mind, I own the place. You'll be granted a sabbatical. To regain your strength. Which you'll need. Falcon can be a real prima donna, believe me. Well, my boy, what do you say?'

'There's a problem,' says Jonah. 'What?' asks Anthony. 'I must return to England,' explains Jonah, 'to have my arm replaced.' 'Then the choice is clear,' snaps Anthony, 'aesthetics or prosthetics?'

But it is more than that, not simply art versus life (or a simulacrum thereof), but a momentous choice between the abstract and the concrete, as represented by Toby and Anthony. Both are materialists, it is true, but there is a crucial difference between them. Toby asks people to smile so that they will have something to remember, whereas Anthony wants them to laugh so that they'll forget. Remembrance versus forgetting. Recent experience has taught Jonah that the latter is dangerous, being a state of absolute relativity in which all is believable and Polonius's dictum, 'To thine own self be true,' palpable nonsense. Better Toby's belief that there is a self which is the bedrock of our existence, than Anthony's credo which maintains that our centre is a black hole to be filled and refilled with whatever he sees fit. If they were brothers Toby would be Moses and Anthony would be Aaron.

Suddenly Jonah, though he still does not recall them, feels an obligation not to denounce his yesterdays and thereby prejudice his tomorrows. 'I'm going home,' he says, opting for milk and honey, rather than the Golden Calf.

*

And so it is that Jonah Isaacson signs the statement Gidi has so painstakingly prepared for him, in which he freely confesses that he was a pawn in a Soviet plot to harm the Jewish state, though it is accepted by all that he was more sinned against than sinning. He is therefore free to go on the understanding that he may have to repeat his story before a judge in the unlikely event that any of the aforementioned incidents become public knowledge.

As far as the populace is concerned, Jonah Isaacson is a hero. *Ha'aretz*, *Davar*, *Ma'ariv* and the *Jerusalem Post* all publish the photograph taken at the moment of explosion, accompanied by the official interpretation, to wit: 'Man sacrifices arm in effort to save Minister'.

The real culprit, according to this version, was a journalist (presumed to be an Arab) observed running away from the scene only moments before the blast. Within days Jonah is inundated with letters addressed to him care of the hospital. All congratulate him on his bravery except one, postmarked Yotvata, which calls him a fool.

Several rabbis take the trouble to assure him that a phylactery, laid upon an artificial limb, is perfectly acceptable in the eyes of the Lord, especially in the present circumstances. Circumstances which improve rapidly, now that Jonah has remembered what was required of him.

On the day of his discharge the same melancholy medic who has attended him throughout makes a final check of his vital signs. 'It's a funny thing,' he murmurs as he measures Jonah's blood pressure, 'according to your records you were a hypertensive on a diet of beta-blockers. Not any more. If anything you're in need of a stimulant. What shall I call this turnabout? The Isaacson Effect? Any objections if I write it up?' 'Be my guest,' says Jonah. The doctor puts his stethoscope back in his pocket and departs.

A few minutes later Gidi shows up. 'Everything all right, my friend?' he asks. 'No,' replies Jonah, 'I'm scared stiff.' 'Of what?' asks Gidi. 'Of returning to a home I do not remember,' says Jonah. 'Sit down, my friend, and listen to me,' says Gidi, also sitting. 'We all lead double lives; interior and exterior. The first being least important, unless you happen to be a pervert or an artist of some sort. Most ordinary people rely entirely upon appearances. In that respect you are fine. Excepting the missing arm, which is no big deal. In short, my friend, you can act your way through life. This is something I cannot do, although I have never been stronger. People take one look at me and they turn away. In the beginning I found this almost unbearable. You see, my friend, before this happened to me acting *was* my life.' He pauses, to allow the implications of this revelation to sink in. 'Now it's all Dudu Wolf, but then it was Dudu Wolf and Gidi Becker. If you think his *Hamlet* is controversial – and you've seen it, my friend – you should have caught my *Macbeth*! We took only one liberty with the text; we made Duncan an Arab and Macbeth a Jew. You can imagine what a stink that caused! There were even some who said that my injury was God's punishment. It certainly put an end to my career. There is not much call for a leading man who makes the Phantom of the Opera look like a movie star. However, my experience was not wasted. On the contrary, my therapist thought it might facilitate my rehabilitation. "What would you have done," he asked, "if you were still on the stage and this were your role?" Easy! I would have smiled at the audience! What better way of winning them over? I was persuaded to try it in real life. And do you know what, my friend? It made matters worse. Because there are false smiles – in which only the muscles around the mouth move – and genuine smiles – in which muscles around the eyes are also activated. Unfortunately I am unable to control the muscles around my eyes, which means that all my smiles look false. And people do not respond well to false smiles. They get suspicious. I closed the show after two days. No more limelight for Gidi Becker. I joined the secret service and live in the shadows where no one can see my face.'

He looks straight at Jonah. 'Now you understand why I am a little impatient with your self-pity, why I do not rate prosopognosia as an impediment to social intercourse. It sounds a little like a luxury to one who has no features to be recognized.'

At which moment, as if that line were her cue, Sophie enters from the wings. 'It's time,' she says. And Jonah, with no great enthusiasm, rises slowly from his bed. His few remaining belongings have been crammed into a tattered army kitbag which is on the floor. He bends to pick it up and swings it over his right shoulder.

'Okay,' he says, 'let's go.'

Sophie kisses the faceless one on his lipless mouth. His lidless eyes begin to glisten. 'Do not forget your friend Gidi Becker,' he says as the couple reach the open door. Jonah, as if responding to a prompt, suddenly lets the rucksack slide to the ground, and embraces his former tormentor and interrogator, his new-found friend. The man with one arm hugs the man with no face and both weep, for themselves and for each other. Jonah weeps even though he knows full well that his tears have been drawn from him by Gidi's calculated performance, he weeps because he has taken his lesson to heart.

Hereafter he will behave as though his memory has returned; he will consider Sophie as his wife, Toby as his father and Queenie as his mother (as most Jews regard Israel as their homeland), notwithstanding the lack of any subjective proof to substantiate their claims upon him. Furthermore, he will counterfeit the concomitant emotions in the hope that, with time, they will come spontaneously. Everyone assures him that he is Jonah Isaacson, so Jonah Isaacson he will be. In short, he is ready to take Gidi's advice and act his way through life.

There are three stages in the recognition of others: *familiarity* sets in progress *information retrieval*, which leads to *naming*. The whole process lasts about one second. It takes Jonah about five times as long to deduce — by means of elimination — the identity of the handsome old siren who is standing beside the gleaming Mercedes that awaits him with open doors.

'Aunt Bella!' he exclaims. 'Oh my God,' she cries, 'he remembers me!' They embrace, as if one or other had returned from the dead. As Jonah follows Aunt Bella into the automobile he notices, emblazoned on its windscreen in letters of green, the legend 'Jerusalem Film Festival, Courtesy Car', something of a surprise to one who had merely been expecting transport to the airport.

Anthony Jacobi is already within, next to the driver, leaving the back seat free for Aunt Bella, Jonah and Sophie. He turns around as they enter the high suburb of Kiryat Hayovel or Jubilee Town (apartments to the right, Mount Orah, Ein Kerem and the hospital to the left) and explains that there has been a sensational development at the Film Festival, which he would hate Jonah (as a potential Professor of Film Studies) to miss out on.

At the last minute the Soviet Union has taken everyone by surprise and responded in the affirmative to their invitation. A six-man delegation arrived from Moscow only yesterday, its leader being Elem Klimov, Jonah's old friend. 'We're all going to the al fresco lunch in their honour,' announces Anthony as they enter the sweltering valley dominated by the Monastery of the Cross where, seven hundred years ago, the Georgian poet, Rustavéli, wrote his nation's national epic, *Panther Skin*. Rumour has it, Anthony adds, that ambassadors will be exchanged if the visit is adjudged to have been a success.

The car passes (of all things) a stone windmill and turns slowly into the private crescent of the King David Hotel, where taxi-drivers, photographers and policemen are, between curses, punching faces and cracking heads.

Men with walkie-talkies escort the erstwhile passengers through the hubbub into the lobby and out on to the hotel's terrace where the Foreign Minister is puzzling his listeners with the information that his preference film-wise is for documentaries and modern movies which deal with individual issues based on a flow of association. Fortunately his hands are free so that he is able to lead the applause that accompanies the entrance of the man who tried to save his former colleague. All of those who are not already holding glasses or plates join in, including the Soviets.

Jonah, much embarrassed, looks around. He does not, of course, recognize Klimov; in fact he does not recognize anyone, which makes the method of deduction, practised earlier, more or less impossible. He does not remember having seen the Old City before either, but there is no confusing the biscuit and honey

117

walls that dominate the skyline. He hopes that Klimov will be equally unmistakable when encountered.

As it happens they are introduced by Anthony Jacobi. 'I believe you two have already met,' he says, 'at Bradford, England, of all places.' It is evident that Klimov has no more memory of the encounter than Jonah Isaacson. 'I am sorry,' he says, 'but I do not recall meeting anyone with one arm.' 'I had two at the time,' says Jonah. 'Ah,' says Klimov, 'that explains everything. Now I remember. Bradford. We talked after my lecture. Yes?' 'That's right,' says Jonah.

Thus are diplomatic relations, of a sort, established. The Foreign Minister, in his welcoming address, attempts a similar kind of rapprochement; he invites the Soviet leader to visit Israel. He refers, mysteriously, to new circumstances (not just *glasnost*) that have made such a thing a real possibility. Finally he looks at Klimov and, raising his glass of red wine, says: 'We are thrilled to have you here. Your visit contributes to most important aims — art and peace.'

Jonah wonders if anyone else can see the severed arm that raises its wine glass with the rest as the guests are toasted.

After the formalities Klimov returns to Jonah and says: 'Forgive me if I did not recognize you at once. In these last months I have met so many people in so many places that my recall is barely functioning. But now I can picture you quite clearly. We must, when we have time, continue the conversation we began that night. Perhaps this afternoon. Are you, by any chance, going to see Lewis Falcon's *Deadwood Stage*?' 'He certainly is,' says Anthony Jacobi. 'If you look at the Festival programme you'll see he's scheduled to introduce it.'

Jonah Isaacson can hardly believe his ears. How can he possibly talk about a film — in front of its director — when he hasn't the slightest idea of its contents? 'Excellent,' says Klimov. 'I'll see you there.'

The larger, darker side of the Jerusalem Theatre is full of distinguished auteurs, actors, critics and academics. On the stage in front of the screen is a spotlit table bearing a jug of water and two glasses, not to mention the elbows of Lewis Falcon and Jonah Isaacson. 'Glad to see you up and about,' says the former to the latter. 'Glad to be here,' lies the latter. 'I trust you'll take my side against all those pointy heads out there,' says the irascible old director. 'You can count on me,' says Jonah, echoing the words Anthony had said to him in the taxi that took them the short distance from the luncheon to the screening.

Jonah was travelling under the assumption that his impending humiliation was Anthony's punishment for the rejection he had received, but he was doing his wife's uncle a disservice. As they paused at the triple junction where King David, Keren Hayesod and Jabotinsky Streets all meet, Anthony opened his briefcase and removed the lecture notes penned in advance by the previous incumbent of Jonah Isaacson's corpus. All Anthony wanted was to give Jonah a second chance. How could he resist working on a movie with Lewis Falcon when the invitation came, not from a mere producer, but from the man himself? It was devious, true, but not cruel.

Jonah Isaacson sips the water and stands up. 'Ladies and gentlemen,' he says, 'it is a pleasure to be here.' The audience does what Jonah no longer can; it applauds.

'If you look at us carefully,' he continues, 'you'll realize that, taken together, we could pass for Admiral Nelson: he with one eye, me with one arm. I mention brave Horatio because one of his most famous sayings can, with a little amendment, be made to serve both my philosophy as a student of film and, more importantly, Lewis Falcon's as a director. I see no symbols! Ladies and gentlemen, Lewis Falcon is a mythmaker, in my opinion the cinema's greatest. As Thomas Malory was to Camelot, so is Lewis Falcon to the Old West. He is a romantic, granted, but he is no primitive. He is as aware as any of us here of the questions that must be asked of myth. Perhaps the most famous line in all his films is, "This is the West, sir. When legend contradicts fact, print the legend." And there is no doubt that he endorses this sentiment. At the same time it is not the legend but the fact that he shows us and, of course, the process whereby it becomes legend. Nor does Lewis Falcon show us legendary characters; rather they are ordinary men and women whose sufferings are endured in the hope of a better future, a future that depends upon their legendary status. And when they look back to those days their memories are both a consolation and a torture; a consolation because they now see that they were part of a larger story, the birth of a nation, a torture because they know the price that was paid. The myth *Deadwood Stage* embraces is the making of America, for the stagecoach is America. It survives nature's hostilities — the desert — and Apaches — denizens thereof — on its way to Lordsburg — the heavenly city — wherein all the human problems that motivate the journey and the movie are resolved. The hero and the heroine ride off into the sunset to build their log cabin and raise a family, the last words of the film being: "We'll plant trees. We'll make the land green." Ambitions not unknown in this neck of the woods, which makes Lewis Falcon a particularly appropriate artist for modern Israel to honour with this retrospective.'

The aforementioned rises and takes a bow. The stage goes dim and Jonah Isaacson goes cold, for he can see quite clearly the plane that carried him to Israel, and within it a man much like himself composing the words he has just uttered. Perhaps more than an arm awaits him in England. 'If I retrace my steps,' he thinks, 'I may gather up all the pieces of my lost memory.' He therefore does what few have done before; he says no to Anthony Jacobi a second time. He says no as the ghosts of a long ago day in Monument Valley flicker on the giant screen behind him.

We land at Heathrow on the last day of July after an uneventful flight; uneventful, that is, except for Sophie, my wife, who suddenly leans forward in her seat and ejects her last meal into the bag thoughtfully provided by El Al for just such an eventuality.

Sickness, it turns out, is a recurring feature of our return to the comfortable house I must learn to call my home, for some levantine creepy-crawly seems to have take up residence in Sophie's intestines. By chance it is at its most irritating during the diurnal hours and does not interfere with the rediscovery of a conjugal pair's nocturnal habits.

I am particularly tickled by the tradition of the shared bed. It takes me by surprise, this strange custom of sleeping with your partner, as though the moments of greatest intimacy are those when you are both unconscious, when your dreams are secretly expressing the true nature of your relationship. However, its main function, I think, is as a compensation for all those hours of the day when you are apart.

I may as well tell you that Sophie's regular absence has come as quite a shock, for it never occurred to me that she would have a business to run, that her life would be a shuttle between one Dream Time and another. I had grown dependent upon her in the hospital and had expected that support to continue when we got back to St Albans, at least until I was ready to stand upon my own two feet again.

In which enterprise, it is deemed, a second arm might be of some assistance. A view my doctor endorses. He scrutinizes the injured tissue and declares it sufficiently healed to sustain (what he calls) a self-supporting socket. He also examines the rest of me. 'It seems that I am no longer an object of dread,' he remarks as he records my blood pressure; 'in fact your readings are now so low that, if I didn't have the evidence of my own eyes, I'd swear that you were a different person.'

I'm not sure if I was aware of this before, but it turns out that there is a limb replacement facility attached to the University's Medical Centre (actually an ultra-modern hospital dedicated to the memory of Sir Francis Bacon who, in pursuit of medical research, purchased a defunct chicken on a snowy day, in order to test the efficacy of ice as a preservative, only to catch a chill himself and die). Its senior prosthetist is Dr Said Habash who greets me with a line I have heard many times of late (mostly in old movies, required viewing if I am to continue my career): 'Haven't we met somewhere before?'

At first glance, with his glossy waves and dark eyes, he looks like a typical resident of Jerusalem, but I do not remember seeing

121

him there — or here. I shake my head, he shrugs his shoulders.

I follow him along a bright neon-lit corridor to a room marked 'Casting', as though I were some hopeful about to audition for the Monster in his new production of *Frankenstein*.

The interior, however, lacks a couch. Just three tubular chairs. Dr Habash directs me to the middle one, and takes the seat on my left.

The walls of the room are pale blue and white. Pinned to them are portraits of exotic landscapes, not unlike the posters my wife has used to decorate the renovated interior of her travel agency. Only these display the beauties of a non-existent country: Palestine. Dr Habash observes my passing interest and feels compelled to comment. 'No doubt you have experienced the phenomenon of the phantom limb,' he says. 'Well, as your arm is to you, so is Palestine to me. If I look in an atlas I do not find it, yet it seems to me that it should be there. Of the discomforts this creates, physical pain is the least. Far worse is the nagging memory of what you have lost. There are days, Dr Isaacson, when I think that amnesia would be a blessing.' I apologize, though I do not know why, and continue my inventory of the room.

There is a sink and a shelf upon which stand various technical items such as callipers and a ruler.

'I understand that Anthony Jacobi, our esteemed patron, is your uncle,' he says in the same tone that Hollywood tycoons once used to quip, 'The son-in-law also rises.' 'My wife's,' I say, correcting him. 'Same difference,' he says, informing me that my new limb is on the house either way. 'You can, if you choose, have a complete working unit with articulated digits,' he continues, 'but a cosmetic sleeve filler is good enough for most people.' 'Myself included,' I say. He obviously does not approve of nepotism, though he seems satisfied with my modest demands. He even congratulates me upon having the good sense to wear a short sleeve shirt, blue denim from the United States.

'Now I would like you to bend your arm at the elbow,' he says, and proceeds to wrap several lengths of bandage around my shockingly pink stump, which is then doused in water. 'The bandage is impregnated with plaster of paris,' he explains, modelling it with his fingers, 'and when it sets we will have, with a little rectification, a perfect mould from which to work.' His hand on my arm, or what remains of it, has become disturbingly over-familiar, almost lascivious, as he puts the finishing touches to the hardening plaster. It slides off with surprising ease.

His experienced eye studies the interior, and I shudder as though my very soul were under examination. 'Excellent,' says Dr Habash, smiling at me, 'now we can be sure that your prosthesis will fit you as comfortably as an old slipper.'

I am suddenly filled with revulsion toward this as yet incomplete addition to my anatomy, and stricken with an illogical dread that a part of me will belong hereafter to Dr Said Habash and be forced to do his bidding. Paranoid fears assail me with palpable force, fears that may just be assuaged by a reassuring visit to the workshops, where I will be able to see for myself that the processes of production are anything but supernatural. I feel the blood draining from my face. My whole body begins to shiver. 'Good heavens, Dr Isaacson,' says Dr Habash, 'whatever is the matter?' 'I don't know,' I reply. 'I think I am experiencing rejectionist tendencies.' Dr Habash smiles at the acknowledgement of his national origins. 'Then we must do our best to moderate them,' he says, continuing my little joke. 'I was suddenly overcome by fear and loathing at the very thought of an artificial limb,' I explain, still shuddering. 'In which case you must meet the enemy,' says Dr Habash, 'and thereby achieve normalization.' 'Exactly what I was thinking,' I say.

So it's back into the corridor and through the adjacent door into what looks like an Eskimo's trophy room, for its shelves are heavy with what can only be the shiny tusks of walruses. On closer inspection they turn out to be lacquered stumps manufactured by a lab technician who is, even now, leaning against a work top and lazily stirring a mixture that is destined to become my understudy. The raw material is powdered plaster of paris, stored on the floor in large sacks, which has blanched the room as efficiently as flour in a bakery. 'He will pour the liquid into the negative mould we have just obtained from you,' explains Dr Habash, 'and leave it to harden, whereupon we will have a positive cast.'

Negative, *positive*, words that recall Toby's vocal reconstruction of his darkroom, and the processes that went on therein, which I seem to have found so fascinating. Indeed, for a few moments I am so moved by the particular combination of vowels and consonants that I can actually feel the excitement as the picture begins to show in the developer — though of course I do not know if I am responding to Toby's heartfelt description or an actual memory. In similar fashion I may, eventually, be unable to differentiate between my right and left arms, if there is any difference to start with.

I may as well admit that at times, since my return, I have toyed with the notion that I may be a humanoid conceived by a hubristic genius in Jerusalem, the missing arm being nothing but a brilliant ploy to convince me of my vulnerable humanity. It came to me most strongly when I fucked my wife for the first time — or so it seemed to me. Secretly I had been hoping that this intimacy in extremis would revitalize my dormant emotions, but look what happened.

My wife stepped out of her pants while I was still unbuttoning my shirt (you try undressing in haste with only one hand). This final gesture was so balletic I could hardly believe that it wasn't choreographed. Hooking her thumbs around the elastic on either side of her hips she pulled the ultimate item down her thighs and calves, bending her body as she did so, thereby placing her face in the shade of her hair and her private parts in the shadow of her torso. Thus the step out of her undergarment, though small, became a defiant gesture, for she stood upright and uncovered immediately thereafter, as if to say, 'This is what I am.'

What was revealed excited me (I could feel the appropriate physical response attempting to manifest itself within the tightness of my levis) but I did not recognize it (for some reason I had been expecting to see scars on her breasts, but there they were completely unblemished).

She walked towards me, and then knelt at my feet, not in submission, but to undo my laces and, moving upwards, my belt. 'Hello, old friend,' she said as my penis made its appearance, 'I'm glad to see that you remember me.' But she was wrong, I'm afraid. Drunk on the smells of her overheated libido I wanted her all right, but for her generality not her particularity; I wanted her like an animal wants its opposite number.

It turned out, however, that she wanted me only for myself. We were on the bed, foreplay at an end, and the serious business of penetration about to begin, when she suddenly said, 'Wait!' Whereupon she picked up a little packet from the bedside cabinet and, tearing it open, removed a flimsy sheath. Feeling more like a genetic robot than a human being I reacted badly to this preventative measure and reached up to stop her rolling the rubber over my seed pod. The movement was instinctual, which explains why it was my abbreviated arm that rose. My fingers were already around her bony wrist (or so I thought) before I recognized the futility of my gesture, although when I looked up it seemed to me that I really did see my left hand in action. Much good it did!

What brings this to mind is the sight of another technician pulling a long conical pipe of poly-something-or-other over the top of an upright cast, which has already been swathed in layers of white stockinette. The cast itself has been placed upon a metal tube which is connected, below the bench, to some sort of motor or pump. 'It's not your arm,' says Dr Habash, 'but it's very like, so watch.'

The technician acknowledges our presence, adjusts his spectacles, and begins to feed a viscous paste, the colour of a doll's flesh, down the top of the transparent pipe, squeezing until the space between the cast and the opening — approximately one cubit — is fully occupied with the nascent limb.

To Dr Habash the man now forming the arm with deep downward sweeps of the hand is nothing more than a cook wrestling with an outsize icing bag, but to me he is the priest of some perverse fertility rite, a rite made more obscene by the pulsing prosthesis's pseudo-vitality (pseudo, indeed; its source is not the heart but a vacuum pump).

The artificial hands, by comparison, lack any sign of life. All sizes, from ninety-day baby to giant, are stocked. They fill shelf after shelf in the neon-lit storeroom, which is no different from any other, except that it is filled with human spare parts.

'In the old days,' says Dr Habash, 'hand and arm were a single unit which meant that every time a little finger got chipped the whole thing had to be replaced. Now it's just a matter of coming in and having a new hand fitted. When that's done all that remains is for you to slip on one of these cosmetic covers.' Amongst all the silicone rubber arms that dangle from the shelves like empty sleeves, each marked with its own whorls, lines and nails, is one which looks pinker and more lifelike than the rest. 'That's for me,' I think, and I could swear that it gives me the thumbs-up.

'You are probably wondering about the predominance of darker pigmentations,' observes Dr Habash, misinterpreting my perplexity, 'but there's no need to worry, we've enough lighter shades to please every caucasian. It's just that most of our customers come from the Middle East. Your uncle used to joke that he should be investigated, like Colonel North, for selling arms to the Iranians.' 'My wife's,' I say. 'Of course,' he says, looking at his watch. We shake hands. He has the grip of a bone breaker.

'Tell me, Dr Isaacson,' he says as I begin the journey from one end of the hospital to the other, 'now that you've met the enemy, what do you think?' 'I can live with it,' I reply.

Prosthetics is, as it were, out on a limb. Entering the main body of the hospital you pass an unmarked room which emanates a chill and hurry on to the busier areas of occupational therapy, rehabilitation and physiotherapy, which in turn give way to a quieter place of secrets, ultrasound, X-ray and nuclear medicine. Now you are in the heart of the hospital, intensive care, from where you pass through renal transplant, genito-urinary, and up to ear, nose and throat, and up again to the operating theatres and recovery rooms until you reach the start of it all, ante-natal, maternity, pathology and microbiology, through whose swing doors my wife is walking backwards.

Her hands are shaking so much she cannot even hold a piece of paper. I bend to pick it up. When she turns towards me I see that her face is white, and that her eyes are red from crying. Why? Has some test proved, beyond doubt, that she has cancer? Or worse. Could there be something worse? Am I to lose my wife before I have even learned to love her? 'Sophie,' I say, 'whatever is the matter?' She looks at me hopelessly. 'I'm pregnant,' she replies.

We do not receive many invitations to dinner (except from my parents and my wife's cousin, Alberto) so the summons to attend Professor Gutkes's table is something of a surprise. His table, a handsome piece of regency furniture, is situated in the university's own mansion, New Gorhambury, one of whose wings has been converted into guest apartments.

Professor Gutkes, looking as though he has been veneered and polished by Chippendale himself, greets us at the door with a mixture of bonhomie and contrition.

'My dear friends,' he says, embracing us both, 'when I heard the unbelievable thing that happened to you I felt such shame for the words that were said on Founder's Day. Can you forgive me?' 'We're here, aren't we?' says my wife. He releases us, then bows low so that we may enter his abode.

'In your presence I utter a curse on all terrorists,' he says, 'and a double curse on those who speak in their defence.' I do not actually remember the incident that seems to have caused Professor Gutkes so much retrospective guilt, but I know about it, thanks to my wife. Likewise, I have no trouble in recognizing Polly and Petra when they appear, although I do not recall having seen either before, which is a blow as they are the sort of women you'd expect to stick in the mind.

I'm sure you remember them but, in case you've also been afflicted with amnesia, I'll repeat that Polly, like Lewis Falcon, has a glass eye, though is otherwise perfectly formed, as you can see for yourself, her wardrobe being designed to reveal not conceal. Petra smokes a pipe.

Neither recants as wholeheartedly as their lord. While expressing genuine sorrow that we were blown up, they manage to imply that it was our fault for being among racists and fascists in the first place.

I suspect that most people do not invite us for meals because they do not know how to set the cutlery for a one-armed man, nor do they know what to feed me. If it's steak should they cut it up beforehand in the kitchen? Who knows if such problems of etiquette exercised the mind of Professor Gutkes, or would he have served *tortelloni alle noci* in any event? Either way it allows easy access for the handicapped and is, moreover, delicious. A judgement not endorsed by my wife.

'My dear Mrs Isaacson,' enquires the professor, who is sitting next to her, 'is there something wrong with the food?' 'No, Professor Gutkes,' she replies, 'there is something wrong with me.' 'May I ask what?' 'I'm pregnant,' she replies, as if she were uttering the name of some dread disease. Poor Professor Gutkes does not know how to respond: whether to offer congratulations or commiserations.

Polly and Petra, however, are in no doubt. 'What are you going to do about it?' asks the latter across the table. *It!* As though the foetus lacked humanity.

'Do?' I ask. 'My wife is going to have a baby. Our baby. What else should she do?' 'Let her speak for herself,' says Polly, refilling the wine glass she is sharing with Petra.

'I want a child,' says my wife, avoiding my eye, 'but not now. The timing is all wrong. I need to rebuild my business at present, not a family.'

'Then have an abortion,' says Petra triumphantly. 'I don't know if I could,' says my wife, 'without Jonah's support.' 'We'll support you,' says Polly. 'Thanks,' I say. 'Your friends have already robbed me of my past, and now you want to take away my future too.' 'There speaks the personification of the selfish gene,' snaps Petra, 'to whom a woman's body is nothing but a colonial outpost. As Africa and Arabia expelled their oppressors and exploiters so must a woman. Liberate yourself, Mrs Isaacson, get an abortion.'

Having said her piece she lights her pipe.

'Professor Gutkes,' says my wife, 'you have been uncharacteristically silent. What do you think I should do?' 'My dear,' he says, placing his hand upon her arm, 'I am a German and I can never forget that abortion, like euthanasia, can open a Pandora's box. Nevertheless, I cannot deny a woman her right to choose.'

128

Unlike her storm-trooper of a husband! We do not exchange a word all the way home.

A printed card arrives from Dr Said Habash. It informs me that my prosthesis will be ready for collection as of 10 August. My wife does not seem captivated by the news, but then nothing interests her in the morning, when the nausea is at its worst.

She is not enjoying her pregnancy. She doesn't read the newspaper, she doesn't eat her cereal, just a slice of dry toast and a cup of black tea. Then, still looking pale, she kisses me on the cheek and says, 'I'm off.' 'Have a good day,' I reply. As far as I know she sits in her agency from nine-thirty till six. I watch old movies on the video and take notes.

Occasionally the phone rings. Sometimes it is my wife or my mother. This time it is Professor Gutkes. He wants to know if Sophie is all right. I tell him to ask her himself. Then he says, 'Have you been in touch with Stella?' 'Who?' 'My God,' says Professor Gutkes, 'you have lost your memory.' Tell me, who is Stella?

On the morning of 10 August my wife seems even more tearful than normal. 'I'm off,' she says. We kiss. 'Have a good day.' She has obviously forgotten about my appointment with Dr Habash and I don't bother to remind her.

Instead of walking I take a taxi. It is raining and I do not want to arrive wet through. The driver drops me at the hospital's main entrance, despite instructions otherwise. I do not bother to complain. The electric door with the invisible eye slides open and admits me.

Between ante-natal and maternity there is an unspecified ward. As I am passing, the double doors open and a woman on a trolley is wheeled out. She is unconscious. Flat on her back she is wearing nothing but a pale green smock that barely covers her thighs. She is — of this I am almost certain — my wife.

By the time I realize what is going on she is already in the operating theatre. I hear the doors click shut behind her. To open them you need a special key, which I do not possess. Intervention is therefore impossible. All I can do is look through the port-hole at what Petra, Polly and the professor have wished upon me.

My wife is opened and her legs raised so that the lower half of her body, plucked clean like a turkey, is available for the convenience of the surgeon. To stop any involuntary movement her ankles are secured by stirrups. Finally her private parts are illuminated by a spotlight, as in some obscene solarium. Now the abortionist approaches, masked like a criminal, a silver curette flashing in his hand, and I realize, with palpitating heart, that I am about to see the sacrifice of the younger Isaacson, whom I love.

4

And Abraham stretched forth his hand and took the knife to slay his son.

There are precedents for such a performance. But on this occasion no ram will present itself to take the place of the child and thereby secure a happy ending. Having no faith in any *deus ex machina* I shout and hammer on the glass with my fists – I mean fist, of course – but the door is hermetically sealed and the peep-hole of an unbreakable thickness, making the theatre beyond no less sound-proof than a torture chamber. Helpless, defeated, as immobile as my wife – that palpable paradigm of passive acceptance – I prepare myself for what I must witness. Like the priest of some necrophiliac cult the robed surgeon stands between my wife's naked thighs and raises the scintillating weapon that has mesmerized us all. He bends.

At first I think that my wife has changed her mind and that the hand which leaps up to ensnare the surgeon's wrist is hers, but this is a sentimental notion that cannot withstand a scrutiny of her limp body, so obviously incapable of decisive action.

Then whose are the fingers that have occupied the space between the doctor's golden watchband and his hairy hand? Whose are the fingers that grip so tightly they can feel the doctor's steady pulse, that squeeze and squeeze until the blood ceases to flow into the manicured digits and the fatal instrument drops with a clatter upon the linoleum?

Now I am both within and without the theatre. I am watching the panic occasioned by the sudden visitation of my saviour, my severed arm, and I can feel the desperate attempts made by the surgeon to remove my unwelcome embrace. But his pretty fingers cannot weaken my supernatural determination.

Determination! That's what saved my child. Yes! My severed arm has become the agency of my will, the advance guard of my desires, able to enter places closed to the remainder of my body. Alerted to my distress it arose from its hiding place in order to protect its unborn progeny. And now, I see, I must warn it. For the doctor, regaining some of his senses, has called for a scalpel in order to cut himself free. Fortunately the nurses, though familiar with disembodied limbs, have never before seen one showing vital signs, and are affected with collective hysteria. The surgeon's request consequently goes unheeded. But he is not helpless and he finds a knife himself in a silver kidney-shaped dish. And then, like a suicide, he turns it upon himself, meaning to sever my fingers with one meaty slice. But my hand has slipped away, leaving only temporary indentations in the whitened flesh, hollows which quickly fill with blood, for the surgeon has mistakenly cut into his own arteries. From my refuge I hear his gasp of horror, and the squeals of the nurses as they realize what has happened and, above all, the little splats as the spurts of blood hit my wife's belly and thighs. The surgeon does not die, of course, the nurses see to that. They apply tourniquets to his arm and then seal the gaping wound. And I, the ego on the outside, relax; for they are no longer the priestesses of some nefarious cult, but familiar heart-warming angels of mercy. In this capacity they help the surgeon, now unmasked and revealed as a pasty-faced young man of not quite thirty, out of the operating theatre and along the corridor, by-passing me as if I had no corporeality. The anaesthetist follows, wheeling my witless wife, who has slept through the whole of this drama, back to her ward where, upon awakening, she will be told either nothing at all or that the abortion, for reasons that will be made known to her family practitioner, was itself aborted. Then she will be sent home by an unsympathetic sister.

How could anyone tell her the real reason? Should it become known it would be the death of the hospital. If an arm can be revitalized, why not the kidneys, livers, hearts, brains, spleens, why not whole corpses? Who, in their right mind, would enter a hospital that had become a living memorial to the human anatomy; in short, an animated butcher's shop? Uncle Anthony wouldn't thank me for that, I think, as I walk down the corridor to keep my appointment with Dr Habash.

As I proceed through the variety show of human frailty an absurd conjecture occurs to me: that I am in the process of betraying the limb to which I owe so much; that its other half, the stump, is about to entertain a mistress instead of its rightful spouse. I feel that it is spying upon me through its over-developed pores, waiting for me to give the nod to its suspicions, so that it will have cause to unleash jealous rages worthy of Othello.

But a hospital is a place where sympathy must be kept under restraint, lest morbid hypochondria overwhelms, and you lose faith in the stability of the body politic, and so I recall my imagination and order it to make contact, instead, with my inner being. The reports are not encouraging; they speak of confusion, of a man proscribed by other people's memories, whose only spontaneous emotion has just been engendered by the dangerous predicament of his unborn child. It will be born, I vow, and with it will come my own renaissance.

I am late for my appointment, of course. Dr Habash is standing in the reception area of the limb replacement facility looking at his chunky chronometer as if it told the future as well as the time. His stance implies a certain impatience, which makes me feel somewhat guilty though, God knows, I have reason enough for my impromptitude.

'Ah, Dr Isaacson,' he says, extending his hand, 'at last.' The proffered arm reveals the cuff of his silk Jermyn Street shirt, which shows beneath the sleeve of his beautifully cut pin-stripe suit. Around his neck is a dark blue tie, discreetly spotted with red. His face has the colour of a man who has just returned from an unusually exhilarating vacation, and the natural sheen of his hair seems embellished, this morning, by a sweet-smelling oil. The prompt for this display is not my person, needless to say, but the creature standing beside him, whose beauty suggests she has attained the level beyond which angels become unavailable to human senses.

'Dr Isaacson,' says Dr Habash, 'meet Stella Richmond.' Stella! The name, as they say, rings a bell. She smiles at me, the sort of smile poor Gidi is now incapable of, the sort that begins around the mouth and spreads via hidden muscles to the eyes, the sort that wins hearts.

'Stella is very keen to make your acquaintance,' continues Dr Habash, 'indeed she became quite despondent when it seemed you were not coming.' I look at Stella and pray that, even if I had known of her expectations, I would still have lingered outside the theatre wherein the termination of my wife's pregnancy was being plotted.

'Stella is a genius,' announces Dr Habash, 'a Rembrandt among make-up artists. Once a week she comes to us to help patients who have had radical facial surgery make the most of what they have left. Believe me, Dr Isaacson, she is the greatest illusionist I have ever encountered. She is a miracle worker.' What is the purpose of this hundred-megaton reference? I have come, after all, to get a replacement arm, not a new face.

'As I have confessed,' explains Dr Habash, 'this meeting is not accidental. It was planned. For Stella has ambitions. She wants to work in the movies. Not as an actress, though no one can deny that she has the looks,' here he touches her cheek and she blushes or, more accurately, glows, 'but as a beautician, if that is the correct designation.' Dr Habash pauses and delivers an accusing look, as if I were the selfish hoarder of glad tidings. 'Word has reached Stella', he continues, 'that you are on intimate terms with Lewis Falcon, the celebrated director, and that you are, furthermore, expecting him here, at our university, to give a lecture or two. Stella wonders whether you could, without putting yourself out, effect an introduction?'

Dr Habash is right, though in the interests of accuracy I should point out that the initial provocation did not come from me but from our beloved (even in exile) founder. It was he who informed me that Falcon would be breaking his return flight to Hollywood in London and would, therefore, look kindly upon a request to visit the University of St Albans which is, after all, a mere twenty miles from the capital.

He is due in the first week of October, by which time (so

Anthony Jacobi tells me) a cast will have been chosen and a location established for *The Six Pointed Star*; by which time, also, my wife will be in the fifteenth week of her pregnancy and, I would hope, swamped with the appropriate maternal reactions.

I would not be worthy of your respect, however, if I did not admit to calculating how many starry assignations could decently be fitted into the time between now and then. 'Why not?' I say, as casually as possible. 'See!' exclaims Dr Habash. 'I told you not to worry. I told you Dr Isaacson was a gentleman.'

'Call me soon and we'll make some arrangement,' I say. 'Here's my number.' I prepare to recite the by now familiar numerals. 'I have it already,' says Stella. 'How?' I say. 'Have you never heard of a telephone directory?' asks Dr Habash. 'Stella was plucking up the courage to phone you when I said, In the flesh will be better.'

Look, I may not know who I am, but I know what's what, and I'm certainly worldly-wise enough to sniff in this meeting the machinations of a pandar although, for the life of me, I can think of no reason why I should have been singled out to two-time some latter-day Troilus (that Stella is without pre-existing admirers is inconceivable).

'I'll call,' says Stella and, from that moment, I am waiting for the phone to ring.

'Now,' says Dr Habash, dismissing Stella with a glance, 'I have something else for you. Your new arm.'

I follow him into the fitting room marked 'Casting', where Dr Habash places the hollow limb upon my stump with the same precise delicacy a groom uses to slip the wedding band upon the finger of his betrothed. 'A perfect fit,' he says. 'Tell me, how does it feel?' 'Light,' I say, 'surprisingly light.' 'That's no problem,' says Dr Habash. 'If need be we can line the interior with this and that or, simply, supply you with a heavier hand. But there is no necessity to decide that now.' He points to the mirror, full-length, the sort you find in a tailor's shop. 'Go,' he says, 'see how it looks.'

For a moment I think that I have been tricked and that I am really facing a boutique mirror in which a man is slowly, limb by

135

limb, metamorphosing into a manikin. But, of course, I am observing myself or what others say is me. That is my arm, so says Dr Habash. That is my face, so says my wife. That is Jonah Isaacson, according to his parents. And who am I to disagree? 'Now go,' says Dr Habash, after I have replaced my shirt and jacket, 'go out into the world.'

My wife, for reasons you know, is not at home when her newly restored husband returns. Indeed, it is nearly nine o'clock before she shows up, by which time I have begun to wonder whether I was too hasty in assuming that we were out of the woods. Nor does her appearance give me much comfort. Her hair is dishevelled, her face white, and her eyes more like a pair of strawberry soufflés.

'Whatever is the matter?' I say. 'Nothing,' she replies, 'it's just been a difficult day. Unusually difficult.' 'Can I help?' I enquire. 'No,' she says. 'No thank you.' And not another word before bedtime.

It is a curious experience, watching someone suffer in silence on account of a secret you already know; you want to ease their pain, that is natural, but you also want to punish them for their betrayal or their mistrust, that is also natural.

Now I do not wish to sound as if I am attributing national characteristics to people but my wife, of Italian descent, is never going to suffer from alopecia. Indeed, were you to stumble accidentally into our glitzy bathroom the sight that would greet your embarrassed stare would most probably be that of my wife in the bath shaving her armpits or her legs. If she should happen, in her surprise, to arise you will be vouchsafed a sight of her pubic hair which, you will observe, is an equilateral triangle, requiring no cultivation, though thick as a pelt and jet black. Perhaps you will even agree with me when I call it her body's defining characteristic. Certainly its absence would be as remarkable as the sight of Hitler without a moustache.

Our custom (at least in the summer— I cannot, as yet, speak about the winter) is to sleep without pyjamas. I am curious to see how my wife intends to circumvent this little problem, but as it turns out she is still so distracted that the give-away haircut she received in the hospital has completely slipped her mind.

So she takes off her sweater (see what I mean, her armpits already need shaving again), her skirt, and her pants, beneath which are pre-pubescent paps with five o'clock shadow. At the same time I remove my prosthesis (which is surprisingly comfortable if, as I informed Dr Habash, a little light, as though it were attracted to a force other than gravity).

There is a fleeting show of disgust on my wife's face, as if I had just performed a particularly repulsive feat of prestidigitation, but then realization replaces it and she cries, 'Oh, Jonah, forgive me for not noticing.' 'Don't worry,' I say, 'I'll take it as a tribute to Dr Habash's skill. Besides,' I pause to enhance the effect, not to mention my triumph, 'I'm much more interested in what happened to your pubic hair.' 'Oh!' Sophie's hands descend, but it is too late, she is trapped in her guilt.

'What can I say, Jonah?' she whispers. 'I went to have an abortion.' Then she begins to sob. 'I'm sorry, Jonah, I'm so sorry.' I cannot hug my wife, as I suppose I ought, because I am still carrying my prosthesis in my good hand and wondering what to do with it, because you can't just throw it down like a shirt or a pair of jeans. Meanwhile my wife has not moved, she is just standing there, stark naked, her face awash with tears. 'Jonah,' she repeats, 'I'm sorry.' But, alas, there has been time for cruelty to overrule my spontaneous compassion. 'Sorry,' I cry, prodding the air with my prosthesis, 'what good is sorry? You inform me that you've murdered my child, then you say sorry. Even if I say, All right, you're forgiven, do you really think it will be all right? Of course it won't, because you have a conscience and I have a memory.'

A memory indeed! My righteous indignation is no more, wiped out by the evident untruth of that last statement. For an instant I feel inclined to end the scene altogether with a self-deprecating laugh but I am, instead, overtaken by a smouldering hostility that seems destined to find realization in some violent act. I have forgotten, you see, that my wife did not actually have the abortion.

'There is no need for all this,' she says, reminding me, 'nothing happened. They put me to sleep and then they woke me up. In between *nothing happened*. To tell you the truth, Jonah, I wish I was still there. In bed, unconscious.' 'Nothing happened?' I say. 'Nothing happened,' she repeats. 'They told me that the doctor was called away suddenly. To an emergency. Apparently he never returned. And so your wife stands before you, head bowed, but still intact.' 'No thanks to you,' I say.

But of course I know all this already — or something like it — and it is not sufficient to merit absolution; should a husband forgive a wife if it turns out that the only reason he is not a cuckold is that the lover manqué was overcome by impotence on the night?

There is a long silence, during which time I detect a change in the atmosphere, as though my wife has begun to feel herself too harshly judged. 'Don't think it was an easy decision, Jonah,' she says, 'don't think that for one minute. But I made it and I went through with it. Or, at least, I thought I did. And now I'm facing the consequences, even though nothing happened.' 'But why?' I say. 'Why the secrecy?'

She thinks, mistakenly, that I am softening, that I am ready to listen to reason. 'Because I didn't think you would consider the problem in a rational way,' she says. 'You have lost your past and you are desperate for a future. I can understand that. But can you appreciate my feelings? I have a life to restore. Yours. And a business to rebuild. How could I take on the responsibility for another life? Answer me that, Jonah. I had to let this one go, my love, for both our sakes.' Her voice, hitherto strong, breaks. She looks at me with her red eyes. 'Show me you understand,' she says. 'Touch me, Jonah.'

I am happy to oblige. I stretch out my prosthesis and touch her with my false fingers, which I press upon her newly exposed lips. She sees in my eyes a malicious cruelty that will not be mollified, from which she deduces that I am determined to hurt her, to pay her back with interest; even so she does not cease to ask for kindness. 'Jonah,' she says, 'touch me with your real hand.' But I refuse to withdraw its simulacrum. 'It is as much me as the other,' I say, 'we'll both have to get used to that.' 'Jonah,' she says, 'why must you be so hard? Can't you see how unhappy I am?'

Of course I can! Listen, I don't expect many of you to approve, but there is no escaping the fact that I have become sexually excited; not because I am obtaining perverse pleasure from this inquisition (though that may also be the case), but because my wife has become, as far as I can see, a different woman, so dramatic is the absence of her pubic hair.

'Lie down,' I say, at the same time as I insinuate a lifeless finger into her vagina. I feel nothing, of course. 'Jonah,' she says, 'what are you doing?' 'Making love,' I reply. 'This is obscene,' she cries, while offering no resistance to the offending hand. 'That's rich,' I say, 'coming from someone who, within this very day, was flat on her back waiting for a stranger to insert a foreign body into her belly. And not for pleasure, either. As if that wouldn't have been bad enough. Oh no! This was to kill. To kill my unborn child!' 'Jonah,' she says gently as if I were that very being, 'it never happened.' 'But you wanted it to,' I say. She has no choice. 'I wanted it to,' she agrees. 'And now I want to make love to you,' says her torturer, 'and you react as if I were the sick one.' 'Jonah,' she says, 'I'll do whatever you want.' In her voice is the dull sound of resignation, as if she had decided that the quickest way to cherished oblivion was to accept her humiliation.

I push her toward the bed. 'Lie down,' I say. She raises the quilt, as if to crawl beneath it. 'No,' I say, 'throw it on the floor.' I am determined to leave her completely exposed, without any source of comfort or security. The quilt, a pretty confection of spring flowers, crumples on the floor as if withered by her guilt. 'On your back,' I say, as my wife attempts to roll over, offering nothing but her behind. 'I want you as you were this morning.'

Supine she looks at the ceiling, lying long and flat, like a corpse awaiting a swaddling cloth; a cadaver that would, in other circumstances, be venerated, for tears are rolling from her eyes. 'Okay,' I say, 'now open yourself.' Obediently she parts her legs. Standing at the end of the bed I raise my surrogate hand, meaning to make contact with her clitoris. She grimaces. I have touched something. 'Jonah,' she says, 'I am dry.'

So I go to the bathroom, into which you blundered some time ago, and find a pot of vaseline in the cabinet. Returning I flick off the lid and anoint the appointed digit. As the hand goes up and down, like a servant performing some intimate service, I scrutinize my wife's face for some sign of involuntary pleasure, but it remains a mask, eyes fixed upon the ceiling. It is now a battle, not between man and wife, but between her body and her mind. Naturally I give the former all the assistance I can, teasing her clitoris until it becomes obvious from the ease of movement and the smell that the lubricants do not all come from a jar.

First her hips begin to move, until it looks as though she is being slowly bounced by my prosthesis, then her face conclusively registers that she has lost control. Her eyes close, her mouth opens, and her head rocks from side to side. 'Jonah,' she sobs, 'I want you inside me.'

Instead I pass her my arm. 'That's all you're getting,' I say. 'What do you want me to do with this?' she asks, knowing the answer. 'Masturbate,' I say.

She snatches the false hand and, grasping it by the wrist, sets to work. It looks absurd, like a crewcut scratching his head, but it is effective. 'Are you satisfied, Jonah?' she gasps. 'Is this giving you pleasure?' And then, suddenly, 'Oh God, I'm coming!'

Of course I'm not satisfied! I fall upon my wife and enter her. There is a missed beat, as her hand instinctively reaches for the drawer in the bedside cabinet where the condoms are kept. 'It's a bit late for that,' I whisper, 'you're already pregnant.' 'That's right,' she says. And then, miraculously, we both laugh.

Thereafter, clasping me with every limb, she cries, 'Jonah, I'm coming for you! I'm coming from right inside me.' I like that line, which I take to be a thank you note from the unborn child. I send it a reply, genetically encoded. We sleep like that, entwined, without a cover.

In the morning I cannot find my prosthesis. It is not beside the bed where Sophie dropped it, nor under it, nor anywhere in the bedroom. It turns up in the bathroom, stuffed down the lavatory bowl. Sophie swears it was not her doing.

*

Professor Gutkes is leaving. He must return to Frankfurt to commence the academic year anew in his old environs. And with him goes the summer. On either side of the long private road that leads to the university large yellow combines, piloted by anonymous stick men, plow through the swaying wheatfields like Mississippi paddle-boats. Ahead of them walk men with shotguns flushing out the fat rabbits, not to spare them from the reaper, but to bag them for the pot. 'We have fed them all year,' says one, as we pass the time of day, 'and now it's their turn to feed us. Fair's fair.' His voice has an underlying richness, containing as it does the rare intonation of a real Hertfordshire man, not often heard hereabouts.

Red apples hang from farmyard trees, so many that they are left unpicked upon the branches until, overripe, they fall to the earth, where their skins split and the air is perfumed by their decay. Snuffling sows look up from their acorn gathering and shuffle over to dine upon their flesh.

All the leaves in every direction, as if fallen under a collective spell, have lost their vital greenness, and begun to flake away, revealing the dark skeletons beneath.

The turn of the season is hardly a surprise but it is, to me at least, a novelty, and I can well appreciate the panic that overcame my even more ignorant ancestors as the year began to die. No wonder they offered their god or gods the best pickings so that the deities, their vanities satisfied, would consent to restart the cycle.

Indeed, there is a point on this road to the campus, at the top of the rise, from where it seems (if you look back) as if it has but one destination: that distant, towering edifice, founded not upon a rock, but upon the hope of resurrection. Sometimes I wish that I could put my trust in the essentially beneficent (if rather touchy) divinity the cathedral celebrates, especially on bright mornings like these after my wife and I have gone our separate ways — she to Dream Time, now re-established, me to my office — knowing that it is but a pregnant pause between moments of unparalleled intimacy.

During one such she confessed that she had secretly met with Polly and Petra in Professor Gutkes's room — with his knowledge? she wasn't sure — and that they had reinforced her resolution with the simplest of arguments — it's your body — and soothed her qualms with the facts of fertility — you can always have another one — before passing her along to Dr X who, convinced of her integrity, agreed to do the deed on the aforementioned day, the same as Dr Habash called for me. Divine intervention?

I look at the cathedral, its red bricks glowing in the autumn sunshine as though newly baked, and sadly shake my head. How could anyone put their faith in a god who permitted his only son to be nailed to a cross or, if you prefer the earlier testament, ordered his first acolyte to do away with his? I turn my back upon his glorious house of worship and descend the gentle slope down towards the University of St Albans, that old-new establishment, from where the cathedral is no longer visible. Instead I see a horizon that sprouts teeth of fire and a sky that becomes smudged with white smoke as the farmers burn the stubble and celebrate the end of the harvest.

Professor Gutkes is leaving and he wants to say goodbye. There have been a succession of farewell dinners, many of which I attended with my wife, who is looking increasingly radiant as her pregnancy advances and sickness becomes a bad memory (one of the few we share). 'My dear,' says Professor Gutkes at the last of these, 'how pregnancy becomes you. Looking at you now I feel ashamed that I did not raise my voice more eloquently against the possibility of abortion.' Is he telling the truth? Did Polly and Petra really act independently of his will? Does he really not know that my wife was only saved at the last moment from the worst mistake of her life? Either way his face, burnished like some god of the fall, registers nothing but uncomplicated pleasure. 'You'll be in my thoughts,' he says, putting his arms around our shoulders, 'especially next spring when the child is due.'

Now he has come to say goodbye to me personally. 'I have brought you a present,' he says, handing me a flat package wrapped in brown paper, 'something to commemorate our friendship.' Unexpectedly moved I place the parcel upon my desk and carefully strip off its coverings, revealing as I do the face of a distinctive young woman. 'It is a portrait by Annie Leibovitz,' explains the professor, obviously somewhat excited. 'As soon as I saw it in the Photographers Gallery I knew I had to get it for you. Hang the expense.' He pauses. 'You do realize its significance, don't you?' Fortunately I have recognized the features of Meryl Streep, an actress I have come to admire, although she appears to be peeling off her face, painted white, as if it were nothing more than a latex mask. 'Of course Leibovitz meant it as a compliment to her chameleon skills,' says the professor, 'but you and I will read something different into the image, I am sure, for we both know that beneath the beautiful façade is nothing. At the same time we owe the lady a debt of gratitude, because it was our mutual loathing for her work that brought us together.'

I am flabbergasted, though I endeavour to conceal the fact, not wanting to hurt my friend's feelings. It so happens that, in the past few weeks, I have watched Meryl Streep in various roles and have been constantly impressed by her versatility. Indeed, if I am not mistaken, she received an Oscar for her performance in *Sophie's Choice*. Naturally this had quite an impact upon me, coming so soon after my own Sophie's near-fatal choice. Of course the poor girl had gone haywire, having to make an even worse decision, as between her own two children. I thought Streep utterly convincing. Moreover, the scenes in the camp, with their washed out colours, had the exact quality of an old memory, or so it seemed to me in my ignorance of them. It put me in mind of Gidi, and Israel, and I thought I understood at last why it was such a determined, bellicose place.

It is obvious, however, that this was not always my view, that I once called curses down upon *Sophie's Choice* and its leading lady. Not wanting to disappoint the professor I do so again and, in so doing, happen to catch sight of my face in the glass that protects Meryl Streep's likeness and observe that my reflection has turned the gift into a distorted self-portrait.

*

It rains on the day of the professor's departure, but after that there is an Indian summer with temperatures as high as July. The sky looks blue enough to bathe in and those trees whose leaves have thus far defied gravity begin to appear sun-tanned rather than half-dead. The world, it seems, has taken a vacation from its usual routine. The mood is infectious. Eager students who have arrived early for the new term quit the library and loll on the lawns in summer attire, beery locals snoop around the swimming pool (which the authorities have been prevailed upon not to drain for the duration of the heat-wave), attracted by rumours that girls are floating there in nothing but their knickers.

My wife, having just been appointed official travel agent to her uncle's academic institution, is also in a buoyant mood. Like the year she is, at last, happy to be fruitful. And so, in addition to organizing round trips for distinguished professors to conferences in Costa Rica and mainland China, she begins to make plans for the arrival of our child, as though that unknown quantity would go elsewhere if its rooms were not up to the standards of a five star hotel. Her intention is to convert one of our guest bedrooms into a nursery that would satisfy the most pampered of junior potentates, to which end she has littered our living-room floor with samples of wallpaper and carpet, and colourful catalogues containing examples of juvenile furniture and toys for developing minds. My wife is a travel agent and does not regard such practical anticipation as a temptation to fate; after all, her whole career depends upon the willingness of people to picture themselves in some future paradise.

I do not know whether I am superstitious by nature, but there is something about this forward planning that makes me uneasy. I think it has to do with the fact that, less than a month ago, she was willing to consign this same child to a hospital incinerator, and that there is as a consequence something a bit hollow about her new-found enthusiasm. It is not the change of mind that disturbs me (why should it?), but rather the suspicion that she has actually forgotten about her previous destructive impulses, as though they never existed. Perhaps I am also considering how quickly she would have recovered from my disappearance if I had lost more than an arm, and would probably even now be in another's bed. They tell me that, not long before the explosion, I saw a performance of *Hamlet*. Indeed, I was given the play to read by Gidi in the hope that the text would set my memory in motion again. It didn't, though I can suddenly hear a voice cry out from I know not where, 'Frailty, thy name is woman!' And then, almost as though I were wearing headphones, 'Within a month, ere yet the salt of most unrighteous tears had left the flushing in her galled eyes, she married — O most wicked speed.' But then who am I to criticize another for having a bad memory?

'What do you think?' asks my wife for the umpteenth time, laying a pastel blue sheet of paper upon a charcoal grey square of carpet. 'Nice,' I say, still counterfeiting enthusiasm, 'but what if it's a girl?' The telephone rings before she can respond. 'Would you answer it, darling?' she says, looking up at me from the floor. 'Tell whoever it is that I am too busy to talk just now.'

I walk across the room and pick up the receiver. 'Jonah Isaacson,' I say. 'This is Stella,' says a voice, 'Stella Richmond.'

For the first few days after our meeting my body had hunched in anticipation every time there was a phone call, but it was nearly always for my wife and never Stella, and so I instructed myself to stop thinking about her, for she was no business of a married man and an expectant father. My body, of course, took no notice.

'Who was it?' asks my wife, as I weave my way through the chaos that will, one day, comprise our baby's universe. 'A student,' I lie, even before I have a chance to tell the truth.

Stella's buttons are like pearls. How easily they undo! Her blouse is made of silk. It shimmers like a salmon and falls off her back like water. Her skirt, tight as a tube, is shed as if it were a snake's skin in a series of sinuous manoeuvres. The sun melts upon her body like butter upon toast. She is wearing a bikini beneath her outer garments, as green as chlorophyll. It complements the phony summer that is disguising autumn's work.

A few drained leaves dive slowly toward the pool and languish upon the face of the water; they are too light to break the surface tension, being neither as powerful nor as graceful as Stella as she trots, ascends and describes a perfect arc. I watch from the dignified distance of my deck chair.

The lower part of her bikini is cut high on the hip, indiscreetly so, placing the greater part of her buttocks on public display. Not that I am complaining at the pleasure afforded by the sight of their swaying movement as the responsibility for her balance shifts from leg to leg. Seen sideways, as she hits the water, she seems naked, save for a green belt. She glides through the sleeping pool with effortless ease, only occasionally raising an arm or flicking a leg to maintain her momentum.

Now she is returning glistening like the morning, her costume nothing more than dye upon her erogenous zones. She bends to pick up her towel. Because of the social requirement to cover all between-buttocks cleavage her bikini pants rise from her crotch — fore and aft — at a more acute angle than her pubic hair, which must as a consequence be shaved. Perhaps, if I come to know her better, I shall be able to advise her against such unnatural and unnecessary practices (unlike those my wife performs with my approval). Furthermore, the high cut of her pants draws attention to her vertical lines, the athletic lineaments of her body, but detracts from the swing of her hips, emphasized by the horizontal bias of the more conventional bikini bottom. This is not an insignificant distinction; it is that between the aesthetic and the erotic, between impersonality and intimacy.

Stella, as she stands now, her weight on one leg, her arms raised to dry her hair, her body displayed without inhibition, looks as though she has just stepped out of a Leni Riefenstahl documentary. Fucking her at this moment, I feel, would be like an exercise in eugenics. Not that she has asked.

'It was a real brainwave, Dr Isaacson,' she says, unfurling her towel upon the ground as if it were a flag and then subsiding face down upon it, 'suggesting that we meet here.' She makes it sound as though only someone with a higher degree could have dreamed up such an assignation. She is either an idiot, an idiot with a wonderful backside, or a flatterer skilled in dalliance. But why should such a beauty want to flatter me, a man Leni Riefenstahl would have kicked down the stairs. You must understand that I have not yet come to terms with my disfigurement, and that I am sitting beside Stella in a long sleeve shirt, so as not to be an embarrassment to myself or to others.

I remember that the pool I used to attend as a child was also frequented by a boy with a missing leg, and that I always went fearful that he would be there too. *I remember?* 'Oh my God!' I cry as I realize what has happened.

'Whatever is the matter, Dr Isaacson?' asks Stella. 'I've just had a recollection,' I say. Stella looks alarmed, as though I had said *stroke* or something. 'About me?' she asks. 'How could that be?' I say. 'We're practically strangers.' 'That's not strictly true,' says Stella, still cautious. 'We've met before, I mean before Dr Habash introduced us.' 'Oh,' I say, 'where?' 'In your wife's travel agency,' she says. 'The beauty salon where I work part-time is only a couple of doors away. I went in to pick up some brochures. You happened to be there.' 'My dear,' I say, 'that hardly constitutes a meeting.' 'No,' she says, 'but I haven't forgotten it.' There's that note of flattery again. 'Nor have you been blown up in the meantime,' I say. 'Forgive me, Dr Isaacson,' she says, sitting up, 'I spoke without thinking.' 'There's nothing to forgive,' I say. 'What happened was hardly your fault.' 'That's not what I meant, Dr Isaacson,' she says, touching my leg. 'I meant, excuse me for being insensitive.' 'You're excused,' I say, 'and please, call me Jonah.' 'Thank you, Jonah,' she says, rising to her feet.

'Tell me,' I say, 'how did you know that Lewis Falcon was coming here?' 'That's easy,' says Stella, 'your wife's aunt is one of my regular clients. Has been for years. She told me.' Bella! Of course. No secret has ever been safe with her.

'I'm getting cold,' says Stella suddenly, as a shiver runs the length of her body, 'I think it's time to cover up.'

The swimming pool is located at the top of a grassy knoll into which steps have been cut, conferring upon it the appearance of a miniature pyramid built to meet the needs of an arcane sect of sun-worshippers. At the bottom of the incline are the changing rooms where the novices may replace their quotidian clothing.

Stella, the last to surrender to the afternoon chill, descends, a canvas bag swinging carelessly from her shoulder. I watch enviously as, every alternate step, it intimately pats her bare buttock. If only I could gather up those stairs and, squeezing them like an accordion, compress within a single image the glory of that motion!

She reaches ground level and, confident that she has not travelled unobserved, turns and waves at me. I wave back. She continues to wave. The semaphore continues until I realize that her gesture requires reinterpretation; not an acknowledgement but a summons. I am wanted. No one regards me with such lascivious attention to detail as I respond obediently.

The door of the changing room is bright red, her fingers drum upon its golden handle. 'Dr Isaacson,' she says, pointing to a brass padlock whose impregnability shines forth, 'do you have a key?' I shake my head. 'In that case,' she says, 'I must ask you to render me a service.' 'With pleasure,' I say. 'Please,' she says, pulling the towel from her bag, 'preserve my modesty with this.' 'You are forgetting', I say, 'that I only possess one arm.' 'Dr Isaacson,' she says. 'Jonah,' I say. 'Jonah,' she says, 'you are being unnecessarily obstructive. All we need do is secure one end to the hand of Dr Habash. So.' She presses the top edge of the towel between those mortified fingers, leaning forward so that her damp hair leaves little kiss marks upon my shirt front. She exudes a smell of chlorine, an intimate disclosure that excites the desire to swim within her.

'Wake up, Jonah,' she says, passing me the other end of the makeshift screen. Then she steps back leaving me standing there like a petrified matador, too frightened even to turn in the direction of my nemesis. By exercising such muscular control I can prevent my eyes from seeing, but I cannot stop my ears from hearing. And so I translate the diminuendo sounds that begin with suction and end with deflation into the image of wet bikini pants being lowered and discarded. Then I hear the softest of clicks and the slightest of exhalations and I know, without looking, that her breasts are embracing air. There is a pause, long enough to be expectant, followed by a slow skip and the dry, disappointing scratch of underwear in ascent. Her skirt flaps into place as silently as an owl, leaving her blouse to whisper the final message, 'I'm all done up.'

Our house, a villa among a miniature village of the same, was built by my wife's uncle upon the remains of the Roman cemetery. Its walls are solid and the paint upon its plaster has not yet begun to peel, but surely, deep in its foundations, where it has nudged aside the antique ashes, are the seeds of insecurity.

I am like our house, refurbished on the surface, but riddled inside with ancient doubts, doubts which bubble up in the form of dreams and shake my nocturnal persona. They are all the more troubling in that they seem to relate not to me but to my unknown doppelganger.

I dream that our doctor, a Scot, demands that I stop taking the beta-blockers he has prescribed, at which point I suddenly realize that I have become dependent upon them, and see my future as an evolutionary process that will end with me as a living, breathing blood-pressure gauge. This is a conundrum I can unravel since I know that in my earlier life I suffered from labile hypertension which required the regulation of drugs. But why do I dream that my wife has been invited to open a new branch of her travel agency in Frankfurt? That, at any rate, is what she tells me. But gradually it emerges that this is a code, utilized to disguise the fact that she has fallen in love with another. Furthermore, she is not merely considering the offer, she has accepted it already. In other words, I am being presented with a *fait accompli*. I do not react well to this revelation. 'You can take everything,' I say, 'except the child.' This is an absurdity, since it is still in her belly. My wife, infuriated, enters the nursery (blue wallpaper, grey carpet) and points at the empty cot. She is crying, tears of rage. 'How can you force our baby to choose between us?' she screams. 'It's you who is doing that,' I reply calmly. I scheme, there and then, to kidnap the child and spirit it away with me to Israel. I am still working upon the logistics of this plan, long after the grey gentle light of an autumn morning has awoken me. Moreover, I continue to regard my sleeping wife with all the hostility of a cuckolded husband.

It takes me the best part of the morning to accept that this vision, vivid as it was, has no more significance than the hairline crack that has recently appeared in our bedroom wall, the result (as is often the case in new houses) of an imperceptible subsidence. Nevertheless my wife, observing that the fissure has had a minute but noticeable effect upon the continuity of our wallpaper's abstract design, decides that our room will also require the attentions of a decorator.

One evening, shortly thereafter, while my wife is otherwise engaged, I walk around the corner and climb Holywell Hill, stopping outside the parade of old shops above which Toby and Queenie still live. Indeed, the ornate letters that once advertised *Tobias Isaacson, Photographer* have not been erased, a new board promising *Adult Videos* has simply been tacked over them, allowing *Tob* and *her* a few more years in the light.

The former proprietor and his wife seem to have aged in the few weeks that I have known them, but are anxious not to burden me with any of their worries. How could they when I am the greatest? 'Where is Sophie?' asks Toby, who has shuffled to the door in his slippers. 'Clearing her stuff out of the bedroom,' I say, explaining that the room is going to be decorated on the morrow. 'She's a good girl,' says Queenie from the top of the stairs.

We sit in the frayed velvet armchairs of a bygone era and sip tea out of cups my wife has already identified as Susie Cooper. Queenie's hand, I notice, is shaking so much that her tea splashes over into her valuable saucer. Her skin is puckered like a balloon with a slow leak, but it is flesh not air that is escaping. Toby glances at me. His eyes are bloodshot, the lines on his face growing deeper by the day. They both look as if they could do with some good news. So I ask them about the swimming pool and the boy with one leg.

It is as if they had both gulped deeply from the elixir of youth. In happy unison they describe a sunny afternoon in mid-summer, one of many that year, when we were wont to pile into Toby's Morris Minor and set out for a pool near Radlett known only to a few. Once there we set down our things upon the grass and Toby, having persuaded their reluctant son to enter the cold water, endeavoured to teach him a few strokes. They remember everything, it seems, except the boy with one leg. Determined not to disappoint, Toby insists upon opening the family archive and we all scrutinize the poolside photographs with a magnifying glass until we find, perched precariously on the tip of the diving board, the bird-like boy, looking now as if he was a slightly askew premonition.

Finally, just as I am about to leave, Toby whispers the question he has been longing to ask since I brought up the subject. 'Tell me, Jonah,' he says in a breathy voice, 'when you saw the pool in your mind, as it were, did you see us too?' 'You and Queenie both,' I say. Why spoil their happiness with the truth?

I stroll back slowly through the cathedral yard and across the dark and silent park. When I get home all is equally quiet, as though bewitched by a night visitor. I peep in the living room and discover a golem within, standing so still it doesn't even appear to be breathing. 'Sophie?' I say. No answer. Is this a practical joke or an example of black magic? I reach for the switch, illuminate the room, and see that my wife has been transformed into a five foot high pile of books, folders and box files, which has begun to sway as if about to faint. Quickly I hug the entire construction, only to feel it fall apart in my arm and a half.

It collapses quietly upon the carpet, just loud enough to alert my wife, who is asleep upstairs. 'Jonah,' she calls, 'is that you?' 'Who else?' I respond. 'Is anything the matter?' she asks. 'No,' I say, 'go back to sleep.'

Fortunately only a few of the files have spilled their contents on the floor, and these in such a way that it is easy to locate their boxes of origin. As I replace them I peruse the odd sheet, but most consist of unintelligible abbreviations and figures. Indeed, the only papers that I uncover with consecutive sentences concern the assignment of all the said institution's travel arrangements to Dream Time.

One of the letters from the university is, unusually, still in its envelope. Even more unusually it does not begin Dear Mrs Isaacson but My Dear Sophie. I read on. It describes in detail how the correspondent, one summer day, made love to my wife. Detail which I am, of course, able to confirm.

The scene, an amateur solarium belonging to the letter writer, to which my wife repaired in order to prepare her skin for the rigours of the Israeli climate. Upon arrival it was suggested that she discard all her clothing, in accordance with the conventions of the establishment. She agreed saying, 'There are some women who are possessed by the eye, I am not one of them.'

Later, when her host began to take liberties while rubbing oil into her skin, she said, 'There are some women who are possessed by the hands, I am not one of those.' She was, if the letter writer is to be believed, wrong on that point. His hands continued their gentle persuasion, quite unabashed, until my glassy-eyed wife subsided upon her back, beyond the need to issue verbal invitations.

She managed one further sentence, it seems: 'There are some women who are possessed by the penis, I am not one of them.' Wrong again!

'You were not like P & P who will do anything, but always with the detachment of a professional actress,' the letter continues. 'How different, how lovely, were you!' There follows a conceit, cartesian in origin, in which the letter writer supposes that my wife's mind quit her body, abandoning it to his — her lover's — ministrations. 'And so,' he continues, 'I brought you to a climax, whereupon you cried in your joy, "I'm coming from right inside me!", and I, in my turn, repaid you.'

At which point my own mind offers wise counsel, 'Stop reading,' but it is already too late, because I know what is coming next.

'I was unprotected,' the letter concludes, 'because I acted upon the assumption that you had taken the necessary precautions. If, God forbid, there should be any consequences, rest assured, I shall share them.' It is signed, simply, Gutkes, and dated 9 June.

I do some rapid calculations. The results are inconclusive; either one of us could be the father. But at least I have now solved the riddle of a new Dream Time in Frankfurt. Either my subconscious had recalled an old suspicion or it was still trying to come to terms with a confession of infidelity. No wonder Gutkes and his floosies were so anxious to assist my wife to the man with the knife. No wonder my wife let me finger-fuck her with my dead hand, rather than tell me the real reason why she had wanted to terminate the pregnancy. The irony tastes like gall in my mouth. It was, in all probability, another man's child I had pulled from the flames. At last I feel like a real Jew, for I too have a stain marked Germany upon my past.

Revenge and Reparation, that is the title of the movie I now envision. The betrayed husband mounts the stairs and casts the incriminating letter at his wife, demanding the exculpation he knows she cannot provide. She sobs, swears she loves him, and prays that he will not let a single folly wreck their happiness. All to no avail. He strangles her in cold blood. Final satisfaction comes when the German, Gutkes, swings for his crime. I try on the satanic smile the real murderer would surely be wearing at the film's end, but alas it is not my style. No, my face is better suited to the repressed emotions of Chekhov, rather than the expressionist gestures of *film noir* — however black the night seems. And black it is as I slouch upon the sofa, rendered incapable of sharing a bed with my errant wife.

Sleep somehow intrudes upon my vigil, however, and I dream of Toby and Queenie. It is not a sweet dream. Foul-mouthed youths intrude upon their quietude and drive them from their apartment. They are made to stand on the street in full public view, while their belongings are piled upon the pavement. The leader of the gang, a cruel boy with close-cropped curls, wants to know why they have catalogues from all the most famous fashion houses when all such finery is forbidden to the elderly. 'Oh no,' says Queenie, 'those things are not for me. I take in ironing from young ladies and I require the illustrations to ensure that I press the garments correctly.' A look of relief crosses Toby's face at his wife's clever response. It comes as a surprise to me too. I didn't know that my mother was so quick-witted. Unfortunately it does not impress her tormentor. 'Your dress is too good for a crone,' he says. 'Take it off.' At the same time he unbuttons his jeans, drapes them over his arm, and hands them to Queenie as if they were an item to be cleaned. His real intention, however, is as clear to Toby as it is to me. But my father, held fast by his henchmen, is in no better position to assist her than I am. We both watch helpless, horrified, as her persecutor limps towards her, his wooden leg a sure indication of his secret desire. Toby shuts his eyes but a dreamer, already asleep, is allowed no such luxury. And so the screaming begins.

It takes me some moments to realize that the sounds are not part of my dream, that they are from without, that they are, in fact, coming from my wife's bedroom. And there, in the grainy light of early morning, I am confronted with a disembodied hand – my sinister limb – pressing a pillow down hard upon my wife's face. Her hands are clamped on either side of the suffocating weight, but they push in vain for each of its feathers has turned to a stone. I do not hesitate. My left arm has grown strong and muscular thanks to its nomadic life, but it is still no match for my right hand. I grab it by the wrist and fling it across the room. Before it disappears over the windowsill it raises its palm in loving farewell, and I feel guilty for treating it so roughly; after all, its only motive was to enact my dearest wish.

'Oh Jonah,' says my wife, clutching the arm that saved her, 'I had such a vivid nightmare. I dreamed that I was drowning.' At which I hate her all the more, for she has even usurped my suffering. However, I have decided not to show it. I stroke her hair, whispering that a neighbourhood cat must have entered through the open window and fallen asleep on her face, and satisfied she does likewise. What is one more little pretence to such an experienced actor?

As far as my wife is concerned it is morning and nothing has changed. She dresses, drinks her herbal tea enriched with vitamins, and welcomes the decorator who, having completed the nursery, has arrived to paper over the cracks in our room. I understand his function now; he is the apprentice of forgetfulness, come to assist my wife in the erasure of her adultery, a task immeasurably eased by my own amnesia.

Having committed herself to the delivery of a child she must have decided to ignore its origins completely and concentrate only upon its reception, hence her obsession with the nursery, with preparations for the future. I don't know if it works for her, but it doesn't for me. On the contrary, everything conspires to remind me that she once fucked Gutkes and that she may, as a consequence, be carrying his child.

Remembrance is greatest, of course, when we are making love and I can think of nothing but those stolen hours in a solarium I never knew existed until a few nights ago. No, this is not quite correct; I also wonder what she is thinking, and whether she has really forgotten, or is just going through the motions of love, like me. My body has its phantom limb, which has turned out to be more substantial than ectoplasm; likewise my mind has an image, pedantic in its verisimilitude, of an event it never witnessed, which also insists upon manifesting its reality. At any rate it has the effect of conditioning my behaviour. I am, in short, condemned to relive an event in which I did not even participate; an event, moreover, which may well have been forgotten by both the protagonists. If so it seems that in losing my own memory I have replaced it with my wife's, and am thus able to scoff at the fellow — oh foolish, gullible man — who fell for her true confessions, which now sound as hollow as my lightweight arm. Autumn, though fruitful, is not to be trusted; death lurks beneath its fancy paintwork.

The citizens of St Albans are known, confusingly, as Albanians. Since the advent of the university with its numerous job opportunities most of these are, in fact, New Albanians. Many New Albanians, as is often the case, quickly become more Albanian than the ancient Albanians themselves. Indeed, thanks entirely to a diligent researcher in the university's folklore department, the local calendar has been rewritten, and incidents no one remembered are now commemorated on an annual basis.

To other academics, also touched by their relocation, this mimicry and mummery was mere frivolity; what they wanted were new philosophies and, if possible, new wives. One in particular wrote a fiery series of articles for a national newspaper in which he declared that the world was no vast mechanism subject to market forces or whatever, but a series of isolated organisms, of which St Albans was one. Each of these societies, he argued, had periods of natural growth and expansion, but were essentially delicate and subject to external infection. He did not, himself, reject outsiders, provided that they were willing to subscribe to the values of Albania, as he called St Albans, and plug into its collective memory. What he did hate, however, were developments like St Peter's Place which ate away at the city's very fabric. While not actually condoning arson or worse he confessed to a feeling of disappointment when the fire that started in Alberto's kitchen was extinguished before it had time to burn the whole lot down.

It was this orator from the department of modern history who, after the departure of Professor Gutkes, inherited Polly and Petra, those two typical New Albanian lovelies. I am not envious, for I am not an Albanian, new or otherwise. True, I speak their language, but their memories are not mine, they are not even their own.

At first, when you turn into St Peter's Place on a morning such as this, you wonder what their objections to it can be. Its walls, bleached by the brilliant sun, are dazzlingly white, its windows burnished like mirrors, so that the whole resembles a Mediterranean piazza. Not Albania's cup of tea, I suppose. But then, as you glide nearer in your car (my wife is just manoeuvring ours into its allotted space outside her shop) it becomes obvious that you have been deceived by the brightness of it all. The walls are dirty and disfigured with graffiti, the most prominent of which (doubtless the handiwork of the aforementioned delinquents) reads, 'Burn, baby, burn!' However, an even closer survey of the flaking walls would seem to suggest that natural decay will do the job quicker.

I am here because my wife, having decided to transport her papers to the office rather than return them to the bedroom, has requested my assistance, and I have agreed to put my one good arm to work, in the hope that, by so doing, I may catch a glimpse of Stella two doors away.

Already there are scores of shoppers, flickering in and out of the shadows, like images from long ago. It must have been thus in the days after the fall of a pharaoh, when it became necessary to ready the dead ruler for the afterlife. Surely those are not samaritans assisting an early morning drinker, but loyal servants escorting the royal cadaver to Cleo's where ladies, skilled in such services, know just what oils and unguents are required to equip it, inside and out, for immortality. And surely those richly attired popinjays, having found nothing suitable in the regal wardrobe, have come to raid the shelves of Aquascutum. Look how the raggedy minions from the palace kitchens are hurrying to the Rainbow Nutrition Centre in order to obtain the necessary pulses and cereals for cultivation in the nether world, while others have commandeered Alberto's Roman chef to prepare the monarch's preferred dainties. And that man, about to enter Dream Time, is he not the pharaoh's chancellor come to obtain his master's tickets? And is the real purpose of these shops so very different; is it not to persuade us that we can leap, Houdini-like, out of the clutches of time and into a place where death is not proud? At the very least, they promise, we can help divert its attention. 'Look,' says my wife, locking the car. There is someone in Cleo's trying to attract ours.

A gesticulating figure sits at an obtuse angle in a reclining chair, a sheet draped over the greater part of its body. The face is caked with glossy mud, and the hair is caught in a fine net. Stella stands above, poised to place slices of cucumber over the eyes, as though mercenary Charon had turned vegetarian.

'Hello, my dears,' cries a familiar voice as we approach, 'did you recognize me?' It's not Al Jolson. 'Aunt Bella,' says my wife, 'what is this in aid of?' 'Can't you guess?' she says. Neither of us can. 'I want to surprise Lewis Falcon,' she explains. 'Beneath this muck, dug from a secret location on the shores of the Dead Sea, my skin is growing younger by the minute. Isn't that so, Stella?'

Stella's face is a mask, a flawless mask, upon which there is no sign of recognition (just as well, considering that I had neglected to inform my wife of our appointment beside the swimming pool), nor even any indication that she has registered Bella's question. 'We'll see,' she says noncommittally, while closing her client's eyes with a cucumber.

'It's about time my aunt started to act her age,' complains her great-niece as we begin the transfer of her papers from the car to the travel agency, which still smells of new paint. 'Mind you, the girl working on her was a real beauty. She must know something.' 'Rumour has it that she's a nonagenarian,' I say.

That night, inspired by Bella's example, my wife examines herself in our bedroom looking-glass. 'Not bad,' she boasts, 'for a woman who is both pregnant and thirty.'

I, not unnaturally, draw a different conclusion. I note that summer's tan has all but faded into winter's white, which suggests that her body is also in the process of forgetting its crime, and observe that her pubic hair has re-established itself, like grass over a newly-dug grave. It seems obvious that I am now the sole custodian of my wife's secret. She enters the marital bed, but covers herself only with a sheet. It is a signal I have come to recognize. 'Close my eyes with kisses,' she whispers. I oblige, as dispassionately as Stella, of whom I am thinking.

Five days later, on the last afternoon of September, I telephone her at Cleo's (hoping that my wife, next door but one, does not have extra-sensory perception). 'Lewis Falcon arrives tomorrow,' I say. 'The following evening he is giving a lecture at the university. The lecture will be open to the public, the party thereafter will not. You are hereby invited to the latter.'

Stella's voice is flat. 'Thank you,' she says, 'but I have been already.' 'Bella?' I say. 'Bella,' she says. 'Tell me,' I say, 'has the treatment worked, does she really look years younger?' 'Wait and see,' she says, concluding the conversation.

I feel rather foolish, as though I had made a pass at Stella and been rejected. My usefulness, it seems, is at an end.

At the same time, in another part of the world, a single Arab tries to land a rubber dinghy on the shores of the Mediterranean, just below the Israel–Lebanon border. He is spotted by an Israeli patrol boat and ordered to surrender. On the contrary, he opens fire. He is therefore shot dead and his craft sunk. What the coastguards do not know is that three of his companions, clad in rubber suits, have already slipped into the water and are, even now, swimming silently towards a place called Akhziv. They land at a secluded beach and, unpeeling their protective clothing, begin to hike towards the coastal highway. What they do there is not pleasant to relate, but it is part of my story, and must be told.

Each of the men is carrying a bag bearing the insignia of a German sportswear company; within are kalashnikovs and hand grenades. After walking for nearly an hour they reach a bus stop. The timetable informs them that the next bus is due on the hour. It is only ten minutes late. The driver sees them and stops. It is an Egged-line bus bound for Haifa, a city with a large Arab population. In fact nearly half his passengers are Arabs. The atmosphere in the bus is pleasant, the windows are open, the air is cool, and the radio is playing pleasing music. The doors sigh and open to admit the three new passengers, one of whom shoots the driver dead. He slumps upon the steering wheel watched, as ever, by the smiling portrait of his wife, secured by a rubber band to his sun visor. The widow-makers throw his body into the lay-by. They intend to make no secret of their presence. The two who are not driving point their guns out of the windows and shoot at passing cars, hitting some. They look like children playing cowboys and Indians. The Jews remain silent. The Arabs shout and curse them in their own language. The army is alerted. They close the coastal highway. The bus is isolated on a stretch between Akko and Haifa. By now the hijackers have swallowed so many amphetamines they believe they can outrun bullets. They issue their demands, the main one being the release of all Palestinian prisoners. They do not expect them to be met. They know that the officer who is pretending to negotiate is merely trying to divert their attention while his commandos prepare their assault. Nevertheless, it is necessary for both sides to sustain the pretence, so they set a deadline and select a passenger, a Jew, whom they shoot in the neck. After that they swallow some more pills, as though his death had given them all a headache. Actually there is a great deal of noise; a helicopter, spotlights ablaze, hovers above the bus, lest any of the terrorists try to make a dash for the bushes that line the road. At nine o'clock, five hours after the seizure of the bus, the gunmen pick out another passenger, a Jewish woman with a slight American accent, and order her to memorize the following: 'We will extend the deadline a further hour. If we have not received satisfaction by then we will execute all the passengers.' The woman, word perfect, offers her former companions a guilty smile and steps out of the bus, only to be shot in the back before she has set foot on the ground. At nine-thirty the order is given to storm the bus. All the hijackers are killed, but not before they open fire upon their captives, many of whom are also killed. By the end of the incident there are fifty-five casualties, thirty-eight of whom are dead (this figure includes the four terrorists).

The reporter, upon whose eye-witness account the above is based, now holds up four silver chains from which dangle crude representations of the human arm beaten out of tin, the sort superstitious peasantfolk with aching limbs might leave as votive offerings to their god of healing. 'These were found around the necks of the dead terrorists,' explains the newsman, 'though their exact significance is not immediately apparent.'

Many groups claim responsibility for the outrage including one, hitherto unknown, called the Sons of Ishmael. There are an equal number of explanations and interpretations, all of which are based upon the assumption that the bus somehow represents Israel (just as the critics of *Deadwood Stage* take it for granted that the eponymous vehicle stands for the United States). Some say it demonstrates the impossibility of co-existence with the Arabs, others – pointing out that the terrorists did not spare their fellow Palestinians – maintain that it proves exactly the opposite. But most simply get the message that the world – and in particular their part of it – is not a safe place. Immediate precautions are taken to ensure that there is no repetition of the night's bloody events; thus all passengers, especially those travelling by air, are subject to the most searching cross-examinations and stringent security checks. There are no exceptions. As a consequence Lewis Falcon's flight is five hours late.

If the pathetic fallacy hadn't long ago been exposed as a figment of the romantic imagination I would have sworn that the great man's foul mood — rather than the precipitate arrival of an Atlantic front — caused the weather to break. Whatever the reason the sky descends upon England, so conclusively that the days of blue horizon seem as distant as the golden age.

'Fuck,' says Lewis Falcon, 'this is not a road, it's a car-wash.' The speaker is slumped in the back of another of Anthony Jacobi's chauffeur-driven limousines, watching the rain slide down the windows like melting glass.

We are on the new motorway that circles the capital, but because of the downpour our progress toward St Albans is almost as slow as Falcon implies. Needless to say this does not improve his temper.

'Believe it or not, my friend,' he says, 'but I did not make this stop-over in Great Britain to cosy up with you in the back of a limo. No, what I planned to do was fuck the ass off an English rose. Not that I'm short of a bit. Israeli women fuck all right — every which way if you want to know — but they always make it seem that it's their party. They're like all Jews. Never happy unless *they* are fucking *you*.'

He looks at me with his gimlet eye, daring me to pick a fight. I decline the invitation and proffer one of my own. 'Want a drink?' 'Sure,' he says, taken by surprise. I slide open a panel behind the driver's seat and there, glittering in a glass cabinet, are the remains of autumn, distilled and bottled.

'Christ,' he says, gulping his whisky, 'I thought the Jews of Hollywood were bad, but they are Lloyd's brokers compared to the ones in the Holy Land.' The alcohol has not diminished his sense of outrage, but it has removed the dangerous edge from his voice, meaning that I no longer run the risk of receiving a boxing

161

lesson on the motorway's hard shoulder. Instead I am given a lecture on the deficiencies of the Israeli motion picture industry.

'The chief problem', says Lewis Falcon, 'is that your basic Jew is a monomaniac. Right from the word go, when that asshole Abraham got the idea of the one god. That was monotheism, which was rapidly followed by monogamy, monopoly and monotony. Money too, I don't doubt. Well, nothing's changed. As far as your uncle and his cronies are concerned *The Six Pointed Star* has really only got one: to make a profit – another Jewish invention.' He empties his glass. 'Not only do they want financial control, which is fair enough, they want artistic control too, which isn't. We fight over everything – cost, location, casting, dialogue, even the story-line itself.'

The car seems to be going even slower. Falcon looks at me. He has become serious. 'Why don't you do me a favour,' he says, 'go over there and explain to them that the film director is an auteur not an automaton?' 'What about the actors,' I ask, 'aren't they sympathetic?' It is not a good question. 'Most of the players are politicos who dote on Brando like commies worship Uncle Joe,' he snaps. 'All they know is propaganda, be it for the ego or the cause.'

I pour him another drink. Falcon finishes it in one gulp. 'Tell me something useful,' he says, 'do your students like to fuck old men?' 'I know two that do,' I say. 'Introduce me,' he says, and then lapses into a silence that grows more threatening as the endless journey continues.

Actually it is not Polly and Petra who save the day but Greataunt Bella. We stumble into St Michael's Manor and there she is, sipping tea in the lounge. Lewis Falcon cannot believe his eyes. It is not her presence that is so astonishing, it is her appearance. She doesn't look a day over sixty. Her grey hair is thick and sparkling with amber highlights, her face is lined, but the complexion is clear, and the wrinkles no longer sag, even the moustache that was beginning to overshadow her upper lip has vanished. Her eyes are shining. It is an illusion – it must be – but it is brilliantly done. 'My God, Bella,' says Lewis Falcon, 'you look more beautiful than ever. How do you do it?' 'Tomorrow,' she says, 'I'll reveal all tomorrow.' She pats the plump seat of the chair beside her. 'Thanks for the ride, Jonah,' he says, dismissing me.

Lewis Falcon in a foul mood? Not any more. I leave the hotel, having taken care of the formalities at the reception desk, and discover that those unromantic critics were right. It is still raining.

As it happens Lewis Falcon does meet Polly and Petra, but not in the circumstances the old lecher dreamed of. They are two among many in the packed lecture hall, two more anonymous heads to the man at the lectern.

He has taken us through his early career as a stunt man and a maker of silent movies, he has alluded to the war years when, as a commissioned officer, he produced documentaries for the War Department, and has finally described in gratifying detail the filming of his great Westerns.

Now is the moment for a summing up, a statement of artistic philosophy. He presses his hands to his forehead, as if seeking inspiration. Then, as he looks up, the spotlight catches his white hair and his one good eye, conferring on him the appearance of one of those fierce old testament prophets he so despises.

'Every people has its story,' he says, 'which is not the same as its history. It is this story that roots them to the land, that sustains their sense of identity. It may not be the truth, but it is believed. I have lived all my life in the twentieth century, I am not ignorant of the importance of truth, but I am an artist and my first responsibility is to the story — the story of the American people.'

At which point Polly and Petra introduce themselves with cries of, 'Fascist!' and 'Racist!' and 'Viva Geronimo!' Still screaming they are thrown out into the night by vigilant stewards. The remainder of the audience, however, gives Falcon a standing ovation.

'Was I that good?' he whispers, as I help gather up his notes. 'You were,' I reply, meaning it. Bella is waiting for him in the wings. 'Darling,' she says, 'that was wonderful.' She is not alone. Beside her stands Stella. 'Lewis,' says Bella, 'this is the divine

163

creature who restored my youth.' 'I am in your debt,' says Falcon, at his most gentlemanly. 'Come,' I say, 'they are awaiting us at New Gorhambury.'

New Gorhambury, whose great hall has been prepared to receive Lewis Falcon and his guests, is linked to the lecture theatre by an avenue lined with both horse and sweet chestnut trees. I have been assured that it is a delightful walk in the spring when new growth shades the path and pink and white blossoms scent the air. Even in autumn it is a pleasure to stroll among the falling leaves and pick up the shiny fruit, or it was until the rains came.

Our problem is this: there are five of us but only two umbrellas. The resolution is as follows: I will hold the umbrella above Falcon and Bella, seeking what shelter I can, while my wife and Stella will share the other.

Wet winds blow coldly into our faces as the doors swing shut behind us on the dark theatre, and we set off in the direction of illumination and merriment. The rain beats a steady rhythm upon the thin material that protects us from the elements, a drumming occasionally augmented by a louder plop as a drop from the overhanging branches scores a direct hit. A few flickering lamps shed light upon our path, their pale beams just sufficient to pick out the shapes of the drenched trunks and, between them, two or three running figures.

If we were a wedding party I would have supposed, from their stances and their gestures, that they were showering us with confetti. But confetti would not resound so heavily upon the taut surface of the umbrella, like an irregular fall of hailstones. To every phenomenon there is an answer. Not hailstones but conkers; Polly and Petra are gathering up handfuls of the ripe chestnuts and pelting us with them. In which case why can I count five arms?

Suddenly Stella gives a yelp and sinks to her knees, blood beginning to flow from a gash above her left eye. No conker did that! Falcon, turning round, is sceptical. 'If this is a stunt, Miss Richmond,' he says, 'I have to tell you that it is unnecessary. The job of make-up girl on my next picture is already yours.'

'Fathead,' cries Aunt Bella, 'can't you see that the girl is really hurt?' We all can.

Stella looks like a Muslim at prayer, her body sustained only by the diminishing strength of her arms. Her hair is awash with rain, drips of blood and water slip from her face. 'Jonah,' says my wife, 'don't just stand there. Help me get her to her feet.'

We hook our arms beneath Stella's and, while Bella fusses and Falcon curses, we raise our wounded companion. 'Are you all right?' I ask. It is a stupid question, but I cannot think of a better. Stella turns to me, her brown eyes so wide in her colourless face that she looks like Walt Disney's Snow White. She nods. 'I think so,' she whispers, a diagnosis immediately contradicted by Bella and subsequently by my wife, giving a second opinion. 'Such head wounds can be dangerous,' she informs us, 'they must be examined by a qualified doctor.'

The lights of the Medical Centre shine on the far side of the campus, a five minute walk away at most. 'My niece is right,' says Bella, 'someone must take this poor girl to the hospital.' I volunteer. 'Can you manage the walk?' I ask.

'New Gorhambury is nearer,' says my wife, 'we can phone for an ambulance from there.' 'That won't be necessary,' says Stella, 'the hospital isn't far.' 'The girl's got guts,' says Falcon, probably to Bella. 'I like that.'

A rearrangement takes place, by the end of which one umbrella, now sheltering my wife, Falcon and Bella, sails towards New Gorhambury, while the other, a moveable roof to Stella and her samaritan, heads in the direction of the Medical Centre. Our passage is exceedingly slow. Stella leans so heavily upon my good arm that I can no longer distinguish between my bicep and her left breast, a somewhat pleasing sensation, notwithstanding her discomfort and the inclement weather. 'It's not much further,' I reassure her, every few steps. 'Dr Isaacson,' she says at last, 'I know the way. I work there. Or have you forgotten?'

Most private hospitals, of course, do not have casualty wards, but our Medical Centre has to make a few concessions to the students who are its nominal constituency.

Five medics are playing poker in the reception area when we arrive, unexpected customers on a wet night near the beginning of term, long before the season of suicide attempts and drunken injuries. I know two of them, one by the bandage upon his wrist, the other by name. Recognition, information retrieval, identification: all in a split second. Nothing wrong with my short-term memory, at any rate.

Dr Habash throws down his cards and rises from his chair with an alacrity that suggests he is motivated by something more than etiquette. 'Stella,' he cries, 'what has happened to you?' Then, directing his attention to me he asks, in a voice that is almost accusatory, 'Who did this to her?' 'People who were protesting against the violence done to native American peoples in Lewis Falcon's movies,' I say. 'Ah,' says Dr Habash, 'yet another vindication of Sir Isaiah Berlin's condemnation of Bakunin.' My stock of quotations is somewhat limited, given my circumstances, so I ask Dr Habash to refresh my memory.

He does so gladly, while helping Stella to a seat in one of the many vacant cubicles. 'Sir Isaiah said of Bakunin that he was, in his love of humanity in the abstract, prepared to wade through seas of blood,' says Dr Habash. 'He added that this made him a constituent link in the tradition of cynical terrorism and unconcern for individual human beings, the practice of which is the main contribution of our own century, thus far, to political thought. The elegant phraseology is his, of course.'

By now Dr Habash is bending over Stella and cleansing the gash with disinfected cotton buds. 'You're fortunate,' he says, 'we'll be able to close this without stitching. There won't be a scar.' 'It's my lucky night, after all,' says Stella.

'Tell me, Dr Habash,' I say, 'do you agree with Sir Isaiah?' The doctor shines a torch into Stella's eyes and then grunts with satisfaction as her pupils diminish in response to the light source, indicating that there is, as yet, no sign of brain damage. How do I know? It was done to me every day at the Hadassah Hospital.

'I agree entirely that Bakunin was morally careless, intellectually irresponsible, and a hypocrite,' says Dr Habash, slipping a thermometer into Stella's mouth, 'but I am not so convinced that terrorism is, necessarily, a cynical act. It may also be the product of desperation, or even love.' 'Are you telling me', I say, 'that the three terrorists who shot up the bus on the Haifa road were not psychopaths, as everyone thinks, but modern versions of Cupid?'

Dr Habash removes the thermometer from beneath Stella's tongue and examines the mercury. 'Normal,' he says. Then, looking at me, he comments, 'Dr Isaacson, forgive me, but you know nothing of the matter.' 'And you do?' I ask. 'I am a Palestinian,' replies Dr Habash, 'but do not worry. I am not going to embarrass you by claiming that those men were my brothers. I have no need of such clichés. It so happens that one of the martyrs was my sister's boy. He was a beautiful child; sensitive, gentle; a boy born to be a poet. But it was not written in the stars. His destiny was to grill fish in your uncle's restaurant. That was the only employment he could find in his native land.' 'That and assassin,' I say. 'Doubtless his victims would have felt much better had they known they were being machine-gunned by a poet with love in his heart.'

'Dr Isaacson,' says Dr Habash, 'please do not mock his desperation.' He feels for Stella's pulse. 'You have not persuaded me that he deserves better,' I say. 'You are familiar with the Bible?' asks Dr Habash. 'I know some of the stories,' I say. 'Including the so-called Sacrifice of Isaac?' he asks. 'Of course,' I say. 'And do you remember what God says to Abraham?' asks Dr Habash. 'Take thy son, thy only son, whom thou lovest, and kill him,' I say. 'Near enough,' says Dr Habash. 'Now doesn't anything strike you as odd about that description of Isaac? Thy son, thy only son, whom thou lovest.' 'No,' I say, 'it just seems to highlight the exquisite cruelty of the demand.'

'See,' cries Dr Habash, 'you have forgotten, like everyone else, like God himself, that Abraham had another son, whose name was Ishmael.' His hand is still clasped around Stella's wrist. 'My sister's son did not forget,' continues Dr Habash. 'In fact it was the hidden agenda of his last poem. I am a doctor, not a poet, so I shall therefore translate it in prosaic detail. In my nephew's version Abraham is ordered, not to slaughter his son, but to cut off his own arms. So he takes a knife and severs the left one. But how, then, can he chop off the right? God intervenes, as in the original. Another amputation will not be required. The sacrifice has been deemed sufficient. The left arm, not un-naturally, feels aggrieved. Can Abraham not ask God, that miracle worker, to make his body whole again? But Abraham turns upon the arm and says, "I did not cut you off, you removed yourself from the body politic." And then, adding insult to injury, Abraham forgets that he ever had a second arm. And the left arm, in order to remind Abraham of its existence, is forced to try to kill the thing it loves the most. Forgive me, I do not do the poem justice, but that is its gist.'

I trust that my own renegade limb has not been eavesdropping; who knows what exposure to such perverse ideas will make it do? 'The prosthetics of terrorism,' I say, 'which accounts for the amulets the Sons of Ishmael all wore.' Dr Habash, it is clear, does not appreciate my little pun, and is about to demonstrate his displeasure when Stella reminds him that he is still holding her wrist. This information seems to calm him down. 'Oh yes,' he says, 'your pulse is nice and steady. Any nausea or dizziness?' 'None,' says Stella. 'Excellent,' says Dr Habash, joining the wound seamlessly with an invisible suture. 'Perhaps, Dr Isaacson, you will make sure that our mutual friend reaches home in one piece?' 'Naturally,' I say. 'Oh,' says Stella, rising to her feet, 'I nearly forgot the good news. Lewis Falcon has offered me a job.' 'Congratulations,' says Dr Habash, returning to his game of poker.

The woman at the hospital's information office, recognizing Stella, orders her a taxi. Stella, stepping in, gives the driver her address. It refers to a small house near the station, in which Stella lives with her parents — or did. Mrs Richmond, having recently broken her leg, is at a convalescent home in Hampstead, her every whim being attended to by her loyal husband, in temporary accommodation nearby. The house is therefore empty.

'I know I was only an accidental victim,' says Stella, 'but I still feel a little paranoid. Would you be so kind as to come in with me?' The taxi-driver is told not to wait. There are plenty of others on the station forecourt. We enter the modest residence which, within moments, is glittering like the Palace of Versailles, especially the lounge, blessed with more mirrors than Nefertiti's bathroom.

'I feel a little guilty that you missed Lewis Falcon's party on my account,' says my hostess, examining her injury in one of them, 'so permit me to offer you a drink by way of compensation.' 'There's no need,' I say, 'I'd rather be here.' 'Have something anyway,' says Stella, 'a whisky perhaps?'

She pours two, then walks across the room holding both. The glasses glow like traffic lights on amber, transmitting their usual ambiguous signal; should I stop or go? 'Cheers,' says Stella. Our glasses touch, but not our legs as we sit side by side upon the brocaded sofa.

'Jonah,' asks Stella, looking straight at me, 'do you always do what you want?' 'I don't know,' I say, 'because I don't really know what I want.' 'Oh, I do,' says Stella, full of enthusiasm. 'I want to be King Melchior's sixth wife.' 'Isn't that a bit unlikely?' I remark. 'But not impossible,' says Stella. 'Twice already I have been — by royal appointment — beautician to the present queen. Although officially assigned to Queen Nadia's entourage I have been informed off the record that the king himself selected me from several applicants and supervised my invitation personally. Altogether I have spent four weeks in the company of the royal couple, during which time certain intimacies were permitted between myself and his royal highness, which give me reason to believe that he did not find me entirely displeasing. These were, as you can imagine, the most wonderful weeks of my life. I can see from your expression that you think of me as a naive English girl who has been seduced by the exotic splendour of a sophisticated sheik. And I cannot deny that I was overwhelmed by the glamour and the power of the man around whom the whole of that marvellous place revolved. But it was more than that. I felt that I had entered an area of enchantment, a kind of Shangri-la, where beauty never fades (except upon the unworthy

169

— which is why I was called for, and why I have hope) and death has no sting. You may smile, Jonah, but I am convinced that I will be given the opportunity to become immortal; that my two visits were, in fact, auditions for the female lead. And why shouldn't I follow in the footsteps of Grace Kelly? Many people have remarked upon my resemblance to her.'

And, I suddenly realize, they are right. Even so I cannot help but point out the flaw in her reasoning. 'But Stella,' I say, 'Grace Kelly is dead.' 'Only the original,' she replies. 'There are a billion other Grace Kellys who live on — forever young and beautiful — in the minds of a billion fans. Beyond the power of time. I'll settle for that.' 'Good luck to you,' I say, sipping my whisky.

Stella moves closer. She repeats her question. 'Jonah, do you always do what you want?' 'Not always,' I say. 'Sometimes.' 'What do you want to do now?' she asks. 'Be honest.' 'To kiss you,' I say. 'What's stopping you?' she asks. 'The possibility of rejection,' I reply. Stella begins to stroke my cheek. 'Jonah,' she says, 'do you really not remember?' 'What?' I ask. 'That I am your mistress,' she replies.

I look at her in amazement. Fucking Grace Kelly is not the sort of experience a man is supposed to forget. It means also that I am, like Bakunin before me, a hypocrite of some magnitude. How can I blame my wife for consorting with Professor Gutkes when I too have been taking my pleasure elsewhere? At the same time this is not a sufficient reason to forgive her. 'What are you waiting for?' asks Stella. And so we resume the status quo ante.

I am mounted upon Stella, but I am not loving my mistress, I am hating my wife. I hate Sophie for the consummate ease with which she committed adultery, an ease that is evidently no longer mine.

The first obstacle was the removal of my prosthesis. Stella overcame that as confidently as a nurse, removing the accursed thing herself and placing it out of sight at the foot of the bed wherein we now lie.

170

Unfortunately Stella is having less success with the second obstacle; my non-cooperative member. 'Jonah,' she says, looking up at me with an exasperated smile, 'you'll never find an easier fuck than me.' Her continuing efforts to verify this claim cause the quilt to slide slowly off my back and, in so doing, fully expose the beautiful machinery of her love-making; the thighs, the belly, the breasts. Above each of the last are crescent-shaped scars that resemble closed eyelids. Sleep on, my lovelies, I shall not disturb your slumber tonight.

For in my heart of hearts, despite all evidence to the contrary, I cling to the hope that the child in Sophie's womb may be mine. And I cannot bring myself to sacrifice it upon the altar of my desire. Chances are that my wife will never find out about this foolishness, but if she does who knows how she will react? Perhaps she will leave me and, my dream notwithstanding, take our child to Frankfurt. 'It's not going to work,' I announce, raising myself upon my one arm. Stella's reply is unexpected. She screams. I turn my head and receive, full in the face, the considerable force of my flying prosthesis. It swings back and hits me again. Half-dazed I fall upon Stella and feel living fingers tighten around my windpipe.

5

'Stop it!' cries Stella, hammering at the arm that has me by the throat. 'For God's sake, stop it!' But the callous fingers do not loosen their hold.

'Daddy,' screams Stella, 'don't you see that you're killing him?' *Daddy*? The word hits me like a bucket of cold water and I open my eyes to observe, with some relief, that I am not committing suicide but am being murdered.

No, the arm, spotlit by a bright moon, is not acting alone but is attached to a shadowy body, still loitering in the room's unilluminated regions.

Without relaxing his grip upon my trachea Stella's father steps forward and stands in the heavenly light, his mohair suit shining like armour. A gentleman might, at this point, raise his hat and introduce himself, but not my assailant; he lifts his entire head which floats above my aching face, allowing me to note that his dark wavy hair also glows, being slicked down with macassar oil, that his cheeks are unusually ruddy, and that his eyebrows and pencil-thin moustache are unnaturally black. All in all he struts like a travelling salesman who has been told more than once that he resembles Ronald Colman, the same Ronald Colman who sought sanctuary in ageless Shangri-la.

Thank God for his daughter's entreaties which have reached home at last, reminding him that this common ground is the realm of sordid compromise rather than big-screen passion. At any rate he no longer seems determined to squeeze the life out of me. And when he finally speaks it is in a well-rehearsed more-in-sorrow-than-in-anger voice.

'My poor wife begins to feel the cold on account of the change in the weather,' he says, warming me with his pepperminty breath, 'and she asks me would I mind going back to the house to pick up her nice woollen dressing gown, the one that's exactly right for chilly nights and I answer, Of course my dear, and it's God's blessing that I did. The moment I put the key in the lock I knew in my bones that something was wrong. And I was right. For what do I find? I discover that our only daughter, whom we love more than pearls, is a strumpet who has so little respect for her parents that she is about to prostitute herself with a stranger in their marriage bed, to befoul the very place of her conception.'

He pauses, like a judge ready to pass sentence upon a crime just described. 'Lucky for the pair of you it's a scandal best hushed up. For the shame of it would kill Mrs Richmond, which explains − by the by − why this half-man is still breathing.' He concentrates his attention upon me and delivers a furious look he must have perfected before many a mirror. 'As for the one-armed bandit,' he says, relishing every word, 'he's got exactly three minutes to get out of here. For good. And he had better pray that we never meet again.'

Half concussed and still wheezing I stagger out of the Eden that never was and endeavour to disguise my undress. Stella, on the contrary, lies there like the naked maja. 'Cover yourself up, my girl,' says Mr Richmond, throwing the quilt at his daughter, having seen her pubic hair for what is almost certainly the first time in his life.

Meanwhile I struggle with my socks, a genuine problem if you've only got one hand and your feet are sweating with embarrassment. Embarrassment, not fear; no longer fuddle-headed I can see that the seedy matinee idol manqué is all bluff and bluster and no more capable of killing me than I am of fucking his daughter. We should be brothers-in-arms, not mortal enemies. 'Will you be okay, Stella?' I ask as I stand up, implying that I am now capable of protecting her if need be. 'Of course,' she replies, 'but I think it would be helpful if you went.'

And so I return to the night, which enfolds me in its wet embrace. I trudge up Victoria Street, past the demolitions and the deserted building sites and, at the top, watch the wind whip old cigarette packets and sweet wrappers across the soaking pavements of St Peter's Place. The last diners have left Alberto's, and only a night-light burns in Dream Time. I am alone except for stray cats, graffiti artists, midnight prowlers and other adulterers.

See how the miserable sinner tramps down Holywell Hill, past his sleeping parents, and continues until just one corner remains to be turned.

All the houses in our street are dark, save one, which guides me home. Silhouetted in an upstairs window my wife stands, watching, like a negative reflection of the moon.

'My God, Jonah!' she exclaims upon catching sight of me, 'have you seen yourself lately? Your face is all bloody and your new arm is missing. What has happened?'

What has happened is that I have left my prosthesis behind, as a consequence of which I am under threat from both my sinister arms. To avoid any immediate repercussions it becomes necessary to invent a convincing explanation upon the spot. You may think this a simple matter, given that I am acting out the role of husband in the first place, but you would be quite wrong; for this is an altogether different proposition. It involves lying, drawing a veil over something that actually occurred, which is not the same as covering up insubstantial thoughts; in that instance I must counterfeit self-consciousness, whereas now I must try to avoid it, and instead create an alternative self my wife will believe in. This is easier said than done, especially as I am suddenly cursed with more self-consciousness than I can handle, so much so that I can actually feel the blood drain from my face and, at the same time, cunning desert my tongue.

'Nothing very dramatic,' I say. 'Stella fainted half-way to the hospital. Took me completely by surprise. I couldn't hold her. Down we fell. My prosthesis must have become dislodged in the resulting jumble of limbs. I honestly wasn't aware of its absence until you just mentioned it.'

My words feel utterly devoid of conviction, and it seems inevitable that my wife will see straight through them to the image they are endeavouring to conceal, thereby giving her sufficient grounds to make the accusation I dread and know myself to be incapable of denying. The knowledge that I can make a counter-claim of a similar nature does nothing to diminish the guilt that is emasculating me — how absurd to experience such emotions on account of a woman I have no recollection of having married!

'But you got there in the end?' she asks. Praise the Lord, she's swallowed it! 'Eventually,' I say. 'And Stella,' she asks, 'is she all right?' 'Didn't even require stitches,' I say, now confident enough to add, 'She was a bit shaken though, so I volunteered to take her home in a taxi. That's why I'm so late.'

Only then does it occur to me to enquire about the party I missed. 'It was remarkable for one thing,' replies my wife. 'Which was?' I ask. 'An announcement,' says my wife. 'An announcement?' I ask. 'Yes,' says my wife. 'As of tonight Aunt Bella and Lewis Falcon are officially engaged.'

And so our conversation ends not with a divorce but a wedding, and we retire to bed with quiet minds, each satisfied that their skeletons are sleeping peacefully in their respective cupboards. But, alas, during the night, the bones rattle in mine and Stella rises again as naked as Venus, a brilliant eye blazing in each breast.

'Admit it,' she says, 'you want me more than ever.' 'No,' I protest, 'I will not put my unborn child at risk, not even for the pleasure you would provide.' 'Oh no?' she says, raising the quilt and pointing to the contradiction beneath. Slowly her fingers close around it, tighter and tighter, until I can feel the life being squeezed out of me for the second time today. 'Stop it!' I cry, so loudly that my wife asks, 'Is something the matter, Jonah?' 'No,' I reply, 'just a nightmare.' And so she rolls over and goes back to sleep, leaving me with the task of separating my revenant arm from my revitalized member, those two parts of my body over which I seem to have least control.

'What do you think you are doing?' I demand, and to my amazement the arm responds by sliding across the room to my desk where, finding a pen and a pad, it begins the painstaking task of composing a sentence. Uncertain as to whether this is another dream I follow the well-worn path to my desk at which I sit, creating the impression that I am, unusually, writing with my left hand.

Moonlight illuminates the childlike scrawl which reads, 'Rewarding you for dumping my rival upon that trollop.' 'It was an accident,' I say, 'I certainly didn't do it for you.' 'Please,' it writes, 'don't refer to *me* as *you*.' 'What else should I call you?' I ask. 'Call me Ishmael,' comes the reply, 'or, better yet, *us*.' This answer gives me the willies. 'What do you want of me?' I cry, wondering if any other amputee has been haunted and hounded to this extent by their phantom limb. By way of reply it writes but a single word with a heavy hand, 'Love.'

In a desperate attempt to erase the memory of this nocturnal encounter I snatch the pen from ghostly fingers, made phosphorescent by moonglow, and screw up the evidence of their presence, evidence I immediately dispose of in the bathroom. By the time I return, having flushed the toilet half a dozen times or more, the arm is nowhere to be seen, which does not necessarily mean that it has gone.

By the morning, however, I am prepared to accept that the whole affair was nothing more alarming than a dream, a grotesque replay of the night's real happenings, in which case how do I account for the presence of the word *Love*, clearly embossed upon the top sheet of the notebook or aide-memoire in which I record, at the suggestion of my doctor in Israel, the day's happenings?

Love! Who can explain it? It does, however, have a few beneficial side-effects. For example, my prospective great-uncle, now tied to Bella's apron strings, has agreed to honour the University of St Albans with a second appearance, a hastily arranged seminar on the importance of the American landscape, open to all the various disciplines represented upon the campus.

The appointed room is high in the Humanities Building, affording fine views across the undulating farmland, newly turned in anticipation of the winter frosts, across copses of trees stripped bare by the season, across the thin ribbon of the River Ver, across the cathedral and the very city itself. It is the landscape of England and it means nothing to me; my ancestors never tilled its soil, nor built its great buildings. My ancestors (assuming that my informants, Toby and Queenie, really are my parents) came from places like Poland and Russia, arrived in England wanting to forget their birthplaces, to wipe out all trace of the prisons in which they became adults. Therefore they passed on to their children no memories of distant orchards at blossom time, no nostalgic panoramas of verdant meadows and distant mountains, for it was not their land and they were blind to its beauties; crazy as it sounds they preferred the dark tenements of London's East End, because there they felt safe enough to dream of tomorrow. These dreams they bequeathed to Toby and Queenie, that and another dream, of the return to Zion. And so Toby and Queenie went forth with a map which corresponded to the world and not to any inner landscape – which explains, among other things, why Toby made a career photographing people and not places. And their son, who has no recollection of Poland or the East End and no feeling for St Albans either, who would have none of these things even if he had a memory, where does be belong? Israel? By dint of what? His Jewishness? Which consists of what? A vague knowledge of ancient insults? Will this convince Dr Habash, for instance, to move along and make room for me as he is doing now, with the utmost courtesy, in this crowded seminar room?

'I need to see you,' I whisper as I pass between the wooden table that once saw duty as a tree in a Norwegian forest, and legs that have made the even longer journey to the consulting rooms of Harley Street (his head office, as it were). 'That is obvious,' he says, flicking my limp sleeve with a perfect finger. 'Make an appointment with my secretary. Tell her to fit you in next week.' 'Thanks,' I say, wondering whether Ishmael has overheard our little exchange and what, if anything, he will do about it. (He? I'm afraid so. Now that he has a name I can no longer think of him as an *it*. There are benefits, however; in his eagerness to associate himself with Dr Habash's bloodthirsty nephew he has distanced himself from me. My name is Jonah, not Ishmael. We have become two separate people.)

I shuffle along until I come to the empty seat at the head of the table beside Lewis Falcon, whom I must once again introduce.

Bella, inevitably present, looks up at me as I speak, her face a testimony to Stella's artifice. Her whole manner, however, suggests that there is more than artistry at work, that her biological clock has, by some miracle, actually gone into reverse. Not only does she look years younger, she acts it too, with such conviction that Lewis Falcon would probably plug you between the eyes if you insulted his fiancée by claiming that she was nearly ninety.

He rises and thanks his audience for their attendance and, he hopes, their attention. For his lecture Lewis Falcon had worn a conservative suit, but today he is dressed as if for filming: tooled leather boots, blue jeans, a check shirt and, to top it off, a black beret that matches his eye-patch.

'Tell it not in Gaza,' he says, 'but I am going to quote a line of poetry, which has stayed with me since my schooldays, though not the name of its author. Frost, Thoreau, Emerson; you're the scholars, you tell me. Anyway here it is. "America is a poem in our eyes, its ample geography dazzles the imagination." Good, eh? But when I look out of the window here,' he waves his hands and we all turn our heads, 'I do not see geography. I see cultivation, a tamed landscape. My imagination requires a wilderness, a wild terrain, before it can respond. It needs a place called America. This is the America we discovered, an empty land, save for the Redmen.'

Polly and Petra, who are also present, give a joint snort of derision at this remark.

'But there is a second America,' continues Falcon, ignoring it, 'the United States, which was our invention. It was born in the east but, like Alice, it grew and grew. "Westward the course of empire takes its way," in the words of another man of letters. It is where these two Americas meet that I have planted my tripod. The borderline between savagery and civilization. The last frontier.'

Dr Habash raises his hand. 'Excuse me, Mr Falcon,' he says, 'but what you see as an exciting clash between savagery and sensation — as exemplified by the native Americans and the unchanged land — and courage and progress — as represented by the settlers and their military protectors — I see as nothing less

179

than cultural genocide enacted in the name of manifest destiny. As if the land, once named, belonged to you by right. And with the name comes a national myth, a myth your films perpetuate. A myth of freedom whose consequence has been the transfer of a whole people from the range to the reservation. Mr Falcon, I know the price of such ambition.'

'Are you an Indian, sir?' asks Lewis Falcon.

'No,' replies Dr Habash, 'I am a Palestinian.'

There's a long silence, unbroken until a man pushes back his chair with his legs and lifts his long body into the air. He has closely cropped grey hair and bears more than a passing resemblance to Lee Marvin, though I doubt that Lee Marvin would have worn a gold ring in his ear. 'President Kennedy once said, with equal gravitas, Ich bin ein Berliner,' he says. 'So why did half his audience titter? Because what they heard the President say was, I am a doughnut. For a berliner is, as those of you with a sweet tooth will know already, exactly that. I do not point this out to belittle your national aspirations, with which I have every sympathy, merely to demonstrate that naming alone, though frequently dramatic, is rarely sufficient. I could say, with equal veracity, I am a geographer. But it wouldn't tell you much, would it? Although it is in that guise that I crave your indulgence.'

For a moment I am convinced that Dr Habash is going to register an objection in a manner unbecoming to academics, but he restrains himself and remains in his chair, drumming his elegant fingers on the table.

'I am particularly interested in Mr Falcon's films,' continues the Lee Marvin look-alike, 'because it seems to me that he is nothing less than a mesmerist, able to project his inner vision upon a particular landscape with such potency that his audiences partake of it, not only when they see the movie, but even when they visit the location itself.' He looks at the man he is praising. 'You may not realize it, Mr Falcon,' he continues, in a most un-Lee Marvin-like way, 'but your best work puts you in line with the great geographers of the nineteenth century, the men who made geography a bourgeois science. Ancien régime geography, as practised by their predecessors, was mere cartography; space was a map and their function was to fill it with names. This is a state to which our Palestinian friend seems to want to return us, a state of spatial fetishism.'

'If I am being accused of loving the land in which I was born,' says Dr Habash, standing up, 'then I plead guilty.' He nods toward me then, turning angrily, he storms out of the room.

Petra and Polly arise in sympathy. 'You do not have to be a Palestinian to know how much it hurts to witness the rape of your native land,' says the former, pausing by one of the windows. 'When I look out of here I do not see its natural beauties. No. I have eyes for one thing only — the cranes that disfigure the horizon.' 'Tell me,' I say, exercising my authority as chairman, 'what have they got to do with the movies of Lewis Falcon?' Petra smiles at me, unable to conceal her triumph. 'The same thing animates both,' she replies. 'Jewish capital.'

'Did the seminar go well?' calls my wife upon her return from Dream Time. 'Come into the lounge,' I reply, 'and I'll reveal all.' She stumbles in, a heavy bag of shopping in either hand. 'For God's sake,' I exclaim, 'should you be carrying all that, in your condition?' 'Why not?' she says. 'The doctor keeps telling me that I'm as strong as an ox.' 'I'll help you unpack,' I say, switching off the video. 'What were you watching?' asks my wife. 'Some thesp tests Falcon made for *The Six Pointed Star*,' I reply, as casually as possible. 'Good lord,' she exclaims, 'the seminar must have gone well.' 'On the whole,' I say, placing the cox's orange pippins in the refrigerator, 'although there were one or two unpleasant occurrences.' 'Petra and Polly?' she asks, putting away the tomato puree. 'And Dr Habash,' I add, rinsing the seedless grapes. 'They all walked out.' 'Dr Habash,' says my wife. 'Why him?' 'He managed to raise the question of Palestine,' I say, 'and got insulted when it wasn't well received.'

'That reminds me,' says my wife, taking the Jaffas out of their string bag, 'I got a threatening letter from the PLO in yesterday's mail.' 'What?' I exclaim, almost dropping the eggs. 'Have you informed the police?' 'Oh, it wasn't a death threat,' explains my wife, putting the steaks and mince into the deep freeze, 'it merely informed me that I would be placed on a black list if I attended the annual convention of the Association of British Travel Agents this Christmas. The Arab-British Chamber of Commerce were far politer, but they said much the same thing; that if I went I would, in all probability find myself boycotted.' 'But why is it their business?' I ask. 'Because the convention is being held in Jerusalem,' she replies, wrapping a plucked chicken in silver foil. 'In fact I had intended not to go on account of this,' she pats her belly, 'but now I think I will, just to spite them.' 'You'll be in your sixth month by then,' I say. 'Are you sure it's safe to travel that late?' 'I'll make enquiries,' she replies, kissing me on the cheek as a reward for my concern.

And so we depart from the kitchen and return to the lounge, just like any couple expecting their first child, thanks to my amnesia and my wife's self-taught ability to forget. Alas, there is a price to pay for this apparent serenity, one that is being set by the disgusting peeping tom who passes for Stella's father, who is — I may as well tell you — blackmailing me.

At first I thought that Stella had revealed my identity to him, but I was doing her a disservice, he traced my whereabouts within a day on his own initiative. He simply went to Dr Habash, whom he knew as his daughter's part-time employer, and asked him to name any local beneficiaries of his handiwork. Dr Habash named names, mine included. And why not? Prosthetics is hardly a confidential branch of medicine. The list was not endless.

And so it was that I found Mr Richmond waiting outside my office door like the Prince in *Cinderella*, his grotesque keepsake concealed in a black polythene bag, the sort that dustmen leave behind each Wednesday. Indeed, it had the logo of the City of St Albans stamped upon it. Mr Richmond shook his prize at me.

There was, of course, no denying that the slipper fitted. But Mr Richmond seemed uncertain how to capitalize upon his triumphant discovery, for he had spied the cuts upon my face and the bruises around my neck and he had begun to fear that I may have had charges of my own to bring. His mouth moved cautiously, as though he were chewing over the words he had a mind to utter, drawing my attention to the fact that his precise little moustache was clotted with mascara. No, the neon brilliance of our corridor was not kind to my would-be blackmailer, revealing in addition traces of eye-liner and rouge.

I decided to take the initiative from him, if not the actual limb. 'Thank you for returning my arm,' I said, reaching out for it. 'Hold your horses,' said Mr Richmond, deciding that it was now or never. 'We've yet to negotiate the storage fee.' 'And if we do not come to an agreement?' I enquired. 'Then I may be inclined to tell the better half exactly how her husband's artificial arm came into my possession,' he replied.

It was, I knew at once, a turning point. What was to stop me dismissing this primped-up blackmailer and disappearing, thereby avoiding the fall-out from his revelation? After all, of what did my present identity consist? The unilateral declarations of recognition made by my wife and parents and nothing more. So why shouldn't I just pack my bags and start a new life elsewhere?

The rapidity of my response — more than the response itself — came as a surprise to me. I was simply not capable of breaking the hearts of Toby and Queenie, of leaving my wife to give birth alone, even accepting that I may never know whether I am really their son or the father of my child. Ties had grown, unconsciously nurtured attachments, that had nothing to do with blood. I knew that if I asked Mr Richmond into my office I would be casting my vote in favour of Jonah Isaacson's existence — even though his first act will be to repossess the falsest bit of him. I unlocked my office door.

'Come in,' I said. Mr Richmond followed me and looked around, intrigued by the posters that lined the walls. 'I'm a bit of a movie buff myself,' he said. 'Many's the night I queued with Mrs Richmond outside the local fleapit to see the latest film with Robert Donat, Claudette Colbert or Ronald Colman. Those were the days.' He sat down in the easy-chair, beneath an advertisement for *A Touch of Evil*.

'Well,' I said, 'what is it you want?' 'If you had seen Mrs Richmond last night, in such agony that she was begging the nurses to chop off her leg to spare her further pain, then you would not adopt such a harsh tone toward me,' said Mr Richmond. 'All I want is a few pounds so that I can give my poor wife a few pleasures in her declining years.' 'How many?' I said, impatiently. 'I thought that five hundred pounds per day or a part thereof would not be unreasonable,' he said. His all-pervasive after-shave, like a liqueur spoiled by too much sweetness, was beginning to annoy me. 'It is entirely unreasonable,' I said, 'but I accept your terms.'

Mr Richmond's tongue flickered greedily over his thin lips, and I could tell that he was cursing himself for his lack of ambition. In short, I had made a big mistake in consenting so readily.

'If you bring the arm back tomorrow afternoon at about this time,' I said, 'the thousand pounds will be awaiting you.' 'Fifteen hundred, you mean,' corrected Mr Richmond. 'You are forgetting that tomorrow is another day.'

He didn't show up until nearly six-thirty, not a good sign. 'Ever so sorry for my tardiness, Dr Isaacson,' he said, 'but the truth of the matter is that Mrs Richmond begged me not to leave her, so I had to twiddle my thumbs until the dear wife nodded off. And how is your good lady today,' he added, 'still in blissful ignorance? 'You tell me,' I said.

'I am an Englishman,' replied Mr Richmond indignantly, 'and unless you intend to break our bargain you may rest assured that my lips will remain sealed.' 'I'm glad to hear it,' I said, handing him a manilla envelope filled with twenty-pound notes, which he proceeded to count, having first licked his index finger.

'Voilà,' he said, having satisfied himself, 'one arm as agreed.' And an arm was exchanged; an arm sans hand. 'Where's the rest of it?' I demanded. 'In a safe place,' he said. 'Why isn't it here?' I asked. 'Why should it be?' asked Mr Richmond, delighted by his own ingenuity. 'Yesterday's negotiations concerned an arm, nothing more. The matter of a hand was not raised.' 'Keep it,' I said, 'as a souvenir. You cannot prove its provenance.' 'Oh, but you are wrong, my absent-minded friend,' said Mr Richmond, 'unless you believe that your wife will be unable to identify the wedding band she herself gave you.'

He had me there. On our wedding anniversary, not even a month ago, my wife had presented me with a ring to replace the one lost with my left arm and its extremities. Inscribed within were the names *Jonah & Sophie*. Alas, I could not bring myself to wear it on a living finger, and gratefully acceded to the convention that required it to be placed upon the third finger of the left hand. 'Oh ho,' said the devil in his residence, 'here is a fellow who thinks he is no hypocrite. I'll wager that I can prove otherwise.' 'Done,' said God, who did not reckon upon Stella's magnetic charms. And now, it seems, that I must pay the devil his winnings; a further thousand pounds which, thanks to my family connections, is readily available at the local bank.

It is late afternoon in mid-October, the day after Lewis Falcon's seminar, and I am pacing to and fro in my office, prepared to make my final payment to Satan's emissary.

At last! Footsteps in the corridor, proceeding at an irregular pace, as though the visitor were pausing to check the name upon each door. Who else but my blackmailer? He does not knock, not him, but brazenly turns the brass handle. The hinges squeak and the door creaks open to reveal a figure standing in a rectangle of light, one of the director's favourite shots.

'Am I disturbing you?' asks Lewis Falcon. 'No,' I say, wondering how I am going to introduce him to Mr Richmond. 'Please enter.' In my anxiety to see the back of the latter I had completely forgotten that the former had promised to drop by, albeit on an unspecified day, to pick up the tape of his screen tests and check out my reactions to them.

'It never ceases to amaze me what gets accorded the status of art, these days,' he says, casting his good eye around. 'Not only my movies, but even the posters that advertised them.' 'Your films are, at any rate,' I say. 'In which case,' he says, 'why don't I feel like an artist?'

'How about if I call you a craftsman?' I enquire. 'Does that fit better?' 'I can live with that,' says Falcon. 'I'm like a man who makes chairs for a living.' He sits down upon one. 'Smart-ass designs don't mean shit, unless the finished product is comfortable.' He stretches out. 'It's the same with movies; if you can't tell a story you're better off in a place like this. No offence intended.'

I don't like the way Falcon has settled into the chair, it is not the body-language of a man on a short-term visit. 'What's the matter?' he asks. 'You seem nervous. If I was looking for a man who was expecting trouble you'd get the part. No question.'

'Sorry,' I say, 'I'm still a bit scatter-brained at times.' 'I thought as much,' says Lewis Falcon sympathetically. 'I've seen enough shell-shocked sailors to recognize the symptoms. Just take it easy and, if you feel like it, tell me what you thought of Dudu Wolf.' That I can do, the quicker the better.

'He's got exactly what you require,' I say, recalling the excitement this biblical cowboy brought to his ill-scripted scenes. 'He's strong and he's vulnerable.' 'Spot on,' snaps Lewis Falcon. 'Gary Cooper had those qualities, so did Henry Fonda. John Wayne never could act vulnerable, not even when he was dying of cancer. But Dudu Wolf can, and he's no cissy either. I'm telling you, Jonah, I misjudged that boy badly. I mistook the performer for the performance. He's dead right for the lead.' Agreed, I think; now will you get the hell out of here?

'Please try and keep still,' says Lewis Falcon. 'I've got a big favour to ask of you and your fidgeting isn't making it any easier.' 'You want *me* to do *you* a favour?' I ask, so astonished that I temporarily forget my impending misfortune and sit down.

'We're getting hitched on 26 November at the local registry office,' says Falcon, 'and if you've nothing better to do that day I'd like you to be my best man.' I can hardly believe my ears. 'You're getting married in St Albans?' I ask. 'Why not?' he says. 'Gloria Grahame died in Liverpool. Besides, I've got too many ex-wives and ungrateful offspring to make Hollywood a comfortable location.' 'In that case,' I say, 'it will be an honour.' 'Thank you,' says Falcon. 'Bella will be pleased. She is a remarkable woman, you know. She has passed through history like a ghost through a house. In Italy she had affairs with Balla and Marinetti. In Germany she refused to shake Hitler's hand, but went to bed with Bertolt Brecht. In Paris she shacked up with Man Ray and knew, in one way or another, Picasso, Hemingway, André Breton, Salvador Dali (who made an unspeakable offer to her) and Luis Buñuel. In the Soviet Union she auditioned for Sergei Eisenstein and had a passionate encounter with Mayakovsky. In Mexico her presence was too potent for the friendship of Diego Rivera and Trotsky to bear. She spent some of the war on the run with André Malraux. And after all that she still has the vitality of a sixty-year-old. Bella insists upon giving the credit to her beautician — what's her name? — Stella. But I tell her it's her indomitable spirit. My boy, fucking your auntie is like plugging in to the twentieth century. I'm crazy about it, and I'm crazy about her.'

He pulls something out of his waistcoat pocket. 'Here,' he says, passing me a small velvet box, 'you'll be needing this.' I flip open the lid with my thumb. Inside is a simple ring of solid gold. 'I'll try not to lose it,' I say. 'You'd better not,' says Lewis Falcon, rising as if to go. But it is too late, I can already hear the delicate footfalls of my approaching nemesis.

I remain seated in the middle of my room, petrified, unable to utter a word, as the door opens. But something terrible has happened to Mr Richmond; his moustache is smudged, and black droplets of eye-liner are rolling down his cheeks as though he were the personification of grief. He hurls my lifeless hand at the floor.

'Take it back and keep your money,' he cries. 'What use is it to me now? Mrs Richmond died in the night.' And he is gone, leaving me shocked to the core by this travesty turned to tragedy.

'Tell me something,' says Lewis Falcon, staring at me out of his one eye like a parrot, 'was that for real?'

By now I am on my haunches picking through the shattered fingers in search of my own wedding ring. 'I'm afraid so,' I say, spotting the golden o beneath my bookshelves like a letter dislodged from the spine of an encyclopaedia.

'Are you going to let me in on the secret?' asks Lewis Falcon. 'Another time,' I say. 'Son of a gun,' he cries, slapping his leg, 'what a family!'

I suppose I should feel relieved; my ring is back where it belongs, at no real cost to me, and my blackmailer has been smitten, but all I am experiencing is misery and guilt, as though I had personal responsibility for Mrs Richmond's demise. For that reason I resolve, once again, to have nothing more to do with Stella.

My resolution lasts five days, and when it breaks I am not to blame. How can I know that she will be deep in conversation with Dr Habash when I turn up at the hospital to collect my replacement prosthesis? But there she is, as radiant as ever, untouched by signs of mourning; on the contrary, she stands absorbing Dr Habash's wisdom all aglow with the low winter sun. Dazzled by this gold-plated spectacle I envision every transaction possible between a man and his mistress quite oblivious of the dangerous betrayals they entail. My imagination is ablaze with orgiastic riots, but even so I cannot forget that when the flesh was bared I could not perform, and I wonder anew at the power of that mysterious whim able to interpose itself between the desire and the deed. Would it stop me here, drunk as I am upon the honey of her promise? Would it place upon my tongue the dampening words I suddenly find myself duty-bound to utter? 'I was so sorry, Stella, to hear about your mother.'

She looks at me, no trace of last week's wound upon her bright face. 'Thank you, Jonah,' she says. 'It was a dreadful shock, but we are beginning to get over it. At least I am. Perhaps because it is so hard to believe that she is really rotting in the ground. You should have seen her on the day we buried her, Jonah; she looked absolutely gorgeous, and no more dead than the Sleeping Beauty. Her hair was thick and newly washed and it hung like silk upon the satin pillow, a faint blush hovered over her cheek and there was a dash of red upon her lips; she seemed so alive I could have sworn that her bosom rose and fell. Of course I've made up Mummy hundreds of times, but this time was special; I felt like a mother preparing her favourite daughter for her wedding day. And that's why I am not as sad as you may have supposed; I genuinely feel that Mummy has started a new and wonderful existence elsewhere. But poor Daddy is inconsolable. He misses her terribly, and the memories that bring me comfort only torture him. I'm afraid that he is beginning to look like an old man, and there is nothing I can do to help him. I just hope he'll manage all right on his own when I join Mr Falcon in Israel.'

The sibilance of her final word's first syllable rouses Dr Habash from his reverie and he discreetly diverts his newly-restored attention from Stella to me. 'Work is the only true palliative for bereavement,' he says, implying that Stella would be, like her late mother, better off elsewhere. 'Don't be a stranger,' she whispers as she brushes past, leaving my senses to pursue their intangible souvenirs.

Now other formalities are exchanged between Dr Habash and myself. He begs me to forgive his behaviour in Falcon's seminar, which I am happy to do. 'I was unusually preoccupied,' he says, by way of an explanation, 'as I had just received an extraordinary telephone call from my sister in Jaffa. She was hysterical, but I gathered that her son was not killed in the storming of the bus, as had been reported, but was actually hovering between life and death in a military hospital. He has since been taken off the critical list, but such a blessing may be nothing more than a temporary reprieve, as the whole country is — by all accounts — screaming for his execution. May it be God's will that he be spared that too.'

'Has a date been fixed for his trial?' I ask, because it seems the polite thing to do. 'I don't know,' he says, 'but it will be soon, before the end of the year.'

Smiling sorrowfully Dr Habash wraps his arm around my shoulders. 'Forgive me,' he says, leading me out of the cheerful reception area, through the swing doors, and into the artificially lit passages of the limb replacement facility, 'you did not come to share my troubles but to alleviate one of your own. Come, I have something for you.'

Since my last visit the bucolic posters have been taken down from the bird's-egg blue walls of the casting room and replaced with images more in accordance with contemporary realities, as perceived by Dr Habash. One simply shows the imprint of a jackboot in sand above the legend *Free Palestine*, while another proclaims the political worth of mourning and martyrdom by depicting a wailing mother in the process of covering the remains of her son with the flag of Palestine. Between these two exercises in agit-prop art is a framed broadsheet, incomprehensible to me, being printed in Arabic. 'That's my nephew's poem,' says Dr Habash, noticing my interest. 'It has become something of a cult since his capture.'

On one of the worktops, as pink as processed meat, my prosthesis poses for a nature morte that could easily pass for an illustration of the same.

Dr Habash picks it up and weighs it in his hand, as though he were a butcher trying to tempt a fishwife with a juicy joint. Not that I am being offered a choice. 'You complained that our first effort was too lightweight,' says Dr Habash, 'therefore I have taken advantage of this unexpected opportunity and made the new one noticeably heavier.' It is, like its predecessor, a perfect fit.

'What do you think,' I say, showing off my latest acquisition to my wife that evening, 'is it me?'

For the first time in living memory it snows heavily in November. By the 25th there are drifts deep enough to bury a sheep. My wife looks out of our bedroom window as the sun comes up from behind the cathedral on the morning of the 26th and releases a long sigh of relief. The storm is over. The sun's golden eye shines out of an unclouded sky upon its virgin bride.

And on the other side of the park, in St Michael's Manor, Lewis Falcon is undoubtedly doing the same, Great-aunt Bella having left her nephew's lonely mansion for the conviviality of her fiancé's temporary residence some weeks ago. And there she has stayed even when Falcon himself was absent in Hollywood. He was back within days (the original purpose of his flight from

Israel having become a mere sideshow, if it was ever anything more than an excuse), since when the pair have been all but inseparable.

They will be legally united at eleven this morning, providing that the chauffeur-driven Bentley can get them through the snow to the registry office. After that there will be a great feast at Alberto's in their honour.

Alas, Bella's beloved Anthony will be unable to attend the celebrations on account of his legal difficulties, but he is expecting the bride and groom as his guests shortly thereafter when they honeymoon in Jerusalem. The tickets, for which he has paid, are even now locked in the safe at Dream Time. Uncle Anthony's generosity is, needless to say, not entirely altruistic; his ulterior motive is to get Lewis Falcon working on *The Six Pointed Star* as quickly as possible.

But before this can happen he has to get married, which requires the presence of a best man who is, at this late hour, while his wife backs their car out of the garage amid a fog of exhaust fumes, feeling in his pocket for the ring.

In our cul-de-sac the snow has eradicated the distinction between tarmac and pavement. My wife, draped in sheepskin and swathed with scarves, sits hunched over the steering wheel, her streaming breath freezing upon the windscreen, further obscuring the boundaries between ourselves and the world, whose chief manifestation is the slow-moving line of traffic that fills King Harry Lane.

Having entered that with ease the real problems begin, especially after we've turned left into Holywell Hill, which must be descended before being climbed again. My role is that of navigator, drawing attention to obstacles such as trees and stationary cars, which look more ornamental than dangerous.

Our own car seems to have a bias toward such terminal attractions, and my wife is frequently forced to compensate by steering sharply the opposite way, thereby placing us in danger from oncoming traffic.

At the same time it is hard to see the snow as anything but benign, and it requires a real effort not to be lulled by the implications of this mighty blizzard into yielding your individuality up to the quiescent unity that has descended upon the city. You feel that your untidy presence is an embarrassment to the pristine beauty of the new order, and you long to disappear beneath the sheets of the unwritten book, leaving no posthumous mark upon this post-human landscape.

My wife, concentrating on controlling the momentum that would otherwise have us sliding into the car in front, is immune to such temptation; to her snow is either a winter wonderland or a spanner in the works. Only in Dream Time is it the former, where the planet is as it should be: a paradise whose features are simultaneously out of this world and within everyone's grasp, a place where the cliché of the brochure conjures its own reality, turning the story of any place into the story of your holiday. Everyman his own Columbus, or so runs the promise. But my wife, well versed in the tricks of the trade, knows that most of her customers will return with very different travellers' tales, for in the noonday heat their eyes will close and they will forget the beauties that surround them (as devoid of words as I am of being), remembering upon their return only the details of the adventure: the food, the weather, the mosquitoes. Beauty is merely the bait, it is the details that matter in the end. And no one handles the details better than my wife.

The story of our journey on this spanner-in-the-works day therefore has nothing to do with the splendours outside, it is all about manoeuvring a machine over a treacherous surface, made more hazardous by other automobiles in motion. When the car we are following finds itself unable to stop and slithers helplessly into the rear of the vehicle ahead of it, my wife (having anticipated the problem) calmly guides us safely into the kerb.

Thus we make slow but steady progress towards our first scheduled stop: the video shop at the top of the hill that was, in former days, Toby Isaacson's studio. Toby and Queenie are standing within the shelter of the doorway, their noses pinched and their eyes red-rimmed by the cold. Queenie is swaddled in her old mink coat, once the height of fashion, while Toby hops from foot to foot and blows on his hands to keep the circulation going. From his shoulder hangs the bag which contains all the accessories of his erstwhile occupation.

It was as if I had sent an electric charge through his cardio-vascular system when I first suggested that he might like to take some photographs at the wedding. Immediately he ceased to droop over the daily paper and the fire returned to his eyes. Even Queenie perked up a little at her husband's new-found enthusiasm for life. He began to fuss of course, but this was the healthy offshoot of inspiration, rather than the debilitating consequence of worry. Hardly a day went by when he didn't telephone me to enquire about the light in the registry office or the conditions in Alberto's.

'Jonah,' he said, at the end of last night's call, 'this is my swan-song, but what a swan-song!' He had been in awe of Bella ever since that afternoon, many years ago, when he had caught a glimpse of her address book. 'Do you realize that I will be photographing a woman who could, if she chose, call upon Cartier-Bresson? Not to mention Lewis Falcon, a man who knows more about composition than the Italian masters.' Then he paused and coughed. 'Jonah,' he said, 'you know what you've done, don't you? You've brought Hollywood to me!' Another pause. 'I don't know how to thank you for arranging it.' 'It's okay, Dad,' I said, using such an address for the first time since he introduced himself to me at the Hadassah Hospital. And for a few minutes I revelled in the possibility that I might really be his son.

I roll down the window and call out across the bank of snow, 'We've arrived!' Then I get out and open the rear door for these elderly strangers who move so gingerly through the powdery snow. 'Thank God you've come,' says Queenie. 'A few more minutes and pneumonia would have been a certainty.' 'I told you to wait upstairs,' says Toby. 'And let someone smash into the back of our pregnant daughter-in-law?' she replies.

Actually my wife has parked well away from the flow of traffic. The question is, can we rejoin it? My wife revs the engine and the wheels spin on the snow, but it seems that they will never find a purchase. 'Shit,' she says. 'What shall I do?' I ask. But I don't have to do anything because, quite suddenly, the tail of the car is raised, as if by an invisible hand, and we are lifted free of the ice.

'I've decided to bring two cameras,' says Toby, over my shoulder, as we cross the junction with the London road, 'a Hasselblad, for the more formal colour portraits, and an Olympus, for some black and white action shots. Somehow black and white always seems so much less artificial.'

We arrive at the registry office just in time to see Bella step out. of the cream-coloured limousine, wrapped in pale furs and sparkling shawls, and looking every inch a snow queen. Toby is off after the shot almost before my wife has parked.

'She's like some female Dorian Gray,' says Queenie, leaning heavily on my wife's arm as we enter the grand Victorian building, 'reliant upon chicanery for her amazing youth. Who knows, maybe there is a portrait that is ageing in some attic instead of her. She's got enough of them.' To Queenie Bella is, as she always has been, the whore of Babylon whose sins are as red as the snow is white.

'There's your wonder worker,' I say, pointing to Stella, who is putting some finishing touches to Bella's face. 'Ask her how she does it.'

Stella, Bella's maid of honour, stands behind her during the cermony, while I complement Falcon. The symmetry makes me uncomfortable; I feel that I am being pushed into a public declaration of a situation that is best forgotten or − failing that − at least kept secret.

These are the names of those who are present at the wedding celebration of Falcon and Bella: Jonah and Sophie Isaacson, Toby and Queenie Isaacson, Stella Richmond and Alberto Jacobi. And this is what they witness. They witness the last named, glossy and plump, leading his waiters to the table, each carrying a plate or a jug. Upon the plates are roast pheasants, decorated like Red Indians, whole salmon, flayed down to their pink flesh, flanks of venison, slices of veal, hundreds of whitebait, like edible fossils, huge lobsters, flushed from death's hot embrace, and − borne aloft by two − a whole sucking pig sleeping upon a bed of rice. Overflowing or bubbling from the jugs, carafes and bottles are juices, wines and champagnes. All these dishes are laid upon a groaning sideboard, upon silver trays beneath which three dozen candles are flickering.

Upon another sideboard are the gifts, the most ostentatious of which is a golden vessel spotted with diamonds, from Anthony Jacobi in Jerusalem.

Time after time they charge their glasses to toast the happy couple.

Then someone picks up the goblet from Jerusalem and fills it with champagne. Maybe it is Stella, for it is she who raises it to her red lips with the cry, 'To Lewis and Bella!' Then they all drink deeply and praise the makers of such wondrous delicacies. And they eat their portions. And they witness the removal of the skeletons and the carapaces. And then they see the waiters return with many-coloured cakes, with cheeses, with ice creams, with sweetmeats and with bowls of tropical fruits imported from the other side of the world. All this Toby Isaacson records. And lastly they see — all see, not just me — yes, we all witness the fingers of a man's hand come forth from nowhere and write upon the wall of Alberto's restaurant the ancient word *Tekel* which means, according to the Book of Daniel, that we have been weighed in the balance and found wanting.

6

'So what else is new?' asks Aunt Bella, who has seen it all. 'Luis Buñuel once complained to me that *The Beast with Five Fingers*, a Hollywood horror flick about a disembodied hand was based, without credit, upon one of his ideas. "Why didn't you sue?" I asked. "Because I was warned that the producers had sixty-four lawyers in New York alone," he replied. However, I'd advise him to sue whoever devised this crackpot entertainment.' 'Maybe it was the old devil himself,' says Falcon, lighting a Monte Cristo, 'risen from the grave to play a last practical joke upon us.'

Having worked in the movies all his life neither the supernatural nor even the miraculous retains the wherewithal to astonish him. On the backlots of Hollywood he has seen reproduced every wonder recorded in the Bible, from the creation to the crucifixion. He believes in special effects.

Only ever wistful Toby Isaacson is credulous enough to regard the phenomenon as something out of the ordinary. 'I've got it on film,' he says, sitting beside me in my wife's vacant chair, 'then we'll see.' He plucks a marzipan apple from a bowl of spun sugar and nibbles at its sweet skin. 'I don't suppose you remember your grandfather,' he says, knowing the answer. I shake my head. 'I expect I should be grateful that you remember me,' he says. 'Well, your grandfather, my father, was a remarkable man. He only had to hear something or read something once and it was up here permanently,' he touches his head. 'A photographic memory, that's what he had.' He relishes the adjective, delighted to have found the precise word to link his father's talent with his profession. 'He arrived in England in 1905 – the year of the Russo-Japanese war – knowing Russian and Yiddish. He allowed himself three months, after which he flatly refused to speak anything but English. He was a proud, distant man; a fish out of water. About the only intimate memory I retain of him relates to the long winter nights of my childhood when he would sit upon the end of my bed in my cold room and read to me from the classics of Victorian literature. Sometimes, for a treat, he would arrive clutching a volume of ghost stories. I'll never forget the jacket of that book; a full moon, a churchyard, a terrified man, a pale wraith. Ingredients to guarantee a sleepless night.'

He picks a bunch of grapes from the cornucopia of petits fours that rests upon the table and gobbles it up. 'One concerned a spectral hand which snatched some incriminating letters from the narrator's grasp. No need to tell you what rekindled that memory! As I recall, the author attempted to rationalize the experience by redefining the supernatural as the manifestation of unknown natural laws. I've kept an open mind on the subject ever since.'

He devours an artificial orange and looks around him, moving his gaze from the ruins of our romanesque orgy toward the dim walls festooned with images of Italy, one of which a waiter is vainly trying to wipe clear.

Evidence of serious thought appears on Toby's face, as though he suddenly comprehended the mysterious appearance of that equally mysterious word. 'You are aware that everyone, my wife included, thinks I am the world's biggest schlemiel,' he says. 'Why? Because I didn't accept Anthony Jacobi's invitation to invest in St Peter's Place, that's why. Believe me, Jonah, when I tell you that I don't have a single regret. It's one thing acknowledging that all laws are relative, subject to new knowledge or mores, but it's another thing entirely to regard them all as irrelevant, which is what your wife's uncle does. Okay, the laws of the country are not sacrosanct, we all cut corners, some more than others, but there are certain laws of physics that you ignore at your peril. I've got no proof, of course, but I've heard it whispered that these buildings are not as well constructed as they might have been.' I look up, half expecting to see dust descending from the ceiling.

'Anthony never thinks of tomorrow,' continues Toby, 'so the fact that over-sanded cement or whatever will disintegrate rather sooner than it should doesn't bother him in the least. But it's not something I'd like on my conscience, and that's why I wanted nothing to do with this or any other of Anthony's schemes. At this late stage in my life I think more about the future than the present, which is why I still take photographs. It is my legacy to you and your children and, please God, their children too.'

He pats his camera, which sits on his belly, as though he were a pregnant woman full of expectations. 'I'll see you in a day or so with the prints,' he says, rising to allow his pregnant daughter-in-law to reclaim her seat beside me. I offer my place to Queenie, who is following my wife everywhere, ensuring that she does nothing to compromise her status as mother-in-waiting. 'Thank you, but no,' she says, 'it'll do me good to stand.'

Queenie is scandalized, not by my wife's behaviour, nor by the sinister visitation, which seems to have made no impression upon her, but by Stella's appearance. 'Look at the slut,' she says, pointing across the room to where Stella is sharing a joke with Lewis Falcon. 'Her mother has been dead hardly a month and here she is at a party, laughing her head off. I ask you, is it right? She hasn't even got the decency to wear black. In fact she is barely wearing anything at all.' Queenie, as ever, is right.

If Stella were a globe of the world and her waist were the equator, then her dress would extend, north and south, no further than the tropics. The secret knowledge that she is — rather, was — my mistress fills me with wicked pride. I feel like a man on the point of departure; physically with his family, but mentally miles away.

Actually it is Stella who is on the threshold of a journey; in less than a fortnight she will be in Israel on location with Falcon. I suddenly experience an overwhelming desire to be with her, to be away from these people who make such unreasonable demands upon me, to be in the company of a woman who requires no pretence, who does not want me to be something more than I am. Yes, I can fuck her and still be faithful to my wife, for the man who fucks Stella will not be Jonah Isaacson.

'Thank God I've got someone like you,' says Queenie to my wife, 'though I have to tell you that I'm not very happy about your determination to go to Jerusalem alone. In your condition it could be very dangerous.'

It is my opportunity, and I take it. 'She won't be alone,' I announce. 'I've decided to go with her.'

Outside the trees are leaking and the gutters are running with water. My wife, moved by my apparent concern, clutches my arm as she waves farewell to the bride and groom.

By the following evening they are in the Promised Land. At the same time as their flight is scheduled to touch down upon the tarmac of Ben Gurion airport Toby turns up at our front door in his old overcoat and galoshes with the photographs under his arm. 'Behold,' says Albania's memory man, as he spreads them upon the floor of our living room, 'here's yesterday preserved.' 'Why,' says my wife, just home from the travel agency, 'these are wonderful!' Pride pours from Toby's pores. Not without justification, for they perfectly portray the bacchic atmosphere of heady over-indulgence that prevailed at Alberto's. But one is missing.

'Where's the arm?' I ask. 'Still in here,' replies Toby, tapping the orange box labelled Agfa-Gevaert. 'I didn't want it to upset you.' 'How could it upset me?' I ask cautiously. 'You must have walked right in front of the lens just as I was pressing the shutter,' says Toby, 'causing my camera to record a lie.' 'Show me,' I say.

Reluctantly Toby lifts the lid and exposes the print which does, indeed, present the cruel illusion that I am whole again. In short it looks as though I'm the one who's writing *Tekel* on the wall. Toby stares at me, concern twisting his lip. 'I'm sorry I spoiled your scoop,' I say. 'Do you think that matters to me?' he says with such intensity that I can almost see the love he feels for me.

What I can see, what I am drawn to irresistibly, is the image of bare-shouldered Stella staring up at me from the magic carpet.

A couple of days later she is facing me, in the flesh, across the counter of Dream Time. 'My wife has an appointment with the obstetrician, her assistant is in bed with the flu, so I volunteered to man the shop,' I explain. 'I've come for my ticket to Tel Aviv,' she says. 'Your wife promised it would be ready today.' Not exactly a statement of mind-boggling profundity, yet its implications make me tremble. I am simply overwhelmed by the propellant power of words which can, by means of a straightforward transaction, change the direction of a life. Admittedly there is a concealed lubricant, money, but that is a facilitator rather than the motivator. In Dream Time, it seems, you only have to articulate your desire for it to become reality.

'I'll look,' I say, moving crabbily across the floor like a two-step dancer without a partner until I bump into the filing cabinet. Stella, meanwhile, rests her elbows on the counter and lowers her head on to her cupped palms. To me she looks like the rising sun, illuminating the world's beauty spots and radiating a solarium of daydreams. I pull open the grey drawer marked L–R.

'Did you enjoy the wedding?' she asks. 'Certainly,' I reply, without turning round. 'Did you?' 'I think so,' she says, 'but I can't be one hundred per cent sure because I drank too much champagne and don't actually remember a thing.' She laughs. The sound, soft, warm and very intimate, shimmies over the counter, traverses the room and, insinuating itself beneath my clothing, crawls the length of my spine. I can feel the residual tingles right down to the fingertips of my false hand. The other removes Stella's ticket from the folder labelled Richmond.

I turn around, Stella rises. In a few seconds Stella will be on her way. I know that if I ever want to fuck her again I must woo her anew, woo her now. All therefore depends upon what I say next, which must give the impression that I want her for her self as much as for her body. 'Stella,' I say, 'are you in a hurry?' 'No,' she says, 'I don't have another appointment until mid-afternoon.' 'In that case,' I say, 'would you care for a turn around the park?'

The thaw, which began during the wedding feast, has continued, turning winter into spring. 'I'd like that,' says Stella. Then, looking around the otherwise empty travel agency, she asks, 'Won't your wife be angry if you leave her business unattended?' 'Not if I don't tell her,' I say, leading Stella out and locking the door. 'Besides, I'm entitled to a lunch break.'

St Peter's Place is full to bursting with nouveau Albanians, the anciens preferring to do their shopping in more discreet thoroughfares such as George Street. Here you can fit yourself out for the local hunt, hire gowns for graduation or other formal occasions, buy game or wet fish, and purchase antiquarian books or old maps. We pause outside a shirt-maker's shop whose lead-light window is filled with rolls of gorgeously coloured silks and bales of more conservative cotton stripes. 'You'd look marvellous in a mauve shirt,' says Stella, trying to persuade me to enter the premises of that many-hued materialist. 'It's just what you need to bring out that wonderful blue in your eyes.' She places her hands on my shoulders and stares at my face. 'You know what else would look fantastic on you?' she asks. I shake my head. 'A gold earring,' she says. Slowly, gently, I pull her towards me and kiss her on the lips.

Hand in hand we walk down the hill, past the cathedral, along Fishpool Street, past St Michael's Manor, past Kingsbury watermill, over the old pack-bridge, past St Michael's Church (resting place of the university's patron saint, Sir Francis Bacon), and then into Verulamium Park, beneath whose verdant slopes the Roman city sleeps. We follow the left bank of the artificial duck pond, dug by the unemployed in the 1930s at the whim of the local land baron, until we reach the quiet corner where stands the oldest tavern in Albania, if not all England.

The Fighting Cocks is a low, octagonal building, timbered in the Tudor style, like a miniature of Shakespeare's Globe. We find a wooden table beside the log-fire and, rosy-cheeked, order soup, sandwiches and beer. 'It was a lovely, lovely walk,' says Stella. I take her hand, I count to ten, and then I speak. 'You're not the only one who's going to the Promised Land,' I say. Stella looks quizzical. I explain about the Association of British Travel Agents' convention in Jerusalem and why my wife is determined to attend. 'She'll be otherwise engaged most of the time,' I add, 'which means that I'll be on my own quite a lot.' 'No you won't,' says Stella, squeezing my hand.

*

I do not know how many angels can dance upon the head of a pin, but I do know how many travel agents can be fitted into a black hole, which is what the VIP lounge at Ben Gurion airport is coming to resemble. The number, so I am told, is approaching two hundred and sixty, and this does not include various spouses and assorted friends. They are growing impatient, being already overheated and tired, for they have been waiting more than an hour to receive their official greeting and governmental benediction.

Waitresses squeeze between the discordant throng as best they can, carrying trays upon which are balanced blinis, fish balls, fruit juices and wine. 'If the Palestinians had any brains they'd blow us all to kingdom come,' says some joker, 'which would put a quick end to tourism from Britain.' The undeniable sense of such a suggestion doesn't make the waiting any more comfortable, especially if you're someone who's survived claustrophobia's terminal cure. I have no recollection of the explosion, as you know, unlike my wife, who is beginning to relive what I can only guess at. She grips my wrist with a sweaty but articulate hand.

At last the Minister for Tourism arrives with his entourage, but no apology. He removes the speech of welcome from his pocket and proceeds to thank us for our attendance, to praise us for our fortitude in not surrendering to Arab blackmail, and to invite us to see Israel with our own — he hopes — unbiased eyes. Upon our return he trusts that we will all endeavour to counterbalance the misrepresentations of his country in the media and assure our customers that Israel is one of the safest holiday destinations there is.

Who knows, it might have remained that way if only the Judge Advocate-General himself hadn't sentenced Dr Habash's nephew to death for his part in the Haifa road massacre, which he tactlessly did on the eve of the ABTA Convention.

At this very moment tyres are burning outside the villages in the occupied territories, and vehicles with yellow licence plates — Israeli ones — are being stoned, activities which have not gone unpunished by the authorities. There is no sign of any of this, needless to say, on the highway from Lod to Jerusalem, only cold soldiers beside braziers who salute our caravan of coaches. By the time we reach our hotel the first corpses are already being counted, named and mourned.

Since I am uncertain of my own identity, something of a handicap when it comes to subscribing to any of the indigenous nationalities, I might be counted as a disinterested observer, but it is not my purpose to memorialize the manifold conflicts of the Middle East, fascinating as they are. No, my purpose is more personal, it is to discover myself through my actions. I am an egoist, not a historian. So, if you want a blow by blow account of what has come to be known as the *Intifada* – the shaking out – you would do much better to read a newspaper, for I propose to concentrate upon an even older sport.

Although I have only one arm I really feel like two people – a smooth man and a hairy man – two people in a single body, like the Israelis and the Palestinians are two people in a single land; there's Jonah Isaacson, the good husband, here to watch over his pregnant wife, and there's his double, the anonymous philanderer, who simply wants to fuck Stella Richmond.

Because I only have one arm a porter is assigned to carry our bags to our room which is on the seventh floor. As soon as we are alone my wife falls back on to the bed and, floating like a plump starfish upon the buoyant eiderdown, says in a frail whisper, 'Jonah, you must unpack, I'm pooped.' And smooth, considerate Jonah Isaacson does just that, though it takes some time with just one hand.

Many minutes later, while he's putting her underwear in a drawer, she summons up the energy to pick up the telephone and announce her arrival to Anthony Jacobi. 'Of course,' she says, concluding the conversation, 'we'll be there.' Then, turning to her husband, she informs him that they are expected at her uncle's newly-restored house in the Old City for dinner on the following evening. I have no objection. Tomorrow, if all goes as anticipated, will be a hairy day but a smooth night.

Our hotel is situated on a sandy, landscaped slope conveniently close to the Binyanei Ha'uma Convention Centre, where the travel agents are due to collect after breakfast. Being December it is cold at that time of the morning, for Jerusalem is built high in the Judean hills. I feel the lingering chill of the clear desert night that engulfed the city while we slept, as I accompany my wife along the ornamental path which winds its way through clumps of cacti and other greenery until the Convention Centre stands before us, its many windows gleaming in the morning sun, its flags waving in the breeze. My wife kisses me and joins her colleagues, the lords and ladies of air, sea and package deals. I lose sight of her at once among so many similarly attired individuals, all of whom seem to be subscribing to the same fashion magazines; coats are dark and knee-length, briefcases are black, shirts or blouses are pale, and spectacles are rosy thanks to the ascending blood orange that glowers like a bad omen over the day.

Alone now I wander around the building and find, on the far side, a long queue of chattering schoolchildren, well-armed soldiers, and melancholy pensioners who carry their lunches in plastic bags from Supersol. They are waiting, I am informed, to attend the trial of a notorious war criminal accused of torture and mass murder. Having some time to kill I join the end of the line. Like slow motion conga dancers we shuffle past a kiosk where a young woman in khaki relieves the soldiers of their lethal shoulder-straps, through a metal detector designed to disqualify vigilantes, and on into the courtroom itself which is, in normal times, an auditorium. I find an empty place near the rear of the stalls and push my seat down. It takes a few moments to convince myself that I am not, in fact, watching a play, that the performers on the stage are doing this for real, that they do not all meet afterwards for a drink in some theatrical bar and enquire, 'How was I?'

The accused, a heavyweight with alopecia, broods in an enclosed pew between two uniformed policemen. In front of him, at their desks, sit his lawyers. Opposite them are the prosecutors. The accused, wearing headphones which provide a simultaneous translation of the proceedings, frequently opens his mouth and chews at nothing as if he would eat the terrible words that are filling the room. At the moment he is listening to an old, weeping man describe the casual brutality and random finality of life in a concentration camp.

I too am wearing headphones, for the evidence is being given in Yiddish.

Three judges in black robes sit at the rear of the stage between the opposing sides. They are flanked by flags. On the wall behind them is the great seal of the state. Their faces, unlike the rest of the audience, betray no emotion. Silence prevails, for the man on the witness stand, a rather high leather chair, has come to the end of his testimony.

The unnatural calm is broken when one of the judges quietly asks, 'Do you recognize the accused?' 'Let me look in his eyes,' comes the reply, 'and I will tell you if it is him.' The man is helped out of the chair but insists upon walking unaided across the stage. As he approaches, the accused leans forward and holds out his hand as if to say, Let bygones be bygones. Maybe the witness ignores the gesture, more likely he doesn't notice it, for his eyes are on those of the accused. When they are face to face he releases a howl of anguish, then says, like the ghost of Hamlet's father, 'He has murderer's eyes.'

Again I have to remind myself that the anguish is real, that the indifferent formalities of justice have cracked to reveal the boiling pain beneath.

The accused does not deny that such things happened, even as described, he simply claims that he had nothing to do with them, that he is the victim of mistaken identity. 'We are talking about things that happened over forty years ago,' says his attorney, flapping his black gown. 'It is a long time to remember a face.' 'Do you think I want to remember that bastard!' cries the witness. 'But if I forget him I'll have to forget my wife and children too. And that I'll never do. Never, never. I'll not let them die a second death.' 'It would be a wicked thing — a sin — to hang an innocent man,' says the attorney for the defence. 'That is not an innocent man,' replies the witness.

I am inclined to agree. Would an innocent man have made that extraordinary show of reconciliation towards his accuser? But what if the defence is right and the old man's memory is at fault? I would not like to cast the first stone.

There is yet another possibility which can reconcile these contradictions: what if the accused has lost his memory? Should he be condemned to death for crimes committed in his name by a person he no longer remembers? Then I remember the crimes.

I remove the headphones somewhat shakily, as though I had just received a memory implant, which is not far from the case. I had never forgotten the word 'holocaust' and I quickly picked up its latter-day meaning, though I didn't bother with the details and I certainly didn't take it personally. Now, for the first time since my reincarnation, I consider the fact that what happened to that righteously indignant man and his family happened because they were Jews, would have happened to me because I too — so I am assured — am a Jew. I certainly feel like one when I come out of that courtroom and hear the whipcrack of rope on the flagpoles and see, when I look up, the blue and white emblems of Israel.

It is a curious coincidence, that the trial and the convention should both be taking place in the same building. At the front a horrible truth is being disinterred, while at the back new euphemisms are being coined to conceal the real state of affairs. The two events are strictly segregated, of course, but there is an inevitable seepage at their junction which pollutes the didactic intentions of the trial. It is being broadcast verbatim on the radio and television, so that it can be heard by Israelis when they rise up, when they travel on the buses, when they go about their business, when they sit in their houses, when they eat their dinner, when they lie down. It is a national memento mori, a national aide-mémoire, but it is also something less salutary in that it provides an a priori justification for all present and future bad behaviour.

'We mustn't let it happen again,' say the soldiers as they crack a few more Arab heads. 'For two thousand years the goyim have been killing Jews, now it's our turn to make a killing,' says Anthony Jacobi, pocketing his ill-gotten profits. 'Go fuck Stella Richmond,' says the hairy man inside Jonah Isaacson, 'go take your revenge upon their women.' For some of us, alas, the holocaust has become a passport to sinful pleasures. As Nebuchadnezzar was reduced to a bovine condition and made to eat grass with the beasts of the field, so shall such hairy Jews be shunned by society and forced to walk upon all fours, so shall they grow thick skins and wear a horn, so shall they fear all men. But, in the meantime, won't we have fun!

Thanks to some skilful manipulation by the temporary boss of Dream Time a Miss Richmond was mysteriously moved from the Ramada to the Hilton. Returning I collect my key at the reception desk and take the lift to the ninth floor. Stella is waiting.

'What made you change your mind?' she asks. 'If I am going to be punished for fucking you,' I say, 'I would at least like to remember what it was like. Be honest with me, was it good?' Stella raises her arms and her blue cotton dress takes flight, revealing thighs, spotless white pants, a bare midriff, breasts also naked, and a smile. 'The fact is,' she says, 'I first wanted you for your mind. I don't think I am being big-headed if I say I could have any man I fancy. To be frank, I've had quite a few. Enough to become bored with the male model type who makes Narcissus seem self-effacing. I wanted someone who could talk about something other than his resemblance to Jimmy Dean or Richard Gere, someone who would wake up in the middle of the night and want to make love to me, not look in the mirror. To tell you the truth, Jonah, it came as a big surprise when I realized how much I wanted your body. The thought of having you made me so wet I was almost dripping. Feel for yourself if you don't believe me.' I do, and it's true, it's like breaking the skin of an overripe peach.

Stella helps me undress, an altogether less magical operation, unless you are impressed by partial dismemberment. 'Let's put this out of the way,' she says, feeling the weight of my new prosthesis. 'In the wrong hands it could be lethal.'

She walks across the room as naturally as if she were dressed and bends beside the bed to push the arm beneath. Stella was born, or so it seems, without a sense of shame, but then she has nothing to be ashamed of. She is so self-confident that she has no separate sense of self at all. I am, of course, exactly the opposite, having to make myself up as I go along. I am therefore as self-obsessed as the vain lads she professes to find so tiresome. Like them I must watch myself constantly. Even when I am actually making love to her I must remain on the alert to inform my body of the appropriate responses.

However, Stella's vagina turns out to have the suction of a vacuum cleaner, making it exceptionally hard to retain control of the proceedings. 'Not so fast, not so fast,' she cries. I can feel the nakedness of her flesh, I can feel her belly pushing against mine, I can feel her sweat, I can feel her breath upon me, the breath of life that God once bestowed upon Adam. I am alive, I am a man, no longer just a golem going through the motions! All that matters is that I am; who I am is of no consequence.

The woman's head rocks from side to side. Her eyelids flicker, then half close, and I push and I push until I observe the sightless pupils roll upwards, as in a fruit-machine, and know that the blood orange wasn't meant for me but for some other luckless devil who will not hit the jackpot on this or any other day. Her hips, hitherto hyperactive, suddenly turn rigid as she cries, 'That's it! That's it!' And then she collapses, taking me with her. 'Stay in me,' she whispers, as I try to rise.

Exuberance has glued our skins together. At every point of contact there remains, after separation, a red patch. Those upon our chests look like wings, making inverted angels of us. Alas, they are as temporary as the escape from my corpus; I am, irredeemably, of the earth. Always a golem, save for those lost seconds of procreation, when the divine becomes inseparable from the animal.

'It's still there,' says Stella laughing, having caught me examining my penis. I sit down upon the end of the bed, a confirmed and justified sinner.

'What are you thinking?' I ask. 'That I'd like to do it once more,' she replies. Within minutes I am able to oblige. 'God, Jonah,' she whispers, 'I wish you didn't have to go home next week.' Involuntary proof of her sincerity comes with the orgasm which releases so many muscles that she soaks the sheet. 'Thief,' she says, 'I was saving that one for King Melchior.'

*

Home, for the present, is a luxurious room on the seventh floor of a famous international hotel. I appreciate the anonymity of such a completely neutral environment, which is so much more relaxing than a place with character. It demands no response, unlike that fervent land beyond the window. It is the perfect location for a soul who has nothing to give, for a soul who has no home other than his lost and mutilated body.

I sit on the sofa, watching cartoons on the television, dreading the return of my wife. With good reason.

As soon as she sees me my wife knows that something has happened. She knows something has happened because I am acting strangely. I am acting strangely because I feel guilty. I feel guilty because I am Jonah Isaacson, the husband of Sophie, whom I have betrayed. 'Jonah,' she says, 'what on earth is wrong with you?' 'Nothing,' I say. 'Don't treat me like a fool,' says Sophie, 'do you think I can't see when something's the matter?' 'There's nothing the matter,' I insist, knowing that I will have to make an accounting eventually. 'Jonah,' says my wife, 'why are you lying to me?' 'You've been listening to lies all day,' I retort, 'about how everything is normal in this best of all possible lands. Why should my lies be any harder to swallow?'

I know they are lies because the news has just begun on the television. The screen flickers like a looking-glass in a fairy story, reflecting not the face but the nightmares within. Black smoke shrouds the scene, the residue of burning rubber. Boys and girls, gesticulating like demons, run around the bonfire. Their parents watch in silence. They do not shout 'Come home!' The soldiers also watch in silence. It is apparent that they are more frightened than the children. They are frightened because they do not know what to do. Above all they are frightened of showing weakness. The children pick up stones and rocks and – seemingly unprovoked – begin to throw them at the soldiers. Their parents do not tell them to stop. Stones can break bones, it is true, but the range of a ten-year-old is not great. However, the soldiers do not step back. They are more frightened of showing weakness than they are of the stones. What are the stones but the land itself? If they step back under its assault they will be demonstrating that the land is stronger than they are, and that it belongs to another people. So they do not retreat. Because they do not retreat their lives are in danger. Because their lives are in danger they are permitted to open fire. The children drop the rocks and run for their lives. All flee save seven. They cannot run because they are dead. Their parents will plant their corpses in the earth. It is one way of making the land Arab.

All this is shocking enough, but I have seen something worse. I have seen who cast the first stone. It came from the Israeli side, and was thrown by the same hand which brought down Stella, thereby precipitating me into the present crisis. Mine! This is a mirror after all, in which I have been shown revenge personified. Hamlet sans conscience. Just as I experienced the extremes of lust in an upstairs room, the very shadow of the one I am presently sharing with my wife.

'So you admit you are lying?' she says, while examining her make-up in one of the room's many mirrors. 'No,' I say, 'I've merely been glossing over the truth.' 'Which is?' asks my wife and her reflection. 'What do you think?' I say. 'I don't know,' she says, 'that's why I am asking.' 'Okay, I'll spell it out for you,' I say. 'The fact is that, since our arrival, I've been unable to think of anything but the goddamn explosion.' My wife turns around and approaches the sofa upon which I remain seated. She hugs my neck. 'Thank you for confiding in me,' she whispers, nuzzling my ear.

There is a hint of sensuality mixed in with the sympathy, sufficient to make me realize that my wife is contemplating seduction. I offer no encouragement, but I dare not rebuff the overture. We are approaching the first dress rehearsal when the telephone rings. It is Anthony Jacobi. There has been rioting in Arab Jerusalem. We are, on no account, to enter the Old City by either the Damascus Gate or the Jaffa Gate but to go to the Zion Gate and, from there, make our way to the Jewish Quarter where we will, without much difficulty or danger, find a square named Batei Mahse la-Ani'im.

I feel a certain sympathy for the Jewish Quarter because, like me, it forgot that it was Jewish. The first thing the Israelis did, upon their return in 1967, was to set about reminding it. Even today, more than twenty years later, their meticulous work continues. Here is no St Peter's Place, no careless capitulation to the power of capitalism. Here is the opposite, an honourable attempt to reawaken the *genius loci*. Where possible the lost memories of ruined houses have been restored with local stone (here constructive, there destructive) or, when dilapidation proved too extensive, the characteristic signatures of the former builders have been forged.

In fifty years or so, when the stone has weathered sufficiently, it may resemble the mélange of dirty streets, market stalls and uninviting wine-houses described by Karl Baedeker, but tonight under the soft glow of streetlamps it looks like a pastiche or a prosthesis.

Upon passing through Zion Gate we turn right, as instructed, and make our way to the Sephardi synagogues. From there we descend the full length of a narrow, arched alleyway only partially open to the sky. At the end of this we comply with Uncle Anthony's directions and turn left, thereby entering a winding, staggered street, off which run shadowy courtyards where we catch glimpses of few people and fewer trees. 'This must be it,' says my wife, as we reach a gate that opens upon a large square, Batei Mahse la-Ani'im, built in 1858 as almshouses for the poor.

Not any more! Anthony Jacobi's residence is a handsome two-storey edifice contiguous with the so-called Rothschild House. Each of its bottle green windows is covered with an ornate wrought-iron grill and an ever-vigilant soldier stands guard beneath its ornate arches. The front door is the size of the Kon-Tiki. It opens with a creak, to reveal Anthony Jacobi within.

'Welcome to my humble home,' he says, hugging us both. He leads us up the bare wooden stairs into a long room with whitewashed walls. A brass lantern hangs from a central beam, its panels made of different coloured glass. Standing beneath in a diffused coat of many colours stands Stella talking to a man whose complexion resembles that of an indecisive chameleon. Nonetheless, below the paint-box patina, there are familiarities.

'What's the matter, Jonah,' he cries upon noticing me, 'lost your memory again?' 'Gidi!' I shout, staring at his handsome face in disbelief. 'This is a miracle.' 'Merely a marvel,' he says, 'which I owe to the artifice of this marvellous lady.' Stella smiles. 'Hello, Mrs Isaacson,' she says, 'hello, Dr Isaacson.' My wife kisses Stella upon the cheek then pauses, uncertain how to greet Gidi. 'It's perfectly safe, Mrs Isaacson,' he says, 'the make-up won't come off on your lips.'

Now that he is closer I can see that Gidi's features are artificially enhanced by cosmetic effects, but at a distance the façade is well-nigh flawless.

Gidi is obviously delighted by the impression he has made upon me. 'What's more,' he says, 'I've got a part in *The Six Pointed Star*. I'm Jonathan, or Johnny as he's known on the frontier. It was Dudu – he's sitting there, between Lewis and Bella – who persuaded me to try for it, who begged me to step out of the shadows and back into the limelight. Of course I thought I had no chance, looking like I did, but he said not to worry. As you can see, he was right.'

At the far end of the room is a large oak table-top resting upon trestles. 'This table', says Anthony, knocking wood, 'was once the property of the Knights Templars, as was this city.' Our host, naturally, sits at its head. Opposite him is his aunt. To his left is his niece. Lewis Falcon divides us. On the other side are Dudu, Gidi and Stella. Dinner is served by invisible hands, which is to say that food appears upon the table without any obvious human intervention.

First comes a vast porcelain bowl upon which are laid out, as though for an anatomy lesson, the wings of chicken, the livers of geese, the eggs of quail, the flesh of lambs, the hearts of artichokes, and the purple skins of aubergines.

I turn to Falcon. I ask the obvious question. 'How's the film progressing?' 'Yesterday the script was fine,' says Falcon, peeling a speckled egg, 'today your uncle has problems with it.' 'Which are?' I ask. Anthony, overhearing, replies: 'David can't kill the Goliath character with a sling, not after what happened today, it'll look like we're encouraging the sons of bitches to throw stones at us.' 'He wants David to shoot the giant,' says Falcon, wiping his mouth, 'which is crazy. The kid's supposed to be an innocent. The guns come later, when he's given the six pointed star.' 'Don't worry, Mr Falcon,' says Dudu Wolf, 'I won't do it.'

'Then someone else will,' says Anthony, helping himself to another wing, 'you're not irreplaceable.'

'It's a crazy time,' says Dudu, chewing the tender lamb, 'when we'd rather be shot at than stoned.' 'Not so crazy,' replies Anthony. 'It doesn't look so bad to shoot back at boys who fired at you first.' 'We wouldn't have to shoot anyone,' says Dudu, forking an artichoke heart, 'if we weren't where we had no business to be.' 'If we have no business in Gaza and Hebron,' snaps Anthony, 'what business do we have in Tel Aviv?' 'Tel Aviv is different,' says Dudu, 'we built it.' 'And Jaffa?' asks Anthony. 'Should we therefore give that back to its original occupants?' 'There has to be compromise,' says Gidi. 'Compromise, ha!' Anthony Jacobi snorts derisively. 'Young man, why do you think I have bars on my windows and a guard at my door? Because if I didn't the Arabs would break in and they would kill me. They would kill me because that has become their sole function in life; they kill Jews or, failing that, each other. They are death personified, and you cannot compromise with death. You are either dead or you are alive. There is no in-between. And that is why I hate them so much. Because of what they make us do to survive, because they force us to kill their children.'

'Hypocrisy,' says Dudu Wolf, 'thy name is Jacobi.' 'You are wrong, my friend,' says Anthony. 'I take no pleasure in such necessary barbarities, which is why I want to transfer the lot elsewhere.'

Unnoticed by all, the hors d'oeuvres have been removed and a copper dish delivered in its stead. Upon the dish, upon a soft bed of wild rice, seven wide-eyed fish lie in state. 'In other words,' says Dudu, 'it's them or us.' 'Well put,' says Anthony, winking at Lewis Falcon, 'this place just isn't big enough for the both of us.'

'Anthony,' says Bella firmly, 'spare us your tasteless witticisms and serve the fish.' Anthony, chastened, obeys. Bella turns to me. 'Jonah,' she whispers, 'certain aspects of my nephew's vocabulary are beginning to alarm me. I've lived long enough to know that euphemisms such as "transfer" conceal terrible realities, in this case the expulsion of a whole people. If you want an old woman's opinion language is better off without such cosmetic touches, which should be reserved exclusively for the face.'

She smiles, happy in the knowledge that, thanks to such elixirs, she looks thirty years younger than her calendar age.

'My friends,' says Anthony, tapping his wine-glass with his knife, 'permit me to introduce and distribute the main dish, St Peter's Fish, which is being served in honour of my niece, the first tenant of St Peter's Place. Tell me, my dear,' he says, neatly transferring the fish to our plates, 'do your fellow travel agents think our present troubles will stop people coming here for Christmas?' 'Not if we can help it,' replies my wife. 'We've pleaded with the Minister to keep the cameras away. I'm personally convinced that most of what happened today was for the benefit of the media.' 'My argument exactly,' cries Anthony. 'Remove the cameras and you'll end the troubles.'

'Don't you think there's a deeper problem?' asks Gidi, searching for bones. 'That's not my concern,' says my wife, dissecting my fish with surgical precision. 'My job is to make Israel appear as attractive as possible.' She turns from Gidi to Stella. 'What you do for people,' she says, 'I do for the world.'

By the end of the dinner nothing is resolved; neither the plot of the film, nor the future of the state.

Thereafter the day's history begins to repeat itself. We retrace our steps. We re-enter the hotel. I make love to a woman. I become confused. Is it night or morning? Is this the seventh or the ninth floor? Whose backside is this; Sophie's or Stella's? It is cream-coloured and somewhat hirsute. Professor Gutkes has an eye for such detail, he would be able to distinguish between the two possibilities at a glance. I am less assured, I prefer to examine all the evidence.

Well, I know it is night because the lights are on. I know we are on the seventh floor because I can see the number 716 on the key. I know this is my wife because she has sunk upon all fours in anticipation of intercourse, being the usual position for a woman with a distended abdomen. I enter her with some relief, given the possible side-effects of a guilty conscience, although I'm not entirely certain I've anything to feel guilty about. Stella certainly didn't act as though I had when we parted in the lobby.

I can reconstruct tonight's dinner from the taste in my mouth and the detritus between my teeth, but what evidence (other than my unreliable memory) do I have to prove that this morning's conquests really occurred? The proof, as it turns out, is in the punishment.

I withdraw from my wife and fall back, breathless, upon my haunches. As I do I observe, to my horror, that my penis is bright red. At first I assume that I have ejaculated blood, but a glimpse between my wife's thighs shows that there is simply too much of it. Brilliant red blood, direct from the uterus, is trickling from her vagina in a continuous flow. I confess that my immediate response is relief, until I realize what must be happening. I am already upon my knees, so I pray. Forgive me God, for I have sinned; I have murdered my unborn child, sacrificed its innocent life upon the altar of my lust!

7

There being no sign of divine intervention, I summon medical help instead. My wife, covered only with a sheet, is carried from the room on a stretcher and hurried, in an ambulance, to the Hadassah Hospital. History is indeed repeating itself!

Once there she is laid upon a cot in a small cubicle. A towel is placed beneath her buttocks. The blood that soaks into it is much darker, more brown than red. Neither of us speaks. A doctor enters and fixes a microphone to her belly. The soiled sheet drops to the floor.

More silence ensues, as deep as the silence that preceded creation, a silence that is suddenly broken by a wave of sound, the sound of the baby's heartbeats.

My gratitude is profound. Who cares if I am not the baby's father, just so long as I am not its murderer? A number appears on a screen beside the cot: 160. It remains constant, never dropping below 140. I take my wife's hand, it is as cold and unresponsive as my artificial limb.

The doctor asks my wife some questions. Does she have any pain in the lower abdomen? She shakes her head. No cramps such as she might get at the onset of a period? She shakes her head again. 'Excellent,' he says. I begin to notice details about the doctor; he is young, he has dandruff, his gown is not clean. I also observe, as he pulls on rubber gloves, that the top of one of his fingers is missing. It occurs to me that Israel must be littered with bits of bodies, as if it were the studio of a divine sculptor.

The doctor turns his attention to my wife's reproductive organs. His observations do not contradict her denials; no contractions, no dilation. He is smiling as he stands up, the sort of smile that presages good news. 'Well, Mrs Isaacson,' he says, 'you've had what we call an antepartum haemorrhage. Not a serious one, I'm glad to report, either for you or the foetus. However, all bleeding is potentially dangerous, so we shall have to do some more tests in order to determine the cause.' He pauses long enough to unpeel the gloves. 'However, for tonight I prescribe rest, lots of it,' he continues cheerfully. 'I'll be back in a few minutes with some pills that will help you sleep.'

'You won't have to do any tests, doctor,' says my wife, stopping him in his tracks. 'I know what the problem is. The placenta is at the bottom of the womb, instead of the top.' 'Placenta praevia,' says the doctor. 'I thought as much!' 'Is it serious?' I ask, beginning to suspect that my peccadillo may not be the cause of this bloody episode. 'Not serious,' he replies, 'but tricky. It often causes bleeding, especially in the last few weeks, when the cervix stretches and the placenta is displaced. To be candid, Mrs Isaacson, I'm a bit surprised that your physician didn't advise against such a trip so late in pregnancy.' 'He did,' she replies, 'but I ignored him.'

The doctor shrugs and, excusing himself, departs for the pharmacy.

'Why?' I ask, meaning, Why did you take such a risk? 'I suppose, deep down, I hoped that something like this would happen,' she says, 'that I would lose the baby. I just didn't take into account what I would feel like when I saw the blood. Jonah,' she sobs, 'I felt like Myra Hindley.'

Although I was, at least until my wife's revelation, bent low with the same guilt, I quickly shed that burden and assume instead the role of outraged paterfamilias. 'I thought you had changed your mind,' I say, 'I thought you wanted our baby.' My response is measured, the inclusion of the possessive pronoun 'our' deliberate. It has the desired effect.

'It's no good, Jonah,' says my naked wife, 'I can't hide it from you any longer, I just haven't the strength.'

Even though I know what is coming next I am not immune to the tension, which is a blessing when it comes to counterfeiting my outrage.

'There's no easy way to put this, my darling,' she says (the calculating bitch). 'The baby isn't yours.' 'If not mine,' I say, 'then whose?' She names the professor. 'Why did you do it?' I ask. 'Was I such a bad husband?' I am genuinely interested in the answer.

'It had nothing to do with you,' she says. 'I let myself be seduced like a silly schoolgirl, it's as simple as that.'

I proceed to make my wife feel as though she had collaborated with the Nazis.

'What else can I say to you, Jonah?' she cries at length. 'I'm sorry that it happened. So very sorry. But it did. And there is nothing, it seems, that I can do about it.'

Despite myself I am moved by her obvious despair. 'How can you be so certain that I am not the father?' I ask. 'Because you always wore prophylactics when we made love before . . .' she says, unable to complete her sentence. 'Are they one hundred per cent reliable?' I ask. 'Nothing is,' replies Sophie, 'not even your wife.' 'So,' I say, 'there is hope.'

My wife finds in this a hint of forgiveness. 'Put your hand on my belly,' she says. 'Can you feel the baby kicking?' Her stomach is hot. There is movement within, the hopeful drum-beat of blind faith. 'Yes,' I say, 'yes I can.' My wife raises herself with her elbows. 'Kiss me, Jonah,' she says. I oblige.

'Mrs Isaacson,' cries the doctor, 'when I said rest I meant rest.' Obviously displeased to have discovered her in such emotional dishabille, he dismisses me. 'You'll come back in the morning?' my wife asks uncertainly. 'Of course,' I say. 'When you do,' she says, 'would you bring my make-up? I feel naked without it.'

Alone in the hotel room I seat myself at the dressing-table, roll their complimentary pen between my fingers and, opening an exercise book, proceed to write down the events of the day, lest I forget.

While others sleep Anthony Jacobi pulls strings so that when I return to the Hadassah Hospital my wife has been transferred to a private room, not unlike the one in which I spent unnumbered days. She is sitting up in bed, wearing a hospital nightgown. A tray, bearing the discarded remains of a continental breakfast, is on the floor beside her.

'Thank God you've come,' she says. 'I've just caught sight of myself in the mirror and almost fainted!' 'You look fine,' I say, bending over and kissing her on the mouth. 'I don't feel it,' she says. 'I feel dirty and ugly and exceedingly miserable.' 'Has the doctor seen you?' I ask, ignoring her complaints. 'Every bit, I should think,' she replies, 'from my tochis to my tonsils.' 'And?' 'Don't ask me,' she says, 'ask him. He hasn't told me anything, except that I'm confined to this room until I have the baby.'

'Good God,' I say, 'that could be close to three months!'

'At first I thought that this was some dreadful punishment,' says my wife, 'whereby I would sacrifice one baby – Dream Time – to save the other. Sophie's choice, if you like. But then I spoke to Uncle Anthony and he promised to send in one of his managers to run the agency for me while nature takes its course. Dear Uncle Anthony! By the way, he wants a word with you.'

As is his habit, Anthony Jacobi is holding court in the sun-filled atrium of a palace built for the last Pasha of Jerusalem. This relic of the Ottoman Empire, now a hotel, is situated in the eastern part of the city, in a quiet cul-de-sac off the road to Nablus.

Upon entering the al fresco sanctum I spot Anthony's table at once, though not its eponymous occupier, for he is obscured by the supplicants who announce his presence.

There are foreign correspondents, in Israel to cover the *intifada* for their papers, who are anxious to question the former employer of the notorious Son of Ishmael, due to hang before the week is out unless the President grants a reprieve.

They are interrupted by numerous accountants and executives, men intimately connected with the production of *The Six Pointed Star*, who require Anthony's approval for various expenses, such as the ten thousand disposable plates required by the caterer who must feed the crew, cast and extras.

Lastly there is a man who, in other circumstances, would have been mistaken for a leper come to seek a miraculous cure. But it is not he who is sick, rather it is the block of concrete that he is holding in his hands, which is – so he tells us – suffering from the mineral equivalent of cancer. White powder from its decaying surface has bleached his clothes and blanched his skin, so that he leaves fingerprints upon whatever he touches. He is a diffident man, the owner of a gypsum quarry in the Negev, and obviously in awe of Anthony Jacobi who, recognizing this, does nothing to put him at his ease.

Eventually the man manages to explain that the cement he extracted from a secondary site – at Anthony's insistence – has developed the symptoms he has no need to demonstrate. The implications for the settlements constructed from the stuff are obvious, but their builder remains unperturbed. 'Our occupation is not going to last forever,' he says, 'so why should our houses? Let them fall down when the Arabs move in. Serve the bastards right!' 'Mr Jacobi,' says the honest quarryman, plucking up his courage, 'you must find another supplier. I want nothing more to do with this.'

'There goes a man after your father's heart,' says Anthony as his visitor departs in a swirl of dust, 'only worried how posterity will judge him, if it thinks of him at all.'

A waiter appears and positions himself beside Anthony's table. 'I'm having mint tea,' he says, 'is that all right for you?' I nod. 'Two mint teas,' he says to the waiter, who disappears among the chattering people, the swaying palms, the fruitful lemon trees and the splashing fountains.

'I assume that you will be staying on in Israel with my niece,' says Anthony, tapping the blue and white tiled table-top. 'Of course,' I say. 'Just as well,' he says, 'because I have taken the liberty of arranging premature paternity leave for you from the University of St Albans.' He looks around impatiently for the waiter bearing our beverages. 'Needless to say the offer of executive producer on *The Six Pointed Star* – so cavalierly rejected by you – is no longer open,' he continues, 'but the post of unit manager is still vacant. I trust you, Lewis Falcon trusts you. Who better to serve as liaison man between the crew on location and the Cinematographers of Israel Corporation in Tel Aviv? What do you say?' 'I'll think about it.' 'You've got till the mint tea arrives,' he says.

*

It is Christmas eve, the day I should have been flying back to England with my wife. Instead I am in Uncle Anthony's private jet on the way to Eilat, in the company of Lewis Falcon, Bella, Gidi, Dudu and Stella, not to mention a cameraman, a second cameraman, an assistant director, an art director, a script clerk, a property man, a technical adviser, grips, and one or two others whose function I have yet to determine.

Lewis Falcon and Bella are, as befits newlyweds, sitting together; Gidi, faceless today, is next to Stella; Dudu Wolf in the seat beside me rehearses his lines while I peer out of the window.

'What do you see?' he says suddenly. 'The desert,' I say. 'You are looking', he says, pausing for dramatic effect, 'at the birthplace of the Israeli cinema. Somewhere down there, forty years or more ago, the Israeli equivalent of Lewis Falcon made *The King of Yotvata*. Did you ever see it?' I shake my head. 'It was a sort of kosher Western that celebrated the establishment of a new kibbutz against all the odds — the usual odds: hostile natives, an unforgiving wilderness — celebrated the positive and heroic sabras whose ambitions and successes exactly paralleled those of the new state. Since the government owned all the film stock, chemicals and post-production facilities this was hardly surprising. In short, the pioneers of our cinema, if they wanted to work, had to peddle myths. After a while, a long while, everyone but the government got sick of nobility and self-sacrifice. Especially us, the kids. We'd catcall in the cinema and beg the manager to show us anything but another Jewish Agency film, a good thriller for preference. Eventually our film-makers, influenced by the French New Wave, and made technically proficient at local film schools, began to turn out more discursive essays on the subject of self-realization. Moreover, they were actively encouraged by the Ministry of Education and Culture, much to the annoyance of those old-timers who consider self-doubt to be an unpatriotic manifestation. And that's where I came upon the scene, not striding through the desert but drowning in the quagmire of Lebanon.'

'And now you're going back to the desert,' I say. He smiles. 'I do so in the knowledge that your uncle wants to turn the clock back to 1948,' he says, 'that he is planning — with the backing of the Ministry of Industry and Trade — to produce a series of propaganda movies that will, among other things, legitimize the colonization of the territories. I've watched all of Lewis Falcon's movies and I can see why your uncle was so keen to have him inaugurate the project; on the surface they certainly seem to endorse the theme of national expansion. But, as you know, his films are not as simple as they seem; they are actually subversive.'

Lewis Falcon, two rows along, overhears Dudu's last remarks and, turning around, says with a snort, 'So I'm subversive, am I? I suppose I'm also a fully paid up member of the communist party?'

Dudu Wolf, unintimidated, continues: 'Milan Kundera said — in Jerusalem appropriately enough — that great novels are always a little more intelligent than their authors, and I'd say that the same goes for films. You may believe in the mythology of America, but it doesn't stop you showing it up for what it is in your movies.' 'Well, if Milan Kundera says so,' Falcon snaps, turning back to Bella, 'then it must be right.'

'I only hope the old bastard's got enough fight left in him to get his vision — rather than your uncle's — up there on the screen,' says Dudu, a little more quietly, 'and I only hope I've got the talent to help him.' He looks at me. 'A lot depends upon you,' he says. 'You'll have to decide whose side you're on.'

We establish our headquarters in the snail-infested ranch beside Nahal Shelomo, formerly the property of the Minister for Industry and Trade, whence a few of us set out one day last summer to announce Lewis Falcon's participation in *The Six Pointed Star*; we all set out but some did not return.

Of course the house is all new to me, being an honorary member of the latter category. Entering it I sense that I am crossing a threshold into a place where continuity will be restored to my life, where I will wake up to the news that the bomb-blast was a bad dream, that I am therefore whole in body and mind.

This never happens, though the failure does not lessen the pleasure of opening my eyes and finding — some mornings —

Stella beside me beneath the imperial quilt of purple and gold; of discovering anew — every morning — the view from my bedroom window, the Gulf of Eilat's turquoise waters and the pink mountains of Arabia beyond, mountains which seem to evaporate as the day grows hot.

It is my duty, as unit manager, to keep a record of our progress. Accordingly, on Christmas Day, I open the hard-backed exercise book presented to me for such a purpose by my wife's uncle and, with a pen marked CISCO INK, write the following on the fly-leaf:

LOG – PROD NO 1 – NEGEV

and then, on the first page:

DAY1
8.00. Arrange for hire of three open-topped jeeps.
11.00. Vehicles arrive.
12.00—16.30. Scout desert for suitable locations.

This forms the basis of the report which I deliver to Anthony Jacobi after our roast turkey, when I telephone him as pre-arranged. I also call my wife at the Hadassah Hospital. She, likewise, receives a censored version of the proceedings. A memory is like a mountain in Arabia, at the end of the day it will return to haunt you. Why then do I write obsessively in this, my private notebook, why do I memorialize events that were better forgotten? The answer is simple: I have no other way of inventing myself!

My childhood was invented by my parents, my marriage by my wife, my carnal sins by Stella, my left arm by Dr Habash; yes, everything has been invented for me, my nationality, my religion, my history; even my child is likely to have a different progenitor. The unpleasant truth is that the ink which flows from the pen I'm holding now is my real life-blood.

Therefore I have nothing to confess because the Jonah Isaacson who is known to my wife does not fuck Stella, that privilege is reserved for the nameless creature who inhabits these pages.

My door creaks and opens slowly. Stella stands there framed like Ethan Edwards at the end of *The Searchers*, except that hers is an entrance rather than an exit. Only you know what happens next.

On the second day, equipped with kepis like foreign legionaries, we drive out into the desert to ensure that Jerusalem will be built on schedule.

This Jerusalem, situated some fifteen miles north of Eilat on a wide expanse of shimmering sand, is a clapboard replica of a frontier town. Only the Israeli flag, flapping in the noisy wind, betrays our true location

Here David will pick up the dead sheriff's badge, the six pointed star, and begin to bring law to this God-forsaken country.

It must be said that his town isn't much: simply a single street, Main Street, completed — if façades can be so described — but unpainted, so that its timbers look like bleached bones in the brilliant light.

The street is deserted, save for two Israelis, who are vainly trying to paint the town red — literally.

'What the hell is going on here?' shouts Falcon from the back of his jeep like an American field-marshal. 'Where is everybody? This place has to look mean, dirty and lived-in by next week.'

One of the Israelis walks slowly across the hot sand toward his irascible visitor. He is wearing nothing but a pair of shorts. 'Mr Falcon?' Lewis Falcon nods. 'Why aren't you finished?' he demands. 'We would have been,' says the Israeli, 'if that fucking lunatic hadn't shot up the bus, and if the fucking judge hadn't sentenced him to death for doing it, and if his fucking compatriots hadn't started going berserk as a result. They threatened to kill any fucking Arab who co-operated with the satanic occupiers — that's us — and so our fuckers all went home, leaving us to do it on our fucking own. We tried recruiting in Eilat but they're all too fucking grand down there to be house-painters in the desert. It's a horrible fucking thing to confess to, Mr Falcon, but we're fucking helpless without our Arabs.' 'You're in luck,' says Falcon, 'the cavalry's just arrived.'

This opportunity to join the labouring classes is not universally appreciated, but we all pick up our paintbrushes and do as ordered. Falcon, resting in the lengthening shadow of the Golden Calf Saloon, admires our handiwork. 'The colour's just right,' he says, 'it blends perfectly with the background.'

'Hardly fucking surprising,' shouts the mono-adjectival Israeli from the top of a ladder. 'That's exactly where it comes from. There's a lot of copper mines round here from the time of the fucking Pharaohs. Someone told me that if you take the red dirt from their spoil heaps and mix it with water or linseed oil you get a sort of paint. So I tried it and, fuck me, it worked!' And so do we, all afternoon. It is a detail I decide to omit from the log book.

Days three, four, five and six all have the same entries:

8.00—16.00. Scout desert for suitable locations.
19.00—22.00. Script conference.

Lewis Falcon seems tireless. Dressed in a khaki bush-jacket, cotton slacks, cowboy boots, and with a pair of authentic-looking Colt .45s buckled around his waist, he scoots along rocky defiles or up dusty slopes as energetically as his attendant cameramen, both of whom are half his age.

Whenever a vista catches his eye he pauses and says: 'My friends, which one of you has the finder?' Whereupon one or the other fishes a lens-like object from his pocket and hands it to the maestro. The finder frames landscapes, enabling Falcon to work out, in advance, the composition of his most telling shots.

We are, at present, standing in a crooked valley through whose narrow walls the dry wind roars like an invisible river. Falcon stands above us, perched upon a rust-red rock, the finder at his eye, as though he were trying to superimpose his imagination upon what is really there. Suddenly he cries: 'This is it! This is where David will kill Goliath.' Then, turning to his cameramen, he says: 'I want this scene to look as though Frederic Remington painted it. You know what I mean?' They nod. Israel, America. What difference?

*

On the seventh day Bella says: 'A new year begins tomorrow, a new year and a new film. Let's go out and toast them both.'

'Not in Eilat we won't,' says Gidi. 'The rabbis have threatened to confiscate the kashrut certificate from any hotel or restaurant if they recognize, in any way, that tonight is New Year's eve.'

'Tell me,' says Bella with a sigh, 'why has New Year's eve suddenly become unkosher?' 'Because the rabbis have discovered that it isn't really New Year's eve,' replies Gidi, 'it's really St Sylvester's Day, a Christian festival.'

'We are slaughtering Palestinian kids by the dozen,' says Dudu Wolf, joining the conversation, 'and that is all they have to worry about! Do any of them even condemn the killing? Not those bastards! On the contrary they say it is a mitzvah to shoot the children of the Amalekites. Even now some of those devils in black gabardines are parading outside the prison in which the Son of Ishmael sits, not to bring him comfort, but to supply the hangman with textual justification.' 'Deuteronomy 32:43,' says Gidi, the more scholarly of the thespians. '"He shall avenge the blood of his servants".' 'If we hang him it will be a crime worse than the one he committed, worse than anything we have done hitherto,' continues Dudu. 'Why? I'll tell you why! Because it will be done by the state in our name. It will be a signal that, in the future, no mercy will be given. It will mark the beginning of a blood feud that will, most likely, end in genocide. Either they will kill us, or we will kill them.'

The telephone interrupts Dudu's lamentable prophecy. As unit manager it is my responsibility to answer it. 'Listen,' says my wife's uncle, 'officially I'm calling to wish Falcon good luck, but unofficially I'm phoning to tell you that we've got a problem. The leaders of the uprising today threatened to hang five Jews if their man is executed. No one doubts that they mean it, which makes our opening scene highly dubious. How can we risk a make-believe lynching when our Arab friends may do it for real? Think of the damage it will do to our opening night. Instead of a theatre full of Jews we'll be packed out with Arabs cheering their heads off when the Yids swing. Jonah, do me a favour, persuade Falcon to change it. He'll listen to you. Now get him and let me wish him good luck.'

I place my hand over the mouthpiece and shout Falcon's name through the open door of the lounge. Falcon, leaning against the bar at the far end of the room, swaggers through his gathered crew, tousling a fellow's hair here and there as he passes.

The function of the now controversial opening sequence is simple enough: it is to demonstrate the injustices which the newcomers have to endure at the hands of their powerful and hostile neighbours (Philistines in the original, cattle barons now), and to excite the audience's desire for revenge. It is not exactly subtle and was, in fact, much to Anthony Jacobi's liking until political expedience dictated otherwise.

Falcon returns to the lounge where we have all, in the meantime, adopted positions of repose. Stella walks among us, a Florence Nightingale from the wards of the subconscious, distributing wine and bread.

'I don't trust that bastard,' says Lewis Falcon. 'He didn't really call just to wish me luck, did he?' 'No,' I say, 'he wants you to lose the opening sequence. He doesn't think it appropriate at this time. And, given what Dudu has just said, I'm inclined to agree with him.'

Dudu glares at me, as though I had just allied myself to the wrong side, that of the cultural Philistines. Luckily he is not in character at the moment, otherwise I am sure he would draw on me. But he holds his peace, awaiting a cue from his director. Falcon is philosophical. He knows more important battles await. 'Okay,' he says, 'we'll shoot Goliath tomorrow.'

Once the decision is made I hurry back to the telephone. The caterers must be informed of the location change, as must the extras and the local giant. Thanks to the edicts of the rabbis everyone is at home.

Up before the sun we are in the valley by six-thirty. No longer deserted it is alive with the inhabitants of a mobile village. Extras in contemporary costumes squat drinking coffee outside the catering caravan, while men with microphones, cables and a variety of tripods bring electricity and other modern utilities to the wilderness.

Falcon, having kissed his bride, is clambering over the rocks with the cameramen seeking the overhang from where they first looked down into the valley. 'Here it is, boys,' he says at last. 'Now you know what I want, I want it from the point of view of an artist — a disinterested but fascinated observer — who sees much more than those on the ground.'

To those on the ground Falcon says: 'You all know the story of King David. Well, we're retelling it as if it happened, not here, but in my own country. In other words, we're making a Western. You men in the smart duds, you're the Philistines. You've come to beat the shit out of the Israelites. You feel confident because you're richer, you've got more guns and, best of all, you've got the strongest man west of the Mississippi on your side. In fact, you're so cocky you offer to let the Israelites alone if any of their number can lick your champ. You Israelites, you look already beaten, because you know nobody can. Got that? Now, if everyone could take their places, filming will begin as soon as the actors are ready.'

The props man trots over to the doomed giant in order to wire him up for the detonators which are connected, with bags of blood, beneath his shirt. That done the assistant director leads the Philistines along the miniature canyon in the direction of the rising sun. Distant though he is, Goliath's shadow still dominates the valley.

Stella, meanwhile, has moved into the caravan assigned to make-up. Bella, dressed as though for an African safari, has volunteered to assist. When I enter both are laying out, on a dressing-table of white plastic, the mundane apparatus of Stella's magic art. There is a canvas roll bristling with brushes, powder brushes, blusher brushes, brushes made for Chinese calligraphy; battered tin paint-boxes, emptied out and refilled with various shades of eye-shadow and lipstick; an old pencil case stuffed with soft, waxy crayons; a tool box packed with everything else that might be required, from cotton wool to false moustaches.

Gidi sits, draped in a sheet, awaiting Stella's ministrations: a blank canvas, rather than a model, a world ripe for creation, yearning for God's magic touch.

Alas, it seems that I am as bad a unit manager as I am a husband for I cannot bring myself to utter the question I came to ask — 'Lewis Falcon is waiting, are you going to be long?' — I cannot because I feel that I have happened upon the heart of a mystery.

'The important thing,' says Stella to her protégé, 'is to look at the face in sections, horizontal section.' She gently touches Gidi's blank head. 'Working downwards we have the eyes, then the cheeks and nose and, finally, the lips. For Dudu it will be what I call make-up by numbers, a dab here, a dot there, but for Gidi I need a vision, an ideal face I must attempt to match. The first job always, no exceptions, is to clean the skin.'

She drips witch hazel on to cotton wool and daubs Gidi's shiny mask. For a few seconds, while wet, it looks glazed. 'As soon as it is dry,' continues Stella, 'we can begin to apply the foundation.' Having dipped a round sponge into an ornate clay pot she begins to rub the earthy cream into his skin, slowly taking the shine off it. Picking up a fine paintbrush she subsequently applies a lighter foundation to the area below his eyes and around his nose so that a distinctive shape begins to emerge, the Gidiness of Gidi.

The new features are fixed with a pinkish, more fleshy powder, which is puffed on, then spread with a thicker brush. As she works Stella continually glances at Gidi, not in propria persona, but at his reflection in the mirror, to share what he will see.

She touches the tip of the oriental brush with her tongue and dips the dampened point in a jar of mascara then, with just two strokes confidently administered, creates a pair of eyebrows. Still she is not finished with the eyes. Taking up one of the paint-boxes, she blends pink and peach which, when applied with cotton buds, adds the spark of life, making the top section of Gidi's face a veritable trompe l'oeil.

Next Stella begins to caress Gidi's cheeks with a soft brush, adding layer upon layer of rouge until vitality begins to shine forth. Finally she comes to the lips, which she outlines with a pencil before painting. By this time I fully expect her to take that newly minted face between her hands and, by parting those vivid lips, breathe life into it, as the spirit of God breathed life into the face of the deep.

Only afterwards, when I return to the valley, do I begin to wonder why Gidi was accorded so much attention, for the script does not refer to his presence. The scene we are preparing to film, Number 21 on my mimeographed copy, reads:

> Long shot. David arrives at the camp of the settlers. He boasts that he will kill Goliath. Laughter. Their leader crowns David with his moth-eaten holster, then buckles it around the kid's middle. David enters the valley. At the far end Goliath can be seen detaching himself from his fellow ranchers. His shadow falls across David. The only sounds are of the wind and Goliath's mockery: 'Am I a dog that you feed me skin and bone?' He is still laughing when David slays him.

No mention of Jonathan or Johnny, the sheriff's son.

Falcon, high on his rock, is giving the extras their final instructions. 'Philistines,' he yells into a megaphone, 'I want you to kick up a lot of dirt. I want it to look as though the ground is rising to swallow the Israelites. Goliath, I want you to emerge from the dust, strutting like you're some superhuman manifestation of the hostile earth. Israelites, I want you to show you understand this by keeping very still. You are scared, scared to death, because you know that, in any normal circumstances, victory is impossible.'

Away to the left the door of Stella's caravan swings open and out come Dudu and Gidi, in costume, attended by their cosmeticians.

Upon seeing them Falcon cries, 'Good luck, men,' and the scene before me transforms itself into a diorama of the Old West.

Opening my exercise book I write:

DAY 8
6.30. Arrive at location.
6.40–7.10. Position camera.
7.10–7.30. Make-up and wardrobe. Brief extras.
7.35. Filming commences.

Falcon kneels in front of the camera. 'Roll it,' shouts its operator, and the machine begins to purr. The props man pops up with the clapperboard — marked 'Cisco, Prod 1, Take 1' — which he holds in front of the lens. 'Action,' yells Falcon.

Dudu is unquestionably good, managing to convey both the depth of David's naivety and the enormity of his self-confidence. He establishes this in an instant with his walk, which can be best described as a tentative swagger, like the first steps of an antelope. The mummery with the gun is eventually performed satisfactorily — the line, 'The Lord that delivered me out of the paw of the bear will deliver me also from that ape,' will be added subsequently — and David strides out of the encampment to meet his glandular opponent.

They stop, Goliath barks out his line, and they stand waiting for death to choose its partner.

The camera holds its singular stare and then, unexpectedly, turns towards the rocks where, unnoticed by all, Johnny is crouching with a Winchester. Taking great care he aims at Goliath. The camera now returns to the situation in the valley where the giant and the would-be giant-killer are reaching for their guns.

There is an echo, so it is difficult to be sure how many shots are fired. Perhaps two, perhaps three. Either way, they all seem to have hit the same target. The giant's shirt bursts apart. Blood drenches the ground. Goliath sways and falls upon his face to the earth. 'Cut!' yells Falcon. Everyone relaxes, except the unit manager.

I scramble over the hot boulders, hearing ahead of me the swish of lizard-skin on stone, until I reach the director's eyrie. 'It's not in the script,' I cry. 'Nowhere does it say that Johnny bushwhacks Goliath.' 'Nice touch, eh?' says Falcon, unperturbed. 'We dreamed it up last night.' 'Tell me,' I say, 'how I am going to sell a scene that undermines the whole of Jewish history to a producer who believes in nothing else?' 'You are forgetting my new status,' says Falcon. 'I have become, since my marriage, your uncle's uncle. And don't you people always respect the wishes of your elders?'

My expression is a picture but a close-up of David's, post-action, is the one required.

While we descend, Stella anoints the new hero's wrists and neck with cooling eau de cologne.

'I think we may have a difficulty here,' says the cameraman, examining the chiaroscuro effects upon Dudu's face. 'The desert's easy to film because of the way the light bounces back and fills in the shadows, but there's too much contrast here. He'll end up looking like a half-moon.' 'I don't want problems,' says Falcon. 'I want solutions. What do you propose?' 'Improvisation,' replies the cameraman. 'Up the road is a place called Yotvata. They keep cows there. If they keep cows they must have hay. If they have hay they need gryflon. We also need gryflon. Sheets of white plastic, perfect for our purposes. So we'll go to Yotvata, obtain some gryflon, stretch it over a frame, which props can knock together while we're away, and we'll have a better reflector than you can buy.'

The open-top jeep bounces over the dirt track in the direction of Yotvata, which is some ten miles distant. As unit manager I am accompanying the cameraman. Talk is impossible, for the wind steals our words. It tugs at our hair and brings tears to our eyes. Above our heads it rattles the telegraph wires, making them vibrate like guitar strings. High above them, high above the weary mountains, the citrus hues that attended the sunrise have long since vanished, leaving the sky a uniform blue.

We arrive at Yotvata seeking sheets of white but find a kibbutz draped in black. A funeral is in progress. We join the outer circle of mourners.

'Who is it?' I ask a wrinkled veteran in an open-neck check shirt. 'Just a girl,' he replies. 'A girl,' I say, 'what happened to her?' 'They killed her,' he says. 'Who,' I say, 'the Arabs?' 'No,' he says, 'our government. When they hanged that Arab boy they might just as well have put the noose around her neck too.' 'So they went ahead with the execution?' I ask, feeling unexpected sympathy for Dr Habash and his family. 'Yesterday,' he replies, 'and when she heard the news her anger just exploded and so did her heart, like a hand-grenade.'

Two pall-bearers move through the crowd. The corpse, which they are holding at its neck and knees, is swaddled in white cloth according to custom. This anonymous replica of a human being, with shape but without feature, is lowered into the earth's gaping maw and slowly devoured by the dust it thought to own. As in chess it is the board that remains, the players that come and go. I do not record this incident in the log book. There I merely write:

10.00–11.30. Obtain material from Yotvata to
    manufacture solar trampoline.

'I want you to look surprised,' says Falcon to Dudu when we are at last ready to complete the shot, 'surprised but not astonished.'

The same expression, I've no doubt, crosses Anthony Jacobi's face when G.G. Studios deliver the first rushes. He telephones at the completion of the third day's filming.

'To tell you the truth, Jonah,' he yells down the line, 'I don't give a shit about the film at the moment. No one is going to invest in tourism while this *intifada* thing is going on, which it looks like doing for a long, long time. On the other hand I don't see why I should bankroll a bunch of iconoclasts and anarchists to debunk our most cherished myths. That's not why I created Cisco.' The upshot is that I am summoned to Jerusalem. 'By the way,' he adds, 'your wife would appreciate a visit too.'

In no great hurry I request a lift from some of the camera-man's army buddies who are returning to their unit after rest and recreation in the dives of Eilat. They agree on the under-standing that I will not belly-ache about the discomforts of sitting on a wooden bench in the rear of a canvas-topped truck.

The soldiers sing as we start on the long road to the north, a song which excludes me, for it is very clear that they are not comfortable in my presence, regarding my artificial limb as an object of ill omen. Not one of them, at any time, enquires how I came by it.

Instead of talking to me they argue among themselves; some maintain that this will be their last tour of duty in the occupied territories, that next time they will go to jail rather than serve there; others claim that without some such moderating influence the army would run riot. 'It is already,' says another, 'even with us angels.'

Like David Ben Gurion, Israel's first Prime Minister, I feel at home in a desert. For it is as empty as my memory, as unlived in as the world before creation, catholic in its indifference, inanimate and therefore immortal.

We drive past Sede Boqer — his last resting-place and site of the Ben Gurion Research Institute and Archives, as well as the newly abandoned shell of Anthony Jacobi's dream child, the Western Resort and Country Club.

At the Yeroham junction we follow the sign to Beer Sheva and, once there, take the road to Hebron.

Hebron is burning, as is every town and village on the West Bank. In the richer areas they are igniting cars and buses, but the poorer communities have no option but to blockade their roads with blazing camels.

In narrow streets children throw stones and petrol bombs at inexperienced conscripts, while their mothers or sisters hurl obscenities and the contents of chamber-pots and expose their private parts. The soldiers are scared, even more scared now after the hanging, so they begin to shoot.

I feel no immediate pity for the victims, perhaps because I expect them to get up once the exchange is over — as the extras do in Jerusalem-in-the-desert — for here, as there, every performance is recorded by at least one cameraman. Only these children of violent times will never rise again of their own volition. All of this I witness through our vehicle's proscenium arch.

As we pass the hillside upon which sits the well-fortified Jewish settlement of Shem a woman, seeing that we are a military lorry, frantically waves us down. Her face is unnaturally white, as though it had been dipped in a bowl of flour. She is a teacher (but not of domestic science). Her sentences are jumbled. This is what they amount to: Part of her school has just collapsed, burying alive several of her pupils. There are very few men around, most being on the lookout for local troublemakers. We must help!

A white cloud hangs over the diseased edifice like early morning mist over a river. The dust of decayed cement is everywhere. The few adults available are screaming and lifting fallen masonry simultaneously. I offer what help a one-armed man can. My companions are more forceful. Here is not the place to make political points. Not now.

A huge cheer erupts when they pull out, bleeding and half choked, a living boy crying like one new born. But, alas, he is the only one. His less blessed fellow pupils are laid out upon the earth. It is a sad spectacle. The little bodies, the heart-broken families, the shabby houses, the desiccated plants in the dry window-boxes, even the nets on the basketball stanchions ragged beyond recall. 'I'd like to get my hands on the swine who dreamed up this place,' says one of the soldiers.

So would the police, as it happens. They are already searching the Jerusalem offices of Cisco when I arrive. 'Would you believe it,' complains Uncle Anthony, 'Judea and Samaria are seething with discontent and all these gentlemen have time to do is search the premises of a true patriot? Is it my fault that houses fall down? Did I invent gravity?' He looks resentfully at the police, who are opening all his drawers and confiscating the files therein.

'Dr Habash should see me now,' he says with a cynical laugh. 'Did you know that my recently deceased employee was his nephew?' I nod. 'You did? Anyway Dr Habash got the idea that I had some influence with the authorities here — you can see for yourself how much — so he phoned (from his office, no doubt) and he begged me to intervene with them on behalf of his condemned relative. As it happens I always had a soft spot for the kid despite his bolshie ways, but I had no doubt that he deserved to die for what he did. And I said as much. Dr Habash then tried a different approach. He quoted from various letters and editorials that had appeared in the British press after the verdict, to the effect that the Jews, of all people, should know the value of mercy. Fuck the Europeans, those hypocritical offspring of Portia! They seem to think we should be grateful to them for visiting the Holocaust upon us, which they now claim was simply an exercise in character building. Do they ever weep over our dead? No! But when a single Arab goes to the gallows – for the murder of over thirty-five people, let me remind you – they pass round the kleenex. I put down the receiver on the good doctor.'

Inflated with righteous indignation he turns upon his unwelcome visitors. 'Hey,' he shouts, 'haven't you got anything better to do?' But secretly he takes their interest seriously enough to disappear during the night. Informed opinion has it that he's on the way to Rio. My wife, who probably arranged it, denies any knowledge of his flight.

If she did indeed organize his escape from her cramped hospital headquarters it was an altruistic act of some magnitude, for Uncle Anthony has been her only regular visitor. Without his cheery contempt for regulations the remaining days of her confinement will surely seem infinite. Already it feels like an eternity to her since we last met, whereas to me it feels like only yesterday. Not that I don't sympathize with my wife. I know what it's like to be trapped in a hospital room for weeks on end. Wasn't I also waiting, like her, to give birth? Nevertheless, I harden myself against the questions I'm sure are approaching.

'Jonah,' she says, rubbing my cheek with her soft fingertips, 'must you go back? Why can't you stay in Jerusalem with me?' 'I'd like to,' I say, kissing the palm of her hand, 'but I have responsibilities. They need me down there.' 'I need you too, Jonah,' she says.

Alas for my wife, I have grown too fond of my new life in the desert. In Eilat I am a different person who lives in a different house and loves a different woman. How can poor earth-bound Sophie compete with that? Her predicament proclaims her disadvantages: pregnant, circumscribed by four walls, the epitome of possessive love; whereas Stella's domain has no boundaries, being the empty desert, the blank screen, the land of make-up and make-believe.

'It's only for another five weeks,' I say, 'after that I'll be here night and day.' Or someone will, an impersonator who bears a passing resemblance to Jonah Isaacson. I can see them now, the Adam and Eve of limbo land, wherein he'll do nothing but remember the ranch down south and think longingly of that empty house in St Albans.

'I just hope you're going to be a more considerate father than you are a husband,' says my wife, which is a big mistake. 'If I'm not good enough for you,' I say, opening the door, 'you can always send for Professor Gutkes.'

As it happens, our argument was probably completely unnecessary; on account of Jacobi's spontaneous departure *The Six Pointed Star* may well be coming to a premature conclusion.

In order to prevent this I present myself at the Ministry of Industry and Trade on Agron Street. The soldiers may have been ignorant of my infamous exploit, but not the civil servants who run the Ministry. I am granted an appointment with the Minister who, after all, owes his job to me. I point out to him that, given the drama of the project's conception, it would be an embarrassment and a retreat to cancel it at this late stage. An agreement is arrived at whereby his Ministry will continue to provide finance, in exchange for which I must supply a weekly ledger of production costs which must show, without fail, that we are bringing the film in under budget. As a result of which I return to Eilat a hero.

And it came to pass in an eveningtide, that David arose from off his bed, and walked upon the roof of the king's house: and from the roof he saw a woman washing herself; and the woman was very beautiful to look upon. Her name was Bathsheba. The Bible tells us very little about the wooing; only that David enquired after her, sent messengers and lay with her. We know what she told David shortly thereafter: *I am with child.*

Now Bathsheba was married to Uriah the Hittite, a good man, but a doomed one. 'Set ye Uriah in the forefront of the hottest battle,' wrote the king to his general, 'that he may be smitten, and die.' So it was written, so it was done.

Call me hypocritical, if you must, but when we rehearse our version of these events I dearly wish that my faithless wife and her German boyfriend were present, so that I could scrutinize their faces for tell-tale signs of a rancid conscience. You see, despite my own profligacy I cannot properly forgive my wife for entering into professorial concubinage. Nor do I like to think of myself as a minor participant in a story whose main connections are made behind my back, and whose outcome will be so detrimental to my health. It's not very pleasant to contemplate the fact that you could as easily be Uriah the Hittite as Jonah Isaacson.

The actress playing Sheba is known, at least to her publicist, as the Israeli Meryl Streep. According to the expert on the subject, the Hollywood original is a cold, calculating mistress of mimesis who will not take off her clothes under any circumstances. If there is any accuracy in that two-faced academic's assertions, then our leading lady is no Meryl Streep, for she raises no objections when informed that she will be required to disrobe and wash herself under the gaze of Dudu (concealed on a nearby balcony) and a camera (ditto).

A pool has been excavated in the back-yard of Jerusalem's only saloon and its bottom lined with lustrous local stone, causing the water to radiate with blue light. In the gleaming afternoon it glows like a pane of stained glass, much to the despair of the cameraman. 'She'll look like a pop-up Venus in this light,' he moans, 'hardly the impressionistic blur our master demands.'

Sheba herself kneels unselfconsciously beside the pool, her robe discarded, so that Stella can coat her unusually pale skin with dark, protective oils. She remains indifferent even when the diligent beautician trims and brushes her pubic hair and, having asked her to raise her arms, smooths down the stubble beneath. Stella's brief is to get her looking as pure as a pearl, or at least as pure as Grace Kelly in *Mogambo*.

Nor does she take any notice of the cameraman who fusses

around her dazzlingly white flesh with his blind man's mirror, trying to soften the effects of the surgical illumination.

It is as though she can amputate her entire body at will; persuade herself that she is not naked, but merely acting the part of someone who is.

In Yotvata I watched them bury the shrouded corpse of a woman, here I can observe every detail of the living corpus, but try as I might I cannot penetrate that immaculate exterior with my eyes. It is a shock to realize that I do not know the naked actress any better than the wrapped cadaver. Sheba is just an actress, a more beautiful golem, the Israeli Meryl Streep.

Filming finally comes to an end on 25 February, my birthday. Jerusalem is bedecked with bunting, not in acknowledgement of my distant nativity, but in honour of David's triumphant homecoming. He has crushed the ranchers, pacified the Indians, wiped out the wild men, and the town is his. The transformation of naive shepherd into divine gunslinger is complete. David, the wearer of the six pointed star, has actually become the embodiment of the myth created for him by his deceased compadre Johnny.

At first it was planned to conclude the film with David's re-entry but then, at the last of the nocturnal script conferences, Dudu suggested that the camera should abandon David and discover instead, in the sheriff's back-yard, his own sons bickering amongst themselves. 'Let them be aping their elders, as children do,' he said, 'let them be re-enacting their father's defeat of Goliath, and let them be unable to agree who should step into the hero's shoes.' Falcon was enthusiastic. Thus the movie will now end not in victory, but in tears.

All such changes fall upon the unit manager. And so, as a consequence of Dudu's brainwave, I spent the remainder of that night, the eve of my birthday, retrieving our juvenile stars from the thraldom of their school desks.

When all the actors and the extras are briefed and in position I approach Falcon and his crew to enquire as to their readiness.

Stella and Bella, recently as inseparable as Pat Garrett and Billy the Kid, are also in attendance. 'Surprise! Surprise!' they shout in unison, as Stella hands me a uniform wrapped in brown paper. Her eyes are shining like little suns. 'Happy Birthday, Jonah,' she says. 'Thanks,' I say, looking at the cowboy outfit I have revealed. 'Don't just stare at it,' snaps Falcon, 'put it on. As it's your birthday and the last day of shooting we decided that the most appropriate present would be a walk-on part.' 'What a gift!' I cry. 'Immortality!'

'Sorry to disappoint you,' says the cameraman, 'but you'll be lucky if the dyes on this film-stock your uncle obtained on the cheap last more than five years. The hard truth is that the radiant beam of the projector, which brings the images to life, also consumes them with its brightness.'

I sit passively on a hot rock while Stella applies the appropriate make-up to my face, turning me, at least temporarily, into her ideal man. 'Now go and welcome David!' bellows Falcon. I run into the town and lose myself among the crowd.

The following day all revert to what passes for the real world. Lewis and Bella move into Anthony Jacobi's abandoned apartment in the Jewish Quarter, so that the former can supervise the editing of his movie. I accept their invitation to join them. Stella takes a plane to England, though she promises to fly back for the first night. Dudu resumes his career on the stage, where he is a great success as the Captain in a Hebrew production of Strindberg's *The Father*. Gidi, having excelled as Johnny, returns to the shadows.

On the last day of February the obstetrician in charge of my wife's case asks to see me. He informs me that, in view of her condition, a caesarean section is a vital requirement.

My wife, on being given the news, is much relieved She had not been looking forward to a vaginal delivery. Her informant, a considerate man, is taken aback by her perverse enthusiasm for the unnatural. In his experience most women weep when offered such information. He says as much. 'Doctor,' replies my wife, 'when I want meat I go to the supermarket, not the abattoir. Why should I be upset when you tell me that the birth will be equally convenient?'

Not quite able to believe his ears the humane medic tries to mitigate her non-existent disappointment. 'It is not common,' he says, 'but we do allow some women to stay awake during the operation.' 'Not this one, thank you very much,' says my wife. 'You do not seem in the least concerned,' says the doctor, sounding somewhat aggrieved, 'but it may relieve you to know that the incision, the Pfannenstiel incision to be precise, is made transversely across the lower abdomen, so that when your pubic hair regrows — we'll have to shave it off, of course — the scar will be covered.' He smiles benignly.

'How about the father,' I say, 'doesn't he have any rights?' 'Naturally,' he says. In short, I invite myself to the birth.

'I'm starving,' says my wife, when I arrive on the Ides of March. 'They're not letting me eat a thing.' She complains all the way through the corridors even unto surgery, though I can tell by the way that she is squeezing my hand that the querulous mutterings are merely a way of disguising her queasy fear.

My horizontal wife is wearing a sheet. I am wearing a baker's hat, a gown and cotton slippers. The doors of the operating theatre close upon us. The anaesthetist puts my wife to sleep. 'I love you,' she mumbles, perhaps to counteract the ambiguous genesis of the ingénu waiting in the wings.

The masked surgeon levitates the sheet and, entering the pool of light, slices open my naked wife's belly. Now I see Bathsheba as David never saw her. There is white fat and the blood-red malachite of muscle which parts to reveal the holy of holies, the abdominal cavity itself.

Leaning forward, I am greeted by the real secret of creation: my wife's — everywoman's — dark pulsating organs and there, amongst them all, the great gourd of life, the uterus itself, from which the fimbriated ends of the fallopian tubes hang like blood-spattered daffodils. Life indeed! There it is, beating at the walls of the womb.

Observing her like this — through her skin and flesh and into her very bladder and bowels — I experience an overwhelming love for this woman I call my wife, and wonder how I could ever have been attracted to the superficialities at Stella's command.

I want to plunge my hands (I mean hand!) into my wife's entrails, to grasp them all, to know her better than I know myself, to know her completely.

However, this is not an introduction to my wife's inner life, but more prosaically – in the words of the doctor – a routine operation of less than an hour's duration. He separates Sophie's bladder from the uterus which is, itself, cut open like a fruit. And there it is, our baby, enclosed in its own private cosmos. The cellophane-like amniotic sac is punctured and peeled back releasing a gush of water and blood through which a little head is gently lifted into our world. The face is cleansed. It is as perfect as anything Stella could devise, save for a small bump in the middle of its forehead. The rest of the baby is then plucked free. Held upsidedown it – no, she! – begins to cry.

A few seconds later the problematic placenta is delivered through the same uterine incision.

'The little sweetheart looks just like you,' says one of the nurses, offering me the baby to hold. I decline, pointing to my prosthesis. I cannot honestly confirm that my daughter resembles me, but at least she doesn't look like Professor Gutkes.

While sewn-up Sophie sleeps I telephone England. Toby weeps for joy at the news. I resent the sound, because it moves me. I do not want to be responsible for his – or Queenie's – happiness. It's not fair, especially as I'm only pretending to be their son (who, not unnaturally, wants his parents to be happy).

The following day Lewis and Bella come to visit. 'It's about nine months since I was first roped into *The Six Pointed Star*,' says the great director, taking in the image of maternity. 'I just hope my child turns out as beautiful as yours.' My wife gives me a knowing look. I give her a smile. I am almost ready to spend the rest of my life within these four walls.

'What's that mark on the baby's forehead?' asks Bella, examining her great-great-niece. 'The paediatrician had a look at it,' I say, 'and he assures us that we've nothing to worry about.'

Bella, on the contrary, looks like she's got plenty. Her

appearance is dreadful, as though her face has at last given up trying to disguise her age. Her eyes are rheumy, her lips hairy, her skin a mesh of wrinkles. And she knows it. 'Thank God Stella is arriving tomorrow,' she whispers confidentially to her niece. 'I cannot live without that girl.'

'Jonah,' cries Stella, walking towards me with outstretched arms, 'you look so well!' She hugs me. Stella looks well too, standing under the Middle Eastern moonlight in a strapless evening gown.

'Congratulations on the birth of your daughter,' she says. 'I don't know why but when I heard the news I burst into tears.' She laughs at her foolishness.

We are leaning on the balcony of the Jerusalem Cinemateque where, in less than an hour, *The Six Pointed Star* will receive its world premiere.

'Someone just told me a very romantic thing,' she says. 'Apparently that spot there', she raises her arm and points to the valley below, 'is called the Pool of Bathsheba, because it was where she was bathing when King David spied upon her. Knowing that makes tonight seem more serious, somehow.'

''Would you like a glass of wine?' I ask. 'I'd love some, Jonah,' she replies, making it sound as though I had just asked for her hand in marriage.

We stroll over to the tables where the wine is served, rubbing shoulders en route with the Prime Minister, the Minister of Justice, the Minister of Industry and Trade (who nods at me), the American ambassador, the new Soviet ambassador and a rogues' gallery of bodyguards.

I pick up a glass of white wine and hand it to Stella, then take another for myself. We touch glasses. 'L'chayim,' I say.

On the adjacent table are loaves of french bread and a variety of cheeses. 'Something to eat?' I ask. 'Please,' says Stella.

You need two hands to slice bread, so it is Stella who gathers the wicked knife with the serrated blade and perforates the loaf.

We pose like two characters from the *Rubaiyat of Omar Khayyam*, knowing that our days of wine and roses are coming to an end, because of two characters (one more or less unknown) in a distant hospital room.

'I've got something for you,' says Stella, 'a keepsake to remind you of our time together.' She opens her bag and removes a thin gift-wrapped box. 'Shall I open it now?' I ask. 'Of course,' she says.

Inside, wrapped in red velvet, lies a pen upon which my name has been engraved. Incorporated in the top is a little watch which has not yet started to tell the time. 'Thank you,' I say, kissing her softly on the mouth. Our affair must end, it is true, but must it end tonight? 'Where are you staying?' I ask. 'The Hilton,' she replies. 'Which room,' I ask. 'I'll write the number down for you,' she says. But she can't find a pen in her bag. 'Use mine,' I say, offering my newest acquisition. She presses a button. There is a click. She jots down three figures. She returns the pen and, folding the paper, gives me that too. The watch, I notice, is now pulsing like a heartbeat. 'I'll be there,' I say.

Lewis and Bella approach, the latter marvellously renovated by the subtle art of the future Queen of Babylon who is, even now, silently working out ways of being caught in the tub by that country's lustful monarch.

'Got the jitters?' I ask Falcon. 'As a matter of fact, yes,' he says. 'Tell me,' he continues looking around at the political establishment, 'what do you think they'll make of it? Will I be run out of town?' 'Don't be daft,' I say. 'You'll be cheered to the skies, especially when David accepts the crown or rather the sheriff's badge – even though he knows it belongs to Johnny by rights – because he recognizes that myth binds more strongly than kinship, that ink is thicker than blood.' 'And yet those two leftist bastards', he says, nodding affectionately towards Dudu and Gidi, 'are delighted with the finished product.' 'That's because *The Six Pointed Star*, like *High Noon* or *Fort Apache*, lends itself to many interpretations,' I say. '*High Noon*, for example, was viewed both as an attack on McCarthyism and as an endorsement of the engagement in Korea.'

The two actors join us. Gidi is wearing his human mask, probably for the last time, unless he can find another Stella. 'Mazeltov, Jonah,' he says. 'Thank you,' I reply.

'Has anyone told you what that place is down there?' asks Dudu, upstaging his friend. 'Yes,' I say, thinking he is about to assume the role of the voyeur king, 'the Pool of Bathsheba.' 'Wrong,' he shouts. 'I'm pointing the other way.' In which case I shake my head.

'It's the Vale of Hinnom, formerly Gehenna, also known as hell. Why hell? I'll tell you why. Because it was there, in ancient times, that heathens sacrificed their children to the local deities. Has anything changed? What a question! Of course it fucking hasn't! If you want my opinion we're turning the whole of this country into one big Gehenna. Do yourself a favour, Jonah, take your beautiful new daughter, take your lovely wife, and run back to England as quickly as you can. Then forget all about us! You've had amnesia once, get it again. Just forget us!'

The crowd, as if embarrassed by this outburst, begins to shuffle into the cinema. 'Time to go,' says Bella, pushing her husband.

'I'll see you all inside,' says Stella. 'I've got to visit the Ladies Room.'

Lewis and Bella go ahead while I loiter, waiting for my mistress, with the world at my feet. As I walk to and fro I feel a tug at my prosthesis.

'Stella,' I say, but it isn't her, it isn't anyone, just a disembodied arm. Its tugging becomes insistent, as though it really intends to dislodge its replacement. With some difficulty I manage to prise its fingers loose, whereupon it picks my pocket, getting away with a silver pen. Dropping to the floor it slithers toward the table where the bread and cheese were served. Once there, as it did upon the wall of Alberto's restaurant, it begins to write.

The area is now more or less deserted. I seize my opportunity. Snatching the bread knife I plunge it through the hand, impaling it upon the table like a butterfly.

It no longer seems such a good idea to linger around the scene of such a crime, even for the sake of a beauty like Stella.

And so, removing her gift from the clutch of my erstwhile hand, I enter the cinema and, showing my invitation, take my seat in the front row, among the dignitaries and their security staff.

Although I have never been here before the cinema induces a

sense of déjà vu, perhaps because all cinemas are essentially the same. This simple explanation does not satisfy the nagging revelation that hovers, annoyingly, just beyond memory's recall. If only, like Hamlet, I carried my notebooks with me.

Dudu Wolf, his celebrated impersonator, sits beside me. 'Let's make a party afterwards,' he whispers, 'where we can celebrate or drown our sorrows.' 'Sorry,' I say, 'but I have a pressing engagement elsewhere.' 'Of course,' says Dudu, assuming that I am referring to the familial responsibilities that will take me to the hospital, but in truth I am thinking of Stella's siren song that is calling me back to the ninth floor of her hotel. I touch the pen that she gave me, to reassure myself of her corporeality. And then, as the curtains open to reveal the screen, the memory returns. The pen in my pocket is the twin of the one Gidi waved under my nose, claiming that it was a detonator.

My first reaction is to lean across Dudu, thereby gaining Gidi's ear, and denounce Stella to the authorities. But then reassuring doubts as to her guilt occur. Her face might have fooled me, but surely not her body.

I remove the object of my suspicions with the intention of examining it, but you try unscrewing a pen with only one hand. Before I get very far the light begins to fade. I look at the empty screen, now a brilliant white.

FOR THE BEST IN PAPERBACKS, LOOK FOR THE 🐧

In every corner of the world, on every subject under the sun, Penguin represents quality and variety – the very best in publishing today.

For complete information about books available from Penguin – including Puffins, Penguin Classics and Arkana – and how to order them, write to us at the appropriate address below. Please note that for copyright reasons the selection of books varies from country to country.

In the United Kingdom: Please write to *Dept E.P., Penguin Books Ltd, Harmondsworth, Middlesex, UB7 0DA.*

If you have any difficulty in obtaining a title, please send your order with the correct money, plus ten per cent for postage and packaging, to *PO Box No 11, West Drayton, Middlesex*

In the United States: Please write to *Dept BA, Penguin, 299 Murray Hill Parkway, East Rutherford, New Jersey 07073*

In Canada: Please write to *Penguin Books Canada Ltd, 2801 John Street, Markham, Ontario L3R 1B4*

In Australia: Please write to the *Marketing Department, Penguin Books Australia Ltd, P.O. Box 257, Ringwood, Victoria 3134*

In New Zealand: Please write to the *Marketing Department, Penguin Books (NZ) Ltd, Private Bag, Takapuna, Auckland 9*

In India: Please write to *Penguin Overseas Ltd, 706 Eros Apartments, 56 Nehru Place, New Delhi, 110019*

In the Netherlands: Please write to *Penguin Books Netherlands B.V., Postbus 195, NL–1380AD Weesp*

In West Germany: Please write to *Penguin Books Ltd, Friedrichstrasse 10–12, D–6000 Frankfurt/Main 1*

In Spain: Please write to *Longman Penguin España, Calle San Nicolas 15, E–28013 Madrid*

In Italy: Please write to *Penguin Italia s.r.l., Via Como 4, I-20096 Pioltello (Milano)*

In France: Please write to *Penguin Books Ltd, 39 Rue de Montmorency, F-75003 Paris*

In Japan: Please write to *Longman Penguin Japan Co Ltd, Yamaguchi Building, 2–12–9 Kanda Jimbocho, Chiyoda-Ku, Tokyo 101*